*The*

'An excellent thril ... ne
as one of the stars

*Sunday Times*

'The real thing, and the best of its kind since *Silence of the Lambs* . . . An unputdownable masterclass in thriller writing' *Time Out*

'A cracker . . . it fairly coruscates with all that goes to make a good crime thriller' *Irish Times*

'Most impressive . . . rich in detail, strong on character, with a fascinating plot that functions on several emotional levels . . . Connelly has, with great skill, given us a detective who inhabits a world filled only with torment, fear and danger' *People Magazine*

'Impressive . . . convincing ambience, a mass of procedural detail, authentic dialogue, a speeding plot and a flawed hero' *The Times*

'His methods of killing and eluding detection are infernally ingenious, adding an intellectual charge to the visceral kick of the hunt' *New York Times*

'One of the most authentic pieces of crime writing I've ever read. It is an extraordinary story, one that engages the reader on the first page and never lets go' James Lee Burke

'In-depth knowledge informs every turn of a wonderfully Byzantine plot . . . If you are an aspiring crime writer, buy this bravura display of technique' *Sunday Times*

'Intensely clever, entirely credible . . . thrilling, suspenseful and securely anchored in procedure and purpose. Not a false note; deeply satisfying stuff' *Literary Review*

A former police reporter for the *Los Angeles Times*, Michael Connelly is the author of six acclaimed Harry Bosch novels including *The Black Echo*, which was the winner of the Edgar Award. Michael Connelly lives in Los Angeles.

*Books by Michael Connelly*

The Black Echo
The Black Ice
The Concrete Blonde
The Last Coyote
The Poet
Trunk Music
Blood Work
Angels Flight

# BLOOD WORK

Michael Connelly

ORION

An Orion Paperback

First published in Great Britain by Orion in 1998
This paperback edition published in 1998 by
Orion Books Ltd,
Orion House, 5 Upper St Martin's Lane,
London WC2H 9EA

Second impression 1998



A CIP catalogue record for this book
is available from the British Library.



Typeset by Deltatype Ltd, Birkenhead, Merseyside
Printed and bound in Great Britain by
Clays Ltd, St Ives plc

*This is for Terry Hansen*
*and Myra McCaleb*

*HER LAST THOUGHTS were of Raymond. She would see him soon. He would awaken as he always did, his welcome-home embrace warm and sustaining.*

*She smiled and Mr Kang, behind the counter, smiled back, thinking her brightness was for him. He smiled at her every night, never knowing that her thoughts and smiles were actually for Raymond, for the moment still to come.*

*The sound of the bell shaken by the opening door behind her made only a peripheral entry into her thoughts. She had the two dollar bills ready and was handing them across the counter to Mr Kang. But he didn't take them. She then noticed that his eyes were no longer on her but focused on the door. His smile was gone and his mouth was opening slightly as if to form a word that wouldn't quite come.*

*She felt a hand grip her right shoulder from behind. The coldness of steel pressed against her left temple. A shower of light crashed across her vision. Blinding light. In that moment she saw a glimpse of Raymond's sweet face, then everything turned dark.*

# 1

McCaleb saw her before she saw him. He was coming down the main dock, past the row of millionaires' boats, when he saw the woman standing in the stern of *The Following Sea*. It was half past ten on a Saturday morning and the warm whisper of spring had brought a lot of people out to the San Pedro docks. McCaleb was finishing the walk he took every morning – completely around Cabrillo Marina, out along the rock jetty and back. He was huffing by this part of the walk, but he slowed his pace even more as he approached the boat. His first feeling was annoyance – the woman had boarded his boat uninvited. But as he got closer, he put that aside and wondered who she was and what she wanted.

She wasn't dressed for boating. She had on a loose summer dress that came to mid-thigh. The breeze off the water threatened to lift it and so she kept one hand at her side to keep it down. McCaleb couldn't see her feet yet but he guessed by the taut lines of the muscles he saw in her brown legs that she wasn't wearing boat shoes. She had raised heels on. McCaleb's immediate read was that she was there to make some kind of impression on someone.

McCaleb was dressed to make no impression at all. He had on an old pair of jeans ripped by wear, not for style, and a T-shirt from the Catalina Gold Cup tournament a few summers before. The clothes were spattered with stains – mostly fish blood, some of his own blood, marine polyurethane and engine oil. They had served him as both fishing and work clothes. His plan was to use the weekend to work on the boat and he was dressed accordingly.

He became more self-conscious about his appearance as he drew closer to the boat and could see the woman better. He pulled the foam pads of his portable off his ears and turned off the CD in the middle of Howlin' Wolf singing 'I Ain't Superstitious'.

'Can I help you?' he asked before stepping down into his own boat.

His voice seemed to startle her and she turned away from the sliding door that led into the boat's salon. McCaleb figured she had knocked on the glass and was waiting, expecting him to be inside.

'I'm looking for Terrell McCaleb.'

She was an attractive woman in her early thirties, a good decade or so younger than McCaleb. There was a sense of familiarity about her but he couldn't quite place it. It was one of those déjà vu things. At the same time he felt the stir of recognition, it quickly flitted away and he knew he was mistaken, that he did not know this woman. He remembered faces. And hers was nice enough not to forget.

She had mispronounced the name, saying Mc-*Cal*-ub instead of Mc-*Kay*-Leb, and used the formal first name that no one ever used except the reporters. That's when he began to understand. He knew now what had brought her to the boat. Another lost soul come to the wrong place.

'McCaleb,' he corrected. 'Terry McCaleb.'

'Sorry. I, uh, I thought maybe you were inside. I didn't know if it was okay to walk on the boat and knock.'

'But you did anyway.'

She ignored the reprimand and went on. It was as if

what she was doing and what she had to say had been rehearsed.

'I need to talk to you.'

'Well, I'm kind of busy at the moment.'

He pointed to the open bilge hatch she was lucky not to have fallen into and the tools he had left spread out on a drop cloth by the stern transom.

'I've been walking around, looking for this boat, for almost an hour,' she said. 'It won't take long. My name is Graciela Rivers and I wanted –'

'Look, Miss Rivers,' he said, holding his hands up and interrupting. 'I'm really ... You read about me in the newspaper, right?'

She nodded.

'Well, before you start your story, I have to tell you, you're not the first one to come out here and find me or to get my number and call me. And I'm just going to tell you what I told all of the others. I'm not looking for a job. So if this is about you wanting to hire me or have me help you some way, I'm sorry, but I can't do it. I'm not looking for that kind of work.'

She didn't say anything and he felt a pang of sympathy for her, just as he had for the others who had come to him before her.

'Look, I do know a couple of private investigators I can recommend. Good ones that will work hard and won't rip you off.'

He stepped over to the stern gunwale, picked up the sunglasses he had forgotten to take on his walk and put them on, signaling the end of the conversation. But the gesture and his words went by her.

'The article said you were good. It said you hated it whenever somebody got away.'

He put his hands in his pockets and hiked his shoulders.

'You have to remember something. It was never me

alone. I had partners, I had the lab teams, I had the whole bureau behind me. It's a lot different than one guy running around out there on his own. A lot different. I probably couldn't help you even if I wanted to.'

She nodded and he thought that he had gotten through to her and that would be the end of this one. He started thinking about the valve job on one of the boat's engines that he'd planned to complete over the weekend.

But he was wrong about her.

'I think you could help me,' she said. 'Maybe help yourself, too.'

'I don't need the money. I do okay.'

'I'm not talking about money.'

He looked at her for a beat before replying.

'I don't know what you mean by that,' he said, injecting exasperation into his voice. 'But I can't help you. I've got no badge anymore and I'm not a private investigator. It would be illegal for me to act as one or to accept money without a state license. If you read the story in the paper, then you know what happened to me. I'm not even supposed to be driving a car.'

He pointed toward the parking lot beyond the row of docks and the gangway.

'You see the one wrapped up like a Christmas present? That's mine. It's sitting there until I get my doctor's approval to drive again. What kind of investigator would that make me? I'd be taking the bus.'

She ignored his protest and just looked at him with a resolute expression that unnerved him. He didn't know how he was going to get her off the boat.

'I'll go get those names for you.'

He walked around her and slid open the salon door. After going in, he pulled the door shut behind him. He needed the separation. He went to the drawers below the chart table and began looking for his phone book. He hadn't needed it in so long he wasn't sure where it was.

He glanced out through the door and watched her step to the stern and lean her hips against the transom as she waited.

There was reflective film on the glass of the door. She couldn't see him watching her. The sense of familiarity came over him again and he tried to place her face. He found her very striking. Dark almond-shaped eyes that seemed both sad and understanding of some secret at the same time. He knew he would easily remember if he had ever met her or even just observed her before. But nothing came. His eyes instinctively went to her hands in search of a ring. There was none. He had been right about her shoes. She wore sandals with two-inch cork heels. Her toenails were painted pink and showed off against her soft brown skin. He wondered if this was how she looked all the time, or if she had dressed to entice him into taking the job.

He found his phone book in the second drawer and quickly looked up the names Jack Lavelle and Tom Kimball. He wrote their names and numbers on an old marine service flier and opened the slider. She was opening her purse as he stepped out. He held up the paper.

'Here are two names. Lavelle is LAPD retired and Kimball was with the bureau. I worked with both and either will do a good job for you. Pick one and call. Make sure you tell him you got his name from me. He'll take care of you.'

She didn't take the names from him. Instead she pulled a photo out of her purse and handed it to him. McCaleb took it without thinking. He realized immediately that this was a mistake. In his hand was a photo of a smiling woman watching a small boy blowing out candles on a birthday cake. McCaleb counted seven candles. At first he thought it was a picture of Rivers a few years younger. But then he realized it wasn't her.

The woman in the photo had a rounder face and thinner lips. She wasn't as beautiful as Graciela Rivers. Though both had deep brown eyes, the eyes of the woman in the photo did not have the same intensity as the eyes of the woman now watching him.

'Your sister?'

'Yes. And her son.'

'Which one?'

'What?'

'Which one is dead?'

The question was his second mistake, compounding the first by drawing him further in. He knew the moment he asked it that he should have just insisted that she take the names of the two private detectives and been done with it.

'My sister. Gloria Torres. We called her Glory. That's her son, Raymond.'

He nodded and handed the photo back but she didn't take it. He knew she wanted him to ask what had happened but he was finally putting on the brakes.

'Look, this isn't going to work,' he finally said. 'I know what you're doing. It doesn't work on me.'

'You mean you have no sympathy?'

He hesitated as the anger boiled up in his throat.

'I have sympathy. You read the newspaper story, you know what happened to me. Sympathy was my problem all along.'

He swallowed it back and tried to clear away any ill feeling. He knew she was consumed by horrible frustrations. McCaleb had known hundreds of people like her. Loved ones taken from them without reason. No arrests, no convictions, no closure. Some of them were left zombies, their lives irrevocably changed. Lost souls. Graciela Rivers was one of them now. She had to be or she wouldn't have tracked him down. He knew that no matter what she said to him or how angry he got, she didn't deserve to be hit with his own frustrations as well.

'Look,' he said. 'I just can't do this. I'm sorry.'

He put a hand on her arm to lead her back to the dock step. Her skin was warm. He felt the strong muscle beneath the softness. He offered the photo again but she still refused to take it.

'Look at it again. Please. Just one more time and then I'll leave you alone. Tell me if you feel anything else?'

He shook his head and made a feeble hand gesture as if to say it made no difference to him.

'I was an FBI agent, not a psychic.'

But he made a show of holding the photo up and looking at it anyway. The woman and the boy seemed happy. It was a celebration. Seven candles. McCaleb remembered that his parents were still together when he turned seven. But not much longer. His eyes were drawn to the boy more than the woman. He wondered how the boy would get along now without his mother.

'I'm sorry, Miss Rivers. I really am. But there is nothing I can do for you. Do you want this back or not?'

'I have a double of it. You know, two for the price of one. I thought you'd want to keep that one.'

For the first time he felt the undertow in the emotional current. There was something else at play but he didn't know what. He looked closely at Graciela Rivers and had the sense that if he took another step, asked the obvious question, he would be pulled under.

He couldn't help himself.

'Why would I want to keep it if I'm not going to be able to help you?'

She smiled in a sad sort of way.

'Because she's the woman who saved your life. I thought from time to time you might want to remind yourself of what she looked like, who she was.'

He stared at her for a long moment but he wasn't

really looking at Graciela Rivers. He was looking inward, running what she had just said through memory and knowledge and coming up short of its meaning.

'What are you talking about?'

It was all he could manage to ask. He had the sense that control of the conversation and everything else was tilting away from him and sliding across the deck to her. The undertow had him now. It was carrying him out.

She raised her hand but reached past the photo he was still holding out to her. She placed her palm on his chest and ran it down the front of his shirt, her fingers tracing the thick rope of the scar beneath. He let her do it. He stood there frozen and let her do it.

'Your heart,' she said. 'It was my sister's. She was the one who saved your life.'

# 2

Out of the corner of his eye he could just see the monitor. The screen was grainy silver and black, the heart like an undulating ghost, the rivets and staples that closed off blood vessels showing like black buckshot in his chest.

'Almost there,' a voice said.

It came from behind his right ear. Bonnie Fox. Always calm and comforting, professional. Soon he saw the snaking line of the scope move into the monitor's X-ray field, following the path of the artery and entering the heart. He closed his eyes. He hated the tug, the one they say you won't feel but you always do.

'Okay, you shouldn't feel this,' she said.

'Right.'

'Don't talk.'

Then, there it was. Like the slightest tug on the end of a fishing line, a scrap fish stealing your bait. He opened his eyes and saw the line of the scope, as thin as a fishing line, still deep in the heart.

'Okay, we got it,' she said. 'Coming out now. You did good, Terry.'

He felt her pat his shoulder, though he couldn't turn his head to look at her. The scope was removed and she taped a gauze compress against the incision in his neck. The brace that had held his head at such an uncomfortable angle was unstrapped and he slowly straightened his neck, bringing his hand up to work the stiff muscles. Dr Bonnie Fox's smiling face then hovered above his.

'How you feeling?'

'Can't complain. Now that it's over.'

'I'll see you in a little while. I want to check the blood work and get the tissue over to the lab.'

'I want to talk to you about something.'

'You got it. See you in a bit.'

A few minutes later two nurses wheeled McCaleb's bed out of the cath lab and into an elevator. He hated being treated as an invalid. He could have walked but it was against the rules. After a heart biopsy the patient must be kept horizontal. Hospitals always have rules. Cedars-Sinai seemed to have more than most.

He was taken down to the cardiology unit on the sixth floor. While being wheeled down the east hallway, he passed the rooms of the lucky and the waiting – patients who had received new hearts or were still waiting. They passed one room where McCaleb glanced through the open door and saw a young boy on the bed, his body tied by tubes to a heart-lung machine. A man in a suit sat in the chair on the other side of the bed, his eyes staring at the boy but seeing something else. McCaleb looked away. He knew the score. The kid was running out of time. The machine would only hold him up for so long. Then the man in the suit – the father, McCaleb assumed – would be staring at a casket with the same look.

They were at his room now. He was moved from the gurney onto the bed and left alone. He settled in for the wait. He knew from experience that it could be as long as six hours before Fox showed up, depending on how quickly the blood work was run through the lab and how soon she came by to pick up the report.

He had come prepared. The old leather bag in which he had once carried his computer and the countless case files he had worked on was now stuffed with back issues of magazines he saved for biopsy days.

*

Two and a half hours later Bonnie Fox came through the door. McCaleb put down the copy of *Boat Restoration* he had been reading.

'Wow, that was fast.'

'It's slow in the lab. How are you feeling?'

'My neck feels like it had somebody's foot on it for a couple hours. You've already been to the lab?'

'Yup.'

'How'd everything come out?'

'It all looks good. No rejection, all the levels look good. I'm very pleased. We might lower your prednisone in another week.'

She spoke as she spread the lab report out on the bed's food table and double-checked the good results. She was referring to the carefully orchestrated mix of drugs that McCaleb took every morning and night. Last he'd counted, he was swallowing eighteen pills in the morning and another sixteen at night. The medicine cabinet on the boat wasn't big enough for all the containers. He had to use one of the storage compartments in the forward berth.

'Good,' he said. 'I'm tired of shaving three times a day.'

Fox folded the report closed and picked the clipboard up off the bed table. Her eyes quickly scanned the checklist of questions he had to answer every time he came in.

'No fever at all?'

'No, I'm clean.'

'And no diarrhea.'

'Nope.'

He knew from her constant drilling and double-checking that fever and diarrhea were the twin harbingers of organ rejection. He took his temperature a minimum of twice a day, along with readings of blood pressure and pulse.

'The vitals look good. Why don't you lean forward?'

She put the clipboard down. With a stethoscope she first warmed with her breath, she listened to his heart at three different spots on his back. Then he lay back and she listened through his chest. She took her own measure of his pulse with two fingers on his neck while she looked at her watch. She was very close to him as she did this. She wore a perfume of orange blossoms, which McCaleb had always associated with older women. And Bonnie Fox was not one of them. He looked up at her, studying her face while she studied her watch.

'Do you ever wonder if we should be doing this?' he asked.

'Don't talk.'

Eventually, she moved her fingers to his wrist and measured the pulse there. After that she pulled the pressure collar off the wall, put it on his arm and took a blood pressure reading, maintaining her silence all the time.

'Good,' she said when she was done.

'Good,' he said.

'Whether we should be doing what?'

It was like her to suddenly continue an interrupted or forgotten bit of conversation. She rarely forgot anything McCaleb said to her. Bonnie Fox was a small woman about McCaleb's age with short hair gone prematurely gray. Her white lab coat hung almost to her ankles because it had been designed for a taller person. Embroidered on the breast pocket was an outline of the cardiopulmonary system, her specialty as a surgeon. She was all business when it came to their meetings. She had an air of confidence and caring, a combination McCaleb had always found rare in physicians – and in the last years there had been many. He returned the confidence and caring. He liked her and trusted her. In his most secret thoughts there had once been a hesitation when he considered he would one day put his life in the hands of this woman. But the hesitation quickly left and caused him only a feeling of guilt. When the time came for the transplant, it had been her smiling face that was the last he had seen as he was put to sleep in pre-op. There had been no hesitation in him by then. And it was her smiling face that welcomed him back to the world with a new heart and new life.

McCaleb took the fact that in the eight weeks since the transplant there had not been a hitch in his recovery as proof his belief in her was valid. In the three years since he had first walked into her office, a bond had developed between them that had gone far beyond the professional. They were good friends now, or so McCaleb believed. They had shared meals a half dozen times and countless spirited debates on everything from genetic cloning to the O. J. Simpson trials – McCaleb had won a hundred bucks from her on the first verdict, easily seeing that her unwavering belief in the justice system had blinded her to the racial realities of the case. She wouldn't bet him on the second.

Whatever the subject, half the time McCaleb found himself taking the opposing opinion just because he liked battling with her. Fox now followed her question with a look that said she was ready for another joust.

'Whether we should be doing *this*,' he said, waving a hand around as if to encompass the whole hospital. 'Taking out organs, putting in new ones. Sometimes I feel like Frankenstein's monster, other people's parts in me.'

'One other person, one other part. Let's not be so dramatic.'

'But it's the big part, isn't it? You know, when I was with the bureau, we had to qualify on the range every year. You know, shoot at targets. And the best way to qualify was to go for the heart. The circle around the heart on those targets scores more than the head. It's called the ten ring. Highest score.'

'Look, if this is the aren't-we-acting-like-God debate again, I thought we were well past that.'

She shook her head, smiled and looked him over for a few seconds. The smile eventually dropped away.

'What's really wrong?'

'I don't know. I guess I'm feeling guilty.'

'What, about living?'

'I don't know.'

'Don't be ridiculous. We've been through this, too. I have no time for survivor's guilt. Look at the choices here. It's simple. You've got life on one side and then you've got death. Big decision. What is there to be guilty about?'

He raised his hands in surrender. She always put things in their clearest context.

'Typical,' she said, refusing to let him back off. 'You hang around almost two years waiting for a heart, draw your string out and nearly don't even make it, and now you wonder if we should have even given it to you. What's really bothering you, Terry? I don't have time to be bullshitting with you.'

He looked back at her. She had developed a skill at reading him. It was something all the best bureau agents and cops he had known had. He hesitated and then decided to say what was on his mind.

'I guess I want to know how come you didn't tell me that the woman whose heart I got had been murdered.'

She was clearly taken aback. The shock of his statement showed on her face.

'Murdered? What are you talking about?'

'She was murdered.'

'How?'

'I don't know exactly. She got caught in the middle of

a robbery in some convenience store up in the Valley. Shot in the head. She died and I got her heart.'

'You're not supposed to know anything about your donor. How do you know this?'

'Because her sister came and saw me on Saturday. She told me the whole thing ... It sort of changes things, you know?'

Fox sat on the hospital bed and leaned over him. A stern look came over her face.

'First of all, I had no idea where your heart came from. We never do. It came through BOPRA. All we were told was that an organ was available with a blood work match to a recipient we had on call and at the top of our list. That was you. You know how BOPRA works. You watched the film during orientation. We get limited information because it works best that way. I told you exactly what we knew. Female, twenty-six years old, if I remember. Perfect health, perfect blood typing, perfect donor. That's it.'

'Then I'm sorry. I thought maybe you knew and just held that back.'

'I didn't. We didn't. So if we didn't know who and where it came from, how did the sister know who and where it went? How did she find you? This could be some kind of a scam she's –'

'No. It's her. I know.'

'How do you know?'

'The newspaper article last Sunday, that "Whatever Happened to ..." column in the *Times* Metro section. It said I got the heart on February ninth and that I'd been waiting a long time because my blood type was rare. The sister read it and put it together. She obviously knew when her sister died, knew her heart was donated and knew she also had a rare blood type. She's an ER nurse up at Holy Cross and figured out it was me.'

'It still doesn't mean you have her sister's –'

'She also had the letter I wrote.'

'What letter?'

'The one everybody writes afterward. The anonymous thank you note to the family of your donor. The one the hospital mails. She had mine. I looked at it and it's mine. I remember what I wrote.'

'This is not supposed to happen, Terry. What does she want? Money?'

'No, not money. Don't you see? She wants me to find out who did it. Who killed her sister. The cops never closed it. It's two months later and no arrest. She knows they've given up. Then she sees this story about me in the paper, about what I used to do for the bureau. She figures out I got her sister's heart and thinks maybe I can do what the cops apparently can't. Break the case. She spent an hour walking around the San Pedro marinas looking for my boat Saturday. All she had was the name of the boat from the paper. She came looking for me.'

'This is crazy. Give me this woman's name and I'll –'

'No. I don't want you to do anything to her. Think if you were her and you loved your sister. You'd do what she did, too.'

Fox got off the bed, a wide-eyed look on her face.

'You're not actually thinking of doing this.'

She said it as a statement, a doctor's order. He didn't answer and that in itself was an answer. He could see anger once again working itself into Fox's expression.

'Listen to me. You are in no condition to be doing anything like this. You are sixty days post-transplant surgery and you want to run around playing detective?'

'I'm only thinking about it, okay? I told her I'd think about it. I know the risks. I also know that I'm not an FBI agent anymore. It would be a whole different thing.'

Fox angrily folded her thin arms across her chest.

'You shouldn't even be thinking about it. As your doctor, I am telling you not to do this. That's an order.'

Her voice then changed in tone and softened.

'You have to respect the gift you were given, Terry. This second chance.'

'But that respect goes two ways. If I didn't have her heart, I'd be dead by now. I owe her. It's that –'

'You don't owe her or her family anything more than that note you sent them. That's it. She'd be dead whether you or anybody else got her heart. You are wrong about this.'

He nodded that he understood her point but it wasn't enough for him. He knew that just because something makes sense on an intellectual level, it doesn't play any better in the twists of your guts. She read his thoughts.

'But what?'

'I don't know. It's just that I thought if I ever found out what happened, I would find out it was an accident. That's what I prepared myself for. That's what they tell you in orientation and even you told me when we started. That ninety-nine out of a hundred times it's an accident leading to fatal head injury. Car crash or somebody falls down the steps or dumps their motorcycle. But this is different. It changes things.'

'You keep saying that. How can it be different? The heart is just an organ – a biological pump. It's the same no matter how its original owner dies.'

'An accident I could live with. All that time I was waiting, knowing that somebody had to die for me to live, I was getting myself ready to accept it as an accident. With an accident it's like it was fated or something. But a murder ... that comes with evil intent attached. It's not happenstance. It means that I'm the benefactor of an act of evil, Doctor, and that's why it's different now.'

Fox was silent for a few moments. She shoved her hands into the side pockets of her lab coat. McCaleb thought that she was finally beginning to see his point.

'That's what my life was about for a long time,' he added quietly. 'I was searching out evil. That was my job. And I was good at it but in the long run it was better than me. It got the best of me. I think – no, I know – that's what took my heart. But now it's like none of that meant anything because here I am, I have this new heart, a new life, this second chance you talk about, and the only reason I have it is because of this evil, hateful thing that someone did.'

He blew out a deep breath before going on.

'She went into that store to get a candy bar for her kid and she ends up – look, it's just different. I can't explain it.'

'You're not making a lot of sense.'

'It's hard for me to put it into the words I want. I just know what I'm feeling. It makes sense to me.'

Fox had a resigned look on her face.

'Look, I know what you're going to want to do. You're going to want to help this lady. But you're not ready. Physically, no way. And emotionally, after hearing what you just said, I don't think you're ready to investigate even a car accident. Remember what I told you about the equilibrium between physical and mental health? One feeds off the other. And I'm scared that what you have going on in your head now is going to affect your physical progress.'

'I understand.'

'No, I don't think you do. You are gambling with your own life here. If this goes south, if you start getting infection or rejection, we're not going to be able to save you, Terry. We waited twenty-two months for that heart you have now. You think another one with matching blood work is going to just pop up because you messed up this one? No chance. I've got a patient down the hall on a machine. He's waiting on a heart that isn't coming.

That could be you, Terry. This is your one chance. Do not blow it!'

She reached across the bed and placed her hand on his chest. It reminded him of what Graciela Rivers had done. He felt its warmth there.

'Tell this woman no. Save yourself and tell her no.'

# 3

The moon was like a balloon being kept aloft by children poking at it with sticks. The masts of dozens of sailboats stood raised beneath it, ready to keep it from falling. McCaleb watched it hover in the black sky until it finally escaped by slipping behind the clouds somewhere out over Catalina. As good a hiding spot as any, he thought, as he looked down at the empty coffee cup in his hand. He missed being able to sit in the stern at the end of the day with an ice-cold beer in one hand and a cigarette in the other. But cigarettes had been part of the problem and were gone for good now. And it would be a few months before the medication therapy would relax enough to allow a dose of alcohol into the mix. For now, if he had just one beer, it might give him what Bonnie Fox called a fatal hangover.

McCaleb got up and went into the boat's salon. First he tried sitting at the galley table but soon got up, turned the TV on and started flipping through the channels without really looking at what was on. He turned the tube off and checked the clutter on the chart table but found there was nothing for him there, either. He moved about the cabin, looking for a distraction from his thoughts. But there was nothing.

He moved down the stairs into the forward passageway and into the head. He took the thermometer from the medicine cabinet, shook it and dipped it under his tongue. It was an old-style glass tube instrument. The electronic thermometer with digital reading display the hospital had provided was still in its box on the cabinet shelf. For some reason he didn't trust it.

Looking at himself in the mirror, he pulled open the collar of his shirt and studied the small wound left by the morning's biopsy. It never got a chance to heal. There had been so many biopsies that the incision was always just about covered with new skin when it was opened up again and the artery probed once more. He knew it would be a permanent mark, like the thirteen-inch scar running down his chest. As he stared at himself, his thoughts drifted to his father. He remembered the permanent marks, the tattoos, left on the old man's neck. The coordinates of a radiation battle that served only to prolong the inevitable.

The temperature reading was normal. He washed the thermometer and put it back, then took the clipboard with the temperature log sheet off the towel hook and wrote the date and time. In the last column, under TEMPERATURE, he drew another dash indicating no change.

After hanging up the board, he leaned into the mirror to look at his eyes. Green flecked with gray, the corneas showing hairline cracks of red. He stepped back and pulled the shirt off. The mirror was small but he could still see the scar, whitish pink and thick, ugly. He did this often, appraised himself. It was because he couldn't get used to the way his body looked now and the way it had so fully betrayed him. Cardiomyopathy. Fox had told him it was a virus that could have been waiting in the walls of his heart for years, only to bloom by happenstance and to be nurtured by stress. The explanation meant little to him. It didn't ease the feeling that the man he had once been was gone now forever. He sometimes felt when he looked at himself he was looking at a stranger, someone beaten down and left fragile by life.

After pulling his shirt back on, he went into the forward berth. It was a triangular-shaped room that followed the shape of the bow. There was a double bunk on the port side and a bank of storage compartments to starboard. He had turned the lower berth into a desk and used the overhead berth for storage of cardboard boxes full of old bureau files. Marked on the side of these boxes were the names of the investigations. They said POET, CODE, ZODIAC, FULL MOON and BREMMER. Two of the boxes were marked VARIOUS UNSUBS. McCaleb had copied most of his files before leaving the bureau. It was against policy but no one stopped him. The files in the boxes came from various cases, open and closed. Some filled whole cartons, some were thin enough to share space in the same boxes. He wasn't sure why he had copied everything. He hadn't opened any of the boxes since he had retired. But at various times he had thought he would write a book or maybe even continue his investigations of the open cases. Largely, though, he just liked the idea of having the files as a physical accounting or proof of what he had done with that part of his life.

McCaleb sat down at the desk and turned on the wall-mounted light. Momentarily, his eyes fell on the FBI badge he had carried for sixteen years. It was now encased in a Lucite block and hanging on the wall above the desk. Tacked to the wall next to it was a photo of a young girl with braces, smiling at the camera. It had been copied from a yearbook many years before. McCaleb frowned at the memory and looked away, his eyes falling to the desk clutter.

There was a handful of bills and receipts scattered on the desk, an accordion file full of medical records, a stack of manila files that were mostly empty, three fliers from competing dry-docking services and the Cabrillo Marina dockage rules book. His checkbook was open and ready to be put to use but he couldn't bring himself to wade into the mundane task of paying bills. Not now. He was restless but it was not because of a paucity of things on his mind. He couldn't stop thinking about the visit from Graciela Rivers and the sudden change it had put him through.

He sorted through the clutter on the desk until he found the newspaper clip that had brought the woman to his boat. He had read it the day it was published, cut it out and then tried to forget about it. But that had been impossible. The story had drawn a procession of victims to his boat. The mother whose teenage daughter's body was found mutilated on the beach down in Redondo; the parents whose son had been hanged in an apartment in West Hollywood. The young husband whose wife had gone clubbing on the Sunset Strip one night and had never come back. All of them zombies, left nearly catatonic by grief and the betrayal of their faith in a God who wouldn't allow such things to happen. McCaleb couldn't comfort them, he couldn't help them. He sent them on their way.

He had agreed to the newspaper interview only because he was in the reporter's debt. When he had been with the bureau, Keisha Russell had always been good to him. She was the kind of reporter who gave some and didn't always take. She had called him on the boat a month earlier to collect on that debt. She'd been assigned the story for the *Times*'s 'Whatever Happened to ...' column. Since a year earlier she had written a story about McCaleb's wait for a heart, she wanted to update it now that he had finally received the transplant. McCaleb wanted to decline the invitation, knowing it would disrupt the anonymous life he was now living, but Russell had reminded him of all the times she had helped him – either holding back details of an investigation or putting them into a story, depending on what McCaleb thought would be useful. McCaleb felt he had no choice. He always made good on his debts.

On the day the story was published, McCaleb had taken it as his official badge of has-been status. Usually, the column was reserved for updates on hack politicians who had disappeared from the local scene or people whose fifteen minutes of fame had long ago lapsed. Every now and then it featured a washed-up TV star who was selling real estate or had become a painter because it was his true creative calling.

He unfolded the clip now and reread it.

**New Heart, New Start for Former FBI Agent**

*By Keisha Russell*

*TIMES* STAFF WRITER

It used to be that Terrell McCaleb's face was a routine fixture on the nightly newscasts of Los Angeles and his words always found space in the local newspapers. It was not a nice routine for him or the city.

An FBI agent, McCaleb was the bureau's point man in the investigations of the handful of serial killers that plagued Los Angeles and the West in the last decade.

A member of the Investigative Support Unit, McCaleb helped focus the investigations of the local police. Media-savvy and always quotable, he often took the spotlight – a move that sometimes rubbed the locals and his supervisors in Quantico, Va., the wrong way.

But it has been more than two years since he has made even a blip on the public radar screen. These days, McCaleb no longer carries a badge or a gun. He says he doesn't even own a standard-issue navy blue FBI suit anymore.

More often than not he wears old blue jeans and torn T-shirts and can be found restoring his 42-foot fishing boat, *The Following Sea*. McCaleb, who was born in Los Angeles and grew up in Avalon on nearby Catalina Island, currently lives on the boat in a San Pedro marina but plans eventually to moor the vessel in Avalon Harbor.

Recovering from heart transplant surgery, McCaleb says hunting serial killers and rapists is the furthest thing from his mind these days.

McCaleb, 46, says he gave his heart to the bureau – his doctors say severe stress triggered a virus that led to the near-fatal weakening of his original heart – but doesn't miss it.

'When you go through something like this, it changes you more than just physically,' he said in an interview last week. 'It puts things in perspective. Those FBI days seem like a long time ago. I've got a new start now. I don't know exactly what I'm going to do with it but I'm not too worried. I'll find something.'

McCaleb almost didn't get the new start. Because he has a blood type found in less than one percent of the population, his wait for a suitable heart lasted almost two years.

'He really strung it out,' said Dr Bonnie Fox, the surgeon who performed the transplant. 'We probably would have lost him or he would have become too weak to undergo the surgery if we'd had to wait much longer.'

McCaleb is out of the hospital and already physically active after only eight weeks. He says that only on occasion does he think about the adrenaline-pumping investigations that once occupied him.

The former agent's case list reads like a Who's Who of a macabre walk of fame. Among the cases he worked locally were the Nightstalker and Poet investigations and he took key roles in the hunts for the Code Killer, Sunset Strip Strangler and Luther Hatch, who became known after his arrest as the Cemetery Man because of his visits to the graves of his victims.

McCaleb had been a profiler in the unit's Quantico

base for several years. He specialized in West Coast cases and was flown to Los Angeles often to assist local police in investigations. Finally, the unit's supervisors decided to create a satellite post here and McCaleb was returned to his native Los Angeles to work out of the FBI field office in Westwood. The move put him closer to many of the investigations in which the FBI was called upon for assistance.

Not all of the investigations were successful and eventually the stress took its toll. McCaleb suffered a heart attack while working late one evening in the local field office. He was found by a night janitor, who was credited with saving the agent's life. Doctors determined McCaleb suffered from advanced cardiomyopathy – a weakening of the heart's muscles – and placed him on a transplant list. As he waited, he was given a disability retirement by the bureau.

He traded his bureau pager for a hospital pager and on Feb. 9 it sounded; a heart from a donor with matching blood was available. After six hours of surgery at Cedars-Sinai Medical Center, the donor's heart was beating in McCaleb's chest.

McCaleb is unsure what he'll do with his new life – other than go fishing. He has had offers from former agents and police detectives to join them as a private investigator or security consultant. But his focus so far has been on restoring *The Following Sea*, a twenty-year-old sport-fishing boat he inherited from his father. The boat was left to deteriorate for six years but now has McCaleb's full-time attention.

'At the moment I'm content to take things a little at a time,' he said. 'I'm not worried too much about what's ahead.'

His regrets are few but like all retired investigators and fishermen, McCaleb laments the ones that got away.

'I wish I had solved all the cases,' he said. 'I hated it when somebody got away. I still do.'

For a moment McCaleb studied the photo they had used with the story. It was an old head shot they had used many times before during his days with the bureau. His eyes stared boldly into the camera.

When Keisha Russell had come around to do the story on him, she had come with a photographer. But McCaleb wouldn't let them take a fresh shot. He told them to use one of the old photos. He didn't want anybody to see the way he looked now.

Not that anyone could tell much, unless he had his shirt off. He was about thirty pounds lighter but that wasn't what he wanted to hide. It was the eyes. He had lost that look – the eyes as piercingly hard as bullets. He didn't want anyone to know he had lost that.

He folded the newspaper clip and put it aside. He tapped his fingers on the desk for a few seconds while brooding over things and then looked at the steel paper spike next to the phone. The number Graciela Rivers had given him was scratched in pencil on the scrap of paper that sat at the top of the stack of notes punctured by the spike.

When he was an agent, he had carried with him a bottomless reservoir of rage for the men he hunted. He had seen firsthand what they had done and he wanted them to pay for the horrible manifestations of their fantasies. Blood debts had to be paid in blood. That was why in the bureau's serial killer unit the agents called what they did 'blood work'. There was no other way to describe it. And so it worked on him, cut at him, every time one didn't pay. Every time one got away.

What happened to Gloria Torres now cut at him. He was alive because she had been taken away by evil.

Graciela had told him the story. Gloria had died for no reason other than that she was in the way of somebody and a cash register. It was a simple, stupid and ghastly reason to die. It somehow put McCaleb in debt. To her and her son, to Graciela, even to himself.

He picked up the phone and dialed the number scratched on the paper. It was late but he didn't want to wait and he didn't think she would want him to. She answered in a whisper after only one ring.

'Miss Rivers?'

'Yes.'

'It's Terry McCaleb. You came by my –'

'Yes.'

'Is this a bad time?'

'No.'

'Well, listen, I wanted to tell you that I, uh, have been thinking about things and I promised you I'd call you back no matter what I decided.'

'Yes.'

There was a hopeful tone in just her one word. It touched his heart.

'Well, this is what I think. My, um, my skills, I guess you'd call them, they're not really suited to this kind of crime. From what you described about your sister, we're talking about a random occurrence with a financial motive. A robbery. So it's different from, you know, the kind of cases I worked for the bureau, the serial cases.'

'I understand.'

The hopefulness was bleeding out.

'No, I'm not saying I'm not going to – you know, that I'm not interested. I'm calling because I am going to go see the police tomorrow and ask about this. But –'

'Thank you.'

'– I don't know how successful I'm going to be. That's

what I'm trying to say. I don't want to get your hopes up, is what I'm saying. These things ... I don't know.'

'I understand. Thank you for just being willing to do this. Nobody –'

'Well, I'll take a look at things,' he said, cutting her off. He didn't want her thanking him too much. 'I don't know what kind of help or cooperation I'll get from the LA police but I'll do what I can. I owe your sister at least that much. To try.'

She was silent and he told her he needed to get some additional information about her sister as well as the names of the LAPD detectives on the case. They talked for about ten minutes and when he had all of the information he needed written down in a small notebook, an uneasy silence played across the telephone line.

'Well,' he finally said, 'I guess that's it, then. I'll call you if I have any other questions or if anything else comes up.'

'Thank you again.'

'Something tells me I should be thanking you. I'm glad I'll be able to do this. I just hope it helps.'

'Oh, it will. You've got her heart. She'll guide you.'

'Yes,' he said hesitantly, not really understanding what she meant or why he was agreeing. 'I'll call you when I can.'

He hung up and stared at the phone for a few moments, thinking about her last line. Then again he unfolded the newspaper clip with his picture. He studied the eyes for a long time.

Finally, he folded the newspaper clip closed and hid it under some of the paperwork on the desk. He looked up at the girl with the braces and after a few moments nodded. Then he turned off the light.

# 4

When McCaleb had been with the bureau, the agents he worked with called this part the 'hard tango'. It was the finesse moves they had to make with the locals. It was an ego thing and a territorial thing. One dog doesn't piss in another dog's yard. Not without permission.

There was not a single homicide cop working who did not have a healthy ego. It was an absolute job requirement. To do the job, you had to know in your heart that you were up to the task and that you were better, smarter, stronger, meaner, more skilled and more patient than your adversary. You had to flat-out know that you were going to win. And if you had any doubts about that, then you had to back off and work burglaries or take a patrol shift or do something else.

The problem was that homicide egos were often unchecked to the point that some detectives extended the view they had of their adversaries to those who wanted to help them – fellow investigators, especially FBI agents. No homicide cop on a stalled-out case wants to be told that maybe someone else – particularly a fed from Quantico – might be able to help or could do it better. It had been McCaleb's experience that when a cop finally gave up and put a case into cold storage, he secretly didn't want anyone taking it out and proving him wrong by solving it. As an FBI agent McCaleb was almost never asked into a case or called for advice by the lead detective. It was always the supervisor's idea. The supervisor didn't care about egos or hurt feelings. The supervisor cared about clearing cases and improving statistical reports. And so the bureau would be called and McCaleb would come in and have to do the dance with the lead detective. Sometimes it was the smooth dance of coordinated partners. More often it was the hard tango. Toes got stepped on, egos got bruised. On more than one occasion McCaleb suspected that a detective he was working with was holding back information or was secretly pleased when McCaleb was unsuccessful in helping identify a suspect or bringing closure to a case. It was part of the petty territorial bullshit of the law enforcement world. Sometimes consideration of the victim or the victim's family wasn't even on the plate. It was dessert. And sometimes there was no dessert.

McCaleb was pretty sure he was facing a hard tango with the LAPD. It didn't matter that they had apparently hit the wall with the Gloria Torres investigation and could use the help. It was territorial. And to make matters worse, he wasn't even with the FBI anymore. He was going in naked, without a badge. All he had with him when he arrived at seven-thirty on Tuesday morning at the West Valley Division was his leather bag and a box of doughnuts. He was going to be dancing the hard tango without music.

McCaleb had chosen his arrival time because he knew that most detectives started early so they could get done early. It was the time when he had the best chance of catching the two assigned to the Gloria Torres case in their office. Graciela had given him their names. Arrango and Walters. McCaleb didn't know them, but he had met their commanding officer, Lieutenant Dan Buskirk, a few years earlier on the Code Killer case. But it was a superficial relationship. McCaleb didn't know what Buskirk thought about him. He decided, though, that it would be best to follow protocol and start with Buskirk and then, hopefully, get to Arrango and Walters.

West Valley Division was on Owensmouth Street in Reseda. It seemed to be an odd place for a police station. Most of the LAPD's stations were placed in the tough areas where police attention was needed most. They had concrete walls erected at the entranceways to guard against drive-by shootings. But West Valley was different. There were no barriers. The station was in a bucolic, middle-class, residential setting. There was a library on one side and a public park on the other, plenty of parking at the front curb. Across the street was a row of signature San Fernando Valley ranch houses.

After the cab dropped him off out front, McCaleb entered through the main lobby, threw an easy salute at one of the uniformed officers behind the counter and headed toward the hallway to the left. He showed no hesitation. He knew it led to the detective bureau because most of the city's police divisions were laid out the same way.

The uniform didn't stop him and this encouraged McCaleb. Maybe it was the box of doughnuts but he took it to mean he still had at least some of the *look* – the confident walk of a man carrying a gun and a badge. He was carrying neither.

After entering the detective bureau, he came to another counter. By pressing against it and leaning over, he could look to the left and through the glass window of the small office he knew belonged to the detective lieutenant. It was empty.

'Can I help you?'

He straightened up and looked at the young detective who had approached the counter from a nearby desk. Probably a trainee assigned counter duty. Usually, they used old men from the neighborhood who volunteered their time or cops assigned light duty because of injury or disciplinary action.

'I was hoping to see Lieutenant Buskirk. Is he here?'

'He's in a meeting at Valley bureau. Can I help you with something?'

That meant Buskirk was in Van Nuys at the Valley-wide command office. McCaleb's plan to start with him was out the window. He could now wait for Buskirk or leave and come back. But go where? The library? There wasn't even a nearby coffee shop he could walk to. He decided to take his chances with Arrango and Walters. He wanted to keep moving.

'How about Arrango or Walters in homicide?'

The detective glanced at a plastic wall-mounted board with names going down the left side and rows of boxes to be checked that said IN and OUT as well as VACATION and COURT. But there were no check marks of any kind made after the names Arrango and Walters.

'Let me check,' the frontman said. 'Your name?'

'My name is McCaleb but it won't mean anything to them. Tell them it's about the Gloria Torres case.'

The frontman went back to his desk and punched in three digits on the phone. He spoke in a whisper. McCaleb knew then that as far as the frontman was concerned, he didn't have the *look*. In a half minute the call was done and the frontman didn't bother getting up from the desk.

'Turn around, back down the hall, first door on the right.'

McCaleb nodded, took the box of doughnuts off the counter and followed the instructions. As he approached, he put the leather bag under one arm so he could open the door. But it opened as he was reaching for it. A man in a white shirt and tie stood there. His gun was held in a shoulder harness under his right arm. This was a bad sign. Detectives rarely used their weapons, homicide detectives even less than others. Whenever McCaleb saw a homicide detective with a shoulder harness instead of the more comfortable belt clip, he knew he was dealing with a major ego. He almost sighed out loud.

'Mr McCaleb?'

'That's me.'

'I'm Eddie Arrango, what can I do for you? My guy up front said you're here about Glory Torres?'

They shook hands after McCaleb awkwardly transferred the box of doughnuts to his left hand.

'That's right.'

He was a large man, more in horizontal than vertical proportions. Latino, with a full head of black hair feathered with gray. Mid-forties, with a solid build, no stomach over the belt. It went with the shoulder harness. He took up the whole door and made no move to invite his visitor in.

'Is there a place we can talk about this?'

'Talk about what?'

'I'm going to be looking into her murder.'

So much for finesse, McCaleb thought.

'Oh, shit, here we go,' Arrango said.

He shook his head in annoyance, glanced behind him and then back at McCaleb.

'All right,' he said, 'let's get this over with. You got about ten minutes before I toss you outta here.'

He turned around and McCaleb followed him into a room crowded with desks and detectives. Some of them looked up from their work at McCaleb, the intruder, but most didn't bother. Arrango snapped his fingers to draw the attention of a detective at one of the desks along the far wall. He was on the phone but looked up to see Arrango signal him. The man on the phone nodded and held up one finger. Arrango led the way to an interview room with a small table pushed against one wall and three chairs. It was smaller than a prison cell. He closed the door.

'Have a seat. My partner will be in in a minute.'

McCaleb took the chair opposite the table. This meant Arrango would likely take the chair to McCaleb's right or be forced to squeeze behind him to go to the chair on his left. McCaleb wanted him on the right. It was a small thing, but a routine he had always followed as an agent. Put the subject you are talking to on the right. It means they look at you from the left and engage the side of the brain that is less critical and judgmental. A psychologist at Quantico had once given the tip while teaching a class on techniques of hypnosis and interrogation. McCaleb wasn't sure if it worked but he liked to have any edge he could get. And he thought he might need one with Arrango.

'You want a doughnut?' he asked as Arrango took the chair on his right.

'No, I don't want any of your doughnuts. I just want you on your way and out of *my* way. It's the sister, isn't it? You're working for the goddamn sister. Let me see your ticket. I can't believe she's wasting her money on –'

'I don't have a license, if that's what you mean.'

Arrango drummed his fingers on the scarred table as he thought about this.

'Jesus, you know it's stuffy in here. We shouldn't keep it closed up like this.'

Arrango was a bad actor. He delivered the line as if he were reading it off a chart on the wall. He got up, adjusted the thermostat on the wall by the door and then sat back down. McCaleb knew that he had just turned on a tape recorder as well as a video camera hidden behind the air duct grill over the door.

'First off, you say you are conducting an investigation of the Gloria Torres homicide, is that correct?'

'Well, I haven't really started. I was going to talk to you first and then go from there.'

'But you're working for the victim's sister?'

'Graciela Rivers asked me to look into it, yes.'

'And you have no license in the state of California to operate as a private investigator, true?'

'True.'

The door opened and the man Arrango had signaled earlier stepped into the room. Without turning around and looking at his partner, Arrango held a hand up, fingers spread, signaling him not to interrupt. The man McCaleb assumed was Walters folded his arms and leaned against the wall next to the door.

'Do you understand, sir, that it is a crime in this state to operate as a private investigator without a license? I could arrest you on a misdemeanor right now.'

'It's illegal, not to mention unethical, to take money to conduct a private investigation without the proper license. Yes, I'm aware of that.'

'Wait. You're telling me you're doing this for free?'

'That's right. As a friend of the family.'

McCaleb was quickly growing tired of the bullshit and wanted to get on with what he was there for.

'Look, can we skip all the bullshit and turn off the tape and the camera and just talk for a few minutes? Besides, your partner is leaning against the microphone. You're not picking anything up.'

Walters jumped away from the thermostat just as Arrango turned around to see that McCaleb had been right.

'Why didn't you tell me?' Walters said to his partner.

'Shuddup.'

'Hey, have a doughnut, guys,' McCaleb said. 'I'm here to help.'

Arrango turned back to McCaleb, still a bit flustered.

'How the fuck did you know about the tape?'

'Because you've got the same setup in every detective bureau in the city. And I've been in most of them. I used to be with the bureau. That's how I knew.'

'The FBI?' Walters asked.

'FBI retired. Graciela Rivers is an acquaintance. She asked me to look into this, I said I would. I want to help.'

'What's your name?' Walters asked.

Obviously he was coming to everything late because he had been on the phone. McCaleb stood up and extended his hand. Walters shook it as McCaleb introduced himself. Dennis Walters was younger than Arrango. Pale white skin, slim build. His clothes were loose, baggy, suggesting that his wardrobe had not been updated since he had experienced a dramatic loss in weight. He wore no holster at all that McCaleb could see. He probably kept his gun in his briefcase until he went out on the street. McCaleb's kind of cop. Walters knew it wasn't the gun that made the man. His partner didn't.

'I know you,' he said, pointing a finger at McCaleb. 'You're that guy. The serial guy.'

'What are you talking about?' Arrango said.

'You know, the profilers. The serial killer squad. He was the one they sent out here permanently, since most of the nuts are out here. He worked the Sunset Strip Strangler, what else, the Code Killer, that cemetery guy, a bunch of cases out here.'

He then put his attention back on McCaleb.

'Right?'

McCaleb nodded. Walters snapped his fingers.

'Didn't I read about you recently? Something in the *Slimes*, right?'

Once again McCaleb nodded.

'The "Whatever Happened to ..." column. Two Sundays back.'

'That's it. Right. You got a heart transplant, right?'

McCaleb nodded. He knew that familiarity bred comfort. Eventually, they would get down to business. Walters remained standing behind Arrango but McCaleb saw his gaze drop to the box on the table.

'You want a doughnut, Detective? I'd hate to see them go to waste. I didn't get breakfast but I'm not going to have one if you guys don't.'

'Don't mind if I do,' Walters said.

As he came forward and opened the box, he glanced anxiously at his partner. Arrango's face was a stone. Walters took out a glazed doughnut. McCaleb took a cinnamon sugar and then Arrango broke and reluctantly took a powdered sugar. They ate silently for a few moments before McCaleb reached into his sport coat and pulled out the stack of napkins he had grabbed at Winchell's. He tossed them onto the table and everyone took one.

'So, the bureau pension's so short you've gotta pick up PI work, huh?' Walters said, his mouth full of doughnut.

'I'm not a PI. The sister's an acquaintance. Like I said, I'm not being paid.'

'An acquaintance?' Arrango said. 'That's the second time you said that. How exactly do you know her?'

'I live on a boat down at the harbor. I met her at the marina one day. She likes boats. We met. She found out what I once did for the bureau and asked me to take a look at this. What's the problem?'

He didn't know exactly why he was shading the truth to the point of lying. Other than that he had immediately taken a disliking to Arrango, he didn't feel he wanted to reveal his true connection to Gloria Torres and Graciela Rivers.

'Well, look,' Arrango said, 'I don't know what she told you about this, but this is a convenience store robbery, FBI man. This isn't Charlie Manson or Ted Bundy or Jeffrey Fucking Dahmer. It's not rocket science. This is some mope with a mask and a gun and the right ratio of balls to brains to use it all to make a couple dollars. This isn't what you're used to seein', is what I'm saying.'

'I know that,' McCaleb said. 'But I told her I'd check into it. It's been what, going on two months now? I thought maybe you guys wouldn't mind a fresh set of eyes on something you can't be spending much time on anymore.'

Walters took the bait.

'Our team's pulled four cases since then and Eddie's been in trial the last two weeks in Van Nuys,' he said. 'As far as Torres goes, it's –'

'Still active,' Arrango said, cutting his partner off.

McCaleb looked from Walters to Arrango.

'Right ... Sure.'

'And we've got a rule that we don't invite amateurs in on active cases.'

'Amateurs?'

'You got no badge, no private ticket, that says amateur to me.'

McCaleb let the insult go by. He guessed Arrango was just taking his measure anyway. He pushed on.

'That's one of those rules you bring up when it's convenient,' he said. 'But we all know here that I might be able to help you. What you need to know is that I'm not here to show you guys up. Not at all. Anything I come up with, you'll be the first to know. Suspects, leads, anything. It all goes to you. I'd just like a little cooperation, that's all.'

'Cooperation in exactly what form?' Arrango asked. 'Like my partner who talks too much says, we're kind of busy here.'

'Copy me the murder book. Also any video you have. I'm good on crime scenes. That was sort of my specialty. I might be able to help you there. Just copy me what you've got and I'll get out of your way.'

'What you're saying is you think we fucked up. That the answer's sitting there in the book ready to jump out at you 'cause you're a fed and the feds are so much smarter than us.'

McCaleb laughed and shook his head. He was beginning to think he should have counted his losses and left as soon as he saw the macho-man holster. He tried once more.

'No, that's not what I'm saying. I don't know if you missed anything or not. I've worked with LAPD many times. If I was betting, I'd bet you missed nothing. All I'm saying is that I told Graciela Rivers I'd check into things. Let me ask you something, does she call you much?'

'The sister? Too much. Week in and week out and I tell her the same thing every time. No suspects, no leads.'

'You're waiting on something to happen, right? Give it new life.'

'Maybe.'

'Well, this could at least be your way of getting her off your back. If I see what you've got and go back to her and say you boys did what you could, she might back off. She'll believe it from me because she knows me.'

Neither of them said anything.

'What have you got to lose?' McCaleb prodded.

'We'd have to clear any kind of cooperation with the lieutenant,' Arrango said. 'We can't just give out copies of investigative records without his say-so, rules or no rules. In fact, you fucked up there, bro. You should've gone to him before you came to us. You know how the game's played. You didn't follow protocol.'

'I understand that. I asked for him when I got here but they said he was at Valley bureau.'

'Yeah, well, he should be back soon,' Arrango said, checking his watch. 'Tell you what, you say you're good with crime scenes?'

'Yeah. If you got a tape, I'd like to take a look at it.'

Arrango looked at Walters and winked, then he looked back at McCaleb.

'We got better than a crime scene tape. We got the crime.'

He kicked back his chair and stood up.

'Come on,' he said. 'Bring those doughnuts with you.'

# 5

........

Arrango opened a drawer in one of the desks crammed into the squad room and took out a videotape. He then led the way out of the homicide squad office, down the hall and then through the half door of the main detective bureau counter. McCaleb could see they were headed for Buskirk's office, which was still empty. McCaleb left the doughnuts on the front counter and followed the others in.

Pushed into one corner of the room was a tall steel cabinet on wheels. It was the kind of setup used in classrooms and roll-call rooms. Arrango opened the two doors and there was a television and a videocassette player inside. He turned the equipment on and shoved in the tape.

'So look at this and tell us something we don't know yet,' he said to McCaleb without looking at him. 'Then maybe we go to bat for you with the lieutenant.'

McCaleb moved until he stood directly in front of the television. Arrango hit the play button and soon the black-and-white image came up on the television screen. McCaleb was looking at the view held by an overhead surveillance camera in a small convenience store. The frame was drawn around the front counter area. It was glass-topped and full of cigars and disposable cameras and batteries and other high-end items. A printed date and timeline ran across the bottom of the screen.

The frame was empty for a few moments and then the

top of the gray-haired counterman's head came into view in the lower left corner as he leaned over the cash register.

'That's Chan Ho Kang, the owner,' Arrango said, punching the screen with a finger and leaving a smudge of doughnut grease. 'He's spending his last few seconds on the planet here.'

Kang had the cash drawer open. He broke a roll of quarters against the corner of the counter case and then dumped them into the appropriate section of the drawer. Just as he shoved it closed, a woman entered the frame. A customer. McCaleb recognized her instantly from the photo Graciela Rivers had showed him on the boat.

Gloria Torres smiled as she approached the counter and placed two Hershey's candy bars down on the glass. She then pulled her purse up, opened it and took out her wallet as Mr Kang punched keys on the register.

Gloria looked up, money in hand, when suddenly another figure entered the frame. It was a man with a black ski mask covering his face and wearing what looked like a black jumpsuit. He moved up behind Gloria unnoticed. She was still smiling. McCaleb looked at the time counter, saw it said 22:41:35 and then looked back at what was happening in the store. It gave him a strange feeling to watch the action take place in this surreal black-and-white silence. From behind, the man in the ski mask put his right hand on Gloria's right shoulder and in one continuous move of the left hand put the muzzle of a handgun against her left temple. Without hesitation he pulled the trigger.

'Badda-BING!' Arrango said.

McCaleb felt his chest clench like a fist as he watched the bullet tear into Gloria's skull, a horrifying mist of blood jettisoning from the entry and exit wounds on either side of her head.

'Never knew what hit her,' Walters said quietly.

Gloria jerked forward onto the counter and then bounced backward, collapsing into the shooter as he brought his right arm up around her and across her chest. Stepping backward, Gloria in front of him as a shield, he raised his left hand again and fired a shot at Mr Kang, striking him somewhere in the body. The store owner bounced off the wall behind him and then forward, his upper body crashing down over the counter and cracking the glass. His arms flung out across the counter and his hands grappled for a hold like a man going over a cliff. Finally, he let go, his body flopping to the floor behind the counter.

The shooter let Gloria's body slide to the ground and her upper body fell outside the view of the video frame. Only her hand, as if reaching across the floor, and legs stayed in the picture. The shooter moved toward the counter, quickly leaning over and looking down at Mr Kang on the floor. Kang was reaching into a shelf below the counter, frantically pulling out stacks of brown bags. The shooter just watched him, until finally Kang's arm came out, a black revolver in his hand. The man in the ski mask dispassionately shot Kang in the face before he ever got the chance to raise his gun.

Leaning further over the counter, his feet in the air, the shooter grabbed one of the bullet shells that had ejected and fallen next to Kang's arm. He then straightened up, reached over and took the bills from the open cash register drawer. He looked up at the camera. Despite the mask, it was clear the man winked and said something to the camera, then quickly left the frame to the left.

'He's picking up the other two shells,' Walters said.

'No sound on the camera, right?' McCaleb said.

'Right,' Walters said. 'Whatever he said there, he said to himself.'

'Only one camera in the store?'

'Only one. Kang was cheap. That's what we were told.'

As they continued to watch, the shooter made one more pass through the corner of the screen on his way out.

McCaleb stared blankly at the television, stunned by the harshness of the violence, despite his experience. Two lives spent for the contents of a cash drawer.

'You ain't gonna see that on *America's Favorite Home Videos*,' Arrango said.

McCaleb had dealt with cops like Arrango for years. They acted as though nothing ever got to them. They could look at the worst crime scenes and find the joke. It was part of the survival instinct. Act and talk as if it means nothing to you and you've got a shield. You won't get hurt.

'Can I see it again?' McCaleb said. 'Can you slow it down this time?'

'Wait a minute,' Walters said. 'It's not over.'

'What?'

'The Good Samuel comes in just about now.'

He said it with a Hispanic pronunciation. Sam-*well*.

'The Good Samuel?'

'Good Samaritan. Mexican guy comes in the store, finds them and tries to help. He kept the woman alive but there was nothing he could do for Kang. Then he goes out to the pay phone out front and makes – there he is.'

McCaleb looked back at the screen. The timeline now read 22:42:55 and a dark-haired, dark-complected man in jeans and a T-shirt had entered the picture. He first hesitated on the right side of the screen, apparently looking at Gloria Torres, and then went to the counter and looked over it. Kang's body lay on the floor in a lake of blood. There were wide, ugly bullet wounds in his chest and face. His eyes were open and still. He was obviously dead. The Good Samaritan returned to Gloria. He knelt on the floor and apparently hunched over her upper body, which was off-screen. But almost immediately he was up again and out of the picture.

'He went down the aisles looking for bandages,' Arrango said. 'He actually wrapped her head with masking tape and a Kotex. A supersize.'

The Good Samaritan returned and went to work on Gloria, although all of this was off-screen.

'The camera never picked up a great shot of him,' Arrango said. 'And he didn't stick around. After he made the call to nine one one out front, he split.'

'He never came in later?'

'Nope. We went on the TV news with it. You know, asking for him to come forward because he might've seen something that would help the investigation. But nothing. This guy went up in smoke.'

'Weird.'

On the screen the man stood up, his back still to the camera. As he was moving out of the frame, he glanced to his left and a brief profile of his face was visible. He had a dark mustache. He then disappeared from view.

'He now calls the cops?' McCaleb asked.

'Nine one one,' Walters said. 'He said "ambulance" and they put him through to the Fire Department.'

'Why didn't the guy come in?'

'We got a theory on that,' Arrango said.

'Care to share it?'

'The voice on the nine one one tape had an accent,' Walters said. 'Latino. We figure the guy was an illegal. He didn't stick around because he was afraid if we talked to him, we'd find out and ship him back.'

McCaleb nodded. It was plausible, especially in LA, where there were hundreds of thousands of illegals avoiding authorities.

'We put out fliers in the Mexican neighborhoods and

went on Channel Thirty-four,' Walters continued. 'Promised he wouldn't be deported if he'd just come in and tell us what he saw, but we got nothing. Happens a lot in those neighborhoods. Hell, the places they come from, they're more scared a' the cops than the bad guys.'

'Too bad,' McCaleb said. 'He was there so soon, he probably saw the shooter's car, maybe got the plate.'

'Maybe,' Walters said. 'But if he got the plate, he didn't bother giving it to us on the tape. He did give a half-ass description of the car – "Black car, like a truck," was how he described it. But he hung up before the girl could ask if he got a plate.'

'Can we watch it again?' McCaleb asked.

'Sure, why not?' Arrango said.

He rewound the tape and they silently watched it again, this time with Arrango using the slow motion button during the shooting. McCaleb's eyes stayed on the shooter for every frame that he was on film. Though the mask hid his expression, there were times that his eyes were clearly seen. Brutal eyes that showed nothing as he gunned down two people. Their color indiscernible because of the black-and-white tape.

'Jesus,' McCaleb said when it was over.

Arrango ejected the tape and turned off the equipment. He turned and looked at McCaleb.

'So, tell us something,' he said. 'You're the expert. Help us out here.'

The challenge was clearly evident in his voice. Put up or shut up. They were back to the territorial thing.

'I'd have to think about it, maybe watch the tape some more.'

'Figures,' Arrango responded dismissively.

'I'll tell you one thing,' McCaleb said, looking only at Arrango. 'This wasn't the first time.'

He pointed at the dead TV tube.

'No hesitation, no panic, the quick in and out ... the

calm handling of the weapon and the kick, the presence of mind to pick up the brass. This guy's done this before. This isn't the first time. And probably not the last. Plus, he'd been in there before. He knew there was a camera – that's why he wore the mask. I mean, it's true that lots of places like that have cameras but he looked right up at this one. He knew *where* it was. That means he'd been in there before. He's either from the neighborhood or he came in earlier to case the place.'

Arrango smirked and Walters looked quickly from McCaleb to his partner. He was about to say something when Arrango held up his hand to silence him. McCaleb knew then that what he had just said had been accurate and that they already knew it.

'What?' he asked. 'How many others?'

Arrango now held both hands up in a hands-off gesture.

'That's it for now,' he said. 'We talk to the lieutenant and we let you know.'

'What is this?' McCaleb protested, finally losing his patience. 'Why show me the tape and stop there? Give me a shot at this. I might help you. What have you got to lose?'

'Oh, I'm sure you can help. But our hands are tied. Let us talk to the lieutenant and we'll get back to you.'

He signaled everybody out of the office. McCaleb thought for a moment about refusing to leave but dismissed it as a bad idea. He walked through the door, Arrango and Walters behind him.

'When will I hear from you?'

'As soon as we know what we can do for you,' Arrango said. 'Give me a number, we'll be in touch.'

# 6

McCaleb stood outside the station's lobby waiting for the cab to show. He was steaming about how he had allowed Arrango to play him. Guys like Arrango got off on holding something out to a person and then snatching it away. McCaleb had always known people like Arrango – on both sides of the law.

But there was nothing he could have done about it. For now it was Arrango's show. McCaleb wasn't really expecting to hear from him again. He knew that he would have to call him for an answer. That was how the game was played. McCaleb decided he would give it until the next morning before he would call.

When the cab got there, McCaleb got in the back behind the driver. It was a way of discouraging conversation. He checked the name on the dashboard license card and saw it was Russian and unpronounceable. He pulled the small notebook out of his bag and gave the driver the address for the Sherman Market in Canoga Park. They headed north on Reseda Boulevard and then west on Sherman Way until they came to the small market near the intersection of Winnetka Avenue.

The cab pulled into the lot in front of the small store. The place was nondescript, unimpressive, its plate-glass windows plastered with brightly colored sale signs. It looked like a thousand other mini-markets in the city. Except someone had decided that this one was worth robbing and that it was worth killing two people in order to accomplish that goal. Before getting out, McCaleb studied the signs covering the windows. They blocked off a view of the interior. He knew that was probably the reason the shooter had chosen this store. Even if passing motorists glanced over, they wouldn't see what was going on inside.

Finally, he opened the door and got out. He stepped to the driver's window and told the man to wait for him. As he went into the store, he heard the tinkling of a bell from above the door. The cash register counter depicted in the video was set up near the back wall directly across from the door. An old woman stood back behind the counter. She was staring at McCaleb and she looked scared. She was Asian. McCaleb realized who she might be.

Looking around as if he had come in with a purpose other than to gawk, he saw the display racks full of candy and picked out a Hershey's bar. He stepped to the counter and placed it down, noticing that the glass top of the case was still cracked. The full realization that he was in the same spot where Glory Torres had stood and smiled at Mr Kang then hit him. He looked up at the old woman with a pained expression on his face and nodded.

'Anything else?'

'No, just this.'

She rang it up and he paid her. He studied her hesitant movements. She knew he wasn't from the neighborhood or a regular customer. She still was not at ease. She probably never would be.

When she gave him his change, McCaleb noticed that the watch she wore on her wrist had a wide, black rubber wristband and a large face. It was a man's watch and it dwarfed her tiny, seemingly fragile wrist. He had seen the watch before. It had been on Chan Ho Kang's wrist in the surveillance video. McCaleb remembered focusing on the watch as the video depicted the wounded

Kang scrambling for purchase on the counter and then finally falling to the floor.

'Are you Mrs Kang?' McCaleb asked.

She stopped what she was doing at the register and looked at him.

'Yes. I know you?'

'No. It's just ... I heard about what happened here. To your husband. I'm sorry.'

She nodded.

'Yes, thank you.' Then, seemingly needing an explanation or salve for her wounds, she added, 'The only way to keep evil out is to not unlock door. We can't do that. We must have business.'

Now McCaleb nodded. It was probably something her husband had told her when she worried about his operating a cash business in a violent city.

He thanked her and left, the bell ringing overhead again as he went through the door. He got back in the cab and appraised the front of the market again. It made no sense to him. Why this place? He thought of the video. The shooter's hand grabbing the cash. He couldn't have gotten much. McCaleb wished he knew more about the crime, more of the details.

The phone on the wall to the right of the store's windows caught his eye. It was the one the unidentified Good Samaritan had apparently used. He wondered if it had been processed for prints after they realized he wasn't coming forward. Probably not. By then it was too late. It was a long shot anyway.

'Where to?' the driver said, his accent discernible in only two syllables.

McCaleb leaned forward to give the man an address but hesitated. He drummed his fingers on the plastic backing of the front seat and thought for a moment.

'Keep the meter running. I've got to make a couple calls first.'

He got out again and headed to the pay phone, once more taking his notebook out. He looked up a number and charged the call to his card. It was answered right away.

'*Times*, Russell.'

'Did you say *Times* or *Slimes*?'

'Funny, who is this?'

'Keisha, it's Terry McCaleb.'

'Hey, how're you doing, man?'

'I'm fine. I wanted to thank you for that story. I should've called sooner. But it was nice.'

'Hey, you're cool. Nobody else ever calls to thank me for anything.'

'Well, I'm not that cool. I was also calling because I need a favor. You got your terminal on?'

'You really know how to spoil a good thing. Yes, my terminal is on. What's up?'

'Well, I'm looking for something but I'm not sure how to find it. You think you could do one of those key-word searches for me? I'm looking for stories that would be about a robber who shoots people.'

She laughed.

'That's it?' she said. 'You know how often people get shot up in robberies? This is LA, you know.'

'Yeah, I know, that was stupid. Okay, how about adding in *ski mask*. And maybe only go back about eighteen months. Think that will narrow it?'

'Maybe.'

He heard her keyboard start clicking as she tapped into the newspaper's computerized library of story files. By using key words like *robbery* and *ski mask* and *shooting* she would be able to draw up all stories that had contained those words.

'So what's going on, Terry? I thought you were retired.'

'I am.'

'Doesn't sound like it. This is like the old days. Are you doing some kind of investigation?'

'Sort of. I'm checking something for a friend and the LAPD's being the LAPD. And it's worse when you don't have a badge.'

'What's it about?'

'It's not newsworthy yet, Keisha. If it turns out that way, you'll be the first I let know.'

She blew out her breath in exasperation.

'I hate it when you guys do that,' she protested. 'I mean, why should I help you when you won't let me decide whether something's a story or not? I'm the newspaper reporter, not you.'

'I know, I know. I guess what I'm saying is that I just want to keep this to myself until I see what is what. I'll tell you about it after that. I promise, first crack at it. It probably won't pan out, but I'll tell you one way or the other. Did you get anything?'

'Yes,' she said in a mock pout. 'Six hits in the last eighteen months.'

'Six? What are they?'

'Six stories. I'll read you the headlines and you tell me if you think you want me to call up the stories.'

'Okay.'

'Okay, here goes. "Two Shot in Robbery Attempt", then we have "Man Shot, Robbed at ATM". After that we have "Deputies Seek Help in ATM Shooting". Let's see, the next three look like one related case. The headlines are "Store Owner, Customer Shot in Robbery", followed by "Second Victim Dies; Was *Times* Employee" – oh, shit, I never heard about that. I'll have to read this one myself – and the last one is "Police Seek Good Samaritan". Those are the six.'

McCaleb thought for a moment. Six stories, three different incidents.

'Could you pull up the first three and read them if they're not too long?'

'Why not.'

He listened as her keyboard started clicking. His eyes wandered out past the cab to Sherman Way. It was a four-lane street, busy even at night. He wondered if Arrango and Walters had been able to come up with any witnesses to the shooter's getaway, anybody besides the Good Samaritan.

McCaleb's eyes moved across the street and in the parking lot of a strip mall he saw a man sitting in a car. The man raised a newspaper just as McCaleb noticed this and his face disappeared. McCaleb checked the car. It was an old beater, foreign make, which dissuaded him from the possibility that maybe Arrango had put a quick tail on him. He dismissed it as Keisha started reading the newspaper story on her computer screen.

'Okay, the first one ran on October eighth last year. It's just a short. "A husband and wife were shot and wounded Thursday by a would-be robber who was then wrestled to the ground and captured by a group of passersby, Inglewood police said Thursday. The couple were walking along Manchester Boulevard at eleven when a man wearing a ski mask approached and –"'

'The guy was captured?'

'That's what it says.'

'Okay, skip that one. I'm looking for unsolveds, I think.'

'Okay, the next story ran Friday, January twenty-fourth. Headline is "Man Shot, Robbed at ATM". No byline. It's another short. "A Lancaster man who was withdrawing cash from an automatic teller machine was fatally shot Wednesday night in what Los Angeles County sheriff's deputies called a senseless killing. James Cordell, thirty, was shot once in the head by an unknown assailant who then took the three hundred dollars he had just withdrawn from the machine. The shooting took place at approximately ten P.M. at a Regional State Bank branch in the eighteen-hundred block of Lancaster Road. Sheriff's detective Jaye Winston said a portion of the shooting was captured on the ATM security camera but not enough to identify the gunman. The one glimpse of the gunman on the camera's tape showed he was wearing a dark knit ski mask over his head. However, Winston said that the tape revealed that there was no confrontation or refusal on Cordell's part to turn over the money. 'It was absolutely cold-blooded,' Winston said. 'This guy just walked up, shot the victim and took the money. It was very cold and brutal. This guy didn't care. He just wanted the money.' Cordell collapsed in front of the well-lighted machine but his body was not found until another customer came approximately fifteen minutes later. Paramedics pronounced him dead at the scene." Okay, that's that one. You ready for the next?'

'I'm ready.'

McCaleb had been jotting down some of the details from the story into his notebook. He underlined the name *Winston* three times. He knew Jaye Winston. He thought Winston would be willing to help him – more so than Arrango and Walters had been. Jaye Winston was not a hard tango. McCaleb felt he had finally caught a break.

Keisha Russell started reading the next story.

'Okay, same thing. No byline. It's short and it ran two days later. "Sheriff's deputies said there were no suspects in the fatal shooting this week of a Lancaster man who was withdrawing money from an automatic teller machine. Detective Jaye Winston said the department wished to speak with any motorists or passersby who were in the area of the eighteen-hundred block of Lancaster Road on Wednesday night and may have seen the assailant before or after the ten-twenty shooting. James Cordell, thirty, was shot once in the head by a robber who wore a ski mask. He died at the scene of the robbery. Three hundred dollars were taken during the robbery. Though part of the incident was captured by the Regional State Bank's security camera, detectives were unable to identify the suspect because of the mask he wore. 'He had to have had it off at one point,' Winston said of the mask. 'He didn't just walk or drive down the street with a mask on. People had to have seen this guy and we want to talk to those people.'" Okay, that's the end.'

McCaleb hadn't taken any notes from the second story. But he was thinking about what Keisha had read and didn't respond.

'Terry, you still there?'

'Yeah. Sorry.'

'Any of it help?'

'I think so. Maybe.'

'And you still won't tell me what it's about?'

'Not yet, Keisha, but thanks. You'll be the first to know.'

He hung up and pulled the business card Arrango had given him out of his shirt pocket. He decided not to wait for Arrango or for the next day. He had a lead he could follow now, whether or not the LAPD cooperated with him. While he was waiting for the call to be answered, he looked across the street. The car with the man reading the newspaper was gone.

The phone was picked up after six rings and he was eventually transferred to Arrango. McCaleb asked if Buskirk was back yet.

'Bad news, amigo,' Arrango said. 'The lieutenant's back all right. But he wants to hold off on turning our book over to you.'

'Yeah, how come?' McCaleb asked, trying to disguise his annoyance.

'Well, I didn't really ask but I think he was pissed that you didn't come in to see him first. I told you that. You should've followed line of command.'

'That was kind of hard to do, being that he wasn't there this morning. And I told you, I did ask for him first. Did you tell him that?'

'Yeah, I told him. I think he was in a bad mood, coming from Valley bureau. He probably got his ass chewed about something so then he chewed mine. That's how it goes sometimes. Right down the food chain. Anyway, look, you're lucky. We showed you the whole thing on tape. You got a good start there. We shouldn't've done that for you.'

'Some start. You know, it's amazing that anything ever gets solved with all the bureaucratic bullshit that goes on. I thought the FBI was unique. We used to call it the Federal Bureau of Inertia. But I guess it's the same all around.'

'Hey, look, we don't need your shit. We have a whole plate full of it here. My boss seems to think I invited you in here and now he's pissed at me. I don't need this. If you want to go away mad, that's your problem. But just go away.'

'I'm gone, Arrango. You won't hear from me until I have your shooter. I'll bring him in for you.'

McCaleb knew it was bullshit grandstanding as soon as he said it. But ever since February ninth he had increasingly found that he had zero tolerance for fools.

Arrango laughed sarcastically in response and said, 'Yeah, right. I'll be waiting for you.'

He hung up.

# 7

McCaleb held up a finger to the cab driver and made another call. He first thought about Jaye Winston but decided to wait. Instead he called Graciela Rivers at the number she had given him for the nursing station in the emergency room of Holy Cross Medical Center. She agreed to meet him for an early lunch, even though he explained that he hadn't accomplished much. He told her to look for him in the emergency room waiting room at eleven-thirty.

The hospital was in a part of the Valley called Mission Hills. On the way there, McCaleb looked out the window at the passing scenery. It was mostly strip shopping centers and gas stations. The driver was making his way toward the 405 so that he could head north.

McCaleb's knowledge of the Valley had come only through cases. There had been many, most of them falling under his review only on paper and photo prints and videotape from the body dumps along the freeway embankments or the hillsides fringing the northern flats. The Code Killer had hit four times in the Valley before he disappeared like the morning marine layer.

'What are you, police?'

McCaleb looked away from the window and over the seat at the rearview mirror. The driver's eyes were on him.

'What?'

'Are you policeman or something?'

McCaleb shook his head.

'No, I'm no one.'

He looked back out the window as the cab labored up a freeway on-ramp. They passed a woman who was holding a sign asking for money. Another victim waiting to be victimized again.

He sat in the waiting room on a plastic chair across from an injured woman and her husband. The woman had internal pain and kept her arms folded across her midsection. She was hunched over, protecting the hurt. Her husband was being attentive, repeatedly asking how she felt and going to the intake window to ask when she would be taken back for examination. But twice McCaleb heard him quietly ask her, 'What are you going to tell them?'

And each time the woman turned her face away.

At quarter to twelve Graciela Rivers came through the double doors of the ER ward. She suggested that they just go to the hospital cafeteria because she had only an hour. McCaleb didn't mind because his taste for food had still not come back since the transplant. Eating at the hospital would be no different to him than eating at Jozu on Melrose. Most days he didn't care what he ate and sometimes he forgot about meals until a headache reminded him that he needed to refuel.

The cafeteria was almost empty. They took their trays to a table next to a window, which looked out on a huge green lawn surrounding a large white cross.

'This is my one chance to look at daylight,' Graciela said. 'Back in the ER rooms there are no windows. So I always try to get a window.'

McCaleb nodded that he understood.

'Way back when I worked in Quantico, our offices were below ground. The basement. No windows, always damp, freezing in the winter even with the heat on. I never saw the sun. It wears on you after a while.'

'Is that why you moved out here?'

'No. Other reasons. But I did figure I'd get a window. I was wrong. They stuck me in a storage closet at the FO. Seventeen floors up but no windows. I think that's why I live on the boat now. I like having the sky close by.'

'What's the FO?'

'Sorry. Field office. It was in Westwood. In the big federal building near the veterans cemetery.'

She nodded.

'So, did you really grow up on Catalina like the paper said?'

'Until I was sixteen,' he said. 'Then I lived with my mother in Chicago ... It's funny, I spent all the time I was growing up on that island just wanting to get off it. Now I'm just trying to get back there.'

'What will you do there?'

'I don't know. I've got a mooring over there my father left me. Maybe I won't do anything. Maybe I'll just drop a line and sit in the sun with a beer in my hand.'

He smiled and she smiled back.

'If you already have a mooring, why can't you go now?'

'The boat's not ready. Neither am I yet.'

She nodded.

'It was your father's boat?'

Another detail from the newspaper. He had obviously said too much about himself to Keisha Russell. He didn't like people knowing so much about him so easily.

'He lived on it over there. When he died, it came to me. I let it sit in dry dock for years. Now it needs a lot of work.'

'Did he name it or was that you?'

'His name.'

She frowned and squinted her eyes as if something was sour.

'Why did he call it *The Following Sea* instead of just *Following Sea*? It doesn't make sense with *The* in front of *Following Sea*.'

'No, it makes sense. It doesn't refer to the act of following behind the sea. There is something known as *the* following sea, or *a* following sea.'

'Oh. What is it?'

'A sea is a wave. You know, how you hear on surf reports that the seas are two to four feet or whatever?'

'Right.'

'Okay, well a following sea is the one you have to watch out for. It's the one that comes up behind a vessel. You don't see it coming. It hits you from behind and swamps you. Sinks you. The rule is that if you're running in following seas, you've just got to be moving faster than they are. Stay ahead of them. He named the boat that because it was like a reminder. You know, always watch over your shoulder. It was something he always said to me when I was growing up. Even when I went over town.'

'Over town?'

'When I left the island. He told me always to watch out for the following sea, even on land.'

She smiled.

'Now that I know the story, I like the name. Do you miss him?'

He nodded but offered nothing else. The conversation drifted away and they began to eat their sandwiches. McCaleb hadn't planned on the meeting being about him. After a few bites he started filling her in on the morning's lack of solid accomplishment. He didn't tell her about watching her sister being murdered on the videotape but he told her about his hunch that the Torres-Kang slayings were connected to at least one other incident. He told her how he was further guessing that that other incident might be the ATM robbery and shooting recounted in the stories Keisha Russell had read him.

'What will you do next?' she asked when he was done.

'Take a nap.'

She looked at him curiously.

'I'm beat,' he said. 'I haven't been running around and doing as much thinking as this for a long time. I'm going back to my boat and resting up. Tomorrow I'll start again.'

'I'm sorry.'

'No, you're not,' he said with a smile. 'You were looking for somebody with a reason to get involved in this. I've got the reason and I'm involved, but I've got to take it slow at first. You being a nurse, I hope you understand.'

'I do. I don't want you to hurt yourself. That would make Glory's dying even more ...'

'I understand.'

They were silent for a few moments before he picked up the conversation again.

'Your take on the LAPD was right on. I think they're in a holding pattern, waiting for something to happen – probably for this guy to hit again. They're definitely not working it. It's a cold case until something happens to warm it up.'

She shook her head.

'They're not working it but they don't want you to have a try at it. That makes a lot of sense.'

'It's a territorial thing. It's the way the game is played.'

'It's not a game.'

'I know.'

He wished he had chosen a better word.

'Then what can you do?'

'Well, in the morning, when I'm fresh, I'll try the

Sheriff's Department on this other case, the one I think is connected. I know the lead on it. Jaye Winston. We worked a case once a long time ago. It went well and I'm hoping that will get me in the door. At least further in than I got with the LA people.'

She nodded but she wasn't all that good at masking her disappointment.

'Graciela,' he said, 'I don't know if you were expecting somebody to just come in and solve this like turning a key in a lock but it's not realistic to believe that. That's movies. This is real. In all my years in the bureau, most of the cases turned on some little detail, some little thing that was missed or didn't seem important at first. But then it comes back around to being the key to the whole thing. It just takes time to get there sometimes, to find that little detail.'

'I know. I know. It just frustrates me that more wasn't done sooner.'

'Yes, when the ...'

He was going to say when the blood was fresh.

'What?'

'Nothing. It's just that with most cases the more time goes by, the harder it gets.'

He knew he wasn't helping her any by telling her the reality of the situation. But he wanted her to be prepared for his eventual failure. He had been good in his day but not that good. He now realized that by agreeing to take the case he had only set Graciela Rivers up for disappointment. His selfish dream of redemption would be another painful dose of reality for her.

'Those men just didn't care,' she said.

He studied her downcast eyes. He knew she was talking about Arrango and Walters.

'Well, I do.'

They finished eating in silence. After McCaleb pushed his plate aside, he watched her as she gazed out the window. Even in her white polyester nurse's uniform with her hair pinned back, Graciela Rivers stirred something in him. She had a kind of sadness about her that he wished somehow to soothe. He wondered if it had been there before her sister died. With most people it is. McCaleb had even seen it in the faces of babies – the sadness already there. The events of their lives seemed only to confirm the sadness they already carried.

'Was this where she died?' he asked.

She nodded and looked back at him.

'She was first taken to Northridge, stabilized and then transferred here. I was here when life support was terminated. I was with her.'

He shook his head.

'It must have been very hard.'

'I see people dying every day in the ER. We joke about it to relieve the stress, say they are "Three-D". Definitely Done Dancing. But when it's your own ... I don't joke about it anymore.'

He watched her face as she shook it off, shifted gears and moved on, away from the trouble spot. Some people have that fifth gear that they can drop into, to get away.

'Tell me about her,' he said.

'What do you mean?'

'That's really why I came. Tell me things about her. It will help me. The better feel that I have for her, the better I'll be at this.'

She was quiet a moment, her mouth curled in a frown as she thought about how to sum her sister up in a few words.

'Is there a kitchen on that boat of yours?' she finally asked.

Her question caught him off guard.

'What?'

'A kitchen. On your boat.'

'Uh, it's actually called a galley.'

'Then galley. Is it big enough to cook real meals?'

'Sure. Why are you asking me about my boat?'

'You want to know my sister?'

'Yes.'

'Then you have to meet her son. Everything that was good about my sister is in Raymond. He's all you have to know.'

McCaleb nodded slowly as he understood.

'So how about I bring Raymond down to your boat tonight and we make you dinner. I already told him about you and about the boat. He wants to see it.'

He thought a moment and said, 'Tell you what. How about we wait until tomorrow. That way I can tell you about how my visit to the Sheriff's Department went. Maybe I'll have something more positive to report.'

'Tomorrow will be fine.'

'And don't worry about cooking dinner. Dinner will be my job.'

'You're turning this all around. I wanted to –'

'I know, I know. But you can save that for one night at your home. You're coming to my home tomorrow and I'll take care of dinner, okay?'

'Okay,' she said, still frowning but realizing he wouldn't be budged. Then she smiled. 'We'll be there.'

Traffic south on the 405 was intense and the cab didn't drop him off at the marina in San Pedro until after two. The cab was not air-conditioned and he caught a slight headache from the mixture of freeway exhaust fumes and the driver's body odor.

After he got inside the boat, he checked his phone machine and found the only message he had was a hang-up call. He felt out of sync because his travels that day had involved more physical activity than he'd had for a long while. His leg muscles were sore and his back was aching. He went down to the head and checked his temperature but there was no fever. Blood pressure and pulse also checked out fine. He logged it all on the clipboard, then went to his stateroom, stripped off his clothes and crawled into the unmade bed.

Despite his physical depletion he had insomnia and lay wide awake on the pillow. His mind churned with the thoughts of the day and images from the video. After an hour of fooling himself, he got up and went up to the salon. He dug the notebook out of the jacket he had draped over a chair and read through the notes he had taken earlier. Nothing stood out but he felt comforted in some way at having started a record of his investigation.

On a fresh page he jotted down some additional thoughts about the video and a couple of questions he wanted to be sure to cover with Jaye Winston the next day. Assuming that the investigators had linked the cases, he wanted to know how solid the connection was and whether the three hundred dollars taken from James Cordell in the first case was actually taken from the victim or from the ATM's cash tray.

He put the notebook aside when he realized he was hungry. He got up, scrambled three egg whites in a skillet, mixed in some Tabasco sauce and salsa and made a sandwich with white toast. After two bites he put on more Tabasco.

When he had cleaned up the galley, he felt the fatigue coming back and finally closing him down. He knew he could sleep now. He took a quick shower, another temperature reading and the evening batch of medications. In the mirror he saw he had what looked like a two-day growth of beard even though he had shaved that morning. It was a side effect of one of the drugs he was taking. Prednisone helped fight organ rejection and stimulated hair growth at the same time. He smiled at his reflection, thinking that the day before he should have told Bonnie Fox that he felt like a werewolf, not

Frankenstein's creation. He was getting his monsters mixed up. He went to bed.

His dream was in black and white. They all were now but they had not been before the operation. He didn't know what this meant. He had told Dr Fox about it and she had just shrugged.

In this dream he was in the market. He was a player in the video he had been shown by Arrango and Walters. He was at the counter smiling at Chan Ho Kang. The store owner smiled back in an unfriendly way and said something.

'What?' McCaleb asked.

'You don't deserve it,' Mr Kang said.

McCaleb looked down at the counter at his purchase but before he could see what it was he felt the cold ring of steel against his temple. He quickly turned and there was the masked man with a gun. McCaleb knew in the way knowledge and logic accompany dreams that the man was smiling behind the mask. The robber lowered the gun and fired into McCaleb's chest, his bullet hitting the ten ring – the circle of the heart. The bullet went through McCaleb as if he were a paper target. But the impact forced him backward a step and then in slow motion he was falling. He felt no pain, only a sense of relief. He looked at the killer as he was going down and recognized the eyes watching through the mask. They were his own eyes. Then came the wink.

And he kept falling and falling.

# 8

........

The distant booming of empty cargo containers being unloaded from a ship in the nearby Port of Los Angeles woke McCaleb before dawn. As he lay in bed, eyes closed but fully awake, he pictured the process. The crane delicately swinging the container the size of a truck trailer off the ship's deck and into the yard, then the ground man giving the drop sign early and the huge steel box dropping the last three feet and producing a concussion like a sonic boom echoing across the nearby marinas. In McCaleb's vision, the ground man was laughing each time.

'Fucking assholes,' McCaleb said, finally giving up on sleep and sitting up. It was the third time in a month it had happened.

He checked the clock and realized he had slept for more than ten hours. He slowly made his way to the head and took a shower. After he had toweled off, he took the morning reading of vital signs and the prescribed complement of assorted pills and liquid chemicals. He logged it all on the progress chart and then got out his razor. He was about to spread shaving cream across his face when he looked in the mirror and said, 'Fuck it.'

He shaved his neck so he would look neat but left it at that, deciding that to shave two or three times a day for the rest of his life, or for as long as he was on prednisone, wasn't an alternative. He had never had a beard before. The bureau wouldn't have allowed it.

After dressing, he took a tall glass of orange juice, his phone book and the portable phone out to the stern and sat in the fishing chair as the sun came up. Between gulps of juice he constantly checked his watch, waiting for it to hit seven-fifteen, which he believed would be the best time to call Jaye Winston.

The Sheriff's Department homicide offices were in Whittier on the far side of the county. From that location, the squad's detectives handled all killings committed in unincorporated Los Angeles County and the various cities the department contracted with to provide law enforcement services. One of those cities was Palmdale, where James Cordell had been murdered.

Because the homicide squad offices were so distant, McCaleb had decided that it would be foolish to take an hour-long cab ride out there without knowing whether Winston would be in when he arrived. So he had decided on the seven-fifteen call rather than the surprise visit with a box of doughnuts.

'Those assholes.'

McCaleb looked around and saw one of his neighbors, Buddy Lockridge, standing in the cockpit of his sailboat, a forty-two-foot Hunter called the *Double-Down*. Buddy's boat was three slips from *The Following Sea*. He was holding a mug of steaming coffee in his hand. He was in a bathrobe and his hair was standing up on one side. McCaleb didn't have to ask whom Buddy was calling assholes.

'Yeah,' he said. 'Not a good way to start the day.'

'Point is they shouldn't be allowed to do that all through the night,' Buddy said. 'Goddamn nuisance. I mean, you gotta be able to hear that from here to Long Beach.'

McCaleb just nodded.

'I talked to them over there in the harbor master's. You know, told them to make a complaint to the Port Authority but they don't give a shit. I'm thinking of gettin' a little petition going. You going to sign it?'

'I'll sign it.'

McCaleb looked at his watch.

'I know, you think it's a waste of time.'

'No. I just don't know if it will work. The port's a twenty-four-hour operation. They're not going to stop unloading ships at night because a bunch of people on their boats in the marina sign a complaint.'

'Yeah, I know. The assholes ... I wish one of them boxes would drop on *them* one day. Then they'd get the idea.'

Lockridge was a wharf rat. An aging surfer and beach bum, he lived a low-cost, low-maintenance life on his boat, subsisting mostly on money from odd jobs around the marina like boat sitting and hull scraping. The two had met a year earlier, shortly after Lockridge had moved his boat into the marina. McCaleb had been awakened by a middle-of-the-night harmonica concerto. When he got up and left his boat to investigate, he traced the sound to a drunken Lockridge lying in the cockpit of the *Double-Down*. He was playing a harmonica to a tune only he heard on his earphones. Despite McCaleb's complaint that night, the two had become friends over time. This was largely due to the fact that there were no other live-aboards in that area of the marina. Each was the other's only full-time neighbor. Buddy had kept an eye on *The Following Sea* while McCaleb had been in the hospital. He also often offered McCaleb rides to the grocery store or a nearby mall because he knew Terry wasn't supposed to drive. In turn, McCaleb had Lockridge over for dinner every week or so. They usually talked about their shared interest in the blues, debated sailboats versus power boats and sometimes pulled out

McCaleb's old file boxes and theoretically solved some of the cases. Lockridge was always fascinated by the details of McCaleb's stories about the bureau and his investigations.

'I've got to make a phone call now, Bud,' McCaleb now called over. 'I'll talk to you later.'

'Sure. Make your call. Take care of business.'

He waved and disappeared down the hatchway into his boat's cabin. McCaleb shrugged and made his call after looking up the number he had for Jaye Winston in his book. After a few seconds he was connected.

'Jaye, it's Terry McCaleb. You remember me?'

After a beat, she said, ' 'Course I do. How is it going, Terry? I heard you got the new ticker.'

'Yeah and I'm doing okay. How about you?'

'Same old same old.'

'Well, you think you'll have a few minutes if I swing by this morning? You got a case I want to talk about.'

'You on the private ticket now, Terry?'

'Nah. Just doin' a favor for a friend.'

'Which one is it, the case I mean?'

'James Cordell. The ATM case on January twenty-two.'

Winston made a *hmmph* sound but didn't say anything.

'What?' McCaleb asked.

'Well, it's funny. That case has gone cold on me but now you're the second person to call about it in two days.'

Shit, McCaleb thought. He knew who had called.

'Keisha Russell from the *Times*?'

'Yup.'

'That's on me. I asked her for the clips on Cordell. But I wouldn't tell her why. That's why she called you. Fishing.'

'That's what I thought. I played dumb. So who is the friend who talked you into this?'

McCaleb recounted how he had been asked to look into the murder of Gloria Torres and how that ultimately led him to the Cordell case. He acknowledged that he was getting no help from the LAPD and that Winston was his only alternate route into the case. He left out the fact that his new heart had come from Gloria Torres.

'So did I hit it right?' he asked at the end. 'Are they connected?'

Winston hesitated but then confirmed his assumption. She also said her case was in a holding pattern at the moment, pending new developments.

'Listen, Jaye, I'll be right up front with you. What I'm hoping to do is come out, maybe take a look at the books and whatever else you care to show me, then be able to go back to Graciela Rivers and tell her all that could be done has been done or is being done. I'm not trying to be a hero or to show anybody up.'

Winston didn't say anything.

'What do you think?' McCaleb finally asked. 'You got some time today?'

'Not a lot. Can you hold on?'

'Sure.'

McCaleb was put on hold for a minute. He paced around the deck and looked over the side at the dark water his boat floated on.

'Terry?'

'Yo.'

'Look, I've got court at eleven downtown. That means I have to be out of here by ten. Can you make it before then?'

'Sure. How's nine or nine-fifteen?'

'That'll work.'

'Okay, and thanks.'

'Look, Terry, I owe you one, so I'm doing this. But

there's nothing here. It's just some scumbag out there with a gun. This is three-strikes shit, that's all.'

'What do you mean?'

'I've got another call on hold here. We'll talk when you get here.'

Before McCaleb got ready to go, he stepped up onto the dock and walked over to the *Double-Down*. The boat was the marina eye-sore. Lockridge had more possessions than the boat was built to hold. His three surfboards, his two bikes and his Zodiac inflatable were stored on the deck, making the boat look like a floating yard sale.

The hatch was still open but McCaleb saw and heard no activity. He called out and waited. It was bad marina etiquette to step onto a boat uninvited.

Eventually, Buddy Lockridge's head and shoulders came up through the hatch. His hair was combed and he was dressed now.

'Buddy, what do you have going for today?'

'Whaddaya mean? The same thing I've always got going. A big goose egg. What'd you think, I was going to Kinko's to update my résumé?'

'Well, look, I need a driver for the next few days, maybe more. You want to do it, the job's yours. I'm paying ten bucks an hour plus any meals. You'd have to bring a book or something because there will be a lot of sitting around waiting for me.'

Buddy climbed all the way up into the cockpit.

'Where're you drivin' to?'

'I've got to go out to Whittier. I need to leave in fifteen minutes. After that, I don't know.'

'What is it, some kind of investigation?'

McCaleb could see the excitement building in Buddy's eyes. He spent a lot of time reading crime novels and often recounted their plots to McCaleb. This would be the real thing.

'Yeah, I'm looking into something for somebody. But I'm not looking for a partner, Buddy, just a driver.'

'That's okay. I'm in. Whose car?'

'We take yours, I pay for gas. We take my Cherokee, I sit in the back. It's got a passenger side air bag. You decide. Either way is fine with me.'

Driving had been forbidden for McCaleb by Bonnie Fox until at least his ninth month. His chest was still closing. The skin was healed but beneath the scarred exterior the sternum was still open. An impact on a steering wheel or from an air bag could be fatal, even in a low-speed accident.

'Well, I like the Cherokee but let's take mine,' Buddy said. 'I'd feel like too much of a chauffeur with you in the back.'

# 9

In the summer of 1993 the body of a woman had been found in a large outcropping of sandstone known as Vasquez Rocks in the Antelope Valley in northern Los Angeles County. The body had been there several days. Decomposition prevented determination of sexual assault but it was assumed. The body was clothed but the panties were inside out and the blouse misbuttoned – a clear indication that the woman had not dressed herself or had done so only under severe duress. Cause of death was manual strangulation, the means of death in most sexual homicides.

Sheriff's detective Jaye Winston drew the Vasquez Rocks killing as lead investigator. When the case didn't break quickly with an arrest, Winston settled in for the long haul. Ambitious but not burdened by an unchecked ego, she contacted the FBI for help as one of her first moves. Her request was relayed to the serial killer unit and she eventually filled out a case survey for the unit's Violent Criminal Apprehension Program.

The VICAP survey was the means by which McCaleb first became acquainted with Winston. The case package she had sent to Quantico was forwarded to McCaleb's storage room office at the Los Angeles FO. In typical bureaucratic fashion, the package had gone all the way across the country only to be sent back nearly to its origin for follow-up.

Through the VICAP data base computer – which

compares an eighty-question survey about an individual killing with those on file – and study of the crime scene and autopsy photos, McCaleb matched the Vasquez Rocks case to another killing a year earlier in the Sepulveda Pass area of Los Angeles. A similar killing method, the dumping of the clothed body on an embankment, other small details and nuances – all matched up. McCaleb believed they had another serial killer working the LA basin. In both of the cases it was determined that the woman had been missing two or three days longer than she had been dead. This meant the killer had held her captive and alive during that period, probably to serve in his ghastly fantasies.

Connecting the cases was only one step. Identifying and capturing the killer were the obvious following steps. However, there was nothing to go on. McCaleb was curious about the lengthy interval between the two murders. The Unknown Subject, as the killer was formally called in FBI documents, had gone eleven months before the urges overtook him and he acted out his fantasies by abducting the second woman. To McCaleb, this meant that the event was so strongly implanted in the killer's mind that his fantasy life could essentially live off it or be fueled by it for almost a year. The bureau's serial killer profiling program showed that this interval would grow shorter and shorter each time and the killer would have to seek fresh prey sooner.

McCaleb worked up a profile for Winston but it wasn't much help and they both knew it. White male, twenty to thirty, with a menial job and existence, the Unknown Subject would also have a prior history of sexual crimes or aberrational behavior. If this history included incarceration for any lengthy periods, it could skew the profiled age span of the subject.

It was the same old story. The VICAP profiles were usually dead-on accurate but they rarely led to the acquisition of a suspect. The profile given to Winston could match hundreds, maybe thousands of men in the Los Angeles area. So after all investigative leads were played out, there was nothing to do but wait. McCaleb made a note of the case on his calendar and went on to other cases.

In March of the following year – eight months from the last murder – McCaleb came across the note, reread the file and gave Winston a call. Nothing much had changed. There still were no leads or suspects. McCaleb urged the sheriff's investigator to begin a surveillance of the two body disposal sites and the graves of the two victims. He explained that the killer was near the end of his cycle. His fantasies would be running dry. The urge to freshly re-create the sensation of power and control over another human would be growing and increasingly hard to control. The fact that the Unknown Subject had apparently dressed the bodies after each of the first two murders was a clear sign of the battle raging inside his mind. One part of him was ashamed of what he had done – he sought in a subconscious way to cover it up by replacing each victim's clothes. This suggested that eight months into the cycle the killer would be engulfed in tremendous psychological turmoil. The urge to act out his fantasy again and the shame the act would bring were the two sides in a battle for control. One way to temporarily placate the urge to kill would be to revisit the sites of his previous crimes in an effort to bring new fuel to the fantasy. McCaleb's hunch was that the killer would return to one of the disposal spots or visit the graves. It would bring him closer to his victims and help him stave off the need to kill again.

Winston was reluctant to instigate a multiple point surveillance operation on the basis of an FBI agent's hunch. But McCaleb had already received approval for himself and two other agents for stake-out duty. He also played upon Winston's professionalism, telling her that if she didn't do it, she would always wonder if the stake-out would have been successful, especially if the Unknown Subject hit again. With that kind of threat to her conscience, Winston went to her lieutenant and counterparts on the LAPD case and a surveillance squad was assembled from all three agencies. While planning the surveillance, Winston learned that by coincidence both of the victims were buried in the same Glendale cemetery, about one hundred yards apart. Hearing that, McCaleb predicted that if the Unknown Subject was going to show, it would be in the cemetery.

He was right. On the fifth night of the surveillance, McCaleb, Winston and two other detectives hiding in a mausoleum with a view of both grave sites watched a man drive into the cemetery in a van, get out and climb over the locked gate. Carrying something under his arm, he walked to the grave of the first victim, stood motionless in front of it for ten minutes and then headed to the grave of the second victim. His actions showed a prior knowledge of the location of the graves. At the second grave, he unrolled what turned out to be a sleeping bag on top of the grave, sat down on it and leaned back against the headstone. The detectives did not disturb the man. They were recording his visit with a night-vision video camera. Before long he opened his pants and began masturbating.

Before he returned to the van, the man had already been identified through its license plates as Luther Hatch, a thirty-eight-year-old gardener from North Hollywood released four years earlier from a nine-year Folsom Prison term for a rape conviction.

The subject was no longer unknown. Hatch became a working suspect. When his years in prison were subtracted from his age, he fit the VICAP profile perfectly. He was watched around the clock for three weeks –

including during two more visits to the Glendale cemetery – until finally one night the detectives moved in as he attempted to force a young woman leaving the Sherman Oaks Galleria into his van. In the van, the arresting officers found duct tape and clothesline cut into four-foot lengths. After receiving a search warrant, the investigators tore apart the interior of the van as well as Hatch's apartment. They recovered hair, thread and dried fluid evidence that was linked through DNA and other scientific analysis to the two murder victims. Quickly dubbed 'The Cemetery Man' by the local media, Hatch took his place in the pantheon of multiple murderers who fascinate the public.

McCaleb's expertise and hunches had helped Winston break the case. It was one of the successes they still talked about in Los Angeles and Quantico. On the night they arrested Hatch, the surveillance team went out to celebrate. During a lull in the din, Jaye Winston turned to McCaleb at the bar and said, 'I owe you one. We all do.'

Buddy Lockridge had dressed for his job as Terry McCaleb's driver as if he were going to a nightclub on the Sunset Strip. Head to toe, he was clad in black. He also carried a black leather briefcase. Standing on the dock next to the *Double-Down*, McCaleb stared at the ensemble without speaking for a long moment.

'What's the matter?'

'Nothing, let's go.'

'Is this all right?'

'It's fine but I didn't think you'd get so dressed up for just sitting in a car all day. You going to be comfortable?'

'Sure.'

'Then let's go.'

Lockridge's car was a seven-year-old silver Ford Taurus that was well maintained. On the way out to

Whittier, he tried three different times to find out what it was McCaleb was investigating but each time the questions were unanswered. Finally, McCaleb was able to deflect the line of questioning by bringing up their old debate over the merits of sailboats versus power boats. They got to the Sheriff's Department Star Center in a little over an hour. Lockridge slid the Taurus into a spot in the visitors' lot and turned off the ignition.

'I don't know how long I'll be,' McCaleb said. 'I hope you brought something to read or you've got one of your harmonicas on you.'

'You sure you don't want me to go in with you?'

'Look, Bud, this might have been a mistake. I'm not looking for a partner. All I need is somebody to drive me. I spent more than a hundred bucks yesterday on cabs. I figured maybe you could use the money instead, but if you're going to be asking me questions and –'

'Okay, okay,' Lockridge said, cutting in. He held his hands up in surrender. 'I'll just sit here and read my book. No more questions.'

'Good. I'll see you.'

McCaleb entered the homicide squad offices on time for his appointment and Jaye Winston was hovering around the reception area waiting for him. She was an attractive woman a few years older than McCaleb. She had blond hair that was straight and kept midlength. She had a slim build and was dressed in a blue suit with a white blouse. McCaleb had not seen her in almost five years, since the night they had celebrated the arrest of Luther Hatch. They shook hands and Winston led McCaleb to a conference room that had an oval table surrounded by six chairs. There was a smaller table against one wall with a double-pot coffeemaker on it. The room was empty. A thick stack of documents and four videocassettes were sitting on the table.

'You want some coffee?' Winston asked.

'Nah, I'm fine.'

'Then let's get started. I've got twenty minutes.'

They took chairs across the table from each other. Winston pointed at the paper stack and the videos.

'This is all yours. I copied everything after you called this morning.'

'Jeez, you kidding? Thanks.'

With two hands McCaleb pulled the pile toward his chest like a man raking in the pot at the poker table.

'I called Arrango over at LA,' Winston said. 'He told me not to work with you but I told him you were the best agent I ever dealt with and that I owed you one. He's pissed but he'll get over it.'

'Is this LA's stuff, too?'

'Yeah, we've copied each other back and forth. I haven't gotten anything from Arrango in a couple weeks but that's probably because there hasn't been anything. I think it's all up to date. Problem is, it's a lot of paper and video and it all adds up to nothing so far.'

McCaleb broke the stack of reports in half and started sorting through them. It became clear that about two-thirds of the work had been generated by sheriff's investigators and the rest by the LAPD. He gestured to the videotapes.

'What are these?'

'You've got both crime scenes there and both shoots. Arrango told me he showed you the market robbery already.'

'Yeah.'

'Well, on ours you get even less. The shooter enters the frame for only a few seconds. Just enough for us to see he was wearing a mask. But anyway, it's there for you to look at if you want.'

'On yours, did the guy take the money from the machine or the victim?'

'The machine, why?'

'I might be able to use that to get some help from the bureau, if I need it. Technically, it means the money was taken from the bank, not the victim. That's a federal offense.'

Winston nodded that she understood.

'So how did you connect these, ballistics?' McCaleb asked, mindful that her time was limited and he wanted as much from her as he could get.

She nodded.

'I was working my case already and then a few weeks later I'm reading the paper and see a story about the other one. Sounded the same. I called LA and we got together. When you watch the videos, Terry, you'll see. There's no doubt. Same MO, same gun, same guy. The ballistics only underlined what we already knew.'

McCaleb nodded.

'I wonder why the guy picked up the brass if he knew the lead would be there. What was he using?'

'Nine-millimeter hardballs. Federals. Full metal jacket. Picking up the shells is just good practice. On my case, the shot was through and through and we dug the slug out of a concrete wall. He probably was guessing – maybe hoping – it was too mashed up for a ballistics comparison. So like a good little shooter, he picked up the brass.'

McCaleb nodded, noting the disdain in her voice for her quarry.

'Anyway, it doesn't really matter,' she said. 'Like I said, watch the tapes. We're dealing with one guy here. You don't need ballistics to know it.'

'Did you or the LAPD take it any further than that?'

'What do you mean, Firearms and Ballistics?'

'Yeah. Who has the evidence?'

'We do. The LA caseload's a little heavier than over here. We agreed, since our case was first, to hold all of the evidence. I had F and B do the regular routine, you know, look for similars, et cetera, but they drew a blank. Looks like just these two cases. For now.'

McCaleb thought about telling her about the bureau's DRUGFIRE computer but decided the time wasn't right yet. He'd wait until he had reviewed the tapes and the murder books before he started suggesting what she should do.

He noticed Winston check her watch.

'You working this by yourself?' he asked.

'I am now. I caught the lead and Dan Sistrunk partnered it with me. You know him?'

'Uh, was he one of the guys in the mausoleum that night?'

'Right, the Hatch surveillance. He was there. Anyway, we worked this one together and then other things happened. Other cases. It's all mine now. Lucky me.'

McCaleb nodded and smiled. He understood how it went. If a case wasn't solved by the team quickly, one player got stuck with it.

'You going to get any flak for giving me this stuff?'

'No. The captain knows what you did for us on Lisa Mondrian.'

Lisa Mondrian was the woman found in Vasquez Rocks. McCaleb thought it was unusual that Winston had referred to her by name. It was unusual because most cops he knew tried to depersonalize the victims. It made it easier to live with.

'The captain was the lieutenant back then,' Winston was saying. 'He knows we owe you one. We talked and he said give you the stuff. I just wish we could pay you with something better than this. I don't know what you'll be able to do with this, Terry. We've just been waiting.'

Meaning they were waiting for the shooter to strike again and hopefully make a mistake. Unfortunately it often took fresh blood to solve old killings.

'Well, I'll see what I can do with it. At least it's something to keep me busy. What was that you said on the phone about it being three-strikes stuff?'

Winston frowned.

'We're getting more and more like these. Ever since they put in the three-strikes law in Sacramento. I don't know since you've been out of the life if you've followed it. But the law says three felony convictions and you're out. Automatic life without parole.'

'Right. I know about it.'

'Well, with some of these assholes, all that did was make 'em more careful. Now they wipe out witnesses where before they'd just rob. Three strikes was supposed to be some kind of deterrent. You ask me, it just got a lot of people killed like James Cordell and the two in that market.'

'So you think that's what this guy's doing?'

'Looks it to me. You saw one of the tapes. There's no hesitation. This scumbag knew what he was going to do before he even went up to that ATM or into that store. He wanted no witnesses. So that's the hunch I've been following. In my spare time I've been going through the files, looking for stick-up men with two or more falls already under their belts. I think the man in the ski mask is one of them. He used to be a robber. Now he's a robbing murderer. Natural evolution.'

'And no luck yet?'

'With the files, nope. But either I'll find him or he'll find me. He's not the type who's going to suddenly go square. And judging by the fact he's shooting people for a few hundred dollars, he's decided that under no circumstances is he going back to the cage. That's for sure. He's going to do this again. I'm surprised it hasn't happened yet – it's been two months since the last one. But when he does, maybe he'll fuck up just a little and we'll get him. Sooner or later, we will. I guarantee it. My victim had a wife and two little daughters. I'm going to get the piece of shit who did this.'

McCaleb nodded. He liked her outrage-fueled dedication. It was a full turn away from Arrango's view of things. He started gathering up the documents and tapes and told Winston he would be calling her after he looked over all of the material. He told her it might be a few days.

'No sweat,' she said. 'Whatever you can do we can use.'

When McCaleb got back to the Taurus, he found Buddy Lockridge sitting with his back to the driver's-side door and his legs stretched across the front seat. He was idly practicing a blues riff on a harmonica while reading a book opened on his lap. McCaleb opened the passenger door and waited for him to move his legs. As he finally got in, he noticed Buddy had been reading a book titled *Inspector Imanishi Investigates*.

'That was pretty quick,' Buddy said.

'Yeah, there wasn't a lot to say.'

He put the stack of reports and videocassettes on the floor between his feet.

'What's all of that?'

'Just some stuff I have to go through.'

Lockridge leaned over and looked at the top sheet. It was an incident report.

'James Cordell,' he read out loud. 'Who's that?'

'Buddy, I'm beginning to think –'

'I know, I know.'

He took the hint, straightened up and started the car. He asked nothing more about the documents.

'So, where to now?'

'Now we just go back. San Pedro.'

'I thought you said you needed me for a few days. I'll stop asking questions, I promise.'

There was a slight protest in his voice.

'It's not that. I still need you. But right now I need to go back and go through some of this stuff.'

Buddy dejectedly tossed his book onto the dashboard, dropped the harp into the door pocket and put the car into gear.

# 10

There was more natural light in the salon than down below in the office stateroom. McCaleb decided to work there. He also had a television and video player built into a cabinet topside. He cleared the galley table, wiped it with a sponge and paper towel and then put the stack of reports Winston had given him down on top. He got a legal pad and a sharpened pencil out of the chart table drawer and brought them over as well.

He decided that the best way to do it would be to go through the material chronologically. That meant the Cordell case came first. He went through the stack, separating out the reports regarding the Gloria Torres killing and putting them aside. He then took what was left and separated the reports into small stacks relating to the initial investigation and evidence inventory, follow-up interviews, dead-end leads, miscellaneous reports, fact sheets and weekly summaries.

When he had worked for the bureau, it was his routine to completely clear his desk and spread all the paperwork from a submitted case file across it. The cases came in from police departments all over the West. Some sent thick packages and some just thin files. He always asked for videotapes of the crime scene. Big or small, the packages were all about the same thing. McCaleb was fascinated and repulsed at the same time. He became angry and vengeful as he read, all while alone in his little office, his coat on the door hook, his gun in the drawer.

He could tune everything out but what was in front of him. He did his best work at the desk. As a field agent, he was average at best. But at his desk, he was better than most. And he felt a secret thrill in the back of his mind each time he opened one of those packages and the hunt for a new evil began again. He felt that thrill now as he began to read.

James Cordell had a lot going for him. A family, nice home and cars, good health and a job that paid well enough to allow his wife to be a full-time mother to their two daughters. He was an engineer with a private firm contracted by the state to maintain the structural integrity of the aqueduct system that delivered water from the snow melt in the mountains in the central state to the reservoirs that nursed the sprawl of Southern California. He lived in Lancaster in northeast Los Angeles County, which put him within an hour and a half by car of any point on the water line. On the night of January twenty-second he had been heading home from a long day inspecting the Lone Pine segment of the concrete aqueduct. It was payday and he stopped at the Regional State Bank branch just a mile from his home. His paycheck had been automatically deposited and he needed cash. But he was shot in the head and left for dead at the ATM before the machine finished spitting out his money. His killer was the one who took the crisp twenties when they rolled out of the machine.

The first thing McCaleb realized as he read the initial crime reports was that a sanitized version of events had been given to the media. The circumstances described in the *Times* story Keisha Russell had read to him the day before did not mesh cleanly with the facts in the reports. The story she had read said that Cordell's body was found fifteen minutes after the shooting. According to the crime report, Cordell was found almost immediately by an ATM customer who had pulled into the bank lot just as another vehicle – most likely the shooter's – was speeding out. The witness, identified as James Noone, quickly called for help on a cellular car phone.

Because the call was relayed through a cell transponder, the 911 operator did not have an automatic address read-out of the exact location from which the call had been made. She had to take that information the old-fashioned way – manually – and managed to transpose two numbers of the address Noone had given when she dispatched an emergency medical unit. In his statement, Noone said he had watched helplessly as a paramedic ambulance went screaming by to a location seven blocks away. He had to call and explain himself all over again to a new operator. The paramedics were redirected but Cordell was dead by the time they arrived.

As he read the initial reports, it was hard for McCaleb to make a judgment on whether the delay in the arrival of paramedics was of any consequence. Cordell had suffered a devastating head wound. Even if paramedics had gotten to him ten minutes sooner, it probably would have made no difference. It was unlikely that death could have been avoided.

Still, the 911 screwup was just the type of thing the media loved to run with. So somebody in the Sheriff's Department – probably Jaye Winston's supervisor – had decided to keep that information quiet.

The screwup was a side matter that held little interest for McCaleb. What did interest him was that there was at least a partial witness as well as a vehicle description. According to Noone's statement, he had almost been creamed by a black blur as he had pulled into the bank's lot. He described the exiting vehicle as a black Jeep Cherokee with the newer, smoother styling. He got only a split-second view of the driver, a man he described only as white and with either gray hair or a gray cap on his head.

There were no other witnesses listed in the initial reports. Before moving on to the supplemental reports and the autopsy protocol, McCaleb decided to look at the videos. He turned on the television and VCR and first popped in the tape made from the ATM's surveillance camera.

As with the tape from the Sherman Market, there was a timeline running across the bottom of the frame. The picture was shot through a fish-eye lens that distorted the image. The man McCaleb assumed was James Cordell came into the frame and slid his bank card into the machine. His face was very close to the camera, blocking out a view of almost everything else. It was a design flaw – unless the real purpose of the camera was not to capture robberies but the faces of fraud artists using stolen or gimmick bank cards.

As Cordell typed in his code number, he hesitated and looked over his right shoulder, his head tracking something passing behind him – the Cherokee pulling into the lot. He finished typing in his transaction and a nervous look came across his face. Nobody likes going to an ATM at night, even a well-lighted machine in a low-crime neighborhood. The only machine McCaleb ever used was inside a twenty-four-hour supermarket, where there always was the safety and deterrent of crowds. Cordell took a nervous glance over his left shoulder, nodded at someone off-screen and then looked back at the machine. Nothing about the person he looked at had alarmed him further. The shooter obviously had not pulled on the mask. Despite his outward calm, Cordell's eyes dropped down to the cash slot, his mind probably repeating a silent mantra of *Hurry up! Hurry up!*

Then almost immediately the gun came into the frame, reaching over his shoulder and just kissing his left temple before the trigger was pulled and James Cordell's life was taken. There was the blast of blood misting the camera lens and the man went forward and to his right, apparently going into the wall next to the ATM and then falling backward to the ground.

The shooter then moved into the video frame and grabbed the cash as it was delivered through the slot. At that moment McCaleb paused the picture. On the screen was a full view of the masked shooter. He was in the same dark jumpsuit and mask worn by the shooter in the Gloria Torres tape. As Winston had said, ballistics weren't necessary. They would only be a scientific confirmation of something Winston knew and now McCaleb knew in the gut. It was the same man. Same clothes, same method of operation, same dead eyes behind the mask.

He flicked the button again and the video continued. The shooter grabbed the cash from the machine. As he did this, he seemed to be saying something but his face was not squared to the camera as with the Sherman Market shootings. It was as if he was speaking to himself this time rather than to the camera.

The shooter quickly moved to the left of the screen and stooped to pick up something unseen. The bullet casing. He then darted to the right and disappeared from the screen. McCaleb watched for a few moments. The only figure in the picture was the still form of Cordell on the pavement below the machine. The only movement was the widening pool of blood around his head. Seeking the lower ground, the blood slid into a joint in the pavement and started moving in a line toward the curb.

A minute went by and then a man entered the video screen, crouching over Cordell's body. James Noone. He was bald across the top of his head and wearing thin-framed glasses. He touched the wounded man's neck, then looked around, probably to make sure he was safe himself. He then jumped up and was gone, presumably to make the call on his cell phone. Another half minute went by before Noone returned to the frame to wait for help. As the time went by, Noone swiveled his head back and forth, apparently fearing that the gunman, if not in the car he had seen speeding away, might still be around. Finally, his attention was drawn in the direction of the street. His mouth opened in a silent scream and he waved his arms above his head as he apparently watched the paramedics speed by. He then jumped up and left the screen again.

A few moments later the screen jumped. McCaleb checked the time and saw that it was now seven minutes later. Two paramedics moved quickly into place around Cordell. They checked for pulse and pupil response. They ripped open his shirt and one of the rescuers listened to his chest with a stethoscope. Another quickly arrived with a wheeled stretcher. But one of the first two looked at the man and shook his head. Cordell was dead.

A few moments later the screen went blank.

After pausing a moment, almost in reverence, McCaleb put in the crime scene tape next. This was obviously taken from a hand-held video camera. It started with some environmental shots of the bank property and the street. In the bank lot there were two vehicles: a dusty white Chevy Suburban and a smaller vehicle barely visible on its other side. McCaleb assumed the Suburban was Cordell's. It was large and rugged, dusty from driving the mountain and desert roads alongside the aqueduct. He assumed the other car belonged to the witness, James Noone.

The tape then showed the ATM and panned downward to the blood-stained sidewalk in front of it. Cordell's body was sprawled in the spot where the paramedics had found it and then left it. It was uncovered, the dead man's shirt open, his pale chest exposed.

Over the next several minutes the video jumped in time through various stages of the crime scene. First a criminalist measured and photographed the scene, then coroner's investigators worked on the body, wrapped it in a plastic body bag and removed it on a gurney. Lastly, the criminalist and a latents man moved in to search the crime scene more thoroughly for evidence and fingerprints. There was a segment showing the criminalist using a small metal spike to work the bullet slug out of the wall next to the ATM.

Finally, there was a bonus McCaleb had not been expecting. The camera operator recorded James Noone's first recounting of what he had seen. The witness had been taken to the edge of the bank property and was standing next to a public phone and talking to a uniformed deputy when the cameraman wandered up. Noone was a man of about thirty-five. He appeared – in comparison to the deputy – to be short and compactly built. He now had on a baseball cap. He was agitated, still pumped by what he had witnessed and apparently frustrated by the screwup with the paramedics. The camera had been turned on in mid-conversation.

'All I'm saying is that he had a fighting chance.'

'Yes, sir, I understand. I'm sure it will be one of the things they take a look at.'

'I mean, I think somebody ought to investigate how this could – and the thing is, we're only what, a half mile from the hospital?'

'We're aware of that, Mr Noone,' the deputy said patiently. 'Now if we could just move on for a moment. Could you tell me if you saw anything before you found the body? Anything unusual.'

'Yes, I saw the guy. At least I think I did.'

'What guy is that?'

'The robber. I saw the getaway car.'

'Can you describe that, sir?'

'Sure, black Cherokee. The new kind. Not one of those that look like a shoe box.'

The deputy looked a bit confused but McCaleb understood that Noone was describing a Grand Cherokee model. He had one himself.

'I was pulling in and it came tearing out of here, almost hit me,' Noone said. 'The guy was a real asshole. I blasted my horn at him, then I pull in and find this man here. I called on my cell phone but then it got all fucked up.'

'Yes, sir. Can you refrain from that kind of language? This might be played in court one day.'

'Oh. Sorry.'

'Can we go back to this car? Did you happen to see a license plate?'

'I wasn't even looking.'

'How many people in the vehicle?'

'I think one, the driver.'

'Male or female?'

'Male.'

'Can you describe him for me?'

'Wasn't really looking. I was just trying not to get plowed into, that's all.'

'White? Black? Asian?'

'Oh, he was white. I'm pretty sure about that. But I couldn't identify him or anything like that.'

'What about hair color?'

'It was gray.'

'Gray?'

The deputy said it with surprise. An old robber. It seemed unusual to him.

'I think,' Noone said. 'It was all so quick. I can't be sure.'

'What about a hat?'

'Yeah, it could have been a hat.'

'What do you mean, the gray?'

'Yeah, gray hat, gray hair. I can't be sure.'

'Okay, anything else? Was he wearing glasses?'

'Uh, I either don't remember or didn't see. I really wasn't looking at the guy, you know. Besides, the car had dark windows. The only time I could really see the guy was through the windshield and I only saw that for a second. When he was coming right at me.'

'Okay, Mr Noone. This is a help. We are going to need you to make a formal statement and the detectives will need to talk to you. Is this going to be an inconvenience?'

'Yes, but what are you gonna do? I want to help. I *tried* to help. I don't mind.'

'Thank you, sir, I'm going to have a deputy take you into the Palmdale station. The detectives will talk to you there. They'll be with you as soon as possible and I'll make sure they know you are waiting.'

'Well, okay. What about my wheels?'

'Someone will take you back here when they are done.'

The tape ended there. McCaleb ejected it and thought about what he had seen and heard and read so far. The fact that the Sheriff's Department did not give the black Cherokee to the media was curious. It would be something he would have to ask Jaye Winston about. He made a note of it on the legal pad he had been writing questions on and then started through the remaining reports on Cordell.

The crime scene evidence inventory was a single page that was almost blank. Collected evidence amounted to the slug removed from the wall, a half dozen fingerprints lifted from the ATM and photographs of a tire mark possibly made by the shooter's car. The video from the ATM camera was also listed.

Clipped to the report were photocopies of photos of the tread mark and a freeze frame from the ATM video of the gun in the shooter's hand. An ancillary report from the crime lab stated that it was the technician's opinion that the tire mark had been on the asphalt at least several days and was not useful in the investigation.

A ballistics report identified the bullet as a slightly pancaked nine-millimeter Federal FMJ. Stapled to the report was a photocopy of a page from the autopsy showing a top-view drawing of the skull. The track of the bullet through Cordell's brain was charted on the drawing. The bullet had entered just forward on the left temple, then tumbled on a straight line through the frontal lobe and out through the right temple region. The track of the tumbling bullet had been an inch wide. As McCaleb read it, he realized it was probably a good thing the paramedics were late. If they had managed to save Cordell, it probably would have been for a life on a machine in one of those medical centers that were nothing more than vegetable warehouses.

The ballistics report also contained an enhanced photo of the gun. Though much of the weapon was hidden in the gloved grip of the shooter, the sheriff's firearms experts had identified it as a Heckler & Koch P7, a nine-millimeter pistol with a four-inch barrel and nickel finish.

The weapon identification was a curiosity to McCaleb. The HK P7 was a fairly expensive weapon, about a thousand dollars on the legitimate market, and not the kind of weapon normally seen in street crimes. He guessed that Jaye Winston must have assumed that the gun itself had to have been taken earlier in a robbery or burglary. McCaleb looked through the remaining supplemental reports and sure enough Winston had pulled crime reports from across the county in which an HK P7 of matching description had been reported stolen. It did not appear that she had taken the lead much further than that. It was true that many gun thefts went unreported because the people who lost the weapons shouldn't have had them in the first place. But as

Winston had undoubtedly done before, McCaleb scanned the list of reported thefts – only five in the last two years – to see if any names or addresses turned a switch. None did. All five of the burglaries Winston had collected were open cases with no suspects. It was a dead end.

After the burglary list was a report detailing all thefts of black Grand Cherokees in the county during the last year. Winston had apparently believed the shooter's car was also a contradiction – a high-line vehicle used in an economically low-line crime. McCaleb thought it was a good jump to consider the car was probably stolen. There were twenty-four Cherokees on the list but no other reports indicating any follow-up. Maybe, he considered, Winston had simply changed her mind after connecting her shooting to the Torres case. The Good Samaritan had described a getaway vehicle from the market shooting that could be a Cherokee. Since that indicated the shooter had not gotten rid of it, it possibly hadn't been stolen after all.

The autopsy protocol was next and McCaleb flipped through the pages quickly. He knew from experience that ninety percent of any autopsy report was dedicated to the minute description of the procedure, identifying the characteristics of the victim's interior organs and state of health at the time of death. Most of the time it was only the summary that was important to McCaleb. But in the Cordell case even that part of the autopsy was irrelevant because it was obvious. He found the summary anyway and nodded as he read what he already knew. Massive brain damage had led to Cordell's death within minutes of the shooting.

He put the autopsy report aside. The next stack of reports dealt with Winston's three-strike theory. Believing the shooter was an ex-convict facing life without parole for another conviction, Winston had gone to the state parole offices in Van Nuys and Lancaster and pulled files on paroled armed robbers who were Caucasian and had two prior felony convictions on their records. These were people facing third-strike penalties if arrested again under the new law. There were seventy-one of them assigned to the two parole offices geographically nearest the two robbery-shootings.

Winston and other deputies had slowly gone through the list in the weeks since the robberies and murders. According to the reports, they had paid visits to nearly every man on the list. Of the seventy-one, only seven of the men couldn't be found. This indicated they had violated parole and had probably left the area or might still be in the area hiding and possibly were more likely to be committing armed robberies and even murders. Nationwide parole pickup bulletins were issued for all these men on law enforcement computer networks. Of the men who were contacted, initial interviews and investigation cleared almost ninety percent through alibis. The remaining eight had been cleared through other investigative means – chiefly because their physical dimensions did not match those of the shooter's upper body on the video.

Aside from the missing seven men on the list, the three-strikes avenue of investigation was stagnant. Winston was apparently hoping that one of those seven would eventually turn up and be tied to the shooting.

McCaleb moved on to the remaining Cordell reports. There were two follow-up interviews with James Noone at the Star Center. His story never differed in these reports and his recollection of the Cherokee driver never got any better.

There also was a crime scene sketch and four field-interview reports on traffic stops of men driving black Cherokees. They had been stopped in Lancaster and Palmdale within an hour of the ATM shooting by deputies made aware of the Cherokee's use in the crime by a sheriff's radio broadcast. The identification of each driver was run through the computer and they were sent on their way after coming up clean. The reports were forwarded to Winston.

The last item McCaleb read was the most recent summary report filed by Winston. It was short and to the point.

'No new leads or suspects at this time. Investigating officer is waiting at this point for additional information that may lead to the ID of a suspect.'

Winston was at the wall. She was waiting. She needed fresh blood.

McCaleb drummed his fingers on the table and thought about all he had just read. He agreed with the moves Winston had made but he tried to think of what she had missed and what else could be done. He liked her three-strike theory and shared her disappointment at not being able to cull a suspect out of the list of seventy-one. The fact that most of the men were cleared through alibis bothered him. How could so many two-strikes dirtbags be able to perfectly account for their exact whereabouts on two different nights? He had always been suspicious of alibis when he was working cases. He knew it took only one liar to make an alibi.

McCaleb stopped his finger roll on the table as he thought of something. He fanned the stack of Cordell reports across the table. He didn't need to look through them because he knew that what he was thinking of was not in the pile. He had realized that Winston had never geographically cross-referenced her various theories.

He got up and left the boat. Buddy Lockridge was sitting in the cockpit of his boat sewing a rip in a wet suit when McCaleb walked up.

'Hey, you got a job?'

'Guy over on millionaires' row wants me to scrape his Bertram. It's the sixty over there. But if you need a ride, I can do his thing whenever I want. He's a once-a-month weekender.'

'No. I just want to know if you have a *Thomas Brothers* I can borrow. Mine's in my car and I don't want to take the tarp off it to get to it.'

'Yeah, sure. It's in the bull.'

Lockridge reached into his pocket and got his car keys out and tossed them to McCaleb. On his way out to the Taurus McCaleb glanced over at millionaires' row. It was a dock with double-wide, long slips to handle the girth of the larger yachts that moored in Cabrillo Marina. He picked out the Bertram 60. It was a beautiful boat. And he knew it had cost its owner, who probably used it no more than once a month, an easy million and a half.

After retrieving the map book from Lockridge's car, returning the key and then returning to his own boat, McCaleb set to work with the Cordell records. First he went through the reports on thefts of Cherokees and HK P7 pistols. He numbered each reported theft and then charted it by address on the appropriate page of the map book. He then went on to the list of three-strike suspects, using the same procedure to chart the home and job locations of each man as well. Lastly, he charted the locations of the shootings.

It took him almost an hour. But by the time he was done, he felt a sense of cautious excitement. One name from the list of seventy-one clearly stood out as being geographically relevant to the Sherman Market shooting and the theft of an HK P7.

The man's name was Mikail Bolotov, a thirty-year-old Russian émigré who had already served two stints in California prisons for armed robberies. Bolotov lived and worked in Canoga Park. His home was off DeSoto near Sherman Way, a mile or so from the market where Gloria Torres and Chan Ho Kang were murdered. His job was at a clock manufacturing plant located on Winnetka only eight blocks south and two blocks east of the market. Lastly, and this was what excited McCaleb, the Russian also worked only four blocks from a Canoga Park home from which an HK P7 had been stolen during a burglary in December. Reading the burglary report, McCaleb noted that the intruder had taken several presents from beneath a Christmas tree, including a new HK P7 that had been wrapped as a gift from the homeowner to his wife – the perfect LA Christmas gift. The burglar left no fingerprints or other evidence behind.

McCaleb read through the entire parole package and investigator's report. Bolotov had a long record of violence, though no previous suspicion of homicide and no tangles with the law since his last discharge from prison three years before. He routinely made his parole appointments and to outward appearance appeared to be on the straight and narrow.

Bolotov had been interviewed on the Cordell matter at his place of employment by two sheriff's investigators named Ritenbaugh and Aguilar. The interview had taken place two weeks after the Cordell murder but nearly three weeks before the Sherman Market murders. Also, the interview had apparently taken place before Winston had pulled the reports on HK P7 thefts. This, he guessed, was why the significance of Bolotov's geographic location was missed.

During the interview, Bolotov's answers had apparently been sufficient to avoid suspicion and his employer had provided an alibi, reporting that on the night James Cordell was murdered, Bolotov had worked his normal two-to-ten shift. He showed the detectives pay records and time cards reflecting the hours worked. That was enough for Ritenbaugh and Aguilar. Cordell had died at about 10:10 P.M. It would have been physically impossible for Bolotov to get from Canoga Park to Lancaster in ten minutes – even if he had used a helicopter. Ritenbaugh and Aguilar moved on to the next name on the list of three-strike candidates.

'Bullshit,' McCaleb said out loud.

He felt excited. Bolotov was a lead that should be rechecked no matter what his boss or the pay records said. The man was an armed robber by trade, not a clock maker. His geographic proximity to key locations relating to the investigation demanded that another look be taken. McCaleb felt he had at least accomplished something that he could go back to Winston with.

He quickly wrote a few notes on the legal pad and then set it aside. He was exhausted from the work done so far and felt the low pounding of a headache coming on. He looked at his watch and saw that time had sped by without his realizing it. It was two o'clock already. He knew he should eat something but he had no desire for any kind of food in particular. He decided instead to take a nap and went below to the stateroom.

# 11

Refreshed from an hour-long nap during which he had no dreams that he could remember, McCaleb made himself a sandwich of white bread and processed cheese. He opened a can of Coke to go with it and went back to the galley table to go through the Gloria Torres case.

He started with the surveillance tape from the Sherman Market. He had seen it twice already in the company of Arrango and Walters but decided he needed to watch it again. He put the tape in and watched it on normal speed, then put what was left of his sandwich in the sink. He couldn't eat any more. His insides were clenched too tight.

He rewound the tape and started playing it again, this time on slow-motion play. Gloria's movements seemed languid and relaxed. McCaleb found himself almost ready to return the smile she showed. He wondered what she was thinking. Was the smile for Mr Kang? McCaleb doubted it. It was a secret smile. A smile for something inside. His guess was that she was thinking about her son and he knew then that she had at least been happy in that final conscious moment.

The tape brought no new ideas, just the rekindling of anger toward the shooter. He put in the crime scene tape next and watched the documentation, measuring and quantification of the carnage. Gloria's body, of course, was not there and the blood on the floor where she had dropped was minimal – thanks to the Good Samaritan.

But the store owner's corpse was crumpled on the floor behind the counter, blood seemingly surrounding it completely. It made McCaleb think of the old woman he had seen in the store the day before. She stood where her husband had fallen. That took a certain kind of courage, a kind McCaleb didn't think he had.

After turning off the tape, he started through the stack of reports. Arrango and Walters had not produced as much paper as Winston had. McCaleb tried not to take this to mean anything significant but he couldn't help it. In his experience, the size of a murder book reflected not only the depth of the investigation but the commitment of the investigators. McCaleb believed there was a sacred bond between the victim and the investigator. All homicide cops understood this. Some took it straight to the heart. Some less so, simply as a matter of psychological survival. But it was there in all of them. It didn't matter if you had religion, if you believed the soul of the departed watched over you. Even if you believed that all things ended with the final breath, you still spoke for the dead. Your name was whispered on the last breath. But only you heard it. Only you knew it. No other crime came with such a covenant.

McCaleb set aside the thick protocols from the autopsies of Torres and Kang to read last. As with the Cordell file, he knew, the autopsies would provide few salient details beyond what was already obvious. He quickly went through the initial crime reports and next came to a thin sheaf of witness reports. They were statements of people who each had a little part of the whole: a gas station attendant, a passing motorist, a *Times* pressroom employee who worked with Gloria. There were also investigative summaries, supplemental reports, fact sheets, crime scene charts, ballistics reports and a chronological record of the travels and calls made by the detectives on the case. Last in this section of the stack was the transcript of the never-identified Good Samaritan's 911 call made after he stumbled into the shooting's aftermath and tried to save Gloria's life. The transcript was of a man speaking English with difficulty as he hurriedly reported a shooting. But when the operator offered to switch him to a Spanish-speaker, he declined.

CALLER: I must go. I go now. The girl is shot very bad. The man, he run. He drive away. A black car, like a truck.

OPERATOR: Sir, please stay on the line ... Sir? Sir?

That was it. He was gone. He had mentioned the vehicle but gave no description of the suspect.

Following this statement there was a ballistics report identifying the bullets recovered during surgery on Gloria Torres and the autopsy of Chan Ho Kang as nine-millimeter Federal FMJs. A photo from the store video was analyzed and the weapon was again identified as the HK P7.

It struck McCaleb as he finished an initial reading of the rest of the reports that what was missing from the murder book was a timeline. Unlike the Cordell case, which had only one witness, the Torres case had a variety of minor witnesses and time markers. The detectives apparently had not sat down with all of these and collated them into a timeline. They had not re-created the sequence of incidents that made up the event as a whole.

McCaleb sat back and thought about this for a moment. Why wasn't it there? Would such a timeline or exact sequence of events even be useful? Probably not initially, he decided. In terms of identifying a killer, it would give little help. And at least initially, that's all that mattered. But a sequential analysis of the event should have been done later, after the dust had settled, so to speak. McCaleb had often advised investigators who sent their cases to him to create a timeline. It could be useful breaking alibis, finding holes in witness accounts, in simply giving the investigator a better command and knowledge of exactly what had happened.

McCaleb was fully aware that he was Monday morning quarter-backing. Arrango and Walters didn't have the luxury of coming into a case two months after the fact. Maybe thought of a timeline got lost. They had other concerns and other cases to worry about.

He got up and went to the galley to turn on the coffeemaker. He was feeling fatigued again and had been awake only ninety minutes. McCaleb hadn't been drinking much coffee since the transplant. Dr Fox had told him to avoid caffeine and on the occasion that he had ignored that advice and had a cup, it sometimes caused a fluttering sensation in his chest. But he wanted to keep alert and finish his work. He took the risk.

After the coffee was ready, he poured himself a mug, then overpowered it with milk and sugar. He sat back down and silently chastised himself for looking for reasons to excuse Arrango and Walters. They should have taken the time to work the case thoroughly. McCaleb was angry with himself for having thought anything else.

He took up the legal pad and began to read through the witness reports again, noting down the salient times and a brief summary of what each witness brought to the case. He then overlaid various time notations from the other crime reports. It took him an hour to do this, during which time he refilled his mug three times without really thinking about it. When he was finished, he had constructed a timeline on two pages of the pad. The problem, he realized as he studied his work, was that the sequence was inexact in all but a couple of references and contained outright conflicts, if not impossibilities.

10:01 P.M. – End of B shift, *Los Angeles Times* pressroom, Chatsworth facility. Gloria punches out.

10:10 P.M. – approximate – Gloria leaves with coworker Annette Stapleton. They talk in the parking lot approximately five minutes. Gloria leaves in her blue Honda Civic.

10:29 P.M. – Gloria at the Chevron gas station on Winnetka at Roscoe. Self-service credit card sale: $14.40. Attendant Connor Davis recalls Gloria as a regular nighttime customer who would ask about sports scores because he often had a game on the radio. Time ascribed to credit card records.

10:40 to 10:43 P.M. – approximate – Motorist Ellen Taaffe traveling east on Sherman Way, windows down, hears popping sound as she passes the Sherman Market. Looks, sees nothing wrong. Two cars in the lot. Sale signs in windows of the market prevent viewing into the store. As she looks, she hears another popping sound but again sees nothing unusual. Timing of sounds ascribed by Taaffe to the beginning of KFWB news report cycle which started at 10:40.

10:41:03 P.M. – Unidentified male with Spanish accent calls 911, says a woman has been shot at the Sherman Market and needs help. Does not stay for police. Illegal alien?

10:41:37 P.M. – Gloria Torres is shot to death, according to store's security video time clock.

10:42:55 P.M. – Good Samaritan enters store and helps Gloria, according to security video time clock.

10:43:21 P.M. – Ellen Taaffe uses her car phone to call 911 dispatch to report sound of possible gunfire. She is told the shooting has already been reported. Her name and number are forwarded to detectives.

10:47 P.M. – Paramedics arrive, transport Gloria to Northridge Medical Center. Chan Ho Kang pronounced dead.

10:49 P.M. – First police arrive on scene.

He read it all again. He knew homicide was an inexact science but the timeline bothered him. According to the first homicide investigation report, the actual shooting was determined by the detectives to have occurred during the sixty seconds between 10:40 and 10:41 P.M. In deciding this, the detectives had used the one source of time they knew to be exact and unassailably correct – the time log at the department's emergency dispatch center. The first call reporting the shooting – from the Good Samaritan – had come in at 10:41:03 to a 911 operator. Using that time and the report by motorist Ellen Taaffe about hearing the shots sometime after the start of the KFWB news report led to the conclusion that the shooting had to have been after 10:40 but before 10:41:03, when the Good Samaritan made the call.

This time frame, of course, was in contradiction to the time of 10:41:37 shown on the store's videotape at the start of the shooting.

McCaleb looked through the reports again, hoping he had missed some page on which there was an explanation of this discrepancy. There was nothing. He drummed his fingers on the table for a few moments while he thought about things. He checked his watch and saw it was almost five. It was unlikely any of the investigators would still be around.

Again he studied the timeline he had constructed,

searching for an explanation for the anomaly. His eyes held on the second call to the dispatch center. Ellen Taaffe, the motorist who had heard the shooting, had called on her mobile phone at 10:43:21 to report the shooting and was told it had already been reported.

He thought about this. The detectives had used her hearing of the shots to set the murders within the minute of 10:40, the very start of the news program. Yet when she called 911, they already knew about the shooting. Why had she delayed more than two minutes to make the call? And was she ever asked if she saw the Good Samaritan?

McCaleb quickly flipped through the stack of reports until he located the Ellen Taaffe witness statement. It was one page, with her signature beneath a statement typed below a two-inch information block. The statement said nothing about how long she had waited between hearing the shots and calling the 911 dispatch center. The statement did say she believed that there were two cars parked in front of the store but she could not identify the type of vehicles they were or remember if there had been any occupants.

He looked at the information box. It said Taaffe was thirty-five years old and married. She lived in Northridge and was an executive with a headhunting firm. She had been driving home from the movies at Topanga Plaza when she heard the shooting. Her home and work phone numbers were contained in the witness information box. McCaleb went to the phone and dialed the work number. A secretary answered, corrected his pronunciation of *Taaffe* and said he had just caught her on her way out the door.

'This is Ellen Taaffe,' a voice said, rhyming the name with *waif*.

'Yes, hello, Mrs Taaffe. You don't know me. My name is McCaleb. I'm an investigator working on that shooting a couple months ago on Sherman Way. The one you heard and talked to the police about?'

He heard her breath going out in a way that indicated she was being put out by the call.

'I don't understand, I already talked to the detectives. Are you with the police?'

'No, I'm ... I work for the family of the woman who was killed there. Is this a bad time?'

'Yes, I'm on my way out the door. I'd like to beat the traffic and ... and, frankly, I don't know what I can tell you. I told everything to the police.'

'This will only take a minute. I just have a few quick questions. This woman had a little boy. I'm just trying to catch the guy who took her away.'

He heard the breath go out again.

'All right, I'll try to help. What are the questions?'

'Okay, one, how long did you wait between hearing the shots and calling nine one one on your car phone?'

'I didn't wait. I called right then. I grew up around guns. My father was a police officer and I went with him to the range sometimes. I knew that what I heard was a gun. I called right away.'

'Well, I'm looking at the police records and they say you thought you heard the shooting around ten-forty but didn't call it in until ten-forty-three. I don't –'

'What they don't tell you in those reports is that I got a tape. I called right away but I got a tape. All the nine one one lines were busy and I was put on hold. I don't know how long. It was aggravating. But when my call finally was put through, they said they already knew about the shooting anyway.'

'How long do you think you were on hold?'

'I just said I'm not sure. Maybe a minute. Maybe more or maybe less. I don't know.'

'Okay. The report says you heard a shot and looked out your window at the store. Then you heard another shot. You saw two cars in the lot. The next question is, did you see anyone outside?'

'No. There was no one there. I told this to the police.'

'It seems like if the inside of the store was lit, you might be able to see if there was anyone in the cars.'

'If there was anyone in either of the cars, I don't remember seeing them.'

'Was one of the cars a sports utility vehicle, like a Cherokee?'

'I don't know. The police already asked that. But my attention was on the store. I looked right past the cars.'

'Would you say they were dark or light colored?'

'I really don't know. I just told you that and I've been over this with the police. They have every –'

'Did you hear a third shot?'

'A third? No, only two.'

'But there were three shots. So you don't know if you heard the first two shots or the last two.'

'That's right.'

He thought about this for a second, deciding that it was probably impossible to decide for sure whether she had heard the first two or last two shots.

'Mrs Taaffe, that's it. Thanks a lot. You've been a help and I'm sorry to have bothered you.'

The brief interview helped answer only the question he had about the delay in her 911 call but it still left the discrepancy between the timing of the Good Samaritan's 911 call and the time on the store's surveillance tape. McCaleb checked his watch again. It was now after five. All the detectives would be gone but he decided to call anyway.

To his surprise he was told when he called West Valley Division that both Arrango and Walters were in and asked which one he wanted. He decided to try Walters, since he had seemed sympathetic to his situation the day before. Walters picked up after three rings.

'It's Terry McCaleb ... The Gloria Torres thing?'

'Right, right.'

'I guess you heard I got the books from Winston over at the sheriff's.'

'Yeah, we're not too happy about that. We also got a call from the *Slimes* about it, too. Some reporter. That wasn't cool. I don't know who you've been talk –'

'Look, your partner put me in a position where I had to look for information where I could get it. Don't worry about the *Times*. They'll sit on the story because there is no story. Not at the moment.'

'And it best stay that way. Anyway, I'm kind of busy here. What've you got?'

'You got a case?'

'Yeah. They just keep dropping like flies out here in the Big Valley.'

'Well, look, I won't hold you up. I've just got one question maybe you can help me with.'

McCaleb waited. Walters didn't say anything. He seemed different from the day before. McCaleb wondered if Arrango was sitting close by and listening. He decided to press on.

'I just want to know about the timing,' he said. 'The video from the store shows the shooting going down at' – he quickly scanned his timeline – 'let's see, ten forty-one thirty-seven. Then you have the nine one one records and they say the call from the Good Samaritan came in at exactly ten forty-one oh three. See what I'm getting at? How'd the guy call it in thirty-four seconds before the shooting actually happened?'

'Simple, the time on the video was off. It was fast.'

'Oh, okay,' McCaleb said, as if the possibility had not occurred to him. 'You guys checked it out?'

'My partner did.'

'Really? I didn't see any report on it in the book.'

'Look, he made a phone call to the security company,

checked it out, no report, okay? The guy who installed that system put it in more than a year ago – right after the first time Mr Kang got robbed. Eddie talked to the guy. He set the camera clock off his own watch back then and hasn't been back in there since. He showed Mr Kang how to set the camera clock in case there was a power outage or something.'

'Okay,' McCaleb said, not sure where this was going.

'So, your guess is as good as mine. Is it showing the original time set off the installer's watch or did the old man set it a few times himself? Either way it doesn't matter. We can't trust it just coming off somebody's watch. Maybe the watch was fast, maybe the camera clock has been gaining a couple seconds every week or two. Who knows? We can't trust it, is what I'm saying. But we can trust the nine-eleven clock. That's the time we know is correct and it's the time we went with.'

McCaleb was silent and Walters seemed to take it as some kind of judgment.

'Look, the camera clock is just a detail that doesn't mean anything anyway,' he said. 'If we worried about every detail that didn't fit, we'd still be working our first case. I'm busy here, man, what else you got?'

'That's it, I guess. You guys never checked the surveillance clock, right? You know, to check the time against the dispatch clock?'

'Nope. We went back a couple days later but there had been a power outage – Santa Anas blew down the line. The time on it was useless to us then.'

'Too bad.'

'Yeah, too bad. I gotta go. Keep in touch. You get something, you call us before Winston or we're not going to be happy with you. All right?'

'I'll call you.'

Walters hung up. McCaleb put the phone down and stared at it for a few moments, wondering what his next move should or would be. He was drawing a blank. But it had always been his practice to go back to the start whenever he hit a stall. The start most often meant the crime scene. But this case was different. He could go back to the actual crime.

He put the video of the Sherman Market murders back in the VCR and watched the tape again in slow motion. He sat there gripping the edges of the table so hard his knuckles and finger joints began to hurt. It wasn't until the third run-through that he picked up on something he had missed earlier and had been there all along.

Chan Ho Kang's watch. The watch his wife now wore. On the video the watch was seen as Kang desperately grasped for purchase on the counter.

McCaleb fished around on the video for a few minutes, backing and forwarding the tape until he froze the image on what he believed was the best view of the watch's face. The best he could do was a clean look at it but the LED readout was not picked up by the video shot from the upper wall. The numbers on the watch – the time – were not readable.

He sat there staring at the frozen image, wondering if he should pursue it. If he could read the time on the watch, he might be able to triangulate the time of the shooting by using the camera clock and the dispatch clock. It might clear up a loose end. But did it mean anything? Walters had been right about one thing. There are always details that don't add up. Always loose ends. And McCaleb wasn't sure if this one was worth the time it would take to tie it up.

His private debate was interrupted. Living on a boat, he had learned to read the subtle rises and falls of his home, to know whether each was caused by a boat wake out in the fairway or the weight of someone coming on board. McCaleb felt the boat dip slightly and immediately looked over his shoulder and out the sliding door.

Graciela Rivers had just stepped onboard and was turning around to help a little boy step on next. Raymond. Dinner. He had completely forgotten.

'Shit,' he said as he quickly turned off the video and got up to go out and greet them.

# 12

'You forgot, didn't you?'

There was an easy smile on her face.

'No – I mean, I sort of forgot for the last five hours. I got lost in all of this paperwork I've been looking through. I meant to go over to the market and –'

'Well, that's okay. We can do it another –'

'No, no, are you kidding? We're going to have dinner. Is this Raymond?'

'Oh, yes.'

Graciela turned to the boy, who was standing shyly behind her at the stern. He seemed small for his age, with dark hair and eyes, brown skin. He wore shorts and a striped shirt. He carried a sweater in his hands.

'Raymond, this is Mr McCaleb. The man I was telling you about. This is his boat. He lives on it.'

McCaleb stepped forward and leaned down with his hand out. The boy was carrying a toy police car in his right hand and had to transfer it to the other. He then tentatively took McCaleb's hand and they shook. McCaleb felt an unexplainable sadness as he met the boy.

'It's Terry,' he said. 'Nice to meet you, Raymond. I've heard a lot about you.'

'Can you fish off this boat?'

'Sure you can. Someday I'll take you out, if you want.'

'That would be good.'

McCaleb straightened up and smiled at Graciela. She looked lovely. She wore a light summer dress similar to the one she had worn the first time she had come to the boat. It was the kind that the breeze off the water easily pushed against her figure. She, too, carried a sweater. McCaleb was in shorts, sandals and a T-shirt that said Robicheaux's Dock & Baitshop on it. He felt a little embarrassed.

'I'll tell you what,' he said. 'Over there they've got a nice restaurant on top of the marine store. They've got good food and a great view of the sunset. Why don't we have dinner there?'

'Sounds good to me,' Graciela said.

'All I have to do is change real quick and, Raymond, I have an idea. Why don't we drop a line off the stern and you see if you can catch something while I go inside and show Graciela a few things I've been working on?'

The boy's face brightened.

'Okay.'

'Okay, then, we'll fix you up.'

McCaleb left them there and went inside. In the salon he took his lightest rod and reel out of the overhead storage rack, went to the tackle box under the chart table and got out a steel leader already set with a number eight hook and a sinker. He attached the leader to the reel line and then went to the cooler in the galley, where he knew he had some frozen squid. Using a sharp knife, he cut off a piece of squid skirt and drove the hook through it.

He returned to the stern with the rod and reel and handed the rig to Raymond. Crouching behind the boy with his arms coming around him, he gave him a quick lesson on casting the bait into the middle of the fairway. He then told him how to keep his finger on the line and to read it for nibbles.

'You okay now?' he asked when the lesson was completed.

'Uh-huh. Are there fish in here by the boats?'

'Sure, I've seen a school of sheepshead swimming right where your line is.'

'Sheepshead?'

'It's a fish with yellow stripes. Sometimes you can see them moving in the water. You watch for them.'

'Okay.'

'Are you all right now if I go in and get your mother something to drink?'

'She's not my mother.'

'Oh, yes, I – I'm sorry, Raymond. I meant Graciela. You okay?'

'I'm okay.'

'Okay, give a holler if you hook one. And then start reeling!'

He pointed a finger into the boy's side and dragged it up his tiny rib cage. McCaleb's father had done the same thing to him when he was holding a fishing pole, his sides unprotected. Raymond giggled and maneuvered away, never taking his eyes off the spot where his line disappeared into the dark water.

Graciela followed McCaleb into the salon and he closed the slider so the boy would not hear them. His face must have been red from the slip-up with the boy. She read him before he got the chance to apologize.

'That's okay. It's going to happen a lot now.'

He nodded.

'Is he going to stay with you?'

'Yes. I'm the only one but that doesn't matter. I've been around since he was born. For him to lose his mother and then me, I think it would be too much. I want him to stay with me.'

'Where's his father?'

'Who knows.'

McCaleb nodded and decided to step out of that area of questioning.

'You are going to be great for him,' he said. 'You want a glass of wine?'

'*That* would be great.'

'Red or white?'

'Whatever you're having.'

'I can't have any right now. In a couple months.'

'Oh, then I don't want you to open a bottle of wine just for me. I can have –'

'Please, I want to. How about a red? I've got some good red and if I open it, I can at least smell it.'

She smiled.

'I remember Glory was like that when she was pregnant. She used to sit right next to me and say she just wanted to smell the wine I was drinking.'

The smile turned sad.

'She was a good person,' McCaleb said. 'I can tell that by the boy. That's what you wanted me to see.'

She nodded. He went to the galley and got a bottle of red wine out of the sea rack. It was a Sanford pinot noir, one of his favorites. While he was opening it, she came over to the counter. He could smell a light scent of perfume. It was vanilla, he thought. It thrilled him. It wasn't so much being close to her as feeling that something was awakening in him after a long dormancy.

'Do you have children?' she asked then.

'Me, no.'

'Were you ever married?'

'Yes, once.'

He poured her a glass and watched her taste it. She smiled and nodded.

'It's good. How long ago was that?'

'What, when I was married? Let's see, I got married about ten years ago. Lasted three years. She was an agent and we worked together in Quantico. Then, when it didn't work out and we got divorced, we still had to work with each other and it ... I don't know, we were cool about it but it wasn't a good thing, you know? About the same time my dad was getting sick out here. So I gave them the idea of sending someone from the unit out here permanently. I sold it to them as a cost-cutting move. I mean, I was flying out here all the time anyway. A lot of us were. I figured they ought to have a little outpost or something out here and save some of that dough. They agreed and I got the job.'

Graciela nodded, turned and looked out the slider to check on Raymond. He was staring intently into the water where he hoped the fish were.

'How 'bout you?' McCaleb asked. 'You ever get married?'

'Once, too.'

'Kids?'

'No.'

She was still looking out at Raymond. Her smile was still in place but straining under the conversation. McCaleb was curious about her but decided to let it go.

'By the way, you were good with him,' she said, nodding in Raymond's direction. 'It's a balance. You have to teach them and let them find out for themselves. That was nice with him.'

She looked at him and he shook his shoulders to indicate it was luck. He took her glass and held it up to his nose to savor its aroma and then handed it back to her. He then poured himself the last from the coffee pot and added some milk and sugar. They clicked mug to glass and drank.

'Sorry,' she said. 'I feel so bad drinking this in front of you.'

'Don't. I'm glad you like it.'

Silence filled the salon. Her eyes fell to the stacks of reports and videotapes on the galley table.

'What did you want to show me?'

'Uh, nothing specific. I just didn't want to talk in front of Raymond.'

He checked on the boy through the glass. He was doing fine. His focus was still intently on the line cutting through the incoming tide. McCaleb hoped he would hook something but guessed it was unlikely. Below the marina's beautiful surface the water was fouled with pollutants. Any fish that survived down there was a bottom feeder with the survival skills of a cockroach.

He looked back at Graciela.

'But I wanted to let you know I met with the sheriff's detective this morning. She was a lot cooler about it than the LAPD guys.'

'She?'

'Jaye Winston. She's good. We worked together before. Anyway, she gave me copies of everything on both cases. That's what I spent all day looking through. There's a lot.'

'And?'

He summarized as best he could, trying to be gentle about details relating to her sister. He didn't tell her he had a videotape of her sister's murder there on the boat with them.

'In the bureau we have this thing called doing a full field,' he said at the end of the summary. 'It means leaving nothing untouched, nothing to chance. The bottom line here is that the investigation of your sister's murder was not a full field but at the same time there's nothing that jumps out at me as a gaping hole in what *was* done. There were some mistakes made, maybe some assumptions that were made before all the facts were in but they weren't necessarily wrong anyway. The investigation was thorough enough.'

'Thorough enough,' she repeated, looking down as she talked. McCaleb realized it had been a poor choice of words.

'I mean –'

'So this guy is just going to get away with it,' she said as a statement. 'I guess I should've known this is what you were going to tell me.'

'Well, I'm not telling you that. Winston, over at the sheriff's department – at least she's still actively pursuing this. And I'm not done, either, Graciela. I'm not saying that. I have a stake in this, too.'

'I know. I don't mean to sound unhappy with you. It's not you at all. But I'm frustrated.'

'I understand that. I don't want you to be. Let's go have a nice dinner and we'll talk more later.'

'Okay.'

'You go on out there with Raymond. I've got to change.'

After changing into a clean pair of Dockers and a yellow Hawaiian shirt with flying slices of pineapple on it, McCaleb led them down the docks to the restaurant. He hadn't bothered reeling in Raymond's line. He'd put the rod in one of the gunwale holders and told the boy they'd check on it when they got back.

They ate at the table with Graciela and Raymond on the side that afforded them a view of the sun just starting to set over the forest of sailboat masts. Graciela and McCaleb ordered the grilled swordfish special, while Raymond had fish and chips. McCaleb repeatedly tried to draw Raymond into conversation but was unsuccessful most of the time. He and Graciela mostly talked about the differences between living on a boat and living in a house. McCaleb told Graciela about how peaceful and restoring it was to be on the water.

'And it's even better when you're out there,' he said, pointing in the direction of the Pacific.

'How long before you have your boat ready?' Graciela asked.

'Not long. As soon as I get the second engine back

together, it will be ready to run. The rest is all cosmetic. I can do that anytime.'

On the way back after dinner, Raymond walked quickly ahead of them along the seawall, an ice-cream cone in one hand and a flashlight in the other, his blue sweater on, his head bobbing this way and that as he hunted with the light for fiddler crabs scaling the walls. The light was almost gone from the sky now. It would be time for Graciela and Raymond to leave when they got back to the boat. McCaleb felt as though he was already missing them.

When the boy got far enough in front of them, Graciela brought up the case again.

'What else can you do at this point?'

'On the case? For one thing, I have a lead I want to follow, something they might have missed.'

'What?'

He explained the geographic cross-referencing he had done and how he came up with Mikail Bolotov. When he saw her getting excited, he quickly cautioned her against it.

'This guy's got an alibi. It's a lead but it may go nowhere.'

He moved on.

'I also am thinking about going to the bureau to get them involved in the ballistics.'

'How so?'

'This guy could've done this elsewhere. He uses a very expensive gun. The fact that he didn't get rid of it between these two cases means he's hanging on to it and so he might've used it before somewhere else. They have some ballistic evidence – the bullets. The bureau might be able to do something with it if I can get them the material.'

She didn't comment and he wondered if her common sense told her that this was a long shot. He moved on.

'I'm also thinking about going back to a couple of the witnesses and interviewing them a little differently. Especially the man who saw part of the shooting up in the desert. And that's going to take some finesse. I mean, I don't want to step on Winston's toes or make her feel I think she dropped the ball. But I'd like to talk to the guy myself. He's the best witness. I'd like to talk to him and then maybe a couple of the witnesses to when your sister was ... you know.'

'I didn't know there were witnesses. There were people in the store?'

'No, I don't mean direct witnesses. But there was a woman who drove by and heard shots. There are also a couple of people in the reports that your sister worked with that night over at the *Times*. I'd just like to talk to all of them myself, see if maybe anything changed in their memories about that night.'

'I can probably help you set that up. I know most of her friends.'

'Good.'

They walked along in silence for a few moments. Raymond was still well ahead of them. Graciela finally spoke.

'I wonder if you'd do a favor for me.'

'Sure.'

'Glory used to go see this lady in our neighborhood. Mrs Otero. She also would leave Raymond with her if I wasn't around. But Glory would go by herself sometimes to talk to her about her problems. I was wondering if you would talk to her.'

'Uh ... I don't ... you mean, you think she might know something about this or is this, like, to console her?'

'It's possible she might be able to help.'

'How would she be able to ...?'

Then it dawned on him.

'Are you talking about a psychic?'

'A spiritualist. Glory trusted Mrs Otero. She said she was in touch with the angels and Glory believed it. And she's been calling and saying she wants to talk to me and, I don't know, I just thought maybe you'd go with me.'

'I don't know. I don't really believe in that sort of stuff, Graciela. I don't know what I'd say to her.'

She just looked at him and it cut him that he thought he saw disapproval in her eyes.

'Graciela ... I saw too many bad things and bad people to believe in that stuff. How can there be angels out there or up there when people do the kinds of things they do down here?'

She still didn't say anything and he knew her silence was a judgment.

'How 'bout I think about it and let you know?'

'Fine,' she finally said.

'Don't be upset.'

'Look, I'm sorry. I got you involved in this and I know it's a big intrusion. I don't know what I thought. I guess I just thought you'd ...'

'Look, don't worry about it. I'm doing it now for me as much as you. Okay? Just don't give up hope. Like I said, there's still a few things I'm going to do and Winston isn't going to let this drop, either. Give me a few days. If I get stalled out, maybe then we'll go see Mrs Otero. Okay?'

She nodded but he could tell she was disappointed.

'She was such a good kid,' she said after a while. 'Having Raymond changed everything for her. She straightened up, moved in with me and just got her priorities right. She was going to school in the mornings at Cal State. That's why she had that night job. She was smart. She wanted to get into the other side of the newspaper business. Be a reporter.'

He nodded and kept silent. He knew it was good for her to keep talking like this.

'She would have been good at it. I think. She cared about people. I mean, look at her. She was a volunteer. After the riots she went down to South-Central to help clean up. After the earthquake she came into the hospital to just be in the ER and tell people it would be okay. She was an organ donor. She gave blood – anytime any hospital called and said they needed blood, she came in. That rare blood ... well, she was rarer. Sometimes I really wish I could've traded places and that it was me who went into that store.'

He reached over and put his arm around her shoulders in a comforting manner.

'Come on,' he said. 'Look at all the people you help at the hospital. And look at Raymond. You're going to be great for him. You can't think about who was more worthy or about switching places. What happened to her shouldn't have happened to anyone.'

'But all I know is Raymond having his own mother would've been better than me.'

There was no way to argue with her. He moved his arm and put his hand on her neck. She wasn't crying but she looked like she might start. He wanted to console her but knew there was only one way he could do that.

They were almost to his dock. Raymond was waiting at the security gate, which was open a couple of inches as usual. The spring return was rusted and the gate never closed on its own.

'We should go,' Graciela said when they caught up to the boy. 'It's getting late and you have school.'

'What about the fishing pole?' Raymond protested.

'Mr McCaleb can take care of that. Now thank him for the fishing and the dinner and the ice cream.'

Raymond put out his little hand and McCaleb shook it again. It was cold and sticky.

'It's Terry. And look, we'll do some real fishing soon. As soon as I get the boat going. We'll take it out then and we'll catch you a big one. I know a spot on the other side of Catalina. This time of year, we'll catch calico bass. Lots of them. We'll go there, okay?'

Raymond nodded silently as if he guessed it would never happen. It sent a shiver of sadness through McCaleb. He looked at Graciela.

'How about Saturday? The boat won't be ready but you guys could come down in the morning and we could fish off the jetty. You could stay over if you want. Plenty of room.'

'Yeah!' Raymond cried.

'Well,' Graciela said, 'let's see how the rest of the week goes.'

McCaleb nodded, realizing the mistake he had just made. Graciela opened the passenger door of her Rabbit convertible and the boy got in. She came over to McCaleb after closing the door.

'Sorry about that,' he said in a low voice. 'I guess I shouldn't have suggested that in front of him.'

'It's all right,' she said. 'I'd like to do it but I might have to juggle some things, so let's wait and see. Unless you need to know for sure right now.'

'No, that's fine. Just let me know.'

She took a step closer to him and held out her hand to shake.

'Thank you very much for tonight,' she said. 'He's quiet most of the time but I think he enjoyed it and I know I did.'

McCaleb took her hand and shook it but then she leaned into him, brought her face up and kissed him on the cheek. As she stepped back, she brought her hand to her mouth.

'Bristly,' she said with a smile. 'Are you growing a beard?'

'Thinking about it.'

This made her laugh for some reason. She walked around the car and he followed so he could hold open the door. When she was in her seat, she looked up at him.

'You know, you should believe in them,' she said.

He looked down at her.

'You mean angels?'

She nodded. He nodded back. She started the car and drove off.

Back at the boat, he went over to the corner of the stern. The fishing pole was still in the slot and the line was still in the water as Raymond had left it. But as he reeled the line in, McCaleb could tell there was no drag on it. When the line finally came out of the water, he saw the hook and weight but no bait. Something down there had cleaned him out.

# 13

On Thursday morning McCalcb was up before the port stevedores had anything to do with it. The caffeine of the day before had surged through his veins without ebb and kept him from sleep. It fueled disquieting thoughts of the investigation, of the differences between angles and angels and of Graciela and the boy. Evcntually, he gave up on sleep and just waited with eyes open for the first light to filter through the blinds.

He was showered and finished measuring vital signs and swallowing pills by six o'clock. He took the stack of investigative reports back up to the table in the salon, put on another pot of coffee and ate a bowl of cereal. In between, he constantly checked his watch and thought about whether to call Vernon Carruthers without talking to Jaye Winston first.

Winston wouldn't be in yet. But three hours ahead at FBI headquarters in Washington, DC, McCaleb's friend Vernon Carruthers would be in his place in the FAT unit of the crime lab. McCaleb knew he shouldn't talk to Carruthers before getting the go-ahead from Winston. It was Winston's case. But the three-hour time difference between LA and Washington had him anxious. At his core McCaleb was an impatient man. The urge to get something going and not lose the day was pressing him.

After rinsing out the bowl and leaving it in the sink, he checked his watch once more and decided not to wait.

He got out his phone book and called Carruthers on his direct line. He picked up on one ring.

'Vernon, it's Terry.'

'Terrell McCaleb! You here in the city?'

'Nah, still in LA. How are you, man?'

'How are *you*? I mean, like long time, no hear.'

'I know, I know. But I'm doing okay. Thanks for the cards you sent to the hospital. Tell Marie I said thanks, too. It meant a lot. I know I should've called or written. I'm sorry.'

'Well, we tried calling you but you're unlisted and nobody in the FO seemed to have the new number. Talked to Kate and she didn't even know. All she knew was you gave up your apartment in Westwood. Somebody else in the FO said you were livin' on a boat now. You really cut yourself off from everybody.'

'Well, I just thought it would be best for a while. You know, until I was mobile and everything. But everything's good. How about you?'

'Can't complain. You coming out here anytime soon? You know you still have the room. Haven't rented it out to anybody from Quantico yet. Wouldn't dare.'

McCaleb laughed and told him that unfortunately there were no immediate plans for a trip east. He had known Carruthers for nearly twelve years. McCaleb had worked out of Quantico and Carruthers had worked out of Firearms and Toolmarks in the crime lab up in DC but it seemed that the two were often working the same cases. Whenever Carruthers came down to Quantico for meetings, McCaleb and his then wife, Kate, had put him up in their spare bedroom. It beat the spare accommodations of a room in an academy dorm. In return, whenever McCaleb was in DC, Carruthers and his wife, Marie, had let him bunk in the room that had belonged to their son. He had died years earlier of leukemia when he was twelve. Carruthers had insisted on the trade-off, even though it meant McCaleb was giving up a decent FBI-paid room at the Hilton near Dupont Circle. At first McCaleb felt like an intruder sleeping in the boy's room. But Vernon and Marie made him feel welcome. And the southern cooking and the good company couldn't be touched by the Hilton.

'Well, anytime,' Carruthers said with a returning laugh. 'Anytime.'

'Thanks, man.'

'So by my estimate, it's gotta be barely the crack a' dawn out there. What're you calling so early for?'

'Well, I'm calling on a bit of business.'

'You? Business? I was about to ask you how the wonderful world of retirement was treating you. Are you really living on a goddamned boat?'

'Yeah, I'm on a boat. But I'm not quite into the pasture yet.'

'Well, what's up, then?'

McCaleb told him the story, including the part about his receiving Gloria Torres's heart. McCaleb wanted Carruthers to know everything, unlike the others involved. He knew he could trust him with it and knew he would understand the bond McCaleb had to the victim. Carruthers had a strong empathy for victims, especially the young ones. The trauma of watching his son die over time in front of him had manifested itself in a dedication to his job that surpassed that of even the best field agents McCaleb had known.

Halfway through the telling, the booming sound of a cargo ship being unloaded began echoing across the marina. Carruthers asked what the hell it was and McCaleb told him as he took the phone down into the forward stateroom and closed the door to get away as much as possible from the noise.

'So what you want is for me to take a look at a slug from this?' Carruthers asked when McCaleb was finished.

'I don't know. That Sheriff's Department out there, they've got good people.'

'I know that. I'm not doubting that. I just want a fresh look and, mostly, I want you to put a laser profile through your computer, if you can. You never know. We might hit something. I've got a feeling about this one.'

'You and your feelings. I remember those. All right, then who am I getting the package from? Them or you?'

'I'm going to try to finesse it. Get the Sheriff's Department out here to send in the package. I don't want you doing this off the books. But if you can, I'd like to put some grease on it. This shooter's a repeater. We might save somebody's life if we can get a line on him.'

Carruthers was silent a few moments and McCaleb guessed he was running his schedule through his head.

'This is the thing. Today's Thursday. I need it by Tuesday morning latest and preferably Monday so I have time to do it justice. Next Wednesday I'm flying out to Kansas City to testify. Mob case. They think I'll be out there the rest of the week. So if you want it expedited, *you've* got to expedite it to me. If you do, I'll give it my immediate attention.'

'That's not going to cause major problems?'

' 'Course it is. I'm backed up two months here, what else is new? But just get me the package and I'll take care of it.'

'I'll get it to you. One way or the other by Monday latest.'

'Okay, buddy.'

'Oh, one last thing. Take my number. Like I said, I'm not acting in any official capacity on this thing. By rights, you should communicate with the Sheriff's Department but I'd appreciate a heads-up if you come up with anything unusual.'

'You got it,' he said without hesitation. 'Give me the

number. *And* the address. Marie will want that for Christmas cards.'

After McCaleb gave him the information, Carruthers cleared his throat.

'So, you talk to Kate lately?' he asked.

'She called the hospital a couple days after the transplant. But I was still out of it. We didn't talk long.'

'Hmmm. Well, you ought to call her just to let her know you're okay.'

'I don't know. How is she doing?'

'Fine, I guess. Haven't heard anything to the contrary. You should call her.'

'It's better just to leave it alone, I think. We're divorced, remember?'

'Whatever. You're the boss. I'll send her an E-mail just to let her know you're still breathing out there.'

After a few more minutes of catching up, McCaleb clicked off the phone and went back up to the salon for more coffee. He was out of milk so he took it black. It was hair of the dog that bit him but he had to keep the momentum. If things went as he hoped, he would be on the road most of the day.

It was now near seven and almost time to call Winston. He went out onto the deck to take a look at the morning. The marine layer had come in strong and thick and the other boats looked ghostlike in the mist. It would be a few hours before it burned off and anybody got a look at the sun. He looked over at Buddy Lockridge's boat and saw no activity yet.

At 7:10 he sat at the salon table with his legal pad and punched Jaye Winston's number into the cordless phone. He caught her just as she was sitting down at her desk.

'I just walked in,' she said. 'And I didn't expect to hear from you for a couple of days. That was a lot of paper I gave you.'

'Yeah, well, once I got into it, I couldn't put it down, I guess.'

'What did you think?'

McCaleb knew she was asking what he thought of her investigation, asking him to make a judgment.

'I think you run a tight show but I already knew that from before. I liked all the moves you made on this one, Jaye. No complaints from me.'

'But?'

'But I've got a few questions I wrote down here if you've got a few minutes. Maybe a couple of suggestions if you want 'em. A lead or two maybe.'

Winston laughed good-naturedly.

'You federal guys always have questions, always have suggestions, always have new leads.'

'Hey, I'm not federal anymore.'

'Well, I guess it sticks in the blood, then. Go ahead.'

McCaleb looked over the notes he had taken the day before and started right in on the Mikail Bolotov angle.

'First off, Ritenbaugh and Aguilar, you close to them?'

'Don't even know them. They're not in homicide. The captain pulled them out of burglaries and gave them to me for a week. That was when we were running down the three-strikes names. What about them?'

'Well, I think one of the names that they scratched off that list needs a second look.'

'Which one?'

'Mikail Bolotov.'

McCaleb heard the rustling of papers as Winston looked for the report from Ritenbaugh and Aguilar.

'Okay, got it. What are you seeing here? Looks like he's got a solid alibi.'

'Have you ever heard of geographic cross-referencing?'

'What?'

He explained the concept and told her what he had done and how it led to Bolotov. He further explained that

Bolotov had been interviewed before the Sherman Market robbery/shooting and therefore the significance of the location of Bolotov's home and employment to the market murders and one of the HK P7 thefts was not as apparent as it was to the other case. When he was done, Winston agreed that the Russian needed to be rechecked but she was not as enthusiastic about the prospect as McCaleb.

'Look, like I said, I don't know those two guys, so I can't vouch for them, but I have to assume they're not fresh off the boat. I have to assume they could handle an interview like this and check out the alibi.'

McCaleb didn't say anything.

'Look, I've got court this week. I can't go check this guy out again.'

'I can.'

Now she didn't say anything.

'I'll be cool,' McCaleb said. 'Just sort of play it by ear.'

'I don't know, Terry. You're a citizen now. This might be going too far.'

'Well, think about it. I've got some other stuff here to talk about.'

'Fine. What else?'

McCaleb knew that if she didn't bring up Bolotov again during the conversation, she was giving him unofficial permission to check the Russian out. She just didn't want to sanction what he was doing.

He glanced down at the legal pad again. He wanted to be careful with what he asked next. He needed to build up to the big questions he had, bring Winston along and not let her think he was second-guessing everything.

'Um, first off, I didn't see anything in there about the bank card in the Cordell case. I know the guy took the money. Did he take the card?'

'No. It was in the machine. It rolled it out but when he didn't take it, the machine automatically swallowed it again. It's a built-in security measure so people don't leave their cards to be taken.'

McCaleb nodded and drew a check mark next to that question on his pad.

'Okay. Next I have a question about the Cherokee. How come you didn't put that out to the media?'

'Well, we did put it out but not right away. On that first day we were still evaluating things and didn't put it into the first press release. I wasn't sure we should put that out because then the guy might see it and just dump the car. A few days later, when nothing was happening and we were hitting the wall, I put out another press release with the Cherokee in it. Trouble is, Cordell was old news and nobody picked it up. A little weekly paper up there in the desert was the only one to run it. I know, it was a screwup. I guess I should've put it all out in the first press release.'

'Not necessarily,' McCaleb said as he drew another check on the pad. 'I can see your reasoning.'

He read through the notes on the page again.

'Couple things ... In both tapes the shooter says something – after the shots. He's either talking to himself or the camera. There were no reports on that. Was anything done to –'

'There's a guy in the bureau here who has a brother who is deaf. He took the tapes to him to see if he could lip-read them. He couldn't be sure but on the first one – the ATM tape – he thought he said, "Don't forget the cashola" just as he took the money from the machine. On the other tape he was less sure. He thought he might have said either the same thing or possibly something along the lines of "Don't fuck with the" something or other. The last word was least clear to him on both tapes. I guess I never typed up a supp on it. You don't miss a thing, do you?'

'All the time,' McCaleb said. 'Would the lip reader know Russian if that was what this guy was saying?'

'What? Oh, you mean if it was Bolotov. No, I doubt his brother knows Russian.'

McCaleb wrote down the possible translations of what the shooter had said. He then drummed the pen against the pad and wondered if he should take his shot now.

'Do you have anything else?' Winston finally asked.

He decided it wasn't the right moment to bring up Carruthers. At least not directly.

'The gun,' he said.

'I know. I don't like it, either. The P7 is not your routine scumbag's choice of firearm. It had to have been stolen. You saw I pulled reports on stolens. But like with everything else, I hit a wall. It got me nowhere.'

'I think it's a good theory,' McCaleb said. 'To a point, I don't like him keeping it after the first shooting. If it was stolen, I see him throwing that thing as far out into the desert as he can about ten minutes after he takes down Cordell. He then goes and steals another for the next time.'

'No, you can't say that,' Winston said and McCaleb envisioned her shaking her head. 'There is no definitive pattern here. He could have been just as likely to keep the gun because he knew it was valuable. And you have to remember, Cordell was a through-and-through shot. He might have figured the lead wouldn't be found or if it had hit the bank – like it actually did – it would be too mangled for comparison. Remember, he picked up the brass. He probably believed the gun had at least one more use.'

'I guess you're probably right.'

They took a breather, neither one of them talking for a few moments. McCaleb had two more things on his page.

'Next thing,' he began carefully. 'The slugs.'

'What about them?'

'You said yesterday that you're holding the ballistics from both cases.'

'That's right. It's all in evidence lockup. What are you getting at?'

'Have you ever heard of the bureau's DRUGFIRE computer?'

'No.'

'It might work for us. For you. It's a long shot but it's worth a shot.'

'What is it?'

McCaleb told her. DRUGFIRE was an FBI computer program designed along similar lines of computerized storage of latent fingerprint data. It was the brainchild of the crime lab in the early 1980s, when the cocaine wars that broke out in most cities, particularly Miami, were responsible for a jump in murders nationwide. Most of the slayings were by gunfire. The bureau, struggling for a means of tracking related murders and killers across the country, came up with the DRUGFIRE program. The unique characteristics of groove marks found on the spent bullets used in drug murders were read by a laser, coded for computer storage and entered into a data bank. The computer's program operated in much the same way as fingerprint computer systems used by law enforcement agencies across the nation. The system allowed for the quick comparison of coded bullet profiles.

Eventually, the database grew as more ballistic entries were added. The program was also widened, though it kept the name DRUGFIRE, to include all cases referred to the FBI. Whether it was a mob killing in Las Vegas or a gang killing in South Los Angeles or a serial killing in Fort Lauderdale, every gunshot case sent to the FBI for analysis was added to the database. After more than a decade, there were thousands of bullets on file in the computer.

'I've been thinking about this guy,' McCaleb said. 'He

hangs on to that gun. Whatever the reason, whether he stole it or not, his hanging on to it is really the only mistake he's made. It makes me think we've got a chance of making a match. Looking at the MO on those tapes, chances are he just didn't start popping people beginning with your case. He's used a gun before – maybe even that particular gun.'

'But I told you, we checked for similars. Nothing on ballistics. We also put out teletypes and a request on the National Crime Index computer. We got blanked.'

'I understand. But this guy's method could be evolving, changing. Maybe what he did with that gun in, say, Phoenix isn't the same as what he did with it here. All I'm saying is that there's a chance that this guy came into town from someplace else. If he did, then he probably used that gun in that other place. And if we're lucky, the data is sitting there in the bureau computer.'

'Maybe,' Winston said.

She went quiet as she brooded over his proposal. McCaleb knew what the considerations were. DRUGFIRE was a long shot and Winston was smart enough to know that. But if she went for it, she would be drawing in federal involvement, not to mention acknowledging that she was taking direction from McCaleb, an outsider with no real standing in the case.

'What do you think?' McCaleb finally asked. 'You only need to send them one bullet. You have, what, four of them from the two cases?'

'I don't know,' she said. 'I'm not so keen on sending our stuff off to Washington. I doubt LA will be, either.'

'LA doesn't have to know. You're the keeper of the evidence. You can send one bullet if you want. And it could be to DC and back inside a week. Arrango wouldn't have to know it was even sent. I already talked to a guy I know in Firearms and Toolmarks. He said he'd grease this one if we got him the package.'

McCaleb closed his eyes. If there was a point at which she might get outright angry, it was now.

'You already told this guy we'd be doing this?' she asked, annoyance in her voice.

'No, I didn't tell him that. I told him I was dealing with a detective out here who was very thorough and dedicated and would probably want to make sure she left no stone uncovered.'

'Gee, where have I heard that before?'

McCaleb smiled.

'There's another thing,' he said. 'Even if we don't get lucky with this, we'll at least have the gun in the computer. Somewhere down the road, it might match up with something.'

She thought about this for a moment. McCaleb was pretty sure he had painted her into the corner. Like watching the cemetery for Luther Hatch. She had to go for it or she'd wonder about it always.

'Okay, okay,' Winston finally said. 'I'll talk to the captain about it. I'll tell him I want to do this. If he gives the go-ahead, I'll send a package. One bullet – that's all.'

'That's all it takes.'

McCaleb filled her in further on Carruthers's need to get the package by Monday evening and urged her to get in with the captain as soon as possible. This created another silence.

'All I can say is, it's worth the shot, Jaye,' he said by way of reinforcement.

'I know. It's just that ... well, never mind. Give me your guy's name and his number.'

McCaleb clenched his fist and punched it into the air in front of him. It didn't matter how long a shot it was. They were rolling the dice. It felt good to him to be getting something going.

After he gave Winston the direct number and address

for contacting Carruthers, she asked if there was anything else McCaleb wanted to talk about. He looked down at his pad but what he wanted to talk about wasn't written down on it.

'I've got one last thing that's probably going to put you on the spot,' he said.

'Oh, no,' Winston said with a groan. 'Serves me right for answering the phone on a court day. Give it to me, McCaleb. What is it?'

'James Noone.'

'The witness? What about him?'

'He saw the shooter. He saw the shooter's car.'

'Yeah, a lot of good it did us. There's only about a hundred thousand of those Cherokees in southern California and his description of the guy is so vague he can't tell if the guy was wearing a hat or not. He's a witness but just barely.'

'But he saw him. It was during a stress situation. The more stress, the deeper the imprint. Noone would be perfect.'

'Perfect for what?'

'To be hypnotized.'

# 14

Buddy Lockridge pulled the Taurus into an open spot in the parking lot of Video GraFX Consultants on La Brea Avenue in Hollywood. Lockridge was not dressed Hollywood-cool for his second day as McCaleb's driver. This time he was wearing boat shorts and a Hawaiian shirt with ukuleles and hula girls floating on an ocean blue background. McCaleb told him he didn't think he would be long and got out.

VGC was a business used mostly by the entertainment industry. It rented professional video equipment as well as video editing and dubbing studios. Adult filmmakers, whose product was almost exclusively shot on video, were its main clients but VGC also provided one of the best video-effects and image-enhancing labs in Hollywood.

McCaleb had been inside VGC once before, working on loan to the field office's bank unit. It was the downside of his being transferred from Quantico to the FO outpost; technically he was under the command of the FO's special agent in charge. And whenever the SAC thought things were slow – if they ever were – in the serials unit, he would yank McCaleb out and put him on something else, usually something McCaleb considered menial.

When he had walked into VGC the previous time, he had a videotape from the ceiling camera of a Wells Fargo Bank in Beverly Hills. The bank had been robbed by several masked gunmen who had escaped with

$363,000 in cash. It was the group's fourth bank robbery in twelve days. The one lead agents had was on the video. When one of the robbers had reached his arm across the teller's counter to grab the bag she had just stuffed her cash into, his sleeve had caught on the edge of the marble counter and was pulled back. The robber quickly pulled the sleeve forward again but for a split second the form of a tattoo was seen on the inside of his forearm. The image was grainy and had been shot by a camera thirty feet away. After a tech in the field office lab said he could do nothing with it, it was decided not to send the tape to Washington HQ because it would take more than a month to have it analyzed. The robbers were hitting every three days. They seemed agitated in the videos, on the verge of violence. Speed was a necessity.

McCaleb took the tape to Video GraFX. A VGC tech took the frame from the video and in one day enhanced it through pixel redefinition and amplification to the point that the tattoo was identifiable. It was a flying hawk clutching a rifle in one claw and a scythe in the other.

The tattoo broke the case. Its description and a photocopy were teletyped and faxed to sixty field offices across the country. A supervisor in the Butte office then retransmitted the information to the smaller Resident Agency in Coeur d'Alene, Idaho, where an agent recognized the tattoo as the insignia he had seen on a flag flown outside the house of a member of a local group of anti-government extremists. The group had intermittently been under bureau observation and suspicion because of its recent purchases of huge tracts of rural land outside the city. The supervisor of the RA was able to provide the Los Angeles FO with a list of members' names and social security numbers. Agents then began checking hotels and soon found seven members of the group staying at the Airport Hilton. The group was placed under surveillance and the following day watched as they robbed a bank in Willowbrook. Thirty agents were poised in surveillance points outside and ready to go in at the first sign of violence. There wasn't any. The robbers were followed back to their hotel and systematically arrested in their rooms by agents posing as room service waiters and house-keeping staff. One of the robbers eventually cooperated with agents and admitted that the group had been robbing banks in order to raise capital to buy more land in Idaho. The group wanted the land so members could safely sit out the Armageddon their leader promised was coming to the United States.

Now McCaleb was back. As he stepped to the reception counter, he noticed that the letter of thanks under the bureau's seal that he had sent following the bank robbery investigation was framed on the wall behind the receptionist. He leaned over the counter until he could read the name of the man he had sent the letter to.

'Can I help you?' the receptionist asked.

McCaleb pointed at the letter and said, 'I'd like to talk to Tony Banks.'

She asked McCaleb his name, didn't seem to recognize it though it was on the letter that hung on the wall above her, and then put in a call. Shortly after, a man McCaleb recognized as Tony Banks came out to greet him. He didn't recognize McCaleb until he started recounting the bank video story.

'Right, right, I remember. You sent the letter.'

He pointed to the framed letter.

'That's me.'

'So what can I do for you? Another bank job?'

He was eyeing the videotape McCaleb had in his hand.

'Well, I've got another case here. I'm wondering if you could take a look at this tape. There's something on it I want to see if I can get a better look at.'

'Well, let's take a look. Always glad to help out.'

He led McCaleb down a hallway of gray carpet past several doors that he knew from his previous visit were editing booths. Business was good. There were Occupied signs on all of the doors. From behind one of them McCaleb heard muffled cries of passion. Banks looked over his shoulder at him and rolled his eyes.

'It's not real,' he said. 'They're editing a tape.'

McCaleb nodded. Banks had explained the same thing to him when he had been there before.

Banks opened the last door in the hallway. He ducked his head inside to make sure the room was empty, then stepped back and signaled McCaleb inside. There were two chairs set in front of a video editing machine with twin thirty-inch monitors above it. Banks turned on the equipment, pushed a button and the left side cassette cradle opened.

'Now this is going to be pretty graphic,' McCaleb said. 'Somebody gets shot. If you want, you can go outside and I'll just move it to the frame I want you to look at.'

Banks took a moment to think about the offer. He was a thin man of about thirty, with limp hair dyed so blond it was almost white. It was long on the top and shaved around the sides. A Hollywood haircut.

'I've seen graphic,' he said. 'Put it in.'

'None like this, I don't think. There's a difference between graphic real life and the stuff they put in movies.'

'Put it in.'

McCaleb put the tape in the slot and Banks began to play it. McCaleb heard the younger man's breath catch as he watched Gloria Torres get grabbed from behind and the gun placed against her head and fired. McCaleb reached over and put his hand on the pause button. At the right moment, after Chan Ho Kang had been shot and his body had fallen across the counter and then slid back, he pushed the button and froze the frame. Then, by using a dial, he could move the picture backward and forward slowly until he had exactly the image he wanted. He looked at Banks. The man looked as though all of the evil of humanity had just been revealed to him.

'You okay?'

'It's horrible.'

'Yes. It is.'

'How can I help you?'

Taking a pen from his shirt pocket, McCaleb pointed at the screen and tapped it on the watch on Kang's wrist.

'The watch?'

'Yes. I want to know if it is possible to blow this frame up or do something that would let me read the watch. I want to know what time it was at this point of the video.'

'Time? What about this?'

He pointed to the timeline running along the bottom of the screen.

'I can't trust that time. That's why I need the watch.'

Banks leaned forward and began fiddling with the dials on the console that controlled the focus and image amplification.

'This is not the original,' he said.

'The tape? No, why?'

'I'm not getting much amplification. Can you get the original?'

'I don't think so.'

McCaleb looked at the screen. Banks had made the image clearer and larger. The screen was filled with Kang's upper body and outstretched arm. But the face of the watch was still a blurred gray.

'Well, then what I can do, if you want to leave it with me, is work with it a little bit, take it to one of the guys in the lab. Maybe bring it up a little, clarify it a bit more with some pixel redefinition. But this is the best I can do with it on this equipment.'

'You think it's worth doing, even without the original? Will we get anything?'

'I don't know but it's worth a try. They can do some wild stuff back there. You're after him, right? This man on the video?'

He gestured toward the screen, though at the moment the shooter wasn't on it.

'Yeah, I'm after him.'

'Then we'll see what we can do. Can you leave this?'

'Yeah. I mean ... uh, can you dub off a copy for me so I can have it with me? I might need to show it to somebody else.'

'Sure. Let me go get a tape.'

Banks got up and left the booth. McCaleb sat there staring at the screen. He had watched how Banks had used the equipment. He backed the tape up and amplified a frame showing the masked shooter. It didn't help much. He hit the fast forward for a bit and stopped it on a close-up of Gloria's face. It felt intrusive to be so close at such a moment, to be staring at a woman who had just had her life taken. Her face was in left profile and the one eye that he could see was still open.

McCaleb noticed the three earrings on her left ear. One was a stud, a small silver crescent moon. Next, going down the curve of the ear, was a small hoop that he guessed was silver and last, dangling below the lobe, was a cross. He knew it was the style among young women to have multiple earrings on at least one ear.

While he continued to wait for Banks, he played with the dials once more and backed the tape up until there was a view of Gloria's right side, just as she entered the frame. He could see only one earring on her right ear, another crescent moon.

Banks came back in with a tape and quickly inserted it into the second cassette cradle while he finished rewinding the first tape. It took him about thirty seconds to make a high-speed dub copy. He ejected it, slid it into a box and handed it to McCaleb.

'Thanks,' McCaleb said. 'How long you think before somebody gets a chance to work on it?'

'We're kind of busy. But I'll go look at the job board and see if we can't get someone on it as soon as possible. Maybe by tomorrow or Saturday. Is that okay?'

'It's okay. Thanks, Tony, I appreciate it.'

'No problem. I don't know if I still have your card. You want me to call you?'

In that moment McCaleb decided to continue the deception. He didn't tell Banks that he was no longer an FBI agent. He thought Banks might push the project a little harder if he thought that the job was being done for the bureau.

'Tell you what, let me give you a private number. If you call and I don't pick up, just leave a message and I'll get back to you as soon as I can.'

'Sounds good. I hope we can help.'

'Me too. And, Tony? Do me a favor and don't show the tape to anybody who doesn't need to see it.'

'I won't,' Banks said, his face reddening a bit. McCaleb realized either he had needlessly embarrassed Banks with a request that did not need to be spoken or he had made the request just as Banks was thinking about whom he could show the tape to. McCaleb thought it was the latter.

McCaleb gave him his number, they shook hands and McCaleb went back down the hall on his own. As he passed the door from which he had heard the feigned sounds of passion, he noticed there was only silence now.

As McCaleb opened the door of the Taurus, he heard the radio playing and noticed Lockridge had a harmonica on his thigh, ready to be played if the right tune came along. Buddy closed a book called *Death of a Tenor Man*. He had marked a spot about halfway through.

'What happened to Inspector Fujigama?'

'What?'

'The book you had yesterday.'

'*Inspector Imanishi Investigates*. I finished it.'

'Imanishi then. You're a fast reader.'

'Good books read fast. You read crime novels?'

'Why would I want to read made-up stuff when I've seen the real stuff and can't stand it?'

Buddy started the car. He had to turn the ignition twice before it kicked over.

'It's a much different world. Everything is ordered, good and bad clearly defined, the bad guy always gets what he deserves, the hero shines, no loose ends. It's a refreshing antidote to the real world.'

'Sounds boring.'

'No, it's reassuring. Where to now?'

# 15

After eating lunch at Musso and Frank's, a place McCaleb loved but hadn't been back to in two years, they drove over the hill from Hollywood to the Valley and got to the building that housed Deltona Clocks at quarter to two. McCaleb had called the business before they set out that morning from the marina and learned that Mikail Bolotov was still working a two-to-ten shift.

Deltona Clocks was a large warehouse structure located behind a small street-front showroom and retail shop. After Lockridge parked the Taurus in front of the retail store, McCaleb reached down to the leather bag on the floor in front of him and removed his gun. It was already snugly held in a canvas holster which he then clipped onto his belt.

'Hey, what are you expecting in there?' Lockridge said after he saw the weapon.

'Nothing. It's more a prop than anything else.'

McCaleb next pulled out an inch-thick sheaf of the sheriff's investigative records and made sure the report on the interview with Bolotov and his employer, a man identified as Arnold Toliver, was on top. He was ready. He looked over at Lockridge.

'Okay, sit tight.'

He noted as he got out of the Taurus that this time Buddy hadn't offered to come in with him. He thought maybe he should carry the gun more often.

Inside the retail shop there were no customers. Cheap

clocks of almost every size were on display. Most had an industrial look, as though they were more likely to be found in a classroom or an auto supply store than in somebody's home. On the wall behind the counter at the rear of the space was a display of eight matching clocks showing the time in eight cities around the world. There was a young woman sitting on a folding chair behind the counter. McCaleb thought about how slowly time must pass for her with no customers and all of those clocks.

'How do I find Mr Toliver?' he asked as he came up to the counter.

'Arnold or Randy?'

'Arnold.'

'I have to call back. Who are you with?'

'I'm not here to buy clocks. I'm conducting a follow-up on a Sheriff's Department inquiry of February third.'

He dropped the stack of paperwork on the counter so she could see that they were official forms. He then raised his hands and put them on his hips, carefully allowing his sports coat to open and expose the gun. He watched her eyes as she noticed it. She picked up a telephone that was on the counter and dialed three numbers.

'Arnie, it's Wendy. There's a man from the Sheriff's Department here about an investigation or something.'

McCaleb didn't correct her. He hadn't lied to her and he wouldn't lie to her about who he was and whom he was with. But if she wanted to make incorrect assumptions, then he wasn't going to correct her. After listening to the phone for a few moments, Wendy looked up at McCaleb.

'What investigation?'

McCaleb nodded toward the phone and held his hand out. The young woman hesitated but then handed the phone receiver to him.

'Mr Toliver?' he said into the phone. 'Terry McCaleb. A couple months ago you talked to a couple of sheriff's detectives named Ritenbaugh and Aguilar about an employee named Mikail Bolotov. You remember?'

After a long hesitation Toliver agreed that he had.

'Well, I'm investigating that case now. Ritenbaugh and Aguilar are onto other things. I need to ask you some additional questions about that. Can I come back?'

Again a hesitation.

'Well ... we are awfully busy back here. I –'

'I won't take long, sir. Remember, it's a murder investigation and I'm hoping you'll continue to help us out.'

'Well, I suppose ...'

'You suppose what?'

'Uh, just come on back. The girl will tell you where I'm at.'

Three minutes later McCaleb had walked the length of the building, past several rows of assembly and packaging benches, to an office at the rear next to a loading dock. There was a short flight of stairs up into the office. Next to the door was a window that allowed Toliver to look out across the workbenches as well as the shipping and receiving dock. As he had walked past the benches toward the office, McCaleb had overheard the conversations of the employees. Three different times he heard a language he believed was Russian.

As McCaleb opened the office door, the man he assumed was Toliver hung up the phone and waved him in. He was a skinny man in his sixties, with brown, leathery skin and white hair fringed around the sides of his head. He had a plastic pocket guard in his shirt pocket, jammed with an assortment of pens.

'I've gotta make this quick,' he said. 'I have to check the lading on a truck going out.'

'Fine.' McCaleb looked down at the report on top of the stack he carried. 'Two months ago you told detectives

Ritenbaugh and Aguilar that Mikail Bolotov was working the night of January twenty-second.'

'That's right. I remember. Hasn't changed.'

'Are you sure, Mr Toliver?'

'What do you mean, am I sure? Yeah, I'm sure. I looked it up for those two guys. It was in the books. I pulled the time card.'

'Are you saying you based it on what you saw in the pay records or did you actually see Bolotov working that night?'

'He was here. I remembered that. Mikail never missed a day.'

'And you remember him working all the way until ten.'

'His time card showed he –'

'I'm not talking about the time card. I'm talking about you remembering he stayed until ten.'

Toliver didn't answer. McCaleb glanced out the window at the rows of workbenches.

'You've got a lot of people working for you, Mr Toliver. How many work the two-to-ten shift?'

'Eighty-eight at the moment.'

'And then?'

'About the same. What's the point?'

'The point is you gave the man an alibi based on a time card. Do you think it could have been possible that Bolotov left early without being noticed, then had a friend punch him out on the clock?'

Toliver didn't respond.

'Forgetting about Bolotov for a moment, have you ever had that problem before? You know, somebody punching out for somebody else, scamming the company that way?'

'We've been in business here sixteen years, it's happened.'

'Okay.' McCaleb nodded. 'Now, could it have happened with Bolotov? Or do you stand at the time clock every night and make sure nobody punches two cards.'

'Anything's possible. We don't stand at the clock. Most nights my son closes up. I'm already home. He keeps an eye on things.'

McCaleb held his breath for a beat and felt the excitement he had been containing build. Toliver's answer, if it were given in court, would be enough to shred Bolotov's alibi.

'Your son, is that Randy?'

'Yeah, Randy.'

'Can I talk to him?'

'He's in Mexico. We've got another plant in Mexicali. He spends one week a month down there. He'll be back next week.'

'Maybe we can call him?'

'I can try but he's probably out on the floor. That's why he goes down there. To make sure the line is running. Besides, how is he going to remember one night three months ago? We make clocks here, Detective. Every night we make the same clocks. Every day we ship them out. One night is no different from the other.'

McCaleb turned away from him and looked out the window again. He noticed that several of the workers were leaving their posts as new workers were taking their places. He watched the shift change until he picked out the man he believed was Bolotov. There had been no photo in the records and only a spare description. But the man McCaleb was now watching wore a black T-shirt with sleeves stretched tightly around his powerful and tattoo-laced arms. The tattoos were all of one ink – jailhouse blue. It had to be Bolotov.

'That's him, right?'

He nodded in the direction of the man who had taken a seat at a workbench. It appeared to McCaleb that it was Bolotov's job to place the plastic casings around completed clock mechanisms and then stack them in a four-wheeled cart.

'Which?'

Toliver had come up next to McCaleb at the window.

'With the tattoos.'

'Yeah.'

McCaleb nodded and thought for a moment.

'Did you tell Ritenbaugh and Aguilar that the alibi you were giving that man was based on what you saw in the pay records and time cards and not what you or your son actually saw on that night?'

'Yeah, I told them. They said fine. They left and that was that. Now, here you are with these new questions. Why don't you guys get your shit together? It would have been a lot easier for my boy to remember after two or three weeks instead of three months.'

McCaleb was silent as he thought about Ritenbaugh and Aguilar. They had probably had a list of twenty-five names they had to cover in the week they were assigned to the case. It was sloppy work but he understood how it could happen.

'Listen, I've got to go out to the dock,' Toliver said. 'You want to wait until I come back or what?'

'Tell you what, why don't you send Bolotov in here on your way out. I need to talk to him.'

'In here?'

'If you don't mind, Mr Toliver. I am sure you want to help us out and continue to cooperate, don't you?'

He stared at Toliver as a final means of ending his unspoken objection.

'Whatever,' Toliver said as he threw his hands up in a gesture of annoyance and headed toward the door. 'Just don't take all day.'

'Oh, Mr Toliver?'

Toliver stopped at the door and looked back at him.

'I heard a lot of Russian being spoken out there. Where do you get the Russians?'

'They're good workers and they don't complain. They don't mind being paid shit, either. When we advertise for help, we do it in the local Russian paper.'

He went through the door then, leaving it open behind him. McCaleb pulled the two chairs in front of the desk away and turned them so they faced each other from about five feet apart. He sat down on the one closest to the door and waited. He quickly thought about how he would handle the interview and decided to come at Bolotov strong. He wanted to engender a response, get some kind of reaction to which he could register his own feel for the man.

He felt a presence in the room and looked at the door. The man he had guessed was Bolotov stood there. He was about five ten, with black hair and pale white skin. But the bulging arm muscles and tattoos – a snake wrapped around one arm, a spider's web covering the other – made his arms the focal point of his image. McCaleb pointed to the empty chair.

'Have a seat.'

Bolotov moved to the chair and sat down without hesitation. McCaleb saw that the spider web apparently continued under the shirt and then came up both sides of the Russian's neck. A black spider sat in the web just below his right ear.

'What is this?'

'Same as before, Bolotov. My name's McCaleb. The night of January twenty-second. Tell me about it.'

'I told them before. I work here that night. It was not me you look for.'

'So you said. But things are different now. We know things we didn't know then.'

'What things?'

McCaleb got up and locked the door and then retook

his seat. It was just a little show, an underlining of his control. Something for Bolotov to think about.

'What things?' he asked again.

'Like the burglary of the house over on Mason, just a few blocks from here. You remember, the one with the Christmas tree and all the presents. That's where you got the gun, wasn't it, Bolotov?'

'No, I am clean on these things.'

'Bullshit. You did the break-in and you got that nice new gun. Then you decided to use it. You used it up in Lancaster and then again around the corner from here at the market. You're a killer, Bolotov. A killer.'

The Russian sat still but McCaleb could see his biceps drawing tight, better defining the artwork on his arms. He pressed on.

'What about February seventh, you have an alibi for that night, too?'

'I don't know that night. I have to –'

'You walked into the Sherman Market and you killed two people that night. You should know it.'

Bolotov suddenly stood up.

'Who are you? You're not cop.'

McCaleb just looked up at him, keeping his seat, hoping not to show the surprise he was feeling.

'Cops are in twos. Who are you?'

'I'm the one who's going to take you down. You did it, Bolotov, and I'm going to prove it.'

'Wha–'

There was an angry knock on the door and McCaleb instinctively turned to look. It was a small mistake but it was all Bolotov needed. McCaleb saw the black blur coming at him in his peripheral vision. Instinctively he began bringing his arms up to protect his chest. He wasn't quick enough. Suddenly he was hit with the impact of the other man's weight and his chair went over with him still in it.

Bolotov had him down on the floor while Toliver or whoever was out there continued to knock angrily on the door. The bigger, stronger man held McCaleb down while he went through his pockets. His hand hit the gun and he tore it off the belt and threw it across the room. Finally he found McCaleb's wallet in the inside pocket of his sports coat. He pulled it out, ripping the pocket, and opened it.

'No badge. See, no cop.'

He read the name off the driver's license, which was held behind a plastic window in the wallet.

'Terr-ell-Mack-Cow-leeb.'

Bolotov then read off the address. McCaleb felt relieved that it was actually the address of the harbormaster's office, where he had a postal box.

'Maybe I pay you a visit one day, yes?'

McCaleb didn't answer or move. He knew there was no chance of overpowering the man. As he was considering his predicament, Bolotov dropped the wallet on his chest and jumped up. He jerked the chair out from beneath McCaleb's hips and raised it over his head. McCaleb raised his arms up to protect his face and head, realizing in the same instant that he was leaving his chest unprotected.

He heard the shatter of glass and looked between his arms to see the chair crashing through the office window. He then watched as Bolotov followed it, leaping with ease through the opening and down to the manufacturing floor. Then he was gone.

McCaleb rolled to his side, folding his arms across his chest and bringing his knees up. He spread a hand flat on his chest, trying to feel the beat. He took two deep breaths and slowly got to his knees and raised himself. The pounding on the door continued, now accompanied by Toliver's panicked demands that McCaleb open up.

McCaleb reached over to unlock the door. He felt a

wave of vertigo hit him then. It was like sliding down a twelve-foot trough into the valley of a wave. Toliver burst into the office and started screaming at him but McCaleb didn't understand his words. He put his hands flat on the floor and closed his eyes, trying to steady himself.

'Shit,' was all he managed to whisper.

Buddy Lockridge jumped out of the Taurus when he saw McCaleb approaching. He ran around the front of the car and came to McCaleb's side.

'Jesus, what happened?'

'Nothing. I made a mistake, that's all.'

'You look like shit.'

'I'm okay now. Let's go.'

Lockridge opened the door for him and then went around to the driver's side and got in.

'You sure you're okay?'

'Come on, let's go.'

'Where?'

'Find a phone.'

'There's one right there.'

He pointed to the Jack in the Box restaurant next door. There was a pay phone on the wall near one of the doors. McCaleb got out and slowly walked to the phone. He was careful to keep his eyes on the pavement in front of him, not wanting to set off another slide into vertigo.

He called Jaye Winston's direct line, expecting to leave a message, but she picked up immediately.

'It's Terry. I thought you had court.'

'I do but it's the lunch break. I have to be back at two. I was just about to call you.'

'Why?'

'Because we're going to do it.'

'Do what?'

'Hypnotize Mr Noone. The captain signed off on it and

I called Mr Noone. He said sure. He just wants us to do it tonight because he's going out of town – back to Vegas, I guess. He's going to be here at six. You can do it then, right?'

'I'll be there.'

'Then we're set. Why were you calling?'

McCaleb hesitated. What he had to tell her might change the evening's plans but he knew he couldn't delay.

'Can you get a photo of Bolotov by tonight?'

'I already have one. You want to show Noone?'

'Yeah. I just paid Bolotov a little visit and he didn't react too well to it.'

'What happened?'

'Before I could ask him three questions, he jumped me and ran.'

'Are you shitting me?'

'I wish.'

'What about his alibi?'

'It's about as solid as a loaf of bread.'

McCaleb briefly recounted his interview with Toliver and then Bolotov. He told Winston she should put out a wanted notice for Bolotov.

'For what, did you or Toliver make a police report?'

'I didn't but Toliver said he was going to make a report on the window.'

'All right, I'll put out a pickup. Are you all right? You sound punchy.'

'I'm okay. Is this going to change things? Or are we still on for tonight?'

'Far as I'm concerned, we're still on.'

'Okay. See you then.'

'Look, Terry, don't put too much stock in Bolotov, okay?'

'I think he looks good for this.'

'I don't know. Lancaster's a long way from where

Bolotov lives. You've got to remember, the guy's a convict. He could have and would have done what he did with you whether he's involved with this or not. Because if he didn't do this, then he did something else.'

'Maybe. But I still like the guy.'

'Well, maybe Noone will make our day and point him out in a six-pack.'

'Now you're talking.'

After hanging up, McCaleb made it back to the Taurus without a problem. Once inside he dug the travel kit he always carried with him out of the leather satchel on the floor. It contained a day's worth of medication and a dozen or so throw-away thermometers called Temp-Strips. He peeled the paper off one and put it in his mouth. While he waited, he signaled Lockridge to start the car. Once the engine had fired, McCaleb reached over to the air-conditioner controls and turned it on.

'You want air?' Lockridge asked.

McCaleb nodded and Lockridge turned the fan up higher.

After three minutes McCaleb took the strip out and checked it. He felt a deep shard of fear cut into him as he looked at the thin red vein stretched past the one-hundred-degree mark.

'Let's go home.'

'You sure?'

'Yes. The marina.'

As Lockridge pointed the car south toward the 101 freeway, McCaleb turned the air vents on his side so that the cool air was flowing right into his face. He opened up another Temp-Strip and put it under his tongue. He tried to calm himself by turning on KFWB on the radio and looking out at the passing street scene. Two minutes later the second temperature reading was better than the first, but he was still running a low-grade fever. His fear eased back some and his throat relaxed. He banged his palms against the dashboard and shook his head, convincing himself in the process that the fever was an aberration. He had been perfect so far. There was no reason for this other than that he had gotten overheated while tangling with Bolotov.

He decided to go back to the boat and take an aspirin and a long nap before preparing for the evening's session with James Noone. The alternative was to call Bonnie Fox. And he knew that such a call would result in his finding himself in a hospital bed for several days of testing and observation. Fox was as thorough at what she did as McCaleb liked to think he was at what he did. She wouldn't hesitate to bring him in. He would lose at least a week lying in bed in Cedars. He would certainly miss his chance at Noone and he would lose the momentum that was the only other thing he had going for him in this investigation.

# 16

To the uninformed – and this included many cops and agents McCaleb had worked with over the years – hypnosis was often seen as a form of voodoo policework, a second-to-last resort just shy of consulting the local psychic. It was considered emblematic of a stalled or failed investigation. McCaleb firmly believed it was not. He believed it was a credible means of plumbing the depths of the mind. In the instances where he had seen or heard of it going wrong, it was usually at the fault of the hypnotist and not the science.

McCaleb had been surprised when Winston said she was in favor of reinterviewing Noone under hypnotic conditions. She had told him that hypnotism had been suggested a couple of times during the weekly homicide bureau meetings when the stalled Cordell investigation came up. But the suggestion had never been acted on for two reasons. The first was the important one. Hypnosis was a tool used often by police until the early eighties, when California's supreme court ruled that witnesses who had memories refreshed through hypnosis could not testify in criminal proceedings. This meant that every time investigators decided whether to use hypnotism on a witness, they had to weigh whether the possible gain from it was worth losing that person as a witness in court. The debate had stalled the use of hypnotism in the Cordell case, since Winston and her captain were reluctant to lose their only witness.

The second reason was that after the supreme court ruling, the Sheriff's Department stopped training detectives in the use of hypnosis. Consequently, the more than fifteen years since the ruling had seen the natural attrition of the detectives who had the skill. There was no one left in the department who could hypnotize Noone, meaning that they would have to go to an outside hypnotherapist. That would further complicate things and cost money.

When McCaleb had told Winston that he had used hypnotism on bureau cases for more than ten years and would be willing to do it, she had brightened on the suggestion even more. A few hours later she'd had the session approved and set up.

McCaleb arrived at the homicide bureau at the Sheriff's Star Center a half hour early. He told Lockridge that he would be a while and encouraged him to go get dinner.

His fever had been trimmed to less than a half a point during an afternoon nap. He felt rested and ready. He was excited by the prospect of digging a solid lead out of the mind of James Noone and accomplishing something that would drive the case forward.

Jaye Winston met him at the front counter and escorted him to the captain's office, talking quickly all the way.

'I posted a wanted on Bolotov. Had a car go by his apartment but he was already gone. He's split. You obviously hit a nerve.'

'Yeah, maybe when I called him a murderer.'

'I'm still not convinced but it's the best thing we've got going at the moment. Typically, Arrango is not happy about what you did. I have to admit, I didn't say we talked about this beforehand. He thinks you were cowboying.'

'Don't worry about it. I don't care what he thinks.'

'Are you worried about Bolotov? You said he has your address.'

'No. He has the marina but not the boat. It's a big place.'

She opened the door and allowed McCaleb to enter first. There were three men and a woman waiting in the cramped office. McCaleb recognized Arrango and Walters from the LAPD. Winston introduced him to Captain Al Hitchens and the woman, an artist named Donna de Groot. She would be available if needed to work up a composite drawing of the suspect, provided that Noone didn't identify Bolotov outright.

'I'm glad you're early,' Hitchens said. 'Mr Noone is already here. Maybe we can get this going.'

McCaleb nodded and looked at the others in the room. Arrango had the smirk of a nonbeliever on his face. A toothpick protruded a half inch from his tight lips.

'This is too many people,' McCaleb said. 'Too much distraction. I need to get this guy relaxed. That won't happen with an audience like this.'

'We're not all going in,' Hitchens said. 'I'd like you and Jaye to be in the room. You bring Donna in at the appropriate time. We're going to videotape it and we have a monitor set up right here. The rest of us will watch from here. That okay with you?'

He pointed to a monitor on a cart in the corner. McCaleb looked at the screen and saw a man sitting at a table with his arms folded in front of him. It was Noone. Even though he was wearing a baseball hat, McCaleb recognized the man from the crime scene and ATM tapes.

'That's fine.'

McCaleb looked at Winston.

'Did you make up a six-pack with Bolotov?'

'Yes. It's on my desk. We'll show it to him first, in case

we get lucky. If he makes the ID there will be no hypnosis, so we can save him for court.'

McCaleb nodded.

'Woulda been real nice,' Arrango began, 'if we had shown Noone the pictures before the bird was flushed.'

He looked at McCaleb. McCaleb thought of a response but decided to keep it to himself.

'Anything in particular you want me to ask him?' he asked instead.

Arrango looked at his partner and winked.

'Yeah, get us the license plate off that getaway vehicle. That'd be nice.'

He smiled brilliantly, the toothpick jutting upward from his lower lip. McCaleb smiled back.

'It's been done before. The victim of a rapist once gave me a complete description of a tattoo on her attacker's arm. Before hypnosis she hadn't even remembered the tattoo.'

'Good, then do it again. Get us a plate. Get us a tattoo. Your pal Bolotov has enough of 'em.'

There had been a clear challenge in his voice. Arrango seemed to insist on putting everything on a personal level, as if McCaleb's desire to bring a multiple killer in was in some way a show of disrespect to him. It was ludicrous but McCaleb had challenged him simply by entering the case.

'Okay, guys,' Hitchens said, cutting it off and trying to diffuse tensions. 'We're just taking a shot at this, that's all. It's worth the shot. Maybe we get something, maybe we don't.'

'Meantime, we lose the guy in court,' Arrango said.

'What court?' McCaleb said. 'You're not going anywhere near court with what you guys have got. This is your last chance, Arrango. I'm your last chance.'

Arrango swiftly stood up. Not to challenge McCaleb physically but to underline his next words.

'Lookit, asshole, I don't need some washed-out fed to tell me how to –'

'Okay, okay, that's it,' Hitchens said, standing up also. 'We're gonna do this thing and do it right now. Jaye, why don't you take Terry into the interview room and get started. The rest of us will wait here.'

Winston guided McCaleb out the door. He looked back over his shoulder at Arrango, whose face had turned dark with anger. Past him McCaleb noticed a quizzical smile on Donna de Groot's face. She had apparently enjoyed the testosterone show.

As they walked through the squad room and past rows of empty desks, McCaleb shook his head with embarrassment.

'Sorry,' he said. 'I can't believe I let him draw me into that.'

'It's okay. Guy's an asshole. It was going to happen sooner or later.'

After stopping by Winston's desk to pick up the file containing the photo lineup, they went down a hallway and Winston stopped outside a closed door. She put her hand on the knob but looked back at McCaleb before turning it.

'Okay, any particular way you want to do this?'

'The main thing is that it works best if only I do the talking once the session begins and I communicate verbally only with him. That way he won't get confused about who I am talking to. So if you and I need to communicate, we can either write notes or point to the door and we can come out here.'

'Fine. Are you all right? You look like shit.'

'I'm fine.'

She opened the door and James Noone looked up from the table.

'Mr Noone, this is Terry McCaleb, the hypnotism expert I told you about,' Winston said. 'He used to work for the FBI. He's going to see if he can't work with you on this.'

McCaleb smiled and reached a hand across the table. They shook.

'Good to meet you, Mr Noone. This shouldn't take long and it should be a relaxing experience. Do you mind if I call you James?'

'No, James is fine.'

McCaleb looked around the room and at the table and chairs. The chairs were standard government issue, with a half inch of foam padding on the seats. He looked at Winston.

'Jaye, you think we can get a more comfortable chair for James? Something with arms maybe? Like the one Captain Hitchens was sitting in.'

'Sure. Hang on a minute.'

'Oh, also, I'm going to need a pair of scissors.'

Winston looked at him quizzically but left without a word. McCaleb took an appraising look around the room. There was an overhead bank of fluorescent lights in the ceiling. No other lighting. The glare from the overheads was magnified by the mirrored window on the left wall. He knew the video camera was set up on the other side of the glass, so he needed to keep Noone in a position facing it.

'Let's see,' he said to Noone. 'I need to get up on the table to get at those lights.'

'No problem.'

Using a chair as a stepladder, McCaleb climbed onto the table and reached up to the light panel. He moved slowly, trying to avoid another bout of vertigo. He opened the panel and began removing the long light tubes, handing them down to Noone and engaging him in small talk, hoping to make the witness feel comfortable with him.

'I hear you're going to Vegas from here? Is that work or play?'

'Uh, work mostly.'

'What do you do?'

'Computer software. I'm designing a new accounting and security system for the El Rio. Still working out the bugs. We'll be running tests for the next week or so.'

'A week in Las Vegas? Boy, I could lose a lot of money there in a week.'

'I don't gamble.'

'That's a good thing.'

He had taken out three of the four bulbs, dropping the room into a dim ambience. He hoped that left enough light for the video. As he got off the table, Winston returned with a chair that actually looked like the one Hitchens had been sitting in.

'You took that from the captain?'

'Best chair in the place.'

'Good.'

He looked at the mirror and winked at the camera behind it. As he did this, he noticed the dark circles beginning to form under his eyes and quickly looked away.

Winston reached into the pocket of the blazer she wore and carefully eased out a pair of scissors. McCaleb took them and put them on the table and then pushed it against the wall below the mirror. He then took the captain's chair and positioned it against the opposite wall. He put two chairs from the table facing the captain's chair but split them apart far enough so as not to block the camera's view of Noone. He directed Noone to the captain's chair and then Winston and he took the remaining seats. McCaleb looked at his watch and noted that it was ten minutes before six.

'Okay,' he said. 'We'll try to do this quick and have

you on your way, James. First off, any questions you have for us about what we're trying to do here?'

Noone thought a moment before speaking.

'Well, I guess I don't know much about it. What will happen to me?'

'Nothing will happen to you. All hypnosis really is is an altered state of consciousness. What we want you to do is go through some progressive stages of relaxation until you reach a point where you can easily move through the recesses of your mind to pull out some of the stored information. Kind of like turning through a Rolodex and pulling out the card you need.'

McCaleb waited but Noone asked nothing else.

'Why don't we start with an exercise. I want you to tilt your head back slightly and look up. Try to roll your eyes upward as far as they can go. Maybe you should take off your glasses.'

Noone took off the glasses, folded them and put them in his pocket. He tilted his head back and rolled his eyes up. McCaleb studied him. He was able to roll them upward enough so that a quarter inch of white cornea was visible below each iris. This was a good indicator of receptivity to hypnosis.

'Okay, that's good. Now, I want you to just relax if you can, take long, deep breaths and tell us what you can recall about the incident on the night of January twenty-second. Just recount what you now remember about what you saw.'

For the next ten minutes Noone told the story about coming upon the tail end of the shooting and robbery at the ATM in Lancaster. His story was no different than the versions he had recounted during various interviews since the night it had all happened. He added no new details that McCaleb picked up on and seemed to leave nothing out from his prior tellings. This was unusual and encouraging to McCaleb. The memories of most witnesses begin fading after two months. They forgot details. The fact that Noone seemed to remember every detail led McCaleb to hope the computer programmer's recessed memory might be just as sharp. When Noone had finished recounting the event, McCaleb nodded to Winston, who then leaned toward Noone and handed him the six-pack file.

'James, I want you to open the file and look at the photos. Tell us if any of the men was the man you saw in the speeding car.'

Noone put his glasses back on and took the file but said, 'I don't know. I really didn't get a –'

'I know,' Winston said. 'But take a look.'

Noone opened the file. There was a piece of cardboard inside with squares cut out in two rows of three. In the squares were photos of men. Bolotov's photo was the third on the top row. Noone stared at the six-pack, his eyes moving from photo to photo, and then shook his head.

'I'm sorry. I just didn't see him.'

'That's fine,' McCaleb said quickly before Winston could say something that Noone might interpret as a negative. 'I think we're ready to go on, then.'

He took the file from Noone and tossed it onto the table.

'So why don't you start by just telling us what you do to relax, James?' McCaleb asked.

Noone looked back at him blankly.

'You know, when are you happiest? When are you the most relaxed and at peace? Me, I like to work on my boat and go fishing. I don't even care if I catch anything. I just like having a line in the water. How about you, James? You like shooting baskets, hitting golf balls? What?'

'Um, I don't know. I guess I like being on the computer.'

'But that's not relaxing mentally, James, is it? I'm not talking about something where you have to do a lot of thinking. I mean, what do you do when you want to let it all go. When you're tired of thinking and you just want to go blank for a while.'

'Well ... I don't know. I like to go to the beach. There's a place I know. I go there.'

'What's it look like?'

'The sand is so white and it's wide. You can rent horses and ride along the edge of the water below the cliffs. The water cuts under the cliffs and it's like a hanging edge. People sit under there in the shade.'

'Okay, that's good. That's real good, James. Now, I want you to close your eyes, rest your arms in your lap and in your mind I want you to think about that spot. Picture in your mind that you are walking on that beach. Just relax and walk along the beach.'

McCaleb was silent for a half minute and simply watched Noone's face. The skin around the corners of his closed eyes began to relax and McCaleb then led him through a set of sensory exercises in which he told him to concentrate on the feel of his socks on his feet, his hands on the fabric of his pants, the glasses on the bridge of his nose, even the hair – what was left of it – on his head.

After five minutes of this, McCaleb went on to muscle exercises, telling Noone to crunch his toes together as hard as possible, hold them that way and then release. Slowly the focus of the exercises was moved up his body, eventually going to every muscle group. McCaleb then started again at the toes and moved back up. It was a method of exhausting the muscles and making the mind more susceptible to the suggestion of relaxation and rest. McCaleb noticed Noone's breathing going deep and long. Things were going well. He looked at his watch and saw it was now six-thirty.

'Okay, James, now without opening your eyes, I want you to hold your left hand out and up in front of your face. Hold it about a foot from your face.'

Noone responded and McCaleb let him hold his arm up for a good minute, all the while counseling him to relax and keep his thoughts on the beach he was walking on.

'Okay, I now want you to very slowly bring your hand toward your face. Very slowly.'

Noone's hand started to move toward his nose.

'Okay, slower now,' McCaleb said, his words slower and softer than before. 'That's it, James. Slowly. And when your hand touches your face you will be totally relaxed and at that point you will drop into a deep hypnotic state.'

He was silent then as he watched Noone's hand move slowly forward until his palm stopped at his nose. At the moment of contact, his head dipped forward and his shoulders slumped. His hand dropped into his lap. McCaleb looked over at Winston. She raised her eyebrows and nodded at him. McCaleb knew they were only halfway there but things were looking good. He decided to run a little test.

'James, you are totally relaxed now, totally at rest. You are so relaxed that your arms are as light as feathers. They weigh nothing at all.'

He watched him but he didn't move, which was good.

'Okay, now I'm going to take a balloon that's full of helium and tie the string to your left hand. I'm tying it on now. There, the balloon is tied to your wrist, James, and I'm letting go of it.'

Immediately, Noone's left arm began to rise until it was stretched upward, his hand up higher than his head. McCaleb just watched. And after half a minute Noone's arm showed no indication of tiring.

'Okay, James, I have a pair of scissors and I'm going to cut the string.'

McCaleb reached back to the table and lifted the scissors. He opened them and closed them sharply on the imaginary string. Noone's arm dropped back into his lap. McCaleb looked over at Winston and nodded.

'Okay, James, you are very relaxed and nothing is bothering you. I want you to picture in your mind that you're walking on that beach and you come to a garden. The garden is green and lush and beautiful and there are flowers and birds singing. It is so beautiful and peaceful. You've never been in any spot as peaceful as this. Now ... you walk through the garden and come to a small building with a set of doors. They're elevator doors, James. They're made of wood with gold trim around the edges and they're beautiful. Everything here is beautiful.

'The doors open, James, and you step on the elevator because you know it takes you down to your special room. A room where nobody else can go. Only you can go down there and you are in total peace when you go there.'

McCaleb got up and stood in front of Noone, just a few feet away. Noone showed no outward sign of acknowledging the close presence of another person.

'The elevator buttons show you are on number ten and you have to go down to your room on number one. You push the button, James, and the elevator starts to go down. You are feeling more relaxed as each floor goes by.'

McCaleb raised his arm and held it parallel to the ground and a foot in front of Noone's face. He then began raising it, bringing it back around and then up again. He knew the disturbance the motion would make in the light hitting Noone's eyelids would add to his sense of descent.

'You're going down, James. Deeper and deeper. That's

the ninth floor ... now the eighth, and seventh ... You are getting deeper and deeper, more and more relaxed. The sixth floor just went by ... now the fifth ... four ... three ... two ... and one ... The doors open now and you step into your special room. You're there, James, and in perfect peace.'

McCaleb went back to his chair. He then told Noone to enter his room and that the most comfortable chair in the world was waiting for him there. He told him to sit down and just melt into the chair. He told him to imagine a pat of butter melting in a frying pan on very low heat.

'No sizzle, just a slow, slow melting. That's you, James. Just melting into your chair.'

He waited a few moments and then told Noone about the television that was sitting right in front of him.

'You've got the remote control in your hand. And this is a special television with a special remote. You can watch whatever you want to on this TV. You can back the picture up, go forward, zoom in or pull back out. Whatever you want to do with it, you can do. Now, turn it on, James. And what we're going to watch on that special TV right now is what you saw on the night of January twenty-second when you were going to the bank in Lancaster to get some money.'

He waited a beat.

'Turn the TV on, James. Is it on now?'

'Yes,' Noone said, his first words in a half hour.

'Okay, good. Now we're going to go back to that night, James. Now tell us what you saw.'

# 17

James Noone told his story as if McCaleb and Winston were there riding with him in his car, if not his head.

'I have the blinker on and I'm turning in. Here he comes! Brakes! He's going to – he almost hit me, the asshole! I could've –'

Noone raised his left arm, made a fist and shot his middle finger up, an impotent gesture at the driver of the car that had blasted by him. As he did this, McCaleb looked closely at his face, noting the rapid eye movement behind his closed lids. It was one of the indicators he always looked for, a sign that the subject was deeply into the trance.

'He's gone and I'm pulling in now. I see, I see the man. There is a man on the ground under the light. By the ATM. He's down – I'm getting out and check to see ... there's blood. He's shot – somebody shot him. Uh, uh, I've got to get somebody – I'm going back to my car for the phone. I can call and get him help. He's shot. There's blood on the ... it's everywhere.'

'Okay, James, okay,' McCaleb said, interrupting him for the first time. 'That's good. Now what I want you to do is take your special remote and back up the picture on the TV until the point that you first see the car coming out of the bank's parking lot. Can you do that?'

'Yes.'

'Okay, are you there?'

'Yes.'

'Okay, now start it again, only this time run it in slow motion. Very slow, so you can see everything. Are you running it?'

'Yes.'

'Okay, I want you to freeze it when you get the best view of the car coming at you.'

McCaleb waited.

'Okay, I got it.'

'Okay, good. Can you tell us what kind of car it is?'

'Yes. Black Cherokee. It's pretty dusty.'

'Can you tell what year?'

'No, it's the newer kind. The Grand Cherokee.'

'Can you see the side of the Cherokee?'

'Yes.'

'How many doors?'

It was a small test to make sure Noone was reporting what he had seen, not what he had been told. McCaleb remembered from the crime scene tape that the deputy who had first interviewed Noone had told him the newer styling on the Cherokee indicated it was the Grand Cherokee model. McCaleb had to confirm the identification of the vehicle and he knew the Grand Cherokee came only in a four-door model.

'Um, two on the side,' Noone said. 'It's a four-door.'

'Good. Now come around to the front. Do you see any damage to the car. Any dents or noticeable scratches?'

'No.'

'Is there any striping on the car?'

'Mmm, no.'

'How about the bumper? Can you see the front bumper?'

'Yes.'

'Okay, I want you to take your remote and zoom in on that bumper. Can you see the license plate?'

'No.'

'Why not, James?'

'It's covered.'

'What's covering it?'

'Uh, there's a T-shirt on it. It's wrapped around the bumper so it covers the plate. Looks like a T-shirt.'

McCaleb glanced over at Winston and could see the disappointment on her face. He pressed on.

'Okay, James, take your remote and zoom up into the car, can you do that?'

'Okay.'

'How many people are in that Cherokee?'

'One. The driver.'

'All right, zoom in on him. Tell me what you see.'

'Can't really.'

'Why not? What's wrong?'

'The lights. He's got the brights on. The glare is too much, I can't –'

'Okay, James, what I want you to do is take the remote and move the picture. Go back and forth until you have the best view of the driver. Tell me when you have that.'

McCaleb looked back at Winston and she looked back with raised eyebrows. They both knew that they would soon find out if this had been worth it or not.

'Okay,' James said.

'Okay, you're seeing the driver.'

'Yes.'

'Tell us what he looks like. What color is his skin?'

'He's white but he has a hat and the brim is down. He's looking downward and the brim covers his face.'

'All of his face?'

'No. I see his mouth.'

'Does he have a beard or mustache?'

'No.'

'Can you see his teeth?'

'No, his mouth is closed.'

'Can you see his eyes?'

'No. That hat is in the way.'

McCaleb sat back and released his breath in frustration. He couldn't believe this. Noone was a perfect subject. He was in a deep trance and yet they couldn't get from him what they needed, a direct look at the shooter.

'Okay, are you sure this is the best view of him?'

'I'm sure.'

'Can you see any of his hair?'

'Yes.'

'What color is it?'

'Dark, like a dark brown or maybe black.'

'What length, can you tell?'

'It looks short.'

'What about the hat? Describe the hat.'

'It's a baseball hat and it's gray. Washed-out gray.'

'Okay, is there any writing on the hat or a team logo?'

'There's a design, like a symbol.'

'Can you describe it?'

'It's like letters overlapping each other.'

'What letters?'

'It looks like a C with a line cut through. A one or a capital I or a small L. And then there's a circle – I mean an oval – around the whole thing.'

McCaleb was silent for a moment thinking about this.

'James,' he then said, 'if I give you something to draw on, do you think you could open your eyes and draw this design for us?'

'Yes.'

'Okay, I want you to open your eyes.'

McCaleb stood up. Winston had already turned the pad she had on a clipboard to a fresh page. McCaleb took it and her pen and handed both to Noone.

Noone's eyes were open and staring blankly at the pad as he drew. He then handed it back. The drawing was as he had described it, a vertical line slashing down through a large C. This design was then captured in an oval.

McCaleb handed the pad back to Winston, who briefly held it up to the mirrored window so those watching on video could see.

'Okay, James, that was good. Now close your eyes and look at the picture of the driver again. You got it?'

'Yes.'

'Can you see either of his ears?'

'One. His right.'

'Is there anything unusual?'

'No.'

'No earring?'

'No.'

'What about below the ear? His neck, can you see his neck?'

'Yes.'

'Anything unusual there? What do you see?'

'Uh, nothing. Uh, his neck. Just his neck.'

'This is his right side?'

'Yes, right.'

'No tattoo on his neck?'

'No. No tattoo.'

McCaleb blew out his breath again. He had just effectively eliminated Bolotov as a suspect after spending the day building him as one.

'Okay,' he said in a resigned voice, 'what about his hands, can you see his hands?'

'On the steering wheel. They're holding the wheel.'

'See anything unusual? Anything on his fingers?'

'No.'

'No rings?'

'No.'

'Is he wearing a watch?'

'A watch, yes.'

'What kind?'

'I can't see. I see the band.'

'What kind of band? What color?'

'It's black.'

'Which wrist is it on, his left or right?'

'His ... right. His right.'

'Okay, can you see and describe any of his clothing?'

'Just his shirt. It's dark. A dark blue sweatshirt.'

McCaleb tried to think of what else to ask. His disappointment in not being able to come up with a substantial lead so far was crowding his focus. Finally, he thought of something he had passed over.

'The windshield, James. Are there any stickers or anything like that on the glass?'

'Mmm, no. I don't see them.'

'Okay, and take a look at the rearview mirror. Anything on that? Like hanging down or hooked to it?'

'Not that I can see.'

McCaleb now slumped in his chair. This was a disaster. They had lost this man as a potential court witness, eliminated a potential suspect and all they got from it was a detailed description of a baseball cap and a dentless Cherokee. He knew the last step was to take Noone forward to his last view of the Cherokee speeding away, but it was likely that if the front license plate had been covered, so too would be the rear plate.

'Okay, James, let's hit fast forward to the point that the Cherokee is past you and you are shooting the guy the bird.'

'Okay.'

'Zoom in on the license plate, can you see it?'

'It's covered.'

'With what?'

'A towel or a T-shirt. I can't tell. Like the front.'

'Zoom back. Do you see anything unusual about the rear of the car.'

'Mmm, no.'

'Bumper stickers? Or maybe the car dealership's name on the rear?'

'No, nothing like that.'

'Anything on the window? Any stickers?'

McCaleb registered the desperation in his own voice.

'No, nothing.'

McCaleb looked at Winston and shook his head.

'Anything else?'

Winston shook her head.

'Do you want to bring the artist in?'

She shook her head again.

'You sure?'

She shook her head one more time. McCaleb turned his attention back to Noone though he couldn't help but think about how this had been a gamble that had not paid off.

'James, over the next few days I want you to think about what you saw on the night of January twenty-second and if anything new comes to mind, if you remember any other details, I want you to call Detective Winston, okay?'

'Okay.'

'Good. Now I'm going to count backward from five and as I do this, you are going to feel your body rejuvenating and you will become more and more alert until I say, "One," and you become fully alert. You are going to have a high level of energy and feel like you've just had eight hours of sleep. You'll stay awake all the way to Las Vegas but when you go to bed tonight, you won't have any trouble sleeping. Okay on all of that?'

'Okay.'

McCaleb brought him out of the trance and Noone looked at Winston with expectant eyes.

'Welcome back,' McCaleb said. 'How do you feel?'

'Great, I guess. How'd I do?'

'You did fine. You remember what we talked about?'

'Yes, I think so.'

'Good. You should. Remember, if anything else comes to the surface, you call Detective Winston.'

'Right.'

'Well, we don't want to hold you up any further. You've got a long drive ahead of you.'

'No problem, I didn't think I'd get out of here until after seven. You're giving me a head start.'

McCaleb looked at his watch and then back at Noone.

'It's almost seven-thirty right now.'

'What?'

He looked at his watch, surprise showing on his face.

'People in the hypnotic state often lose time,' McCaleb said.

'I thought it was only like ten minutes.'

'That's normal. It's called disturbed time.'

McCaleb stood up and they shook hands and Winston walked him out. McCaleb sat back down and clasped his hands together on top of his head. He was bone tired and wished that *he* could feel like he had just had eight hours' sleep.

The door to the interview room opened and Captain Hitchens stepped in. He had a dour expression on his face that was easy to interpret.

'Well, what do you think?' he asked as he sat down on the table next to the scissors.

'Same as you. It was a bust. We got a better description of the car but it still only narrows it down to ten thousand or so. And we got the hat, which there may even be more of.'

'Cleveland Indians?'

'What? Oh, the CI? Maybe, but I think they have a little Indian guy on their hats.'

'Right, right. Well ... what about Molotov?'

'Bolotov.'

'Whatever. I guess we've painted him out now.'

'Looks it.'

Hitchens clapped his hands together and after a few uncomfortable moments of silence, Winston came back in and stood there with her hands in the pockets of her blazer.

'Where's Arrango and Walters?' McCaleb asked.

'They left,' she said. 'They weren't impressed.'

McCaleb stood back up and told Hitchens that if he got off the table he'd put it back in place and then put the light bulbs back into the ceiling. Hitchens said not to bother. He told McCaleb that he had done enough – which McCaleb took to mean in more ways than one.

'Then I guess I'll be going,' he said. Pointing at the mirror, he added, 'You think at some point I could get a copy of the tape or the transcript? I'd like to look at it at some point. Might get a few ideas for a follow-up.'

'Well, Jaye can make you a copy. We've got a transfer machine. But as far as any follow-ups go, I don't see much of a need to pursue this. The guy clearly didn't see our shooter's face and the plates were covered. What else is there to say?'

McCaleb didn't answer. They all left after that, Hitchens pushing his chair back toward his office and Winston leading McCaleb into the video room. She grabbed a fresh tape off a shelf and put it in a tape machine already attached to the one that had recorded the hypnotism session.

'Look, I still think it was worth the shot,' McCaleb said as she pushed the buttons that began dubbing one tape onto the other.

'Don't worry, it was. I'm disappointed only in the lack of results and because we lost the Russian, not in the fact that we did it. I don't know what the captain thinks and I don't care about those LAPD guys, that's how I look at it.'

McCaleb nodded. It was nice of her to put it that way and let him off the hook. After all, he had pushed for the use of hypnotism and it hadn't paid off. She could have dumped all the blame on him.

'Well, if Hitchens gives you grief, just put it all on me. Tell him it was all me.'

Winston didn't reply. She popped the dubbed tape out of the machine, slid it into its cardboard sleeve and handed it to McCaleb.

'I'll walk you out,' she said.

'Nah, that's okay. I know the way.'

'Okay, Terry, stay in touch.'

'Sure.' They were out in the hallway before McCaleb remembered something. 'Hey, did you talk to the captain about the DRUGFIRE thing?'

'Oh, yeah, we're going to do it. A package goes out FedEx tomorrow. I called your guy in DC and told him it was coming.'

'Great. You tell Arrango?'

Winston frowned and shook her head.

'Basically, I get the idea that any idea that comes from you, Arrango isn't interested in. I didn't tell him.'

McCaleb nodded, threw a salute her way and headed for the exit. He walked through the parking lot, his eyes scanning for Buddy Lockridge's Taurus. Before he spotted it, another car pulled up alongside him. McCaleb glanced over and saw Arrango looking up at him from the passenger seat.

McCaleb braced himself for the detective's gloating about the lack of success from the session.

'What?' he said.

He kept walking and the car stayed alongside him.

'Nothing,' Arrango said. 'I just wanted to tell you that was a hell of a show in there. Four stars. We'll put a teletype out on the watchband first thing in the morning.'

'That's funny, Arrango.'

'Just making the point that your little session in there

cost us a witness, a suspect who probably should have never been a suspect, and didn't get us squat.'

'We got more than we had before. I never said the guy was going to give us the shooter's goddamn address.'

'Yeah, well, we already figured out what the CI on the hat means. Complete Idiots – that's what the shooter probably thinks of us.'

'If he does, he was already thinking that before tonight.'

Arrango didn't have an answer for that.

'You know,' McCaleb said, 'you ought to think about your witness. Ellen Taaffe.'

'To hypnotize like that?'

'That's right.'

Arrango barked a command at Walters to stop the car. He popped his door open and jumped out. He came up close to McCaleb, their faces inches apart. Close enough for McCaleb to smell his breath. He guessed that the detective kept a flask of bourbon in the glove compartment.

'Listen to me, bureau man, you stay the fuck away from my witnesses. You just stay the fuck away from my case.'

He didn't back away when he was done. He just stayed there, his whisky breath burning McCaleb's nose. McCaleb smiled and nodded slowly as if he had just come into possession of a great secret.

'You're really worried, aren't you?' he said. 'You're worried I'm going to break this. You don't care about the actual case, about the people killed or hurt by this. You just don't want me doing what you can't.'

McCaleb waited for a response but Arrango said nothing.

'Then be worried, Arrango.'

'Yeah? Because you're going to break this one?'

He laughed in a fake way that had far more venom in it than humor.

'Because I'll let you in on a little secret,' McCaleb said. 'You know Gloria Torres? The victim you don't give a shit about? I've got her heart.'

McCaleb tapped his chest and looked back at him.

'I got her heart. I'm alive because she's dead. And that cuts me into this in a big way. So I don't care much about your feelings, Arrango. I couldn't give a fuck about stepping on your toes. You're an asshole and that's fine, be an asshole. I'll put up with that. But I'm not backing out of this till we get this guy. I don't care if it's you, me or somebody else. But I'm in this one for the whole ride.'

They just stared at each other for a long moment and then McCaleb raised his right hand and calmly pushed Arrango away from him.

'I gotta go, Arrango. See you around.'

# 18

........

He dreamed of darkness. A moving darkness, like blood in water, with darting images in the periphery that he couldn't grab onto with his eyes until they were gone.

Three times in the night he was awakened by some interior alarm. Sitting up so fast he grew dizzy, he would wait and listen and there would be nothing but the sound of the wind through dozens of masts in the marina. He would get up and check the boat, look out across the marina for Bolotov even though he thought it unlikely the Russian would ever show up. He'd then use the bathroom and check the vitals. Status quo each time and he would return to the dark waters of the same indecipherable dream.

At nine o'clock Friday morning the phone woke him. It was Jaye Winston.

'You awake?'

'Yeah. Just getting a slow start today. What's going on?'

'What's going on is that I just heard from Arrango and he told me something that really bothers me.'

'Oh, yeah? What's that?'

'He told me who you got that new heart from.'

McCaleb rubbed a hand across his face. He had forgotten that he had told Arrango.

'Why does that bother you, Jaye?'

'Because I wish you had told me everything. I don't like secrets, Terry. That asshole calls up and makes *me* feel like an asshole because I'm the last one to know this.'

'What's the difference whether you knew or not?'

'It's kind of a conflict of interest, isn't it?'

'No. It's not a conflict. You ask me, it's an enhancement. It makes me want to get this guy even more than you people. Is there something else that's bothering you? Is this about Noone?'

'No, it's not about that. I told you last night, I stand behind doing it. The captain gave me some grief already today but I still think we had to do it.'

'Good. So do I.'

There was a tentative silence after that. McCaleb still thought there was something else she wanted to say and he waited her out.

'Look, just don't go off cowboying on this, okay?' Winston said.

'What do you mean?'

'I'm not sure. I just don't know what you've got planned. And I don't want to have to worry about what you're up to because of your "enhancement", as you call it.'

'I understand. It's not even a point of contention, Jaye. As I've said all along, if I get something, it goes to you guys. That's still the plan.'

'Okay, then.'

'All right.'

He was putting the phone down when he heard her voice.

'By the way, the bullet went to your man today. He'll get it tomorrow if he works Saturdays. If not, Monday.'

'Good.'

'You'll let me know if he gets something, right?'

'He's going to tell you first. You sent the package.'

'Don't bullshit a bullshitter, Terry. He's your man, he's

going to call you. Hopefully, he'll call me real quick after.'

'I'll make sure he does.'

Again he was putting the phone down when he heard her.

'So what are you going to do today?'

He hadn't really thought about it.

'Well ... I don't know. I'm not sure where to go. I'd like to reinterview the witnesses on the Gloria Torres thing but Arrango pretty much threatened me if I went near them.'

'So what's that leave?'

'I don't know. I was thinking about just hanging around the boat today, maybe take another run through the books and the tapes, see if anything comes up. I was quick on the first read-through, but not thorough.'

'Well, that sounds like a boring day. Almost as bad as mine's going to be.'

'Court again?'

'I wish. Trial's in recess Fridays. That means I get to spend the day doing paper. Catching up. And I better get started. I'll see you, Terry. Remember what you said. You'll call me first with the news.'

'You get the news,' he agreed.

She finally hung up and he flopped back on the bed, the phone clutched to his stomach. After a few minutes of trying to recall the dreams of the night before, he lifted the phone and called information to get the number of the emergency room at Holy Cross.

After calling and asking for Graciela Rivers, he waited nearly a minute before she picked up. Her voice was clipped and urgent. He had obviously called at a bad time. He almost hung up but guessed that she might figure out it was him.

'Hello?'

'I'm sorry. I must've caught you in the middle of something.'

'Who is this?'

'It's Terry.'

'Oh, Terry, hi. No, it's not a bad time. I just thought it might be something about Raymond. I usually don't get calls here.'

'Then I'm sorry I alarmed you.'

'It's okay. Are you sick? You don't sound like you. I didn't even recognize your voice.'

She forced a laugh into the phone. He thought she felt embarrassed that she didn't know his voice.

'I'm lying on my back,' he said. 'You ever do that when you're calling in sick? You know, it makes you sound like you really are sick.'

This time her laugh was legitimate.

'No, I never tried that. I'll have to remember.'

'Sure. It's a good tip. You can use it.'

'So what's up? How are things going?'

'Well, on the case not so good. I thought we had something yesterday but then we hit a bit of a stall. I'm going to rethink things today.'

'Okay.'

'I was calling because I was wondering about tomorrow. You know, whether you were thinking of bringing Raymond down so I could take him out to the rocks.'

'The rocks?'

'The jetty. There's good fishing off there. I walk out most mornings and there's always people there, lines out.'

'Well, Raymond hasn't stopped talking about it since we left the other night. So I was planning on it. As long as it's still all right with you.'

McCaleb hesitated, thinking about Bolotov and wondering if he could possibly be a threat. But he wanted to see Graciela and the boy. He felt a need to see them.

'It sounds like maybe we should do it another time,' she said then.

'No,' he said, the specter of Bolotov disappearing from his mind. 'I was just thinking. I want you to come down. It will be fun. And I could make up for that dinner I was supposed to cook the other night.'

'Then good.'

'And you two should stay over. I've got plenty of room. Two staterooms and the salon table collapses and becomes a third bed.'

'Well, we'll see. I like to keep some constants in Raymond's life. Like his bed.'

'I understand.'

They talked about the arrangements a little further and she agreed to come down to the marina the following morning. After hanging up, he continued to lie in bed with the phone sitting on his stomach. His thoughts were on Graciela. He liked being with her and the thought of spending all of Saturday with her made him smile. Then the thought of Bolotov intruded again. McCaleb carefully considered the situation and decided that Bolotov was not a threat. Most spoken threats were never carried out. Even if Bolotov wanted to, it would be difficult for him to find *The Following Sea*. Lastly, the Russian was no longer a suspect in the murders.

Those thoughts led to the next question: If he was not a suspect, then why had he run? McCaleb thought of Winston's explanation the night before. Bolotov had not been the shooter but he was probably guilty of something. He ran.

McCaleb put it aside, rolled out of bed and finally got up.

After he had gotten one cup of coffee down, McCaleb went down to the office and gathered up all of the reports and the tapes and brought them back up to the salon. He then opened the slider to air out the boat and sat back down and began methodically going through all of the videotapes associated with the case.

Twenty minutes later he was watching the shooting of Gloria Torres for the third time in a row when he heard Buddy Lockridge's voice from behind him.

'What the hell is that?'

McCaleb turned around and saw Lockridge standing in the open door of the salon. He hadn't felt him come aboard. He grabbed the remote and flicked off the television.

'It's a tape. What are you doing here?'

'Reporting for duty.'

McCaleb stared blankly at him.

'You told me yesterday you'd need me this morning.'

'Oh, right. Well, I don't think I'm – I'm just going to work around here today, I think. You going to be around later if something comes up?'

'Prob'ly.'

'Okay, thanks.'

McCaleb waited for him to leave but Lockridge just stood there.

'What?'

'Is that what you're working on?' Lockridge asked, pointing at the tube.

'Yes, Buddy, that's it. But I can't talk to you about it. It's a private matter.'

'That's cool.'

'Then what else?'

'Um, well, when's payday?'

'Payday? What are you talk – oh, you mean for you? Oh, anytime. You need some money?'

'Sort of. I could use some today.'

McCaleb went to the galley counter where he had left his wallet and keys. As he was opening the wallet, he computed that he had used Buddy for no more than eight hours. He took out six twenties and handed the bills to Lockridge. Fanning the money in his hands, Buddy said it was too much.

'Some of it's for gas,' McCaleb explained. 'And the extra is for the hanging around and being on call. That okay?'

'Fine with me. Thanks, Terror.'

McCaleb smiled. Lockridge had been calling him that ever since the night they met and McCaleb had been so mad about the harmonica noise.

Lockridge finally left then and McCaleb got back to work. Nothing struck him as significant during his viewing of the videotapes and he went on to the paperwork. On this read-through time was not a factor and he tried to absorb every detail on every page.

He started backward, beginning with the Kang-Torres case. But as he went through the crime reports and investigative summaries, he found nothing aside from the conflict in the timeline he had constructed earlier that tugged at him as being out of order or needing further investigation. Despite his dislike of Arrango's personality and Walters's complacency, he couldn't find anything wrong or anything that had slipped through.

Finally, he came to the autopsy report and the grainy photocopies of the photos of Gloria Torres's body. He hadn't looked at these before. With good reason. Death photos had always been the way he remembered victims. He saw them in death, not in life. He saw what had been done to them. During the first read-through of the murder book, he had decided that he didn't need to see the photos of Gloria. It wasn't what he wanted or needed to know about her.

But now, grasping for anything, he studied the photos. The poor duplication of them by the photocopier made the details murky and softened the impact. He leafed through them quickly and then came back to the first one. It was Gloria's naked body on the steel table, the photo taken before the autopsy. A long incision, made by the surgeon who took her organs, ran between the breasts and down the sternum. McCaleb held the photo in both hands and looked at her violated body for a long moment, feeling a mixture of sadness and the heat of guilt.

The phone rang, startling him. He grabbed the phone before it could ring again.

'Yes?'

'Terry? It's Dr Fox.'

McCaleb inexplicably turned the photo over on the table.

'Are you there?'

'Yes, hi, how are you?'

'I'm fine. How are you?'

'I'm fine, too, Doc.'

'What are you doing?'

'Doing? I'm just sort of sitting here.'

'Terry, you know what I mean. What did you decide about that woman's request? The sister.'

'I, uh ...' He turned the photo back over and looked at it. 'I decided I needed to look into it.'

She didn't say anything but he pictured her at her desk closing her eyes and shaking her head.

'I'm sorry,' he said.

'I'm sorry, too,' she said. 'Terry, I really don't think you understand the risks of what you are doing.'

'I think I do, Doctor. I don't think I have a choice, anyway.'

'I don't think I have one, either.'

'What do you mean?'

'I mean I don't think I can continue to be your doctor if this is what you are going to do. You obviously don't value my advice or feel you should follow my instructions. You are choosing this pursuit of yours over your health. I can't be around while you do this.'

'Are you firing me, Doc?'

He laughed uneasily.

'It's not a joke. Maybe that's your problem. You think it's some sort of joke, that you're invincible.'

'No, I don't feel invincible.'

'Well, your words and actions don't match up. On Monday I'll have one of my assistants gather your files and put together two or three cardiologists I can refer you to.'

McCaleb closed his eyes.

'Look, Doc, I ... I don't know what to say. We've been together a long time. Don't you feel an obligation to see it through?'

'It goes two ways. If I don't hear from you by Monday, I'll have to assume you are going on with this. I'll have your records here at the office ready for you.'

She hung up. McCaleb sat still, the phone still to his ear until it started blaring its hang-up tone.

McCaleb got up and took a walk outside. From the cockpit he surveyed the marina and the parking lot. He saw no sign of Buddy Lockridge or anyone else. The air was still. He leaned over the stern and looked down into the water. It was too dark to see the bottom. He spat into the water and with it went the misgivings he felt over Fox's edict. He decided he would not be swayed.

The photo was there on the table waiting for him when he got back. He picked it up again and studied it once more, this time his eyes traveling up the body to the face. There was some kind of dark salve on the eyes and then he remembered that the eyes had probably been taken along with the internal organs.

He noticed the three small perforations running along

the ridge of the left ear and down to the lobe. On the right lobe there was only one.

He was about to put the photo aside when he realized that earlier he had read through a property report listing the items removed from the victim at the hospital and then turned over to the police.

Curious to make sure all details checked out, he went back to the stack of paperwork and dug out the property report. His finger ran down the list of clothing until he got to the subheading of jewelry.

JEWELRY

1. Timex watch
2. Three earrings (2 crescent moon, one silver hoop)
3. Two rings (birthstone, silver)

He thought about this for a long moment, remembering that on the video of the shooting it was clear that Gloria Torres was wearing a total of four earrings. The hoop, the crescent moon and the dangling cross on her left ear. On her right ear there had been only a crescent moon. This accounting did not fit with the property report, which listed only three earrings. Nor did it jibe with the perforation marks clearly visible on Gloria's ears in the evidence photo.

He turned to the television, thinking that he would look at the tape again, but then stopped. He was sure. He did not imagine something like a cross. Somehow it was not accounted for.

A loose end. He tapped his fingers on the property report, trying to think about whether this was a notable detail or not. What had happened to the cross earring? Why wasn't it on the list?

He checked his watch and saw it was ten minutes after twelve. Graciela would be at lunch. He called the hospital and asked to be transferred to the main cafeteria. When a woman answered, he asked if it would be possible for her to go to the nurse seated at the table next to one of the windows and give her a message. When the woman hesitated, McCaleb described Graciela and gave her name. The woman on the phone reluctantly asked what the message was.

'Just tell her to call Dr McCaleb as soon as she can.'

About five minutes later he got the callback.

'Dr McCaleb?'

'Sorry, I had to do that so she would be sure to give you the message.'

'What's up?'

'Well, I'm going through the case files again and I've got a loose end here. The property report says that they took two crescent moon earrings and a hoop earring off your sister's ears at the hospital after she was brought in.'

'Right, they would have needed to remove those for the CAT scan. They wanted to look at the wound track.'

'Okay, what about the cross earring she wore in her left ear? There's nothing on the property report about –'

'She wasn't wearing it that night. I always thought that was weird. Like it was bad luck, because that was her favorite earring. She usually wore it every day.'

'Like a personal signature,' McCaleb said. 'What do you mean, she wasn't wearing it that night?'

'Because when the police gave me her things – you know, her watch and rings and earrings – it wasn't there. She wasn't wearing it.'

'Are you sure? In the video she's wearing it.'

'What video?'

'From the store.'

She was silent a moment.

'No, that can't be. I found it in her jewelry box. I gave it to them at the funeral home so they could, you know, put it on for when she was buried.'

Now McCaleb was silent and then he put it together.

'But wouldn't she have had two of them? I don't know anything about crosses, but don't you buy earrings in pairs?'

'Oh, you're right. I didn't think about that.'

'So the one you found was the extra one?'

He felt a stirring inside that he immediately recognized but hadn't felt in a long time.

'I guess ...' Graciela said. 'So if she did have one on in the store, what happened to it?'

'That's what I want to find out.'

'But what does it matter anyway?'

He was silent for a few moments thinking about how he should answer. He decided that what he was thinking was too speculative at the moment to share with her.

'It's just a loose end that should be tied up. Let me ask you something, was it the kind of earring that just hooked on or was there a hasp to make sure it didn't fall off easily? You know what I mean? I couldn't tell that from the video.'

'Yes. Um, I think there was like a hook that you sort of clipped after it was on your ear. I don't think it would have fallen off.'

While she was speaking, McCaleb was looking through the stack for the paramedics' report. He ran his finger down the lines of the information box until he found the squad number and names of the two paramedics who had treated and transported Gloria.

'Okay, I'm gonna go,' he said. 'Are we still on for tomorrow?'

'Sure. Um, Terry?'

'What?'

'You saw the video from the store? I mean, all of it? You saw Glory ...'

'Yes,' he said quietly. 'I had to.'

'Was she ... was she scared?'

'No, Graciela. It was very quick. She never saw it coming.'

'I guess that's good.'

'I think so ... Listen, are you going to be all right?'

'I'm fine.'

'Okay then. We'll see you tomorrow.'

The paramedics who had transported Gloria worked out of Fire Station 76. McCaleb called but the crew that had worked the night of January 22nd was off until Sunday. However, the station captain told him that under department policy governing what are called 'crime transports', any property left behind on a stretcher or found anywhere in an ambulance would have been turned over to police custody. This meant that if this had occurred following the transport of Gloria Torres, there would be a property-received report in the murder book. There wasn't. The cross earring remained unaccounted for.

The irony that McCaleb carried inside of him alongside a stranger's heart was the secret belief that he had been the wrong one saved. It should have been someone else. In the days and weeks before he received Glory's heart, he had been prepared for the end. He had accepted it as the way it was to be. He was long past believing in a God – the horrors he had seen and documented had little by little sapped his stores of faith until the only absolute he believed in was that there were no bounds to the evil acts of men. And in those seemingly final days, as his own heart withered and tapped out its final cadences, he did not grasp desperately for his lost faith as a shield or a means of easing the fear of the unknown. Instead, he was accepting of the end, of his own nothingness. He was ready.

It was easy to do. When he had been with the bureau,

he was driven and consumed by a mission, a calling. And when he carried it out and was successful, he knew he was making a difference. Better than any heart surgeon, he was saving lives from horrible ends. He was facing off against the worst kinds of evil, the most malignant cancers, and the battle, though always wearing and painful, gave his life its meaning.

That was gone the moment his heart deserted him and he fell to the floor of the field office thinking he had surely been stabbed in the chest. It was still gone two years later when the pager sounded and he was told they had a heart for him.

He had a new heart but it didn't feel like a new life. He was a man on a boat that never left port. It didn't matter what stock quotes about second chances he had used with a newspaper reporter. That existence was not enough for McCaleb. That was the struggle he was facing when Graciela Rivers had stepped down off the dock and into his life.

The quest she had given him had been a way of avoiding his own inner struggle. But now things were suddenly different. The missing cross earring stirred something deep and dormant in him. His long experience had given him true knowledge and instincts about evil. He knew its signs.

This was one of them.

# 19

McCaleb had been to the sheriff's homicide bureau so often during the week that the receptionist just waved him back without a phone call or escort. Jaye Winston was at her desk, using a three-hole punch on a thin stack of documents which she then slipped over the prongs of an open binder. She snapped it closed and looked up at her visitor.

'You moving in?'

'Feels like it. You get caught up on the paper?'

'Instead of four months behind I'm only two. What's going on? I didn't think I was going to see you today.'

'You still upset about me holding that thing back?'

'Water under the bridge.'

She leaned back in her chair, looked him over and waited for an explanation of why he was there.

'I've sort of come up with something I think bears looking into,' he said.

'Is this about Bolotov again?'

'No, it's something new.'

'Don't become the boy who cried wolf on me, McCaleb.'

She smiled.

'I won't.'

'Then tell me.'

He put his palms down on the desk and leaned over it, so he could speak to her in a confidential tone. There were still plenty of Winston's colleagues around the bureau, working at their desks and trying to get things done before the weekend.

'Arrango and Walters missed something,' McCaleb said. 'So did I on my first go-through. But I picked up on it this morning when I took a second look at the videos and the paperwork. It's something that has to be considered pretty seriously. I think it changes things.'

Winston furrowed her eyebrows and looked at him seriously.

'Quit talking in circles. What did they miss?'

'I'd rather show you than tell you.' He reached down to the floor and opened his leather satchel. He pulled out the copy of the surveillance tape and held it up to her. 'Can we go look at this?'

'I guess so.'

Winston got up and led the way to the video room. She turned the machines on and popped in the tape after looking at it and noting it was not one of the tapes she had given McCaleb on Wednesday.

'What is this?'

'It's the surveillance from the market.'

'Not the one I gave you.'

'It's a copy. I'm having somebody look at the other one.'

'What do you mean? Who?'

'A tech I knew when I was with the bureau. I'm just trying to get some of the images enhanced. Not a big deal.'

'So what are you showing me?'

She had the surveillance tape playing.

'Where's the freeze?'

Winston pointed to a button on the console and McCaleb held his finger over it, waiting for the right moment. On the tape Gloria Torres approached the counter and smiled at Kang. Then came the gunman and the shot that threw her body forward over the counter. McCaleb froze the image and used a pen from his pocket to point at Gloria's left ear.

'It's pretty murky but on a blowup you can see she has three earrings on this ear,' he said. Then tapping the pen at each point on the ear, he added, 'A crescent moon on a stud, a hoop and then dangling from the lobe, a cross.'

'Okay. I can't really see it too well but I'll take your word for it.'

McCaleb hit the freeze button again and the video started playing. He stopped it at the moment Gloria's body rebounded backward, her head turning to the left.

'Right ear,' he said, using the pen again to point. 'Just the matching crescent moon.'

'Okay, what's it mean?'

He ignored the question and hit the replay button. The gun was fired. Gloria was hurled into the counter and then rebounded backward into the shooter. Holding her in front of him, he fired at Mr Kang while stepping backward out of the camera's field of vision and lowering Gloria to the ground.

'The victim is then lowered down out of view of the camera.'

'What, you're saying that was intentional?'

'Exactly.'

'Why?'

He opened the satchel again and drew out the property report and handed it to Winston.

'That's the police property report on the victim's possessions. It was filled out at the hospital. Remember, she was still alive. They took her things there, gave them to a patrol officer. That is his report. What don't you see?'

Winston scanned the page.

'I don't know. It's just a list of – the cross earring?'

'Right. It's not there. He took it.'

'The patrolman?'

'No. The shooter. The shooter took her earring.'

A puzzled look came across Winston's face. She wasn't following the logic. She hadn't had the same experiences or seen the same things that McCaleb had. She didn't see it for what it was.

'Wait a minute,' she said. 'How do you know he took it? It could have just fallen off and gotten lost.'

'No. I've talked to the victim's sister and I've talked to the hospital and the paramedics.'

He knew this was exaggerating his investigation into this aspect but he needed to pin Winston down. He couldn't give her a way out or a way to any other conclusion than his own conclusion.

'The sister says the earring had a safety hasp. It is unlikely that it fell off. Even if it did, the paramedics didn't find it on the stretcher or in the ambulance, and they didn't find it at the hospital. He took it, Jaye. The shooter. Besides, if it was going to fall off, despite the safety hasp, it probably would have been when he fired the round. You saw the impact on the head. If the earring was going to come loose, it would have been then. Only it didn't. It was taken off.'

'Okay, okay, what if he did take it? I'm not saying I believe it yet, but what are you saying it means?'

'It means everything changes. It means this wasn't about a robbery. She wasn't just an innocent nobody who walked into the wrong place at the wrong time. It means she was a target. She was prey.'

'Oh, come on. She ... What are you trying to do, turn this into a serial killer or something?'

'I'm not trying to turn it into anything. It is what it is. And it's been that way all along. Only you people – we, I mean – didn't see it for what it was.'

Winston turned away from him and walked toward the corner of the room shaking her head. She then turned back to him.

'Okay, you tell me what you're seeing here. Because I'm just not seeing it. I'd love to go to the LAPD and tell those two jerks that they fucked up but I'm just not seeing what you're seeing.'

'Okay, let's start with the earring itself. Like I said, I talked to the sister. She said Glory Torres wore this particular earring every day. She played around with the others, switched them, used different combinations, but never the cross. It was always there. Every day. It had the obvious religious implications but for lack of a better description, it was also her good luck charm. Okay? You with me so far?'

'So far.'

'Okay, now let's just assume that the shooter took it. Like I said, I talked to the hospital and the fire department, and it hasn't showed up anywhere. So let's assume he took it.'

He opened his hands and held them up, waiting. Winston reluctantly nodded her agreement.

'So then let's look at that from two angles. How? And why? The first one is easy. Remember the video. He shot her and let her rebound off the counter and then fall back into him and then down to the floor, outside the view of the camera. He could take the earring then without being seen.'

'You're forgetting one thing.'

'What's that?'

'The Good Samaritan. He wrapped her head up. Maybe he took it.'

'I thought about that. It's not beyond possibility. But it's less likely than it being the shooter. The Good Samaritan is the random player in this. Why would he take it?'

'I don't know. Why would the shooter?'

'Well, like I said, that's a question. But look at the item that was taken. A religious icon, good luck charm. She wore it every day. It was a personality signature, its personal significance more important than its monetary value.'

He waited a beat. He had just given her the setup. Now came the closing pitch. Winston was fighting on this but McCaleb hadn't lost sight of her skills as an investigator. She would see what he was saying. He was confident he would convince her.

'Someone who knew Gloria would know the significance of the earring. Similarly, someone who was close to her, who had studied her over a period of days or longer could pick up on it as well.'

'You're talking about a stalker.'

McCaleb nodded.

'In the acquisition period. He watches her. Learns her habits, sets his plan. He'd also be looking for something. A token. Something to take and to remember her by.'

'The earring.'

He nodded again. Winston started pacing around the small room, not looking at McCaleb.

'I've got to think about this. I've got ... let's go someplace where we can sit down.'

She didn't wait for a reply. She opened the door and left the room. McCaleb quickly ejected the tape, grabbed his bag and followed. Winston led him to the meeting room in which they had talked the first day McCaleb had come to see her about the case. The room was empty but smelled like a McDonald's restaurant. Winston hunted around, found the offending trash can under the table and escorted it out into the hallway.

'People aren't supposed to eat in this room,' she said as she closed the door and sat down.

McCaleb took the seat across from her.

'All right, what about my guy? How does James Cordell fit in? First of all, he's a guy. The other's a girl. Plus, there was no sex. This woman wasn't touched.'

'None of that matters,' McCaleb said quickly. He had been anticipating the question. He had done nothing but think about the questions and their possible answers during the drive out with Buddy Lockridge from the marina. 'If I'm right, this would fall into what we called the power kill model. Basically, it's a guy who is doing it because he can get away with it. He gets off on that. It's his way of thumbing his nose at authority and shocking society. He transfers his problems with a particular situation – whether it's a job, self-worth, women in general or his mother in particular or whatever – onto the police. The investigators. From tweaking them, he gets the jolt in self-worth that he needs. He derives a form of power from it. And it can be sexual power, even if there are no obvious or physical sexual manifestations in the actual crime. You remember the Code Killer out here a while back? Or Berkowitz, the Son of Sam killer in New York?'

'Of course.'

'Same thing with both of them. There was no sex in each crime itself but it was all about sex. Look at Berkowitz. He shot people up – men and women – and ran away. But he came back days later and masturbated at the scene. We assumed the Code Killer did the same thing but if he did, our surveillances missed him. What I'm saying is that it doesn't have to be obvious, Jaye, that's all. It's not always the obvious wackos who carve their names in people's skin.'

McCaleb watched Winston closely, leery of talking above her. But she seemed to understand his theory.

'But it's not only that,' McCaleb went on. 'There's another part to this. He gets off on the camera, too.'

'He likes us seeing him do it?'

McCaleb nodded.

'That's the new twist. I think he wants the camera. He wants his work and his accomplishments documented, seen and admired. It increases the danger to him and therefore increases the power reflection on him. The payoff. So to get that situation, what does he do? I think he picks up on a target – he chooses his prey – and then watches them until he has their routine and he knows when it takes them into places of business where the cameras are. The ATM, the market. He wants the camera. He talks to it. He winks at it. The camera is you – the investigator. He's talking to you and getting off on it.'

'Then maybe he doesn't choose the victim,' Winston said. 'Maybe he doesn't care about that. Just the camera. Like Berkowitz. He didn't care who he shot. He just went out shooting.'

'But Berkowitz didn't take souvenirs.'

'The earring?'

McCaleb nodded.

'You see that makes it personal. I think these victims were chosen. Not the other way around.'

'You've thought this all out, haven't you?'

'Not everything. I don't know how he chose them or why. But I've been thinking about it, yeah. The whole hour and a half it took us to get out here. Traffic was bad.'

'Us?'

'I have a driver. I can't drive yet.'

She didn't say anything. McCaleb wished he hadn't mentioned the driver. It was revealing a weakness.

'We have to start over,' McCaleb said. 'Because we thought these people were chosen at random. We thought the locations were chosen, not the victims. But I think it's the other way around. The victims were chosen. They were prey. Specific targets that were acquired, followed, stalked. We've got to background them. There's got to be an intersection. Some commonality. A person, a place ... a moment in time – something that hooks them either to each other or our unknown subject. We find –'

'Wait a minute, wait a minute.'

McCaleb stopped, realizing his voice had been rising in fervor.

'What souvenir was taken from James Cordell? Are you saying the money he took from the ATM is a token?'

'I don't know what was taken but it wasn't the money. That was just part of the robbery show. The money wasn't a symbolic possession. Besides, he took it from the machine, not Cordell.'

'So then, aren't you jumping the gun?'

'No. I'm sure something was taken.'

'We would have seen it. We have the whole thing on video.'

'Nobody picked up on it with Gloria Torres and that was on video, too.'

Winston turned in her chair.

'I don't know. This still seems like a – let me ask you something. And try not to take it too personal. But isn't it possible that you're just looking for what you always looked for before, when you were with the bureau?'

'You mean, like am I exaggerating? Like I want to get back to what I was doing before and this is my way of doing it?'

Winston hiked her shoulders. She didn't want to say it.

'I didn't go looking for this, Jaye. It's just there. It is what it is. Sure, the earring might mean something else. And it might not mean anything at all. But if there is anything I know about in this world, it is this kind of thing. These people. I know them. I know how they think and I know how they act. I feel it here, Jaye. The evil. It's here.'

Winston looked at him strangely and McCaleb guessed that maybe he shouldn't have been so fervent in his response to her doubts.

'Cordell's truck, the Chevy Suburban, wasn't in the video. Did you process his truck? I didn't see anything in the stack you gave me about –'

'No, it wasn't touched. He left his wallet open on the seat and just took his ATM card to the machine. If the shooter had gone into his truck, he would have taken his wallet. When we saw it still there, we didn't bother.'

McCaleb shook his head and said, 'You are still looking at it from the point of view of a robbery. The decision not to process the truck would have been okay – if it had been a real robbery. But what if it wasn't? He wouldn't have gone into the truck and taken something as obvious as the wallet.'

'Then what?'

'I don't know. Something else. Cordell used his truck a lot. Driving all day along the aqueduct. It would be like a second home to him. There could have been lots of things of a personal nature in there that the shooter could've taken. Photos, things hanging from the rear-view, maybe a travel diary, you name it. Where is the truck? Make my day and tell me it's still impounded.'

'No chance. We released it to his wife a couple days after the shooting.'

'It's probably been cleaned out and sold by now.'

'Actually, no. The last time I talked to Cordell's wife – which was only a couple weeks ago – she said something about not knowing what to do with the Suburban. It was too big for her and she said it gave her bad vibes now anyway. She didn't use those words but you know what I mean.'

A charge of excitement went through McCaleb.

'Then we go up there and look at the Suburban and we talk to her and we figure out what was taken.'

'*If* something was taken ...'

Winston frowned. McCaleb knew what she was facing. She already was dealing with a captain who, after the hypnosis and Bolotov fiascos, probably thought she was being controlled too easily by an outsider. She didn't want to have to go back to the man with McCaleb's new theory unless she was sure it was dead-solid perfect. And McCaleb knew it could never be that. It never was.

'What are you going to do?' he asked. 'It's like I'm in the car and ready to go. Are you getting in with me or staying on the sidewalk?'

It had occurred to him that he was not constrained by such worries or by a job, a role, inertia or anything else. Either Winston could get in the car or McCaleb could drive on without her. She apparently realized the same thing.

'No,' she said. 'The question is what are *you* going to do. You're the one who doesn't have to deal with the bullshit around here like I do. After the hypnosis thing, Hitchens has been –'

'Tell you what, Jaye. I don't care about all of that. I only care about one thing – finding this guy. So look. You sit tight and give me a few days. I'll come in with something. I'll go up to the desert and talk to Cordell's wife and take a look at the truck. I'll find something you can go to the captain with. If I don't, then I'll eat my theory. You can cut me loose and I won't bother you again.'

'Look, it's not that you're both –'

'You know what I mean. You've got court, other cases. The last thing you need is to have to overhaul on an old one. I know how it is. Maybe coming in here today was premature. I should've just gone up there and seen the widow. But since it's your case and you've treated me like a human, I wanted to check with you first. Now, you give me your blessing and a little time and I'll go up on my own. I'll let you know what I get.'

Winston was silent for a long moment, then finally she nodded.

'Okay, you got it.'

# 20

Lockridge and McCaleb took a succession of freeways from Whittier until they reached the Antelope Valley Freeway, which would finally take them to the northeast corner of the country. Lockridge drove one-handed most of the way, holding a harmonica to his mouth with the other hand. It didn't give McCaleb much of a feeling of safety, but it cut out the meaningless banter.

As they passed Vasquez Rocks, McCaleb studied the formation and pinpointed the spot where the body had been found that eventually led to his knowing Jaye Winston. The slanted and jagged formation caused by tectonic upheaval was beautiful in the afternoon light. The sun was hitting the front rock faces at a low angle and throwing the crevices into deep darkness. It looked beautiful and dangerous at the same time. He wondered if that was what had drawn Luther Hatch to it.

'Ever been there, Vasquez Rocks?' Buddy asked after tucking the harmonica between his legs.

'Yeah.'

'Neat place. It's named after a Mexican desperado who holed up in the crevices about a hundred years ago after robbing a bank or something. So many places to hide in there, they could never find him and he became a legend.'

McCaleb nodded. He liked the story. He thought about how his histories of places were so different. They always involved bodies and blood work. No legends. No heroes.

They made good time on the front of the wave of rush hour and weekend traffic out of the city and it was just past five when they got to Lancaster. They cruised through a subdivision called Desert Flower Estates, looking for the home where James Cordell had lived. McCaleb saw a lot of desert but not many flowers or homes that met his definition of estate. The subdivision was built on land as flat and most days as hot as a frying pan. The homes were Spanish style with red-barrel roofs and arched windows and doors in the front. There were dozens of matching developments scattered through the Antelope Valley. The homes were large and reasonably attractive. They were bought mostly by families escaping the expense and crime and crowding of Los Angeles.

Desert Flower Estates had apparently offered three different design plans to its buyers. Consequently, McCaleb noticed as they drove through, about every third house was the same and sometimes there were even side-by-side duplicates. It reminded him of some of the post-World War II neighborhoods in the San Fernando Valley.

The thought of living in one of the homes he was passing depressed him. And it wasn't because of anything he saw. It was the distance this place was from the ocean and the feeling of renewal the sea gave him. He knew he'd never last in a neighborhood like this. He would dry up and blow away like one of the tumbleweeds they periodically passed on the street.

'This is it,' Buddy said.

He pointed to a number on a mailbox and McCaleb nodded. They pulled in. McCaleb noticed that the white Chevy Suburban he had seen in the crime scene video was parked in the driveway below a basketball rim. There was an open garage with a mini-van parked on one side and the other side cluttered with bikes and boxes, a tool bench and other clutter. Standing up in the back of the garage was a surfboard. It was an old long board and it made McCaleb think that maybe at one time James Cordell had known something about the ocean.

'I don't know how long I'll be,' he said.

'It's going to get hot out here. Maybe I could just go in with you. I won't say anything.'

'It's cooling down, Buddy. But if you get hot, run the air. Drive around a little bit. There's probably kids selling lemonade around here someplace.'

He got out before any debate could begin. He wasn't going to bring Lockridge into the investigation and turn it into amateur hour. On the way up the driveway he stopped and looked into the Suburban. The back was full of tools and there was clutter in the front seats. He felt a charge. He might be in luck. It looked as though the truck had been sitting untouched.

James Cordell's widow was named Amelia. McCaleb knew that from the reports. A woman he assumed to be her opened the arched front door before he reached it. Jaye Winston had said she would call ahead to smooth his way in.

'Mrs Cordell?'

'Yes?'

'My name's Terry McCaleb. Did Detective Winston call about me?'

'Yes, she did.'

'Is this a bad time?'

'As opposed to a good time?'

'Poor choice of words. I'm sorry. Do you have some time that we can talk?'

She was a short woman with brown hair and small features. Her nose was red and McCaleb guessed she either had a cold or had been crying. McCaleb wondered if the call from Jaye Winston had set her off.

She nodded and invited him in, leading the way to a neatly kept living room where she sat on the sofa and he took the chair opposite her. There was a box of tissues on the coffee table between them. The sound of television was coming from another room. It sounded like cartoons were on.

'Is that your partner waiting in the car?' she asked.

'Uh, my driver.'

'Does he want to come in? It might get hot out there.'

'No, he's fine.'

'You're a private investigator?'

'Technically, no. I'm a friend of the family of the woman who was killed in Canoga Park. I don't know what Detective Winston told you, but I used to work for the FBI and so I have some experience in these kinds of things. The Sheriff's Department, as you probably know, and the LAPD have not been able to, uh, advance the investigation very far in recent weeks. I'm trying to do what I can to help.'

She nodded.

'First off, I'm sorry about what happened to your husband and your family.'

She frowned and nodded.

'I know it doesn't matter what a stranger thinks but you do have my sympathy. From what I've read in the sheriff's files, James was a good man.'

She smiled and said, 'Thank you. It's just so funny to hear him called James. Everyone called him Jim or Jimmy. And you are right, he was a good man.'

McCaleb nodded.

'What questions can I answer, Mr McCaleb? I really don't know anything about what happened. That's what was confusing about Jaye's call.'

'Well, first ...' He reached down to his satchel, opened it and took out the Polaroid that Graciela had given him the day she came to his boat. He handed it across the table to Amelia Cordell. 'Could you look at that and tell me if you recognize the woman or if you think she might be someone your husband could have known.'

She took the photo and stared at it, her face serious and her eyes making small movements as she seemed to study everything about the photo. She shook her head finally.

'No, I don't think so. Is she the one who ...'

'Yes, she was the victim in the second robbery.'

'Is that her son?'

'Yes.'

'I don't understand. How could my husband have known this woman – are you suggesting that they might have –'

'No. No, I'm not suggesting anything, Mrs Cordell. I'm just trying to cover ... Look, to be very honest, Mrs Cordell, some things have come up in the investigation to possibly indicate – and I have to stress *possibly* – that there was more here than meets the eye.'

'Meaning what?'

'Meaning that *possibly* robbery was not a motive here. Or not the only motive.'

She stared blankly at him for a moment and McCaleb knew she was still taking things the wrong way.

'Mrs Cordell, I am not in any way trying to suggest that your husband and that woman had any kind of a relationship. What I'm saying is that somewhere, sometime, your husband and that woman crossed the shooter's path. So you see there *is* a relationship. But it is a relationship between the victims and the shooter. It is likely that your husband and the other victims crossed the shooter's line at separate points but I need to cover everything and that is why I show you the photograph. You are sure you don't recognize her?'

'I'm sure.'

'Would your husband have any reason in the weeks

before the shooting to have spent any time in Canoga Park?'

'Not that I know of.'

'Would he have had any dealings with the *Los Angeles Times*? More specifically, any reason he would have gone to the newspaper's plant in Chatsworth?'

Again her answer was no.

'Was there any problem at work? Anything that he might have wanted to talk to a reporter about?'

'Like what?'

'I don't know.'

'Was she a reporter?'

'No, but she worked where there were reporters. Maybe their paths crossed with the shooter there.'

'Well, I don't think so. If something was bothering Jimmy, he would have told me. He always did.'

'Okay. I understand.'

McCaleb spent the next fifteen minutes asking Mrs Cordell questions about her husband's daily routine and his activities in the weeks before the shooting. He took three pages of notes but even as he wrote them, they didn't seem helpful. Jimmy Cordell seemed like a man who worked hard and spent most of his off time with his family. In the weeks before his death he had been working exclusively on sections of the aqueduct in the central part of the state and his wife did not believe he had spent any time at all to the south. She did not think he had been down into the Valley or other parts of the city since before Christmas.

McCaleb folded his notebook closed.

'I appreciate your time, Mrs Cordell. The last thing I wanted to ask about is whether or not any of your husband's possessions were missing.'

'His possessions? What do you mean?'

Amelia Cordell led McCaleb out to the Chevy Suburban.

They had already discussed her husband's clothing and jewelry. Nothing had been taken, she assured him, just as the ATM video had seemed to attest. That left the Suburban.

'No one's been in it?' he asked as she was unlocking it.

'I drove it home from the sheriff's office. That was actually the only time I ever drove it. Jimmy bought it for work only. He said if we started using it for nonwork driving, he couldn't write everything off. I don't drive it because it's too high up for me to be climbing in and out of all the time.'

McCaleb nodded and leaned into the truck through the open driver's door. The rear seat was folded down and the cargo area was full of surveying equipment, a folding drafting table and other tools. McCaleb quickly dismissed it all. It was equipment, not something of a personal nature.

He concentrated on the front section of the vehicle. A patina of road dust covered everything. Cordell must have been driving in the desert with the windows down. Using one finger, he opened a pocket on the door and saw it was crammed with service station receipts and a small spiral notebook on which Cordell had noted mileage, dates and destinations. McCaleb took the notebook out and flipped through the pages to see if there had been any trips to the west Valley, particularly Chatsworth or Canoga Park. There were none recorded. It appeared Amelia Cordell had been correct about her husband.

He flipped down the driver-side visor and found two folded maps. McCaleb walked them around to the front and opened them on the hood. One was a gas station map of central California and another was a survey map that showed the aqueduct and its many access roads. McCaleb was looking for any unusual notations Cordell might have made on the maps but there were none. He refolded them and put them back.

He now sat in the driver's seat and looked around. He noticed the rearview mirror and asked Amelia Cordell if her husband had ever hung anything off it, knickknacks or otherwise. She said she didn't remember anything.

He checked the glove compartment and the center console. There was more paperwork and several tapes for use in the stereo, an assortment of pens and mechanical pencils, and a pack of opened mail. Cordell liked country music. Nothing seemed amiss. Nothing came to mind.

'Do you know if he had any particular kind of pen or pencil he liked? Like a special pen he might have gotten as a gift or something?'

'I don't think so. Nothing I remember.'

McCaleb took the rubber band off the mail and looked through the envelopes. It appeared to be departmental mail, notices of meetings, reports on problems on the aqueduct that Cordell was to check out. McCaleb put the band back around the stack and placed it back in the glove box. Amelia Cordell watched him silently.

In an open bin between the seats there was a pager and a pair of sunglasses. Cordell had been coming home at night when he stopped at the ATM. That explained why the glasses were not on, but not the beeper.

'Mrs Cordell, do you know why his pager is here? How come he wasn't wearing it?'

She thought a moment and then said, 'He usually didn't keep it on his belt for long rides because he said it was uncomfortable. He said it dug into his kidneys. He forgot it a few times. You know, left it in the car and missed his pages. That's how I know why.'

McCaleb nodded. As he sat there thinking about what to check next, the passenger door was suddenly opened and Buddy Lockridge looked in.

'What's up?'

McCaleb had to squint to look at him because of the sun coming into the car over Buddy's shoulder.

'I'm almost done, Buddy. Why don't you wait in the car?'

'My ass was getting sore.' He looked past McCaleb and nodded at Amelia Cordell. 'Sorry, ma'am.'

McCaleb was annoyed by the intrusion but introduced Lockridge as his associate to Amelia Cordell.

'So what are we looking for?' Buddy asked.

'We? I'm just looking for something that's not here. Why don't you wait in the car?'

'Like something that might've been taken. I see.'

He flipped down the passenger-side visor. McCaleb had already checked it and there was nothing there.

'I got it, Buddy. Why don't you –'

'What went there, a picture?'

He pointed toward the dashboard. McCaleb followed the line of his finger but didn't see anything.

'What are you talking about?'

'There. See the dust? Looks like a picture or something. Maybe he kept a parking pass there until he needed it.'

McCaleb looked again but still didn't see what Lockridge was pointing at and talking about. He shifted to his right and leaned toward Buddy and then turned his head back to look at the dashboard.

Now he saw it.

A coat of driving dust had settled on the clear plastic guard over the display of speedometer and other gauges. On one side of the plastic there was a clearly defined square where there was no dust. Something had been propped on the plastic guard until recently. McCaleb realized how lucky he was. He probably would never have noticed it. It only became apparent when viewed from the passenger side and with the sun coming in at a low angle.

'Mrs Cordell?' McCaleb said. 'Can you walk around and look at this through the other door?'

He waited. Lockridge stepped out of the way so she could look in. McCaleb pointed to the outline on the plastic guard. It was about five inches wide by three inches deep.

'Did your husband keep a picture of you or the kids here?'

She shook her head slowly.

'Boy, I don't really know. He had pictures but I just don't know where he put them. He could have but I don't know. I never drive this. We always take the Caravan – even when just Jim and I would go out. Like I said, I didn't like climbing up there.'

McCaleb nodded.

'Is there anyone he worked with who might know, who might have ridden with him to jobs or to lunch, that sort of thing?'

Driving on the Antelope Valley Freeway back toward the city, they passed a seemingly never-ending line of cars stacked in the lanes going the other way. Commuters heading home or travelers getting out of the city for the weekend. McCaleb barely noticed. He was deep in his own thoughts. He barely even heard Lockridge until he repeated himself twice.

'I'm sorry, what?'

'I said I guess I helped you back there, noticing that.'

'You did, Buddy. I might not have noticed it. But I still wish you had stayed in the car. This is all I'm paying you for, to drive.'

With a double hand gesture McCaleb indicated the car.

'Yeah, well, you might still be back there looking if I had stayed in the car.'

'We'll never know now.'

'So aren't you going to tell me what you found out?'

'Nothing, Buddy. I didn't find out anything.'

He had lied. Amelia Cordell had taken him back inside and allowed him to use her phone to call her husband's office. Buddy had been sent back to the car to wait. Inside, McCaleb talked to James Cordell's supervisor, who gave him the names and numbers of some of the aqueduct maintenance supervisors Cordell would have been working with in early January. McCaleb then called the Lone Pine aqueduct station and talked to Maggie Mason, who was one of those supervisors. She reported that she had joined Cordell for lunch twice in the week before the shooting. Both times Cordell had driven.

Avoiding the leading question, McCaleb had asked her if she had noticed anything of a personal nature on the dashboard of the Suburban. Without hesitation Mason said there had been a photograph of Cordell's family on the dashboard. She said she had even leaned over to get a look at it. She remembered that it was Cordell's wife holding their two little daughters on her lap.

As they were heading home, McCaleb felt a mix of dread and excitement growing inside. Someone, somewhere, had Gloria Torres's earring and James Cordell's family photo. He now knew that the evil of these two killings came together in the form of a person who killed not for money, not out of fear and not for revenge against his victims. This evil went far beyond that. This person killed for pleasure and to fulfill a fantasy that burned like a virus inside his brain.

Evil was everywhere. McCaleb knew that better than most. But he also knew that it could not be confronted in the abstract. It needed to be embodied in flesh and blood and breath, to be a person who could be hunted down and destroyed. McCaleb had that now. He felt his heart rise up in rage, and a horrible joy.

# 21

The Saturday morning mist came in thick and felt like a gentle hand on the back of his neck. McCaleb had gotten up by seven so that he could get into the laundry in the marina's commons building and use several of the machines at once to get all of the bed clothes cleaned. Then he set about getting the boat cleaned up and ready for overnight guests. But as he worked, he found it hard to concentrate on the chores in front of him.

He had talked to Jaye Winston when he got in from the desert the evening before. When he told her about the photo that was missing from Cordell's Suburban, she grudgingly agreed that McCaleb might be onto a viable new lead. An hour later she called back and said a meeting was set for 8 A.M. Monday at the Star Center. She and her captain and a few other sheriff's detectives would be there. So would Arrango and Walters. So would Maggie Griffin from the FBI. Griffin was the agent who had taken McCaleb's place in the VICAP slot in the LA field office. McCaleb only knew her by her reputation which was good.

And that was the problem. First thing Monday morning McCaleb would be on the hot seat, the focus of intense scrutiny. Most, if not all, of those in the meeting at the Star Center would be non-believers. But rather than prepare for the meeting or do what additional investigation he could, McCaleb was going fishing on the jetty with a woman and a little boy. It didn't sit right with him and he kept thinking he should cancel the visit from Graciela and Raymond. In the end, he didn't. It was true that he needed to talk with Graciela, but more than that, he found that he just wanted to be with her. And that was what brought the twin paths of his uneasy thoughts to an intersection: guilt over putting the investigation aside and guilt over his desire for a woman who had come to him for his help.

When he was done with the laundry and the general cleanup, he walked over to the marina center. At the store he bought the makings of the evening's dinner. At the bait shop he bought a bucket of live bait, choosing shrimp and squid, and a small rod-and-reel outfit that he planned to present to Raymond as his own. Back at the boat, he put the rod in one of the gunwale holders and dumped the bait bucket into the live well. He then put away the store items in the galley.

He was finished and the boat was ready by ten. Seeing no sign of Graciela's convertible in the parking lot, he decided to walk over and check with Buddy Lockridge about his availability on Monday morning. He first went up to the gate and made sure it was propped open so Graciela and the boy could enter the marina, then he went to Lockridge's boat.

Adhering to marina custom, McCaleb did not step onto the *Double-Down*. Instead, he called Lockridge's name and waited on the dock. The boat's main hatch was open so he knew Lockridge was awake and around somewhere. After half a minute, Buddy's disheveled hair, followed by his crumpled face, poked up through the hatch. McCaleb guessed he had spent a good part of the night drinking.

'Yo, Terry.'

'Yo. You okay?'

'Fine as always. What's up, we going somewhere?'

'No, not today. But I need you Monday morning early.

Can you drive me out to the Star Center? I mean like we've got to leave by seven.'

Buddy thought a moment to see if it fit with his busy schedule and nodded.

'It's a go.'

'You're going to be all right to drive?'

'You bet. What's going on at the Star Center?'

'Just a meeting. But I've got to be there on time.'

'Don't worry about a thing. We leave at seven. I'll set the alarm.'

'Okay, and one other thing. Keep an eye out around here.'

'You mean the guy from the clock plant?'

'Yeah. I doubt he'll show but you never know. He's got tattoos running up both arms. And they're big arms. You'll know him if you see him.'

'I'll be on the lookout. Looks like you've got a couple visitors right now.'

McCaleb saw that Lockridge was looking past him. He turned and looked back at *The Following Sea*. Graciela was standing in the stern. She was lifting Raymond down into the boat.

'I gotta go, Bud. I'll see you Monday.'

Graciela was wearing faded blue jeans and a Dodgers sweatshirt with her hair up under a matching baseball cap. She had a duffel bag slung over her shoulder and was carrying a grocery bag. Raymond was wearing blue jeans and a Kings hockey sweater. He also had on a baseball cap and carried with him a toy fire truck and an old stuffed animal that looked to McCaleb like a lamb.

McCaleb gave Graciela a tentative hug and shook Raymond's hand after the boy stuck his stuffed animal under his other arm.

'Good to see you guys,' he said. 'Ready to catch some fish today, Raymond?'

The boy seemed too shy to answer. Graciela nudged the boy on the shoulder and he nodded in agreement.

McCaleb took the bags, led them into the boat and gave them the complete tour he had not shown them on their earlier visit. Along the way, he left the grocery bag in the galley and put the duffel bag down on the bed in the main stateroom. He told Graciela it was her room and the sheets were freshly washed. He then showed Raymond the upper bunk in the forward stateroom. McCaleb had moved most of the boxes of files under the desk and the room seemed neat enough for the boy. There was a guard bar on the bunk so that he wouldn't roll out of bed. When McCaleb told him it was called a berth, his face scrunched up in confusion.

'That's what they call beds on boats, Raymond,' he said. 'And they call the bathroom the *head*.'

'How come?'

'You know, I never asked.'

He led them to the head and showed them how to use the foot pedal for flushing. He noticed Graciela looking at the temperature chart on the hook and he told her what it was for. She put her finger on the line from Thursday.

'You had a fever?'

'A slight fever. It went away.'

'What did your doctor say?'

'I didn't tell her yet. It went away and I'm fine.'

She looked at him with a mixture of concern and, he thought, annoyance. He then realized how important it probably was to her that he survive. She didn't want her sister's last gift to be for nothing.

'Don't worry,' he said. 'I'm fine. I was just doing a little too much running around that day. I took a long nap and the fever was gone. I've been okay since.'

He pointed to the slashes on the chart following the one fever reading. Raymond pulled on his pants leg and said, 'Where do you sleep?'

McCaleb glanced briefly at Graciela and turned toward the stairs before she could see his face start to color.

'Come on up, I'll show you.'

When they got back up to the salon, McCaleb explained to Raymond how he could turn the galley table into a single berth. The boy seemed satisfied.

'So let's see what you got,' McCaleb said.

He started going through Graciela's grocery bag and putting things away. Their agreement was that she would make lunch, he would do the same with dinner. She had gone to a deli and it looked like they were going to have submarine sandwiches.

'How'd you know that subs were my favorite?' he asked.

'I didn't,' Graciela said. 'But they're Raymond's, too.'

McCaleb reached over and caught Raymond in the ribs again with a finger and the boy recoiled with a giggle.

'Well, while Graciela makes sandwiches to take with us, why don't you come out and help me with the equipment. We have fish out there waitin' for us!'

'Okay!'

As he ushered the boy out to the stern, he looked back at Graciela and winked. Out on the deck he presented Raymond with the rod and reel he had bought him. When the boy realized the outfit was his to keep, he grabbed onto the pole as if it were a rope being dropped to him by a rescue squad. It made McCaleb feel sad instead of good. He wondered whether the young boy had ever had a man in his life.

McCaleb looked up and saw Graciela standing in the open door to the salon. She also had a sad look on her face, even though she was smiling at them. McCaleb decided they had to break away from such emotions.

'Okay,' he said. 'Bait. We've got to fill a bucket, 'cause

I've got a feeling they're going to be biting out there today.'

He got the floating bucket and dipping net out of the compartment next to the live well and then showed Raymond how to dip the net into the well and bring up the bait. He put a couple netfuls of shrimp and squid into the bucket and then turned the chore over to Raymond. He then went inside to get the tackle box and a couple more rods for himself and Graciela to use.

When he was inside and out of earshot of the boy, Graciela came up to him and hugged him.

'That was very nice of you,' she said.

He held her eyes for a few moments before saying anything.

'I think maybe it does more for me than him.'

'He's so excited,' she said. 'I can tell. He can't wait to catch something. I hope he does.'

They walked out along the marina's main dock, past the stores and restaurant, and then crossed a parking lot until they came to the main channel into the city's marinas. There was a crushed-gravel path here and it led them out to the mouth of the channel and the breakwater, a rock jetty that curved out into the Pacific for a hundred yards. They carefully stepped from one huge granite slab to another until they were about halfway out.

'Raymond, this is my secret spot. I think we should try it right here.'

There was no objection. McCaleb put down his equipment and set to work getting ready to fish. The rocks were still wet from the nightly assault of high seas. McCaleb had brought towels and walked about the spot looking for flat rocks that would make good seats. He spread the towels out and told Graciela and Raymond to sit down. He opened the tackle box, took out the tube of sun block and handed it to Graciela. He then started baiting lines. He decided to put the squid on Raymond's rig because he thought it would be the best bait and he wanted the boy to catch the first fish.

Fifteen minutes later they had three lines in the water. McCaleb had taught the boy how to cast his line out, leave the reel open and let the squid swim with it in the current.

'What will I catch?' he inquired, his eyes on his line.

'I don't know, Raymond. A lot of fish out there.'

McCaleb took a rock directly next to Graciela's. The boy was too nervous to sit and wait. He danced with his pole from rock to rock, anxiously waiting and hoping.

'I should've brought a camera,' Graciela whispered.

'Next time,' McCaleb said. 'You see that?'

He was pointing across the water to the horizon. The bluish outline of an island could be seen rising in the far mist.

'Catalina?'

'Yeah. That's it.'

'It's weird. I can't get used to the idea of you having lived on an island.'

'Well, I did.'

'How did your family end up here?'

'They were from Chicago. My father was a ballplayer. Baseball. One spring – it was nineteen fifty – he got a tryout with the Cubs. They used to come out to Catalina for spring training. The Wrigleys owned the Cubs and most of the island. So they came out here.

'My father and my mother were high school sweethearts. They had gotten married and he got this chance to go for the Cubs. He was a shortstop and second baseman. Anyway, he came out here but didn't make the team. But he loved the place. He got a job working for the Wrigleys. And he sent for her.'

His plan was to end the story there but she prompted more out of him.

'Then you came.'

'A little while later.'

'But your parents didn't stay?'

'My mother didn't. She couldn't take the island. She stayed ten years and that was enough. It can be claustrophobic for some people ... Anyway, they split up. My father stayed and he wanted me with him. I stayed. My mother went back to Chicago.'

She nodded.

'What did your father do for the Wrigleys?'

'A lot of things. He worked on their ranch, then he worked up at the house. They kept a sixty-three-foot Chris-Craft in the harbor. He got a job as a deckhand and eventually he skippered that for them. Finally he got his own boat and put it out for charter. He was also a volunteer fireman.'

He smiled and she smiled back.

'And *The Following Sea* was his boat?'

'His boat, his house, his business, everything. The Wrigleys financed him. He lived on the boat for about twelve years. Until he got so sick they – I mean, me, I was the one – I took him over town to the hospital. He died over here. In Long Beach.'

'I'm sorry.'

'It was a long time ago.'

'Not for you.'

He looked at her.

'It's just that at the end there comes a time when everybody knows. He knew there was no chance and he just wanted to go back over there. To his boat. And the island. I wouldn't do it. I wanted to try everything, every goddamn marvel of science and medicine. And besides, if he was over there, it would be a hassle for me to get out to see him. I'd have to take the ferry. I made him stay in that hospital. He died alone in his room. I was down in San Diego on a case.'

McCaleb looked out across the water. He could see a ferry heading toward the island.

'I just wish I had listened to him.'

She reached her hand over and put it on his forearm.

'There is no sense in being haunted by good intentions.'

He glanced over at Raymond. The boy had settled down and was standing still, looking down at his reel while a steady torrent of line was being pulled out. McCaleb knew that a squid didn't have that kind of pulling power.

'Hey, wait a minute, Raymond. I think you've got something there.'

He put his rod down and went to the boy. He flipped the reel's bail over and the line caught. Almost immediately the pole was pulled down and almost out of the boy's hands. McCaleb grabbed it and held it up.

'You got one!'

'Hey! I got one! I got one!'

'Remember what I told you, Raymond. Pull back, reel down. Pull back, reel down. I'll help you with the pole until we tire that boy out. It feels like a big one. You okay?'

'Yeah!'

With McCaleb doing most of the pulling up on the pole, they began to fight the fish. Meantime, McCaleb directed Graciela to reel in the other lines to avoid a tangle with the live line. McCaleb and the boy fought the fish for about ten minutes. All the while McCaleb could feel through the pole the fight slipping out of it as it tired. Finally, he was able to turn the pole over to Raymond so he could finish the job himself.

McCaleb slipped on a pair of gloves from the tackle box and climbed down the rocks to the water's edge. Just a few inches below the surface he saw the silvery fish weakly struggling against the line. McCaleb kneeled on the rock, getting his shoes and pants wet, and leaned out until he could grab hold of Raymond's line. He tugged the fish forward and brought its mouth up, reached into the water and locked a gloved hand around the tail, just forward of the back fins. He then yanked the fish out of the water and climbed back up the rocks to Raymond.

The fish was shining in the sun like polished metal.

'Barracuda, Raymond,' he said, holding it up. 'Look at those teeth.'

# 22

........

The day had gone well. Raymond caught two barracudas and a white bass. The first fish had been the biggest and most exciting, though the second was hooked while they were eating lunch and almost pulled the unattended pole into the water. After they got back in the late afternoon, Graciela insisted that Raymond rest before dinner and took him down to the forward stateroom. McCaleb used the time to spray off the fishing equipment with the stern hose. When Graciela came back up and they were alone, sitting on chairs on the deck, he felt a physical craving for a cold beer that he could just sit back and enjoy.

'That was wonderful,' Graciela said of the outing to the jetty.

'I'm glad. Think you're going to stay for dinner?'

'Of course. He wants to stay over, too. He loves boats. And I think he wants to fish again tomorrow. You've created a monster.'

McCaleb nodded, thinking about the night ahead. A few minutes of easy silence went by while they watched the other activities in the marina. Saturdays were always busy days. McCaleb kept his eyes moving. Having guests made him more alert for the Russian, even though he'd decided the chances of Bolotov showing up were slim. He'd had the upper hand in Toliver's office. If he had wanted to harm McCaleb, he could have done it then.

But thoughts of Bolotov brought the case intruding. He remembered a question he'd thought of for Graciela.

'Let me ask you something,' he said. 'You first came to me last Saturday. But the story about me ran a week before that. Why did you wait a week?'

'I didn't really. I didn't see the article. A friend of Glory's from the paper called up and said he saw it and wondered if, you know, you could've been the one who got her heart. Then I went to the library and read the story. I came here the next day.'

He nodded. She decided it was her turn to ask a question.

'Those boxes down there.'

'What boxes?'

'Stacked under the desk. Are they your cases?'

'They're old files.'

'I recognize some of the names written on them. The article mentioned some of them. Luther Hatch, I remember him. And the Code Killer. Why did they call him that?'

'Because he – if it was a he – left messages for us or sent messages to us that always had the same number at the bottom.'

'What did it mean?'

'We never found out. The best people at the bureau and even the encryption people at the National Security Agency couldn't crack it. Personally, I didn't think it meant anything at all. It wasn't a code. It was just another way for the UnSub to tweak us, keep us chasing our tails ... nine-oh-three, four-seven-two, five-six-eight.'

'That's the code?'

'That's the number. Like I said, I don't think there was any code.'

'Is that what they decided in Washington, too?'

'No. They never gave up on it. They were sure it meant something. They thought it might be the guy's

Social Security number. You know, scrambled around. With their computer they printed out every combination and then got all the names from Social Security. Hundreds of thousands. They ran them all through the computers.'

'Looking for what?'

'Criminal records, profile matches ... it was one big wild-goose chase. The UnSub wasn't on the list.'

'What is UnSub?'

'Unknown subject. That's what we called each one until we caught him. We never caught the Code Killer.'

McCaleb heard the faint sound of a harmonica and looked over at the *Double-Down*. Lockridge was down below practicing 'Spoonful'.

'Was he the only one of your cases where that happened?'

'You mean where the guy was never caught? No. Unfortunately, a lot of them get away. But the Code case was personal, I guess. He sent letters to me. He resented me for some reason.'

'What did he do to the people he ...'

'The Code Killer was unusual. He killed in many different ways and with no discernible pattern. Men, women, even one small child. He shot, he stabbed, he strangled. There was no handle.'

'Then how did you know it was him each time?'

'He told us. The letters, the code left at the crime scenes. You see, the victims and who they were didn't matter. They were only objects by which he could exercise power and stick it in the face of authority. He was an authority-complex killer. There was another killer, the Poet. He was a traveler, was active across the country a few years ago.'

'I remember. He got away here in LA, right?'

'Right. He was an authority killer, too. See, you strip away their fantasies and their methods and a lot of these people are very much alike. The Poet got off on watching us flailing around. The Code Killer was the same way. He liked to tweak the cops every chance he got.'

'Then he just stopped?'

'He either died or went to jail for something else. Or he moved somewhere else and started a new routine. But it's not something these guys can just turn off.'

'And what did you do in the Luther Hatch case?'

'Just my job. Look, we should talk about something else, don't you think?'

'I'm sorry.'

'It's okay. I just ... I don't know, I don't like all of those old stories.'

He had wanted to talk to her about her sister and the latest developments but now it didn't seem like the right time. He let the opportunity pass.

For dinner McCaleb grilled hamburgers and barracuda steaks. Raymond seemed enthusiastic about eating the fish he had caught but then didn't like the strong taste of the barracuda. Neither did Graciela, though McCaleb didn't think it was bad.

The meal was followed with another walk to the ice-cream store and then a walk along the shops on Cabrillo Way. It was dark by the time they got back to the boat. The marina was quiet again. Raymond got the bad news from Graciela.

'Raymond, it's been a long day and I want you to go to sleep,' she said gently. 'If you're good, you can fish some more tomorrow before we leave.'

The boy looked at McCaleb, seeking either confirmation or an appeal.

'She's right, Raymond,' he said. 'In the morning I'll take you back out there. We'll catch some more fish. Okay?'

In a cranky tone the boy agreed and Graciela took him

down to his room. His parting request was that he be allowed to take his fishing pole to his room with him. There was no objection to that. McCaleb had secured the hook on one of the pole's eyelets.

McCaleb had two space heaters on the boat and he set them up in each of their rooms. He knew that at night it could get cold on the boat, no matter how many blankets you had on.

'What are you going to use?' Graciela asked him.

'I'll be fine. I'm going to use my sleeping bag. I'll probably be warmer than both of you.'

'You sure?'

'I'm sure.'

He left them down there and went topside to wait for Graciela. He poured the last of the Sanford pinot noir he had opened on her first visit into her glass.

He took that and a can of Coke out to the stern. She joined him after ten minutes.

'It gets cold out here,' she said.

'Yeah. Do you think he'll be all right with that heater?'

'Yes, he's fine. He fell asleep almost as soon as he hit the pillow.'

He handed her the glass of wine and she tapped it against his Coke.

'Thank you,' she said. 'He had a wonderful time today.'

'I'm glad.'

He tapped his Coke against her glass. He knew that at some point he needed to finally talk about the investigation with her but he didn't want to spoil the moment. Once again he put it off.

'Who is that girl in the picture down on your desk?'

'What girl?'

'It looks like a photo from a yearbook or something. It's taped to the wall over the desk in Raymond's room.'

'Oh ... it's just ... it's just somebody I always want to remember. Somebody who died.'

'You mean like a case or someone you knew?'

'A case.'

'The Code Killer?'

'No, long before that.'

'What was her name?'

'Aubrey-Lynn.'

'What happened?'

'Something that shouldn't happen to anybody. Let's not talk about it right now.'

'Okay. I'm sorry.'

'It's all right. I should have taken that thing down before Raymond came anyway.'

McCaleb didn't get into the sleeping bag. He just draped it over his body and lay on his back with his hands laced behind his head. He knew he should be tired but he wasn't. Many thoughts raced through his mind, from the mundane to the gut-wrenching. He was thinking about the heater in the boy's berth. He knew it was safe but he worried about it anyway. The talk earlier in the day also resurfaced in a strand of thoughts about his father in the hospital bed. Once more he wished he had brought the old man home to die. He remembered taking the boat out after the ceremony at Descanso Beach and circling Catalina, parceling out the ashes a little at a time so that they lasted until he had come all the way around the island.

But those memories and concerns were only distractions from his thoughts of Graciela. The evening had ended on a wrong note after she had brought up Aubrey-Lynn Showitz. The memory had knocked McCaleb off stride and he stopped talking. He was infatuated with Graciela. He wanted her and had hoped the evening would end with them together. But he had let the grim memories intrude and it spoiled the moment.

He felt the boat gently rise and fall as the tide rolled in. He exhaled loudly, hoping to expel the demons. He readjusted himself on the thin cushion. There was a seam down the middle of the makeshift bed and he couldn't get comfortable. He thought about getting up for some orange juice but worried that if he had a glass, there might not be enough left for Raymond and Graciela in the morning.

Finally, he decided to go down and check the vitals. The old standby for killing time. It would give him something to do, maybe make him tired and finally able to sleep.

He had plugged a night-light into the circuit over the sink in case Raymond had to get up and find the toilet. He decided not to turn on the overhead fixture and stood there in the dim light with the thermometer under his tongue. He looked at his shadowy reflection and saw that the circles beneath his eyes were becoming more pronounced.

He had to lean over the sink and hold the thermometer close to the night-light in order to read it. It looked like he had a slight fever. He took the clipboard off the hook and wrote the date and time and 99 instead of a slash. As he replaced the clipboard, he heard the door of the master stateroom open across the passageway.

He had never closed the door to the head. He looked across the dark hallway and saw Graciela's face peering around the edge of her door. The rest of her body she hid behind the door. They spoke in whispers.

'Are you okay?'

'Yes. You?'

'I'm fine. What are you doing?'

'I couldn't sleep. I was just checking my temperature.'

'Do you have a fever?'

'No ... I'm fine.'

He nodded as he said it. He became aware he was wearing only his boxer shorts. He folded his arms and raised one hand to rub his chin but he was really just trying to hide the ugly scar on his chest.

They looked at each other in silence for a moment. McCaleb realized he had been holding his hand to his chin too long. He dropped his arms to his sides and watched her as her eyes fell to his chest.

'Graciela ...'

He didn't finish. She had slowly opened the door and he could see she wore a pink silk sleep shirt cut high on her hips. She was beautiful in it. For a moment they just stood there and looked at each other. Graciela still held the door, as if to steady herself against the boat's slight movements. After another moment she took a step into the hallway and he took a step to meet her. He reached forward and traced his hand gently up her side and then around to her back. With his other hand he caressed her throat and moved to the back of her neck. He pulled her into him.

'Can you do this?' she whispered, her face pressed into his neck.

'Nothing's going to stop me,' he whispered back.

They moved into the stateroom and shut the door. He left his shorts on the floor and crawled onto the bed with her as she unbuttoned the nightshirt. The sheets and blanket already had her smell, the vanilla he had noticed once before. He moved on top of her and she pulled him down into a long kiss. He worked his face down to her chest and kissed her breasts. His nose found the spot just below her neck where she had touched the perfume to her skin. The deep musky vanilla filled him and he moved his lips back up to hers.

Graciela moved her hand in between their bodies and held her warm palm against his chest. He felt her body tense and he opened his eyes. In a whisper she said, 'Wait. Terry, wait.'

He froze and lifted himself up with one arm.

'What is it?' he whispered.

'I don't think ... It doesn't feel right to me. I'm sorry.'

'What's not right?'

'I'm not sure.'

She turned her body underneath him and he had no choice but to get off her.

'Graciela?'

'It's not you, Terry. It's me. I'm ... I just don't want to rush. I want to think about things.'

She was on her side, looking away from him.

'Is it because of your sister? Because I have her –'

'No, it's not that ... Well, maybe a little. I just think we should think about it more.'

She reached back and caressed his cheek.

'I'm sorry. I know it was wrong to invite you in and then do this.'

'It's okay. I don't want you to do something you might be unhappy about later. I'll go back up.'

He made a move to slide toward the foot of the bed but she grabbed his arm.

'No, don't leave. Not yet. Lie here with me. I don't want you to leave yet.'

He moved back up the bed and put his head on the pillow next to hers. It was an odd feeling. Though obviously rejected, he felt no anxiety about it. He felt that the time would come for them and he could wait. McCaleb began wondering how long he could stay with her before having to return to his sleeping bag.

'Tell me about the girl,' she said.

'What?' he replied, confused.

'The girl in the yearbook picture on your desk.'

'It's not a nice story, Graciela. Why do you want to know that story?'

'Because I want to know you.'

That was all she said. But McCaleb understood. He knew that if they were to become lovers, they had to share their secrets. It was part of the ritual. He remembered years before how on the night he first made love to the woman who would become his wife, she had told him that she had been sexually abused as a child. Her sharing of such a carefully held and guarded secret had touched him more deeply than the actual physical act of their making love. He always remembered that moment, cherished it, even after the marriage was over.

'All of this was put together from witnesses and physical evidence ... and the video,' he began.

'What video?'

'I'll get to that. It was a Florida case. This was before I was sent out here. A whole family ... abducted. Mother, father, two daughters. The Showitz family. Aubrey-Lynn, the girl in the photo, she was the youngest.'

'How old?'

'She had just turned fifteen on the vacation. They were from the Midwest, a little town in Ohio. And it was their first family vacation. They didn't have a lot of money. The father owned a little auto garage – there was still grease under his nails when they found him.'

McCaleb blew his air out in a short laugh – the kind a person makes when something isn't funny but he wished it were.

'So they were on a cut-rate vacation and they did Disney World and all of that and they eventually got down to Fort Lauderdale, where they stayed in one room in this little shitty motel by the I-95 freeway. They had made the reservation from Ohio and thought because the place was called the Sea Breeze, it was near the ocean.'

His voice caught because he had never spoken the

story out loud; every detail about it was pitiful and made him hurt inside.

'Anyway, when they got there, they decided to stay. They were only going to be in town a couple days and they'd lose their deposit if they left for a beach hotel. So they stayed. And on their first night there one of the girls spots this pickup in the lot that was attached to a trailer with an airboat on it. You know what an airboat is?'

'Like with an airplane propeller and it goes in the swamp out there?'

'Right, the Everglades.'

'I saw them on CNN when that plane crashed into the swamp and disappeared.'

'Yeah, same thing. But this girl and her family had never seen one other than on TV or in a magazine and so they were looking it over and a man – the owner – just happens to walk up to them. He's a friendly guy and he tells the family that he'll take 'em on out for a real Florida airboat ride if they want.'

Graciela turned her face into the crook of his neck and pressed a hand against his chest. She knew where the story was going.

'So they said okay. I mean, they were from some town in Ohio with only one high school. They didn't know anything about the real world. So they went ahead and accepted this man's – this stranger's – invitation.'

'And he killed them?'

'All of them,' McCaleb said, nodding in the dark. 'They went out with him and they never came back. The father was found first. A couple nights later his body was found by a frogger working the grass. It wasn't too far from a ramp where they launch those boats. He'd been shot once in the back of the head and dumped off the boat.'

'What about the girls?'

'It took the local sheriffs a couple days to ID the father and trace him to the Sea Breeze. When there was no sign there of the wife and kids, and they weren't back in Ohio, the sheriffs went back out into the 'Glades with helicopters and more airboats. They found the three other bodies about six miles out. The middle of nowhere. A spot the airboaters call the Devil's Keep. The bodies were there. He had done things to all three of them. Then he tied them to concrete blocks and threw them over. While they were alive. They drowned.'

'Oh, God ...'

'God wasn't anywhere around that day. Decomposition gases eventually made the bodies float to the top, even with the concrete blocks attached.'

After a long moment of silence he continued.

'About that time the bureau was called in and I went down there with another agent, named Walling. There wasn't a whole lot to go on. We worked up a profile – we knew it was somebody very familiar with the 'Glades. Most of it's three feet deep anywhere you stop out there. But the women were dropped in a deep spot. He didn't want them found. He had to have known about that spot. The Devil's Keep. It was like a sinkhole or a meteorite crater. He had to have been out there before to have known about it.'

McCaleb was staring through the darkness at the ceiling, but what he was seeing was his own private and horrible version of the events that took place at the Devil's Keep. It was a vision that was never far from memory, always in the dark reaches of his mind.

'He had stripped them, taken their jewelry, anything that would ID them. But in Aubrey-Lynn's hand, when they pried it open, there was a silver necklace with a crucifix. She had somehow hidden it from him and held on to it. Probably praying to her God until the end.'

McCaleb thought about the story and the hold it had on him. Its resonance still moved through his life all these years later, like the incoming tide that gently lifted the boat in an almost rhythmic pattern. The story was always there. He knew he didn't need to display the photo above his desk like a holy card. He would never be able to forget the face of that girl. He knew that his heart had started to die with that girl's face.

'Did they catch that man?' Graciela asked.

She had just heard the story for the first time and already needed to know someone had paid for the horrible crime. She needed the closure. She didn't understand, as McCaleb did, that it didn't matter. That there was never closure on a story like this.

'No. They never caught him. They went through the registry at the Sea Breeze and ran everybody down. There was one person they never found. He had registered as Earl Hanford but it was a phony. The trail ended there ... until he sent the video.'

A beat of silence passed.

'It was sent to the sheriff's lead detective. The family had a video camera. They took it with them on the airboat trip. The tape starts with lots of happy scenes and smiles. Disney World, the beach, then some of the 'Glades. Then the killer started taping ... everything. He wore a black hood over his face so we couldn't ID him. He never showed enough of the boat to help us, either. He knew what he was doing.'

'You watched it?'

McCaleb nodded. He disengaged from Graciela and sat on the side of the bed, his back to her.

'He had a rifle. They did what he wanted. All sorts of things ... the two sisters ... together. Other things. And he killed them anyway. He – ah, shit ...'

He shook his head and rubbed his hands harshly over his face. He felt her warm hand on his back.

'The blocks he tied them to weren't enough to take them right down. They struggled, you know, on the surface. He watched and taped it. It got him aroused. He was masturbating while he watched them drown.'

He heard Graciela crying quietly. He lay back down and put an arm around her.

'The tape was the last we ever heard from him,' he said. 'He's out there somewhere. Another one.'

He looked at her in the darkness, not sure if she could see him.

'That's the story.'

'I'm sorry you have that to carry around.'

'And now you have it. I'm sorry, too.'

She rubbed the tears away from her eyes.

'That's when you stopped believing in angels, isn't it?'

He nodded.

An hour or so before dawn McCaleb got up and went back to his uncomfortable bed in the salon. They had spent the night until that point talking in whispers, holding and kissing, but never making love. Once back in his sleeping bag, sleep still did not come to him. McCaleb's mind kept running over the details of the hours he had just spent with Graciela, the touch of her warm hands on his skin, the softness of her breasts against his lips, the taste of her lips. And during moments when his mind wandered from these sensual memories, he also thought about the story he had told her and the way she had reacted.

In the morning they did not talk about what had happened in the stateroom or what had been said, even when Raymond had gone out to the stern to look into the live well and was out of earshot. Graciela seemed to act as if there had been no rendezvous, consummated or not, and McCaleb acted in kind. The first thing he spoke of while he scrambled eggs for the three of them was the case.

'I want you to do something for me when you get home today,' he said, checking over his shoulder to make sure Raymond was still outside. 'I want you to think about your sister and write down as much as you can about her routines. I mean like places she would go, friends she would see. Anything you can think of she did between the first of the year and the night she went into that store. Also, I want to talk to her friends and boss at the *Times*. It might be better if you set that up.'

'All right. How come?'

'Because things are changing about the case. Remember I asked you about the earring?'

McCaleb told her his belief that it had been the shooter who had taken the earring. He also told her how he had found out late Friday that something of a personal nature had been taken from the victim in the first shooting as well.

'What was it?'

'A photo of his wife and kids.'

'What do you think it means?'

'That maybe these weren't robberies. That maybe this man at the ATM and then your sister were picked for some other reason. There's a chance they might have had some prior interaction with the man who shot them. You know, crossed paths with him somewhere. That's why I want you to do this. The wife of the first victim is doing it for me with her husband. I'll look at the two of them together and see if there are any commonalities.'

Graciela folded her arms and leaned against the galley counter.

'You mean like they did something to this man to cause this?'

'No. I mean that they crossed paths and something about them attracted him to them. There's no valid reason. I think we're looking for a psychopath. There is no telling what caught his eye. Why he chose these two people out of the nine million others who live in this county.'

She slowly shook her head in disbelief.

'What do the police say about all of this?'

'I don't think the LAPD even knows yet. And the sheriff's investigator is not sure whether or not she sees it the way I do. We're all going to talk about it tomorrow morning.'

'What about the man?'

'What man?'

'The store owner. Maybe he was the one who crossed the path. Maybe Glory had nothing to do with it.'

McCaleb shook his head and said, 'No. If he was the target, the shooter would have just gone in and shot him when nobody else was in the store. It was your sister. Your sister and the first man up in Lancaster. There is some connection. We have to find it.'

McCaleb reached into the back pocket of his jeans and pulled out a photo Amelia Cordell had given him. It showed James Cordell in close-up, a bright smile on his face. He showed the photo to Graciela.

'Do you recognize this man? Is he someone that your sister might have known?'

She took the photo from him and studied it but then shook her head.

'Not that I know of. Is he ... the man from Lancaster?'

McCaleb nodded and took the photo back. He put it in his pocket, then told Graciela to go get Raymond to come inside for his breakfast. As she got to the sliding door, he stopped her.

'Graciela, do you trust me?'

She looked back at him.

'Of course.'

'Then trust me about this. I don't care if the LAPD and the sheriffs don't believe me, but I know what I know. With or without them, I'm going to keep pushing on this.'

She nodded and turned back to the door and the boy out in the stern.

# 23

The detective bureau at the Sheriff's Department's Star Center was crowded with detectives when McCaleb entered at eight o'clock on Monday morning. However, the receptionist who had let him walk back to homicide on his own just three days earlier told him he had to wait for the captain. This puzzled McCaleb but before he could ask about it, the receptionist was on the phone making a call. As soon as she hung up, McCaleb saw Captain Hitchens emerge from the meeting room he had sat in with Jaye Winston on Friday. He closed the door behind him and headed toward McCaleb. Terry noticed that the blinds over the meeting room's glass window were drawn and closed. Hitchens beckoned him to follow.

'Terry, come on back with me.'

McCaleb followed him to his office and Hitchens told him to have a seat. McCaleb was getting a bad feeling about the overly cordial treatment. Hitchens sat behind his desk, folded his arms and leaned forward on the calendar blotter with a smile on his face.

'So, where have you been?'

McCaleb looked at his watch.

'What do you mean? Jaye Winston set the meeting for eight. It's two minutes after.'

'I mean Sunday, Saturday. Jaye's been calling.'

McCaleb immediately knew what had happened. On Saturday, when he had been cleaning up the boat, he had taken the phone and the answer machine and placed them in a cabinet next to the chart table. He had then forgotten about it. Calls to the boat and messages left while they had been out on the jetty fishing both days would have been missed. The phone and machine were still in the cabinet.

'Damn,' he now said to Hitchens. 'I haven't checked my machine.'

'Well, we were calling. Could've saved you a trip out.'

'The meeting's been canceled? I thought Jaye wanted –'

'The meeting isn't canceled, Terry. It's just that some things have come up and we feel it's better if we conduct the investigation without outside complications.'

McCaleb studied him for a long moment.

'Complications? Is this because of the heart transplant? Jaye told you?'

'She didn't have to tell me. But it's because of a number of things. Look, you came in here and shook things up. Gave us a number of things – good hard leads – to follow. We're going to do that and we're going to be very diligent in our investigation, but at this point I have to draw the line on your involvement. I'm sorry.'

There was something not said, McCaleb thought as the captain spoke. Something was going on he didn't understand or at least know about it. Good hard leads, Hitchens had said. Suddenly, McCaleb understood. If Winston couldn't get through to him during the weekend, then neither could Vernon Carruthers in Washington, DC.

'My FAT guy found something?'

'Fat guy?'

'Firearms and Toolmarks. What did he get, Captain?'

Hitchens raised his hands palm out.

'We're not going to talk about that. I told you, we thank you very much for the jump start. But let us handle it from here. We will let you know what happens and if good things happen, you will be properly credited in our records and with the media.'

'I don't need to be credited. I just need to be part of this.'

'I'm sorry. But we'll take it from here.'

'And Jaye agrees with this?'

'It doesn't matter if she agrees or doesn't agree. Last I checked, I was running the detective bureau here, not Jaye Winston.'

There was enough annoyance in his tone for McCaleb to conclude that Winston had not been in agreement with Hitchens. That was good to know. He might need her. Staring at Hitchens, McCaleb knew he wasn't going to go quietly back to his boat and drop it. No way. The captain had to be smart enough to realize it as well.

'I know what you're thinking. And all I'm saying is don't get yourself in a jam. If we come across you in the field, there's going to be a problem.'

McCaleb nodded.

'Fair enough.'

'You've been warned.'

McCaleb told Lockridge to cruise around the visitors' lot. He wanted to get to a phone quickly but first he wanted to see if he could get an idea who had been in the meeting room Hitchens had come out of. He knew Jaye Winston was obviously in there and probably Arrango and Walters. But following his hunch that Vernon Carruthers had come up with a ballistics match with the DRUGFIRE laser program, he also suspected that someone from the bureau besides Maggie Griffin was in the meeting room.

As they moved slowly through the parking lot, McCaleb checked the rear driver's-side window of each parked car they passed. Finally, in the third lane, he saw what he was looking for.

'Hold it here, Bud,' he said.

They stopped behind a metallic blue Ford LTD. On the rear driver's-side window was the telltale bar-code sticker. It was a bureau car. A laser reader at the garage entrance of the federal building in Westwood scanned the bar code and raised the steel gate to permit entrance after hours.

McCaleb got out and walked up to the car. There were no other exterior markings to help him identify the agent who had driven it. But whoever had been driving the car made it easy for him. Driving east to the meeting against a rising sun, the driver had turned down the windshield visor and left it down. All the FBI agents McCaleb had ever known kept the government gas card assigned to their car clipped to the visor for easy access. This driver was no exception. McCaleb looked at the gas card and got the serial number off it. He went back to Lockridge's car.

'What's with the car?' Buddy asked.

'Nothing. Let's go.'

'Where?'

'Find a phone.'

'Shoulda guessed.'

Five minutes later they were at a service station with a bank of phones on the side wall. Lockridge pulled up to the phones, lowered his window so he would be able to eavesdrop and shut off the car. Before getting out, McCaleb opened his wallet and gave him a twenty-dollar bill.

'Go fill it up. We're going back up to the desert, I think.'

'Shit.'

'You said you were free all day.'

'I am, but who wants to go to the desert? Don't any clues point to the beach, for cryin' out loud?'

McCaleb just laughed at him and got out of the car with his phone book.

At the phone, McCaleb called the field office in Westwood and asked to be transferred to the garage. The call was picked up after twelve rings.

'G'age.'

'Yeah, who's this?'

'Roofs.'

'Oh, okay,' McCaleb said, remembering the man. 'Rufus, this is Convey up on fifteen. I've got a question you might be able to answer for me.'

'Shoot, man.'

The familiarity McCaleb had put in his voice had apparently worked. He remembered Rufus and had never been much impressed with his intelligence. This was reflected in the poor upkeep of the federal fleet.

'I found a gas card on the floor up here and it's supposed to be in somebody's car down there. Who's got card eighty-one? Can you look it up?'

'Uh ... etty-one?'

'Yes, Roof, eight-one.'

There was a spell of silence while the garage man apparently looked through a log.

'Well, that's Misser Spence. He got that one.'

McCaleb didn't respond. Gilbert Spencer was the second-highest-ranking agent in Los Angeles. Rank notwithstanding, McCaleb had never thought much of him as an investigative team leader. But the fact that he was meeting with Jaye Winston and her captain and who knew who else at the Star Center came as a shock. He began to get a better idea why he had been kicked off the case.

' 'Lo?'

'Uh, yeah, Rufus, thanks a lot. That was eighty-one, right?'

'Yuh. Tha's Agent Spence cah.'

'Okay, I'll get him the card.'

'I don't know. I see his car ain' here right now.'

'Okay, don't worry about it. Thanks, Roof.'

McCaleb hung up the phone and immediately picked it up again. Using his calling card number, he called Vernon Carruthers in Washington. It was just about lunchtime there and he hoped he had not missed him.

'This is Vernon.'

McCaleb blew out a sigh.

'It's Terry.'

'Man, where the hell you been? I tried to give you a damn heads-up on Saturday and you wait two days to call me back.'

'I know, I know. I fucked up. But I hear you got something.'

'Damn tootin'.'

'What, Vernon, what?'

'I gotta be careful. I get the feeling there's a need-to-know list on this and your name's –'

'– not on it. Yeah, I know. I already found that out. But this is my car, Vernon, and nobody's going to drive away without me. So you're going to tell me, what did you find that would bring the assistant special agent in charge of the Los Angeles field office out of his little room and into the field, probably for the first time this year?'

' 'Course I'm going to tell you. I got my twenty-five in. What are they going to do to me? Kick me out and then have to pay me double-time witness fees to testify in all the cases I got lined up?'

'So give it to me then.'

'Well, you really stuck your dick in it this time. I lasered the slug this Winston gal sent me and got an eighty-three percent match on a good-sized frag they dug out of the head of one Donald Kenyon back in November. That's why you got the A-SAC's nuts in an uproar out there.'

McCaleb whistled.

'Damn, not in my ear, man,' Carruthers protested.

'Sorry. Was it a Federal FMJ – the one from Kenyon?'

'No, actually, it was a frangible. A Devastator. You know what that is?'

'That's what Reagan got nailed with at the Hilton, right?'

'Right. Little charge in the tip. Bullet is supposed to fragment. But it didn't with Ronnie. He got lucky. Kenyon wasn't lucky.'

McCaleb tried to think about what this might mean. The same gun, the HK P7, had been used in the three murders, Kenyon, Cordell and Torres. But between Kenyon and Cordell the ammunition had changed from a frangible to a hardball. Why?

'Now, remember,' Carruthers was saying, 'you didn't hear this stuff from me.'

'I know. But tell me something. After you got the match, what did you do, go to Lewin or do some checking first?'

Joel Lewin was Carruthers's by-the-book boss.

'What you're asking is if I got anything to send you, am I right?'

'You're right. I need what you can send me.'

'Already on the way. Put it in priority mail on Saturday before the shit hit the fan around here. I printed out what was on the computer. You got all the internals coming. Should be there t'day or t'morrow. You are going to take me on one hell of a fishing trip for this, man.'

'Absolutely.'

'And you didn't get any of that stuff from me.'

'You're cool, Vernon. You don't even have to say it.'

'I know but it makes me feel better.'

'What else can you tell me?'

'That's about it. It was taken out of my hands. Lewin

took over everything and it went high-level from there. I did have to tell them why I put the push on it. So they know you were looking into it. I didn't tell them why.'

McCaleb silently chastised himself for losing his temper and control with Arrango after the hypnotism session. If he hadn't revealed the real motivation behind his investigation, he might still be a part of it. Carruthers had not revealed the secret, but Arrango certainly had.

'You there, Terry?'

'Yeah. Listen, if you pick up anything else about this, give me the heads-up.'

'You got it, man. But answer your fuckin' phone. And watch yourself on this.'

'All the time.'

After McCaleb hung up he turned around and almost walked into Buddy Lockridge.

'Buddy, come on, you gotta give me room. Let's get going.'

They started walking to the car, which was still parked at one of the pumps.

'The desert?'

'Yeah. We go back up and I see Mrs Cordell again. See if she's still talking to me.'

'Why wouldn't – never mind, don't answer that. I'm just the driver.'

'Now you got it.'

On the way up to the desert, Buddy warbled on a B flat harmonica while McCaleb used some self-hypnosis techniques to relax his mind so that he would better recall what he knew of the Donald Kenyon case. It had been the latest in what had seemingly been a long line of embarrassments to the bureau in recent years.

Kenyon had been president of Washington Guaranty, a federally insured savings and loan bank with branches in Los Angeles, Orange and San Diego Counties. Kenyon was a golden-haired and silver-tongued climber who curried favor with deep-pocketed investors through insider stock tips until he ascended to the president's office by the shockingly young age of twenty-nine. He was profiled in every business magazine. He was a man who instilled confidence and trust in his investors and employees and the media. So much so that over the period of three years that he was president, he was able to siphon a staggering $35 million from the institution through bogus loans to bogus companies without so much as raising an eyebrow. It wasn't until Washington Guaranty collapsed after being thoroughly hollowed out and Kenyon disappeared that anyone, including federal auditors and watchdogs, realized what had happened.

The story played in the media for months, if not years, McCaleb remembered. Stories on retirees left with nothing, stories on the ripple effect of businesses failing, stories on alleged sightings of Kenyon in Paris, Zurich, Tahiti and other places.

After five years on the run Kenyon was found by the bureau's fugitive unit in Costa Rica, where he had been living in an opulent compound that included two pools, two tennis courts, a live-in personal trainer and horse-breeding facilities. The thief, now thirty-six, was extradited to Los Angeles to face charges in federal court.

While Kenyon sat in the federal holding facility awaiting trial, an asset and forfeiture squad descended on his trail and worked for six months looking for the money. But less than $2 million was found.

This was the puzzle. Kenyon's defense was that he did not have the money because he didn't take it, he only passed it on under threat of death – his and his entire family's. Through his attorneys he averred that he was blackmailed into setting up corporations, loaning them millions from his S&L and then turning the money over to the blackmailer. But even though he faced the potential of years in a federal penitentiary, Kenyon refused to name the extortionist who had taken the money.

Federal investigators and prosecutors chose not to believe him. Citing his high-flying lifestyle both while running the S&L and on the run, and the fact that he clearly had some of the money – albeit a fraction of the whole – with him in Costa Rica, they settled for prosecuting only Kenyon.

After a four-month trial in a federal courtroom packed each day with a gallery of victims who had lost their life savings in the S&L collapse, Kenyon was convicted of the massive fraud and US District Judge Dorothy Windsor sentenced him to forty-eight years in prison.

What happened next would result in one more bludgeoning of the reputation of the FBI.

After passing sentence, Windsor agreed to a defense request to allow Kenyon time at home with his family to prepare for prison while his attorneys prepared appeal motions. Over the prosecutor's strenuous objection, Windsor gave Kenyon sixty days to get his house in order. He then had to report to prison forthwith, whether an appeal was filed or not. Windsor further ordered that Kenyon wear a monitor bracelet around his ankle to ensure he did not attempt another flight from justice.

Such an order following conviction is not unusual. However, it *is* unusual when the convict has already shown his willingness to flee authorities and the country.

But whether Kenyon had somehow been able to influence a federal judge to get such a ruling and planned to flee once more would never be known. On the Tuesday after Thanksgiving, while Kenyon was enjoying the twenty-first day of his two-month reprieve, someone entered the Beverly Hills home he was renting on Maple Drive. Kenyon was alone, his wife having left to take their two children to school. The intruder confronted

Kenyon in the kitchen and marched him at gunpoint into the marble-tiled entry of the house. He then shot Kenyon to death just as his wife's car was pulling into the circular drive out front. The intruder escaped out a back door and through the alley running behind the row of mansions on Maple Drive.

Except for the investigation and pursuit of the killer, the story might have ended there or at least taken on the mundane boredom of a cold trail. But the FBI had Lojacked Kenyon – bureau-speak for having placed him under an illegal surveillance that included listening devices planted in his home, cars and attorney's office. At the moment he was shot, a tech van with four agents in it was parked two blocks away. The murder had been recorded.

The agents, aware of their illegal standing, nevertheless raced to the home and gave pursuit to the intruder. But the gunman escaped while Kenyon was being rushed to Cedars-Sinai Medical Center, only to be declared dead on arrival.

The missing millions Kenyon was convicted of looting from Washington Guaranty were never recovered. But that detail was eclipsed when the actions of the FBI were revealed. Not only was the bureau vilified for undertaking such an illegal operation, it was also publicly castigated for allowing a murder to happen right under its nose, for bumbling the chance to intervene and stop the assassination of Kenyon, not to mention capture the gunman.

McCaleb had viewed all of this from afar. He was already out of the bureau and at the time of Kenyon's murder was preparing himself for his own death. But he remembered reading the *Times*, which was at the forefront of the story. He recalled that the newspaper reported that there were demotions all around for the agents involved and calls from politicians in Washington, DC, for congressional hearings on illegal activities by the bureau. To add insult to injury, he also remembered, Kenyon's widow filed an invasion-of-privacy lawsuit against the bureau, seeking millions in damages.

The question McCaleb now had to answer was whether the intruder who killed Kenyon in November was the man who killed Cordell and Torres two and three months later. And if it was the same man, what could possibly be the connection linking a failed savings and loan president with an aqueduct engineer and a newspaper pressroom worker?

He finally looked around and noticed his surroundings. They were well past Vasquez Rocks now. In a few more minutes they would be at Amelia Cordell's house.

# 24

As promised, Amelia Cordell had spent a good part of the weekend going through her memory and filling four pages of a legal tablet with what she recalled of her husband's travels in the two months before his death on the twenty-second of January. She had it ready and sitting on the coffee table when McCaleb arrived.

'I appreciate the time you put into this,' he told her.

'Well, maybe it will help. I hope it helps.'

'Me too.'

He nodded and sat in silence for a moment.

'Um, by the way, have you heard from Jaye Winston or anybody else from the Sheriff's Department lately?'

'No, not since Jaye called me on Friday to say it was okay to talk to you.'

McCaleb nodded. He was heartened by the fact that Jaye hadn't called back to rescind the permission. Again it made him think that she wasn't going along with her captain's decision to drop McCaleb from the case.

'And nobody else?'

'No ... like who?'

'I don't know. I'm just curious about whether, you know, they're following up on the information I've given them.'

McCaleb decided he had better change the subject.

'Mrs Cordell, did your husband have a home office?'

'Yes, he had a small den he used, why?'

'Do you mind if I look around there?'

'Well, no, but I'm not sure what you'll find. He just kept files from work there and he did our bills there.'

'Well, for example, if you have credit card statements for the period of January and December, it might help me isolate where he was at different points.'

'I'm not too sure I want you taking our credit card records.'

'Well, all I can do is assure you that I'm only interested in the billing locations and possibly the items purchased. Not your credit card numbers.'

'I know, I'm sorry. That was silly of me. You're the only one who seems to care anymore about Jim. Why am I suspicious of you?'

It made McCaleb feel uneasy not being totally truthful with the woman and telling her he had lost his official sanction. He stood up so that they could move on and he didn't have to think about it.

The office was small and largely used for storage of skiing equipment and cardboard boxes. But one end of the room was largely taken up by a desk with two drawers and two built-in file cabinets.

'Sorry, it's a mess. And I'm still getting used to doing all the bills. Jim always handled that.'

'Don't worry about that. Do you mind if I just sort of sit and look through things a bit?'

'No, not at all.'

'Um, would it be possible for me to have a glass of water in here?'

'Of course, I'll go get you one.'

She headed to the door but then stopped.

'You don't really want the water, do you? You just want to be left alone and not have me hovering around.'

McCaleb smiled slightly and looked down at the worn green carpet.

'I'll get you the water anyway, but then I'll leave you alone.'

'Thanks, Mrs Cordell.'

'Call me Amelia.'

'Amelia.'

McCaleb spent the next half hour going through the drawers and the paperwork on top of the desk. He worked quickly, knowing that the package from Carruthers was probably waiting for him in his postal box in the harbormaster's office.

At the desk McCaleb took some notes on the legal pad Amelia Cordell had already worked on, and he piled documents and credit card records he wanted to take with him to study later. He made an inventory list of the things he wanted to take so that Amelia Cordell would have a record.

The last drawer he went through was in one of the file cabinets. It was almost empty and had been used by Cordell as the place to file work, insurance and estate planning records. There was a thick file on medical insurance, with billing records dating back to the birth of his daughters and his own treatment for a broken leg. The billing address of one of his treating physicians was in Vail, Colorado, leading McCaleb to guess the bone had been broken in a skiing misadventure.

There was a black binder with a handsome leather slipcover. McCaleb opened it and found that it contained documents relating to the wills of both husband and wife. McCaleb saw nothing unordinary. Each spouse had been the other's beneficiary, with the children following in line in the event of both parents dying. McCaleb didn't spend a lot of time with it.

The last file he looked at was simply labeled WORK and it contained various records, including performance evaluations and various office communications. McCaleb scanned the employment reviews and found that Cordell had apparently been held in high regard by his employers. McCaleb wrote down some of the names of supervisors who signed the reports so he could interview them later. Last he scanned the other correspondence but nothing interested him. There were copies of interoffice memos as well as letters of commendation for Cordell's chairing of the engineering firm's annual blood drive and his volunteer work in a program that provided Thanksgiving meals to the needy. There was also a two-year-old letter from a supervisor praising Cordell for stopping and helping the injured victims of a head-on collision in Lone Pine. Details of what Cordell did were not in the letter. McCaleb put the letters and evaluations back in the file and returned it to the file drawer.

McCaleb stood up and looked around the room. There was nothing else that raised any interest. He then noticed a framed photo on the desk. It was of the Cordell family. He picked it up and studied it for a moment, thinking about how much the bullet had shattered. It made him think of Raymond and Graciela. He envisioned a photo that had the two of them and McCaleb in it, smiling.

He took his empty water glass into the kitchen and left it on the counter. He then stepped into the living room and found Amelia Cordell sitting in the chair she had taken earlier. She was just sitting there. The television was not on, she had no book or newspaper in her hands. She appeared to be just staring at the glass top of the coffee table. McCaleb hesitated in the hallway from the kitchen.

'Mrs Cordell?'

She shifted her eyes to him without moving her head.

'Yes?'

'I'm finished for now.'

He stepped in and placed the receipt on the table.

'These are the things I am taking. I'll get it all back to you in a few days. I'll either mail it or bring it up myself.'

Her eyes were on the list now, trying to read it from three feet away.

'Did you find what you need?'

'I don't know yet. These sorts of things, you never know what is important until it becomes important, if you know what I mean.'

'Not really.'

'Well, I guess I mean details. I'm looking for the telling detail. There used to be a game when I was a kid. I don't remember what it was called but they still might have it around for kids today. You've got a clear plastic tube that stands vertical. There are a bunch of plastic straws running through holes all around the center of it. You load a bunch of marbles into the tube so that they are held up by the straws. The object of the game is to pull a straw out without any marbles dropping. And there always seemed to be one straw that when you pulled it out, everything came down like a landslide. That's what I'm looking for. I've got lots of details. I'm looking for the one that brings the landslide when it's pulled out. Trouble is, you can't tell which one it is until you start pulling.'

She looked at him blankly, the way she had been staring at the coffee table.

'Well, look, I've taken too much of your time. I think I'll be on my way and, like I said, I'll get these things back to you. And I'll call you if anything else comes up. My number is on the inventory list there in case you think of anything else or there is anything I can do for you.'

He nodded and she said good-bye. He turned to head to the door when he thought of something and turned back.

'Oh, I almost forgot. There was a letter in one of the

files commending your husband for stopping at an accident up near Lone Pine. Do you remember that?'

'Sure. That was two years ago, November.'

'Do you remember what happened?'

'Just that Jimmy was driving home from up there and he came across the accident. It had just happened and there were people and debris thrown every which way and that. He called for ambulances on his cell phone and stopped to comfort the people. A little boy died right in his arms that night. He had a hard time with that.'

McCaleb nodded.

'That was the kind of man he was, Mr McCaleb.'

All McCaleb could do was nod his head again.

McCaleb had to wait out on the front driveway for ten minutes before Buddy Lockridge finally drove up. He had a Howlin' Wolf tape playing loud on the stereo. McCaleb turned it down after climbing in.

'Where you been?'

'Drivin'. Where to?'

'Well, I was waiting. Back to the marina.'

Buddy made a U-turn and headed back to the freeway.

'Well, you told me I didn't have to just sit in the car. You told me to take a drive, I took a drive. How am I supposed to know how long you're going to be if you don't tell me?'

He was right but McCaleb was still annoyed. He didn't apologize.

'If this thing lasts much longer, I ought to get a cell phone for you to carry.'

'If this lasts much longer, I want a raise.'

McCaleb didn't respond. Lockridge turned the tape back up and pulled a harmonica out of the door pocket. He started playing along to 'Wang Dang Doodle'. McCaleb looked out the window and thought about Amelia Cordell and how one bullet had taken two lives.

# 25

The package from Carruthers was waiting for McCaleb in his mailbox. It was as thick as a phone book. He took it back to the boat, opened it and spread the documents across the salon table. He found the most recent summary on the Kenyon investigation and began reading, deciding to learn the latest developments and then go back to read from the start.

The investigation of the Donald Kenyon murder was a joint FBI-Beverly Hills police operation. But the case was cold. The lead agents for the bureau, a pair from the special investigation unit in Los Angeles named Nevins and Uhlig, had concluded in the most recent report, filed in December, that Kenyon had likely been executed by a contract killer. There were two theories as to who had employed the assassin. Theory one was that one of the two thousand victims of the savings and loan collapse had been unsatisfied with Kenyon's sentence or possibly feared he would flee justice once again and therefore had engaged the services of a killer. Theory two was that the killer had been in the employ of the silent partner who Kenyon had claimed during the trial had forced him to loot the savings and loan. That partner, whom Kenyon had refused to identify, remained unidentified as well by the bureau, according to this last report.

McCaleb found the outlining of theory two in the report interesting because it indicated that the federal government might now give credence to Kenyon's claim that he had been forced to siphon funds from his savings and loan by a second party. This claim had been derided during Kenyon's trial by the prosecution, which took to referring to this alleged second party as Kenyon's phantom. Now, here was an FBI document which suggested that the phantom might actually exist.

Nevins and Uhlig concluded the summary report with a brief profile of the unknown subject who had contracted the murder. The profile fit both theories one and two: the employer was wealthy, had the ability to hide his or her trail and remain anonymous and had connections to or was even part of traditional organized crime.

Aside from the report breathing life into Kenyon's phantom, the second thing that interested McCaleb was the suggestion that the employer, and therefore the actual killer, was connected to traditional organized crime. Traditional organized crime in FBI parlance meant the Mafia. The tendrils of the Mafia were almost everywhere, but, even so, the mob was not a strong influence in southern California. There was a tremendous amount of organized crime in the area, it just wasn't being perpetrated by the traditional mobsters out of the movies. At any given time there were probably more Asian or Russian mobsters operating in southern California than their counterparts of Italian descent.

McCaleb organized the documents in chronological order and went back to the start. Most were routine summaries and updates on aspects of the investigation that were forwarded to supervisors in Washington. Quickly scanning through the documents, he found a report on the surveillance team's activities the morning of the shooting that he read with fascination.

There had been four agents in the surveillance van at the time of the killing. It was change-of-shift time, eight o'clock on a Tuesday morning. Two agents coming on, two going home. The agent monitoring the bugs took off the headset and passed it to his replacement. However, the replacement was a type A personality who claimed he had once gotten an infestation of head lice from another agent during an earphone exchange. So he took the time to put his own pair of foam cushions on the headset and to then spray the equipment with a disinfectant, all the while fending off insulting barbs from the three other agents. After he finally placed the earphones on his head, he heard silence for nearly a minute, then a muffled exchange of conversation and then finally a shot from Kenyon's house. The sound was muffled because no listening devices had been placed in the entryway of the house, the thinking being that any escape planning Kenyon might do would not be done at the front door. The bugs had been placed in the actual living areas of the house.

The overnight team had not yet left and were continuing the banter in the van. After hearing the shot, the agent on the phones shouted for silence. He listened closely for several seconds while another agent put on a second set of phones. What they both heard was someone in the Kenyon house clearly speak one line near one of the microphones: 'Don't forget the cannoli.'

The two agents on the phones looked at each other and agreed that it had not been Kenyon who had spoken the line. Declaring an emergency, the agents blew their cover and sped to the house, arriving moments after Donna Kenyon had arrived home, opened the front door and found her husband lying on the marble floor, his head bathed in blood. After calling for bureau backup, local police and paramedics, the agents searched the house and the surrounding neighborhood. The gunman was gone.

McCaleb moved on to a transcript of the last hour of

tape from Kenyon's home. The tape had been enhanced in the FBI lab but still not every word was captured. There were the sounds of the daughters having breakfast and the normal morning talk between Kenyon and his wife and the girls. Then, at 7:40, the girls and their mother left.

The transcript noted nine minutes of silence before Kenyon made a phone call to the home of his attorney, Stanley LaGrossa.

LAGROSSA: Yes?
KENYON: It's Donald.
LAGROSSA: Donald.
KENYON: Are we still on?
LAGROSSA: Yes, if you are still serious about it.
KENYON: I am. I'll see you at the office then.
LAGROSSA: You know the risks. I'll see you there.

Another eight minutes went by and then a new unknown voice was picked up in the house. Some of the terse conversation was lost as Kenyon and the unknown man moved through the house, in and out of the reach of the listening devices. The conversation had apparently taken place while the delayed earphone exchange was taking place in the bureau tech van.

KENYON: What is –
UNKNOWN: Shut up! Do what I say and your family lives, understand?
KENYON: You can't just walk in here and –
UNKNOWN: I said shut up! Let's go. This way.
KENYON: Don't hurt my family. Please, I ...
UNKNOWN: (unintelligible)
KENYON: ... do that. I wouldn't and he knows that. I don't understand this. He ...
UNKNOWN: Shut up. I don't care.

KENYON: (unintelligible)
UNKNOWN: (unintelligible)

The report noted that two minutes of silence went by and then the final exchange.

UNKNOWN: Okay, look and see who ...
KENYON: Don't ... She's got nothing to do with this. She ...

Then one shot was fired. And moments later microphone 4, which was hidden in a rear den with a door to the rear yard, picked up the unknown man's final words.

UNKNOWN: Don't forget the cannoli.

The door to the den was found open. It had been used as part of the killer's escape route.

McCaleb read the transcript again, captivated by knowing it was a man's last moments and words. He wished he had an audiotape, so that he would have a better feel for what had happened.

The next document he read explained why the investigators suspected mob involvement. It was a cryptology report. The tape from the Kenyon house had been sent to the crime lab for enhancement. The transcript was then sent to cryptology. The analyst given the assignment focused on the killer's last line, spoken after Kenyon was down and seemingly a non sequitur. The line – 'Don't forget the cannoli' – was fed into the cryptology computer to see if it matched any known code, prior usage in bureau reports or literary or entertainment reference. It scored a direct match.

In the movie *The Godfather*, the film that inspired a legion of true-life Mafia hoodlums, a top capo for the Corleone family, Peter Clemenza, is given the assignment of taking a traitorous family soldier out into the New Jersey meadowlands and killing him. On the morning he leaves his home for the hit, his wife tells Clemenza to stop by a bakery for pastry. As the hugely overweight Clemenza lumbers out to a waiting car containing the man he is tasked with killing, his wife calls after him, 'Don't forget the cannoli.'

McCaleb loved the movie and now remembered the line. It so clearly captured the essence of movie mob life – the ruthless and guiltless brutality alongside family values and loyalty. He understood now why the bureau had concluded that the Kenyon killing was in some way mob related. The line had the audacity and bravura of the mob life. He could see a stone-cold killer adopting it as the imprimatur of his work.

'Don't forget the cannoli,' McCaleb said out loud.

He suddenly thought of something and a little jolt of electricity went through him.

'Don't forget the cannoli,' he said again.

He quickly went to his leather bag and dug through it until he found the video from the James Cordell shooting. He went to the television and jammed the tape in and started playing it. After getting his bearings on where in the tape he was, he fast-forwarded to the moment of the shooting and hit play again. His eyes stayed on the masked man's mouth and as the man began to speak on the silent tape, McCaleb spoke with him out loud.

'Don't forget the cannoli.'

He backed the tape up and did it again, saying it again. His words matched the shooter's lips. He was sure it fit. He could feel excitement and adrenaline surging inside of him now. It was a feeling that only came when you had momentum, when you were making your own breaks. When you were getting close to the hidden truth.

He pulled the tape of the Gloria Torres murder out, put it in the player and repeated the process again. The words fit the lips of the shooter once again. There was no doubt.

'Don't forget the cannoli,' McCaleb said aloud again.

He went to the cabinet next to the chart table and got the phone out. He still had not played the messages that had accumulated over the weekend but he was too hyped to do it now. He punched in the number for Jaye Winston.

'Where have you been and don't you ever check your machine?' she asked. 'I've been trying to call you all weekend and all day to explain. It wasn't my –'

'I know. It wasn't you. It was Hitchens. I'm not calling about that anyway. I know what the bureau told you. I know what you've got – the connection to Donald Kenyon. You've got to bring me back in.'

'That's impossible. Hitchens already said I shouldn't even talk to you. How am I going to bring –'

'I can help you.'

'How? With what?'

'Just answer me this, see if I have this right. This morning Gilbert Spencer and a couple of field agents – I'm guessing they were named Nevins and Uhlig – come out and give you the news that the bullet you sent to Washington matched up with Kenyon. Right?'

'So far, but that's no great –'

'I'm not done. Next, he tells you the bureau would like to look into your case and the LAPD case but that initially there seems to be no likely connection other than the weapon. He says, after all, Kenyon is a professional hit and you guys are working two street robberies. Not only that, his shooter used a Devastator on Kenyon and your guy used something else. Federals. That backs the bureau theory that the professional shooter in the Kenyon case discarded his weapon somewhere and the shooter from your two cases then came along and picked it up. End of connection. How am I doing so far?'

'Dead on.'

'Okay, so you asked Spencer for information on the Kenyon killing just so you could do your own cross-checking but that didn't go over so well.'

'He said the Kenyon case was at a – quote – sensitive point and that he would rather us peons be on a need-to-know basis.'

'And Hitchens agreed to that?'

'He went along for the ride.'

'And did anybody serve the cannoli?'

'What?'

McCaleb spent the next five minutes explaining the cannoli connection, reading her the transcript from the bugs in Kenyon's house and the conclusions of the cryptology report. Winston said these were all facts that Gilbert Spencer had not mentioned during the morning meeting. McCaleb knew that he would not have. McCaleb had been in the bureau. He knew how it worked. Given the opportunity, you brush the locals aside and say that the bureau will handle it from here.

'So the cannoli connection makes it clear this wasn't a throw-away gun that our guy happened to pick up,' McCaleb said. 'It's the same shooter on all three. Kenyon, then Cordell, then Torres. Whether the bureau people knew that going in to your meeting, I don't know. But if you copied them the case file and the tapes, they know it now. The question is, how do these three killings fit together?'

Winston was silent for a moment before finally expressing her confusion.

'Man, I have no – well, maybe they don't connect. Look, if it's a contract killer like the bureau says, maybe they were three separate contracts. You know? Maybe there is *no* connection other than the same killer did all three on three separate jobs.'

McCaleb shook his head and said, 'It's possible, I guess, but nothing makes sense. I mean, what did Gloria Torres have that would make her a pro hitter's target? She worked in the print shop at the newspaper.'

'It could have been something she saw. Remember what you said Friday about there being some connection between the two, Torres and Cordell? Well, maybe it's still the same, only the connection is something they saw or something they knew.'

McCaleb nodded.

'What about the icons, the things taken from Cordell and Torres?' he asked, more to himself than to Winston.

'I don't know,' she said. 'Maybe it's a hitter who likes to take souvenirs. Maybe he had to prove to his employer that he had hit the right people. Is there anything in the reports about anything being taken from Kenyon?'

'Not that I have seen yet.'

His mind was a jumble of possibilities. Winston's question made him realize that in his excitement he had called her too soon. He still had a stack of unread Kenyon files. The connection he was looking for might be there.

'Terry?'

'Yeah, sorry, I was just thinking. Look, let me call you back. I've got some more stuff to go through and I might be able –'

'What stuff do you have?'

'I think I've got everything, or almost everything, that Spencer wasn't telling you.'

'I would say that that is going to buy you back into the captain's good graces.'

'Well, don't say anything to him yet. Let me figure out a little more about this and I'll call you.'

'You promise?'

'Yeah.'

'Then say it. I don't want you pulling any bureau bullshit on me.'

'Hey, I'm retired, remember? I promise.'

An hour and a half later McCaleb finished going through the bureau documents. The adrenaline that had jazzed him before had dissipated. He had learned a lot of new information as he read the reports but nothing that hinted at a connection between Kenyon and Cordell and Torres.

The rest of the bureau documents contained a lengthy printout of the names, addresses and investment histories of the two thousand victims of the savings and loan collapse. And neither Cordell nor Torres had been investors.

The bureau had had to consider every victim of the S&L collapse a suspect in the Kenyon shooting. Each name on the investors list was backgrounded and screened for criminal connections and other flags that might elevate it to viable suspect status. A dozen or so investors were raised to that level but then eventually cleared through full field investigations.

The investigation had then shifted its focus toward theory two, that Kenyon's phantom was real and had ordered the hit on the man who had stolen millions for him.

This theory gathered momentum after it was learned that Kenyon had been about to reveal whom he had turned over the stolen S&L funds to. According to a statement from Kenyon's attorney, Stanley LaGrossa, Kenyon had decided to cooperate with the authorities in hopes of getting the US Attorney's office to petition the judge who sentenced him to reduce his penalty.

LaGrossa said that on the morning Kenyon was murdered, they had planned to meet to discuss how LaGrossa would go about negotiating his cooperation.

McCaleb flipped back through the reports and reread the short transcript of the phone call Kenyon made to LaGrossa just minutes before the murder. The brief exchange between the lawyer and his client appeared to back up LaGrossa's claim that Kenyon was ready to cooperate.

The bureau theory, outlined in a supplemental report to LaGrossa's statement, was that Kenyon's silent partner either was taking no chances and eliminated Kenyon or he eliminated Kenyon after specifically learning that his partner was planning to cooperate with government investigators. The supplemental report noted that federal agents and prosecutors had not yet been approached by the Kenyon camp with the overture of cooperation. That meant that if there was a leak to the silent partner, it came from Kenyon's people, possibly even LaGrossa himself.

McCaleb got up and poured a glass of orange juice, emptying one of the half-gallon cartons he had bought on Saturday morning. As he drank, he thought about what all of the Kenyon information meant to the investigation. It clouded things for sure. Despite the early jolt of adrenaline, he now realized he was basically back to ground zero, no closer to knowing who killed Gloria Torres and why than he was when he opened the package mailed from Carruthers.

As he rinsed out the glass, he noticed two men coming down the main gangway to the docks. They were dressed in almost matching blue suits. Anybody in a suit stood out on the docks – usually, it was a bank loan officer come to chain down a boat for repossession. But McCaleb knew better this time. He recognized the demeanor. They were coming for him. Vernon Carruthers must have been found out.

Quickly, McCaleb went to the table and gathered up the bureau documents. He then split off the sheaf of pages that listed the names, addresses and other information about the savings and loan collapse. He put that thick packet in one of the overhead cabinets in the kitchen. The rest of the documents he shoved into his leather bag, which he then put into the cabinet under the chart table.

He slid the salon door open and stepped out into the cockpit to greet the two agents. He closed and locked the door behind him.

'Mr McCaleb?' the younger one said. He had a mustache, daring by bureau standards.

'Let me guess, Nevins and Uhlig.'

They didn't look happy about being identified.

'Can we come aboard?'

'Sure.'

The younger one was introduced as Nevins. Uhlig, the senior agent, did most of the talking.

'If you know who we are, then you know why we are here. We don't want this to get any messier than it has to be. Especially taking into account your service to the bureau. So if you give us the stolen files, it can all end right here.'

'Whoa,' McCaleb said, holding his hands up. 'Stolen files?'

'Mr McCaleb,' Uhlig said. 'It has come to our attention that you are in the possession of confidential FBI files. You are no longer an agent. You should not be in possession of these files. As I just said, if you want to make this a problem for you, we can make it a problem for you. But all we really want is the files back.'

McCaleb stepped over and sat on the gunwale. He was trying to think about how they knew and it came back to

Carruthers. It was the only way. Vernon must have gotten jammed up in Washington and had to give McCaleb up. But it was unlike his old friend to do that, no matter what pressure they put on him.

He decided to trust his instincts and call the bluff. Nevins and Uhlig knew Carruthers had run the ballistics laser comparison at McCaleb's request. That was no secret. They must have then assumed that Carruthers would have forwarded him copies of the computer files.

'Forget it, guys,' he finally said. 'I don't have any files, stolen or otherwise. You got bad info.'

'Then how'd you know who we were?' Nevins asked.

'Easy. I found out today when you guys went to the sheriff's office and told them to keep me out of the case.'

McCaleb folded his arms and looked past the two agents to Buddy Lockridge's boat. Buddy was sitting in the cockpit, sipping from a can of beer and watching the scene with the two suits on *The Following Sea*.

'Well, we're going to have to take a look around, then, to make sure,' Uhlig said.

'Not without a warrant and I doubt you've got a warrant.'

'We didn't need one after you gave us permission to enter and search.'

Nevins stepped over to the salon door and tried to slide it open. He found it was locked. McCaleb smiled.

'Only way you're getting in there is to break it, Nevins. And that won't look much like permission granted, if you ask me. Besides, you don't want to do that with an uninvolved witness watching.'

Both agents started looking around the marina. Finally, they spotted Lockridge, who held his beer can up as a greeting. McCaleb watched as anger turned Uhlig's jaw rigid.

'Okay, McCaleb,' the senior agent said. 'Keep the files. But I'm telling you right now, smart guy, don't get in the way. The bureau's in the process of taking over the case and the last thing we need is some tin man amateur without a badge or his own heart fucking things up for us.'

McCaleb could feel his own jaw drawing tight.

'Get the fuck off my boat.'

'Sure. We're going.'

They both climbed back up onto the dock. As they headed to the gangway, Nevins turned around and said, 'See you around, Tin Man.'

McCaleb watched them all the way through the gate.

'What was that all about?' Lockridge called over.

McCaleb waved him off while still watching the agents.

'Just some old friends come to pay a visit.'

It was nearly 8 P.M. in the east. McCaleb called Carruthers at his home. His friend said he had already been through the wringer.

'I told them, I said, "Hey, I turned over my information to Lewin. Yes, I put a push on the package at the request of former agent McCaleb, but I did not furnish a copy of the report or any other reports to him." Hey, they don't believe me, then they can shove it. I'm fully vested. They want me out, I'm out. Then they can pay me every time I have to come in to testify on one of my cases. And I got voluminous cases, if you know what I mean.'

He was speaking as if for a third party listening in. And with the bureau, you never knew if there wasn't. McCaleb followed suit.

'Same thing out here. They came around, tried to act like I had reports I don't have and I told them to get off my damn boat.'

'Yeah, you're cool.'

'So are you, Vernon. I'm gonna go. Watch the following sea, man.'

'What's that?'

'Watch your back.'
'Oh. Right. You, too.'

Winston picked up the call on a half ring.
'Where have you been?'
'Busy. Nevins and Uhlig just paid me a little visit. Did you copy them everything you copied to me last week?'
'The files, tapes, Hitchens gave them everything.'
'Yeah, well, they must've made the cannoli connection. They're coming after the case, Jaye. You're going to have to hang on.'
'What are you talking about? The bureau can't just take over a murder investigation.'
'They'll find a way. They won't take it away but they'll take charge. I think they know there's more than the gun connecting the cases. They're assholes but they're smart assholes. I think they figured out the same thing I did once they looked at the tapes you gave them. They know it's the same shooter and that there is something hooking all three of these hits together. They came by to intimidate me, to get me off it. Next it will be you.'
'If they think I'm just going to turn this whole thing over to them and –'
'It's not you. They'll go to Hitchens. And if he doesn't agree to back off, then they go farther up the ladder. I was one of them, remember? I know how it works. The higher you go, the more pressure points.'
'Damn!'
'Welcome to the club.'
'What are you going to do?'
'Me? Tomorrow I'm going back to work. I don't have to answer to the bureau or Hitchens or anybody else. Just myself on this one.'
'Well, you might be the only one with a shot at this. Good luck.'
'Thanks. I could use it.'

# 26

McCaleb didn't get to the notes and financial records he had taken from Amelia Cordell until the end of the day. Tired from all the desk work, he quickly scanned the notes and came across nothing in the widow's recollections that sparked any interest in him. From the bank statements he quickly determined that Cordell was paid every Wednesday by direct deposit. During the three months for which McCaleb had statements, Cordell had made an ATM withdrawal on every payday at the same bank branch at which he was eventually killed. The significance of this was that it confirmed that, like Gloria Torres's nightly stop at the Sherman Market, Cordell had been following a definable pattern when he had been murdered. It gave more credence to the belief that the shooter had watched his victims – in Cordell's case for a minimum of a week, but probably longer.

McCaleb was glancing through the credit card statements when he felt the boat dip and looked out to see Graciela stepping down into the stern. It was a pleasant surprise.

'Graciela,' he said as he stepped out to the stern. 'What are you doing here?'

'You didn't get my message?'

'No, I – oh, I haven't checked messages.'

'Well, I called and said I was coming down. I wrote up some things about Glory. Like you asked.'

McCaleb almost groaned. More paperwork. Instead, he

told her he appreciated her doing the work so quickly after his request.

He noticed that she carried a duffel bag slung over her arm. He took it from her.

'What's in the bag? You didn't write that much, did you?'

She looked at him and smiled.

'My stuff. I'm thinking about staying over again.'

McCaleb felt a little thrill inside, even though he knew that her staying over didn't necessarily mean they would be sleeping together.

'Where's Raymond?'

'With Mrs Otero. She'll also get him to school tomorrow. I'm taking the day off.'

'How come?'

'So I can be your driver.'

'I already have somebody to drive me. You don't have to take –'

'I know but I want to. Besides, I made an appointment for you at the *Times* with Glory's boss. And I want to go with you when you talk to him.'

'Okay, you got the job.'

She smiled and he led her into the salon.

After McCaleb took her bag down to the stateroom and poured her a glass of wine from a new bottle of red, he sat with her in the stern and began going over the case's new developments. As he told her about Kenyon, her eyes widened as she struggled to accept the idea that there was a connection somewhere between her sister and the murdered criminal.

'Nothing obvious comes to mind, right?' he asked.

'No. I have no idea how they could be ...'

She didn't finish.

McCaleb shook his head and slouched in his deck chair. She opened her purse and took out the notebook in which she had written down her sister's activities.

They went over it. Nothing she had written jumped out at McCaleb as being significant. But he told her the information could still be useful as the case continued to evolve.

'It's amazing how much everything has changed,' he said. 'A week ago this was a basic holdup. Now we have possibilities of the motivation being pathological or even being some kind of contract hit. The random possibility is now third.'

Graciela sipped her wine before speaking.

'It makes it harder, doesn't it?' she asked in a soft voice.

'No,' he said. 'It just means we're getting close. You have to open up and let all of the possibilities in. Then sift it out ... All of this just means we're getting close.'

After they watched the sunset, Graciela drove them to a small Italian restaurant in the Belmont Shores section of Long Beach. McCaleb liked the food and they had the privacy of one of the restaurant's three round booths. During dinner McCaleb had tried to change the subject, sensing that Graciela was still depressed by the turns of the investigation. He told her some lame jokes he remembered from his bureau days but they barely brought a smile.

'It must have been hard when this was your full-time job,' she said as she pushed her half-finished plate of gnocchi aside. 'I mean, just dealing with these kinds of people all the time. It must have been ...'

She didn't finish. He just nodded. He didn't think they needed to go there again.

'Do you ever think you'll get past it?'

'What, the job?'

'No, what it did to you. Like that story you told me. The Devil's Keep. The whole thing of what happened to you. Can you get past that?'

He thought for a moment. He sensed that a lot was riding on his answer. She was asking about faith and she was deciding something about him. He knew it was important that his answer be honest yet the correct one. For himself he needed to be correct.

'Graciela, all I can tell you is that I hope I can get past it. I want to be restored. To what, I'm not sure. But I've been empty for a long time and I want to be filled. In my mind, it feels too weird to talk about but it's there. I want you to know that. I don't know if it answers what you need to know about me. But I'm hoping and waiting to have what I think you have.'

He wasn't sure if he was making sense. He slid around in the booth until he was right next to her. He leaned over and kissed her high on the cheek. Shielded by the red-checked tablecloth, he put his hand on her knee and ran it softly across the top of her thigh. It was the kind of caress a lover would undertake. But he was desperate to hold on to her, not to lose her, and he lacked confidence in his words. He had to touch her in some way.

'Can we go?' she asked.

He looked at her a moment.

'Where?'

'To the boat.'

He nodded.

Back at the boat Graciela led him to the stateroom and made love to him without hesitation. As they moved in a slow rhythm, McCaleb felt his heart pounding so strong and hard in his chest that the beat seemed to echo in his temples, a throbbing sensation that urged him on. He was sure she also felt it, pulsing against her own chest, the cadence of life.

At the end, a shudder rolled through his body and he pressed his face hard into the crook of her neck. A short, clipped laugh, like a gasp, involuntarily came from his throat and he hoped she would think it was a cough or a grab for breath. He gently lowered more of his weight onto her and buried his face in the soft nest of hair behind her ear. She ran a hand down his back, then all the way up again, leaving it soft and warm on his neck.

'What's so funny?' she whispered.

'Nothing ... I'm just happy, that's all.'

He pressed his face tighter against her and whispered into her ear, his nose full of her smell, his heart and mind full of hope.

'You are the one bringing me back,' he said. 'You're my chance.'

She brought her arms up around his neck and pulled him tightly down on her. She didn't say a word.

In the dead of night McCaleb awoke. He had been dreaming of swimming underwater with no need to break the surface for air.

He was on his back, his arm against Graciela's naked back. He felt the warmth of the contact. He thought about raising himself to look over her at the clock but he didn't want to break the seam of their touch. As he closed his eyes to return to the dream, the unmistakable sound of the slider upstairs being slowly rolled open brought him awake. He realized that something – a sound – had woken him from the dream. He felt an icicle go through his chest and he became fully alert. Somebody was on the boat.

The Russian, he thought. Bolotov had found him and had come to make good on his threat. But then he quickly dismissed the possibility, returning to his instinctive belief that the Russian would not be that stupid.

He rolled to the edge of the bed and reached down to the remote phone set on the floor. He hit the speed dial combination for Buddy Lockridge's boat and waited for him to answer. He wanted Lockridge to look at *The*

*Following Sea* and tell him if he could see anyone or anything amiss. The thought of Donald Kenyon being marched to his front door and shot with a fragmenting bullet flashed through his mind. And he realized that whoever was up there probably wasn't counting on Graciela's being on the boat. He suddenly knew that no matter what happened in the next few minutes, the intruder must not and would not get to her.

After four rings Lockridge didn't answer and McCaleb knew he couldn't waste any more time. He quickly got out of bed and headed toward the stateroom's closed door, checking the red glowing numerals of the clock and seeing it was ten minutes past three.

As he quietly opened the door, he thought about his gun. It was in the bottom drawer of the chart table. The intruder was closer to it than McCaleb was and possibly had already found it.

He mentally canvased the lower deck, looking for a weapon and coming up with nothing. He had the door all the way open now.

'What is it?' Graciela whispered from behind him.

He quickly and quietly turned around and came to the bed. He put his hand over her mouth and whispered, 'Somebody's on the boat.'

He felt her body go rigid beneath his.

'They don't know about you. I want you to quietly move over the side and lie down on the floor until I come get you.'

She didn't move.

'Do it, Graciela.'

She started to move but then he held her.

'Do you have Mace or any kind of weapon in your purse?'

She shook her head no. He nodded and then pushed her to the side of the bed nearest the wall. He went back to the door.

As McCaleb came quietly up the steps, he could see the slider was half open. There was more light in the salon than below and his vision improved. Suddenly the figure of a man was silhouetted against the exterior light beyond the door. The light seemed to reflect off the figure. McCaleb could not tell if the intruder was staring at him or was turned around, looking out at the marina.

McCaleb knew that the corkscrew he had used to open Graciela's wine earlier was on the galley counter, just to the right at the top of the steps. He could easily get to it. He just had to decide if he would be using it against someone with something better.

He decided there was no choice. As he came to the top stair, he stretched out to reach the corkscrew. The stair creaked and McCaleb saw the silhouette tense. The element of surprise was gone.

'Freeze, asshole!' he yelled as he grabbed the corkscrew and moved toward the dark figure.

The intruder quickly moved to the door, going sideways out through it and using one hand to fling it down its track behind him. Grappling to get the door open, McCaleb lost a few seconds and the intruder was up on the dock and running before he was even out of the boat.

Instinctively, he knew he would not be able to catch the intruder but he leaped up onto the dock and gave full-speed chase anyway, the cool night air hardening his skin, the rough wood of the dock planks biting into his bare feet.

As he ran up the slanted gangway he heard a car engine turn over. He jerked open the gate and ran out into the lot just as a car sped through the exit, its tires squealing as they lost grip on the cold asphalt. McCaleb watched it go. It had been too far away for him to get the plate.

'Shit!'

He closed his eyes and brought his hand up and pinched the bridge of his nose. It was a self-hypnosis technique. He tried to commit as many details of what he had just seen to active memory. Red car, small, foreign, worn-out suspension ... It occurred to him that the car was familiar. But he couldn't place it yet.

McCaleb bent over and put his hands on his knees as a feeling of nausea hit him and his heart seemed to bounce up into a higher gear. He concentrated on long, deep breaths and eventually he felt the beat slow down.

He felt light hit his closed eyelids. He opened his eyes and looked into the beam of an approaching flashlight. It was the marina's security guard, pulling up in his golf cart.

'Mr McCaleb?' the voice behind the light asked. 'That you?'

It was only then that McCaleb finally realized he was naked.

Nothing was missing, nothing was disturbed. At least as far as McCaleb could tell. Nothing appeared out of order. The contents of his leather bag, which he had left on the galley table, seemed to be as he remembered them. He found the thick sheaf of documents he had shoved into the galley cabinet earlier in the day to be where he had left it. McCaleb inspected the sliding door and found scratches from a screwdriver. He knew how easy it was to pop a sliding door with a screwdriver. He also knew that the pop was always louder outside the structure than inside. He had been lucky. Somehow the pop or something else had woken him.

With the security guard, Shel Newbie, watching, McCaleb finished checking every drawer and cabinet in the salon and found nothing amiss.

'What about below?' Newbie asked.

'Not enough time,' McCaleb said. 'I heard him as soon

as he opened the door. I guess I scared him off before he did whatever he was coming to do.'

McCaleb was silent as he thought about the possibility that the intruder had not come to steal anything. He thought about Bolotov again but quickly dismissed it. The figure he had seen move sideways through the sliding door was too small to have been the Russian.

'Can I come up? I could make some coffee.'

McCaleb turned to the stairs. Graciela was there. When he had returned to the stateroom to get dressed, he had told her it would be better if she stayed below. But here she was, wearing her pink nightshirt over a pair of baggy gray sweatpants she had taken from his closet. Her hair was a bit disheveled and she couldn't have looked sexier. He stared at her silently for a moment before finally answering.

'Well, we're about to wrap it up, I think.'

'Should I call Pacific Division?' Newbie asked.

McCaleb shook his head.

'It was probably just some dock punk looking to rip off my Loran or the compass,' he said, though he didn't believe it. 'I don't want to drag the police in. We'll be up all night.'

'You sure?'

'Yeah. Thanks for helping, Shel. I appreciate it.'

'Glad to. I guess I'll go back out then. I'm going to have to write up an incident report. In the morning they might want to make an LAPD report anyway.'

'Yeah, that's fine. I just don't feel like waiting up for them to get over here. That run took it out of me. Tomorrow will be fine.'

'Okay, then.'

Newbie saluted and left. McCaleb waited a few moments and then looked at Graciela, who was still in the stairwell.

'You okay?'

'Yes. Scared is all.'

'Why don't you go back down. I'll be right down.'

She went back to the stateroom. McCaleb closed the slider and worked the lock to see if it was still operable. It was. He reached up to the overhead rod racks and took down the wooden gaff handle. He placed it in the door's track and used it as a wedge to hold the door closed. It would do for the night. But he knew he would have to rethink the boat's security.

When he was finished with the door and reasonably assured of security, McCaleb looked down at his bare feet on the salon's Berber carpet. For the first time he realized that the rug was wet. He then remembered how the marina lights had shone off the body of the intruder as he had stood near the door.

# 27

On the drive up to the *Times* plant in the Valley, McCaleb sat in the passenger seat of Graciela's Volkswagen and was mostly silent. His mind moved over the activities of the night like an anchor dragging across a sandy bottom, seeking but finding no purchase, nothing to grip.

After he had noticed the wet spot on the carpet, he had retraced the chase to the parking lot and found the dock also was wet. It was a cool, crisp night and too early for the morning moisture to have formed. The intruder had clearly been wet when he had broken into the boat. The shine of light on his body indicated he had probably been wearing a wet suit. The question McCaleb could not answer now was *why*?

Before they had left, McCaleb had gone over to Buddy Lockridge's boat to see if his neighbor was there. He found Buddy, looking disheveled as usual, sitting in the cockpit reading a book called *Hocus*. McCaleb asked him if he had spent the night on the boat and he said he had. When asked why he hadn't answered the phone, Buddy insisted that it was because it hadn't rung. McCaleb let it go, thinking either Lockridge had simply been passed out and hadn't heard his call or McCaleb had pushed the wrong speed-dial button.

He told Lockridge that he didn't need him as a driver for the day, but that he wanted to hire him as a diver.

'You want me to scrape your hull?'

'No. I want you to search the hull. And the bottom. And all the piers around the boat.'

'Search? Search for what?'

'I don't know. You'll know it when you see it.'

'Whatever you say. But I ripped my wet suit again doing that Bertram. As soon as I sew it up, I'll go over and check it out.'

'Thanks. Put it on my tab.'

'You got it. Hey, is your lady friend going to be driving you now?'

He was looking past McCaleb at Graciela standing in the stern of *The Following Sea*. McCaleb looked at her and then back at Lockridge.

'No, Buddy. Just today. She's got to introduce me to some people. That okay?'

'Sure. It's okay.'

In the car McCaleb sipped from the mug of coffee he had brought with him and looked out the window, still bothered by Lockridge not having answered his call for help. They were in the Sepulveda Pass, going over the Santa Monica Mountains. Most of the traffic on the 405 was going the other way.

'What are you thinking about?' Graciela asked.

'Last night, I guess,' he said. 'Trying to figure it out. Buddy is going to take a dive under the boat today, maybe find out what the guy was doing.'

'Well, are you sure you want to see this *Times* guy now? We could reschedule it.'

'No, we're already on our way. It can't hurt to talk to as many people as we can. We still don't know what any of this stuff from yesterday means. Until we do, we should keep plugging away.'

'Sounds good. He said we could talk to some of her friends who worked there, too.'

McCaleb nodded and reached down to the leather bag

on the floor. It had grown fat with all the documents and tapes he had accumulated. He had decided to leave nothing from the case behind on the boat, in case of another break-in. And adding to the bag's weight was his gun, a Sig-Sauer P-228. Other than at his interview with Bolotov, he hadn't carried the weapon since he had retired from the bureau. But when Graciela went into the shower, he had removed it from its drawer again and slid the clip into it. He did not chamber a round – following the same safety precaution he had always practiced while with the bureau. He then made room for the pistol in his bag by jettisoning his medical kit. His plan was to be back at the boat before it was time for him to take more pills.

He dug through the stacks of paperwork in the bag until he found his legal pad and he opened it to the timeline he had constructed from the reports in the LAPD murder book. He read the top and found what he wanted.

'Annette Stapleton,' he said.

'What about her?'

'You know her? I want to talk to her.'

'She was Glory's friend. She came over once to meet Raymond. And then she was at the funeral. How do you know about her?'

'Her name is in the LAPD stuff. She and your sister talked in the parking lot that night. I want to talk to her about other nights. You know, see if your sister was worried about anything. The LAPD never spent much time with Stapleton. Remember, they were running the random-holdup angle from the start.'

'Bozos.'

'I don't know. It's hard to blame them. They carry a lot of cases and this one looked the way it was set up to look.'

'Still no excuse.'

McCaleb let it go and turned silent. He didn't particularly feel the need to defend Arrango and Walters anyway. He returned to his thoughts on the events of the night and came to one positive conclusion: he was apparently making enough waves to engage a response from someone, though he didn't know what exactly that response had been.

They got to the *LA Times* plant ten minutes before their appointment with Glory's supervisor, a man named Clint Neff. The *Times* plant was a huge property at the corner of Winnetka and Prairie in Chatsworth in the northwest corner of Los Angeles. It was a neighborhood of slick office buildings, warehouses and upper-middle-class neighborhoods. The *Times* building looked as though it were made of smoked glass and white plastic. They stopped at a guard station and had to wait while a man in uniform called in to confirm their appointment before lifting the gate. After they parked, McCaleb took the legal pad from his bag to take in with him. The bag itself had become too cumbersome to lug around. He made sure Graciela locked the car before they left it.

Through automatic sliding doors they stepped into a two-story lobby of black marble and terra-cotta tile. Their steps echoed on the floor. It was cold and austere, and not unlike the paper's coverage of the community, some critics would say.

A white-haired man in a uniform of matching blue pants and shirt came down a hallway and greeted them. The oval patch above the pocket of his shirt said his name was Clint before he got a chance to say it. A set of professional ear protectors like those worn by ground crews at airports was around his neck. Graciela introduced herself and then McCaleb.

'Miss Rivers, all I can say is that we're all real sorry here,' Neff said. 'Your sister was a good gal. A fine worker and a good friend to us.'

'Thank you. She was.'

'If you want to come back, we can sit down for a minute and I can help you as best I can.'

He led the way back down the hall, walking in front of them and throwing conversation over his shoulder.

'Your sister probably told you, but this is where we print all the papers for the Valley edition and then most of the specials we insert in all the editions. You know, the TV magazine and whatnot.'

'Yes, I know,' Graciela said.

'You know, I don't know what good I'll be to you. I told some of the crew you might want to talk to them, too. They said it would be fine.'

They came to a set of stairs and went up.

'Is Annette Stapleton still on the night shift?' McCaleb asked.

'Uh ... actually, no,' Neff said. He was winded from the climb. 'Nettie ... got sorta spooked after what happened with Glory and I don't blame her, a thing like that. So she's on days now.'

Neff headed down another hallway toward a set of double doors.

'She's here today?'

'Sure is. You can talk to her if you – the only thing I ask is that you talk to these folks on their breaks. Like Nettie for example. She goes to the break room at ten-thirty and maybe we'll be done by then, so you can talk with her then.'

'No problem,' McCaleb said.

After a few steps in silence Neff turned around to look at McCaleb.

'So you were an FBI man, is that right?'

'Right.'

'That must've been pretty interesting.'

'Sometimes.'

'How come you quit? You look like a young man to me.'

'I guess it got a little too interesting.'

McCaleb looked at Graciela and winked. She smiled. McCaleb was saved from further personal inquiry by the noise of the pressroom. They came to the thick double doors which barely contained the roar of the presses on the other side. From a dispenser attached to the wall next to the doors, Neff pulled two plastic packages containing disposable foam earplugs and handed them to McCaleb and Graciela.

'Better put these in while we walk through. We're running the whole line right now. Printing the *Book Review*. A million-two copies. Those plugs'll knock about thirty decibels off the sound. You still can't hear yourself think, though.'

As they opened the packages and put in the plugs, Neff pulled his ear protectors up and into place. He opened one of the doors and they walked along the line of presses. The sensory impact was tactile as much as it was auditory. The floor vibrated as if they had just stepped into a minor earthquake. The earplugs did little to soften the high-pitched keening of the presses. A heavy thumping sound provided an underlying bass line. Neff led them to a door and into what was obviously the break room. There were long lunch tables and a variety of vending machines. The free spaces on the walls were taken up with corkboards cluttered with company and union announcements and safety-related warnings. The noise was greatly decreased when the door swung shut. They crossed the room and through another door entered Neff's small office. As Neff pulled his ear set down around his neck again, McCaleb and Graciela pulled their plugs.

'Better hang on to those,' Neff said. 'You go out the

way you came in. Depending on when that is, we might be rolling out there.'

McCaleb took the plastic bag out of his pocket and put the plugs in it. Neff took the seat behind his desk and signaled them to two in front of it. The vinyl padding of the seat McCaleb was assigned was smeared with ink. He hesitated before sitting.

'Don't worry,' Neff said, 'it's dry.'

For the next fifteen minutes they talked to Neff about Gloria Torres and got very little usable or salient information. It was clear that Neff liked Glory but it was also clear that his relationship was typical of most supervisor-employee interaction. It was primarily job focused and there was little personal information passed back and forth. When asked if he knew of anything that could have been troubling Glory, Neff shook his head and said he wished he knew something that would help. Any disputes with fellow employees? Same shake of the head.

Out of the blue McCaleb asked him if he knew James Cordell.

'Who's that?' Neff said.

'What about Donald Kenyon?'

'What, that savings and loan guy?' Neff smiled. 'Yeah, we were pals. At the country club. Milken and that guy, Boesky, hung out with us, too.'

McCaleb returned the smile and nodded. It was clear Neff was not going to be of much help. His mind drifted and Graciela asked Neff questions about who Glory's friends were. McCaleb thought about the ink-stained chair upon which he sat. He knew where the ink came from. Probably everyone who sat in the chair before him was someone called in off the press line. It was why they all wore the navy blue uniforms. To hide the ink.

A thought occurred to him. Glory had been on her way home from work when she was killed. But she wasn't in any uniform. She had changed. Here. But there had been nothing in the LAPD report about detectives finding work clothes in her car or checking the contents of a locker.

'Excuse me,' McCaleb said, interrupting Neff as he told Graciela about how skilled her sister was at driving a forklift that loaded huge rolls of newsprint into the presses. 'Is there a locker room? Did Glory have a locker?'

'Sure, we got a locker room. Who wants to get into their automobile covered with ink? We've got complete fa—'

'Would Glory's locker have been cleaned out yet?'

Neff sat back and thought a moment.

'You know, we got another hiring freeze here. We haven't been able to get permission to replace Glory. Since we haven't done that, I doubt we've cleaned out her locker.'

McCaleb felt a little jump. Maybe it was a break.

'Then is there a key? Can we look at it?'

'Uh, sure, I suppose so. I have to go get the master from the maintenance supervisor.'

Neff left them in his office while he went to get the master key and to find Nettie Stapleton. Since Glory's locker was obviously in the women's locker room, Neff had said before leaving that Nettie would escort Graciela in to search its contents. McCaleb would have to wait in the hallway with Neff. This did not sit well with McCaleb. It was not that he didn't think Graciela capable of searching a locker. It was just that he would look at and treat the locker in its entirety, taking in the subtleties of what he saw the way he studied crime scenes and crime scene tapes.

Soon Neff was back with Stapleton and introductions were made. She remembered Graciela and offered seemingly heartfelt condolences. Neff then led the entourage downstairs to the hallway leading to the locker rooms.

McCaleb was going to make one last offer, that if the locker room was empty, he be allowed in. But as they approached the door to the women's locker room, he could hear the sound of the showers running. He knew he was going to be left out.

McCaleb had run out of things to ask Neff and was short of small talk. While they waited, he slowly sauntered away from the man so that he could avoid idle conversation and personal questions. There were more bulletin boards affixed to the wall between the locker room doors and he acted as though he was reading some of the posted notices.

Four minutes of silence went by in the hallway. McCaleb had moved from one end of the side-by-side bulletin boards to the other. When Graciela and Nettie finally came out, he was staring at a hand-drawn rendering of a liquid drop on a poster attached to the board. The drop was half shaded in with red, indicating that the employees were halfway toward their goal in an ongoing blood drive. Graciela walked up to him.

'Nothing,' she said. 'Just some clothes, a bottle of perfume and her earphones. There were four pictures of Raymond and one of me taped to the door.'

'Earphones?'

'I mean ear protectors. But nothing else.'

'What kind of clothes?'

McCaleb was still staring at the poster as he spoke.

'A couple of fresh uniforms and a top from home and a pair of jeans.'

'You check all the pockets?'

'Yes. Nothing.'

It hit him then, with the impact of an armor-piercing bullet. He leaned forward and put his hand up against the bulletin board for support.

'Terry, what is it?' Graciela said. 'Are you okay?'

He didn't respond. His thoughts were racing. Graciela

put her hand to his forehead to feel for fever. He brushed it aside.

'No, it's not that,' he said.

'Is there a problem?' Neff chimed in.

'No,' McCaleb said, a little too loudly. 'We just have to go. I need to get to the car.'

'Is everything all right?'

'Yes,' McCaleb said, again too loudly. 'I'm sorry, but everything's fine. We just have to go.'

McCaleb nodded his thanks to Annette Stapleton and headed down the hallway toward what he believed was the entrance lobby. Graciela followed and Neff called after them, telling them to take their first left.

# 28

'What was that about? What's going on?'

McCaleb was walking quickly toward the car. He felt that maintaining velocity would somehow help keep the growing dread he was feeling from entirely overtaking his thoughts. Graciela had to trot to keep up.

'The blood.'

'The blood?'

'They both gave blood. Your sister and Cordell. It was right there in front of me all the – I saw that poster and I remembered I saw a letter at Cordell's house ... and I just knew. Do you have your keys?'

'Listen, slow down, Terry. Slow down.'

He reluctantly slowed his pace and she came up next to him, digging the car keys out of her purse.

'Now tell me what you are talking about.'

'Open the car and I'll show you.'

They reached the car. She unlocked his door first and started around to her side. He slipped in and reached across to open her door. He then leaned forward and started going through the bag on the floor. It was so jammed with paperwork, he had to pull the gun out and place it on the floor mat just so there was room to look through the documents. Graciela got in the car and started watching.

'You can start it,' he said without turning his attention from his task.

'What are you doing?'

He pulled out the Cordell autopsy.

'I'm looking for – shit, this is just the preliminary report.'

He flipped through the protocol to make sure. It was incomplete.

'No toxicology and blood.'

He shoved the autopsy report back into the bag and then the gun. He straightened up.

'We've got to find a phone. I'll call his wife.'

Graciela started the car.

'Fine,' she said. 'We will – we'll go to my house. But you have to tell me what it is you're thinking, Terry.'

'Okay, just give me a minute to think first.'

He slowed the jumble of thoughts streaming through his mind and tried to analyze the jump he had just made.

'I'm talking about the match,' he said. 'The link.'

'What link?'

'What have we been missing? What have we been looking for? The link between these cases. At first the connection was simply the randomness of crime. That's what the cops thought. That's what I thought when I first started looking at it. We had two holdup victims – no connection other than the killer and the chance crossing of his path with the paths of these individuals. This is LA, this sort of thing happens all the time. The capital of random violence, right?'

Graciela turned onto Sherman Way. They were just a couple of minutes from her home.

'Right.'

'Wrong. Because then we read more into it. We discover a killer who takes personal icons and this suggests something more involved than random collisions of shooter and victim. This suggests a deeper relationship – the targeting, stalking and acquisition of each victim.'

McCaleb stopped. They were passing the Sherman

Market and they both wordlessly looked at the store as they went by. McCaleb waited a moment longer before continuing.

'Then all of a sudden we get another wrinkle, another layer of the onion is peeled back. We get the ballistics and it's a whole new ball game. Now we have another murder and what looks like a professional running through this. A hitter. Why? What could possibly be the connection between your sister, James Cordell and Donald Kenyon?'

Graciela didn't answer. She was coming up on Alabama now and moved the car into the left-turn lane.

'Blood,' he said. 'Blood has got to be the link.'

She pulled into the driveway of her home. She turned the engine off.

'Blood,' she said.

McCaleb stared straight ahead at the closed garage door. He spoke slowly, the dread finally catching up with him.

'All this time I've been thinking, What did she see, what did she know? Whose path could she have crossed that would have gotten her killed? You see, I looked at her life and made a judgment. I decided that she didn't have anything that anyone would want to take, so the reason had to be elsewhere. But I missed it. Missed it completely. Your sister was a good mother, a good sister, good employee and friend. But the one thing she had that made her almost unique was her blood. That made what she had inside her so very valuable ... to someone.'

He waited a beat. He still didn't look at her.

'Someone like me.'

He heard her breath leaving her body and he felt as though it was the hope going out of him. His hope of redemption.

'You're saying she was ... taken for her organs. You look at a poster back there and can say that?'

He finally looked over at her.

'I just knew it. That's all.'

He opened his door.

'We call Mrs Cordell. She'll tell us her husband's blood type. It will be AB with CMV negative. Perfect match. Then we get Kenyon's blood. It, too, will match. I'd bet on it.'

He turned his body to get out.

'It doesn't make sense,' she said. 'Because you told me Mr Cordell died right there. At the bank. His heart wasn't taken. His organs. It's not the same. And Kenyon. Kenyon died at his house.'

He got out and then leaned down and looked in at her. She was looking out through the windshield now.

'Cordell and Kenyon didn't work out,' he said. 'The shooter learned from them. He finally got it right with your sister.'

McCaleb shut the door and walked toward the house. It was a while before Graciela caught up to him.

Inside, McCaleb sat down on a sectional couch in the living room and Graciela brought him the phone from the kitchen. He realized he had left Amelia Cordell's number in his bag in the car. He also realized that the car was unlocked and his gun was in the bag as well.

As he stepped back outside and approached the car, his eyes casually swept the street. He was looking for the car from the night before at the marina. He saw nothing that remotely matched and no other cars parked along the curb with occupants inside.

Back in the house again, he sat on the couch and punched Amelia Cordell's number into the phone while Graciela sat down in the far corner of the couch and watched him with a distant look on her face. The phone rang five times before a machine picked up. McCaleb left his name, number and the message that he needed

James Cordell's blood type as soon as she could get it to him. He clicked off the phone and looked at Graciela.

'Do you know if she works?' she asked.

'No, she doesn't. She could be anywhere.'

He clicked the phone back on and called his own machine to check for messages. There were nine, the machine having accumulated them unplayed since Saturday. He listened to four messages from Jaye Winston and two from Vernon Carruthers that were outdated by events. There was also Graciela's message that she would be coming to the boat Monday. Of the two remaining messages, the first was from Tony Banks, the video tech. He told McCaleb that he had completed the job on the video he had dropped off. The other message was from Jaye Winston again. She had called that morning to tell McCaleb that his prediction had come true. The bureau was increasing its involvement in the investigations of the murders. Hitchens had not only promised full cooperation but was abdicating lead status to agents Nevins and Uhlig. She was frustrated. McCaleb could easily read it in her voice. But so was he. He clicked off and blew out his breath.

'Now what?' Graciela asked.

'I don't know. I need to confirm this ... this idea before I take the next step.'

'What about the sheriff's detective? She should have the complete autopsy. She'd know the blood type.'

'No.'

He didn't say anything else by way of explanation. He looked around what he could see of the house from the couch. It was small, neatly furnished and kept. There was a large framed photo of Gloria Torres on the top shelf of a china cabinet in the adjoining dining room.

'Why don't you want to call her?' Graciela asked.

'I'm not sure. I just ... I want to figure things out a

little bit before I talk to her. I think I should wait a little while and see if I hear from Mrs Cordell.'

'What about calling the coroner's office directly?'

'No, I don't think that would work, either.'

What he was leaving unsaid was the fact that if he confirmed his theory, it would mean that anyone who benefited from Glory's death would rightly have to be considered a suspect. That included him. Therefore, he did not want to make any inquiry to authorities that might set that into motion. Not until he was ready with a few more answers with which to defend himself.

'I know!' Graciela suddenly said. 'The computer in the blood lab – I can probably confirm it there. Unless his name's been deleted. But I doubt that. I remember coming across the name of a donor who had been dead four years and he was still on there.'

What she was saying made little sense to McCaleb.

'What are you talking about?' he asked.

She looked at her watch and jumped up from her chair.

'Let me change and then we have to hurry. I'll explain everything on the way.'

She then disappeared down a hallway and McCaleb heard a bedroom door close.

# 29

They got to Holy Cross shortly before noon. Graciela parked in the front lot and they went into the hospital through the general admissions entrance. She did not want to go through the emergency room, since that was where she worked. She explained on the way over that she had been taking a lot of personal days off with little notice to be with Raymond since Gloria's death. But the patience of her supervisors was wearing thin. She didn't think it would be wise to take the day off on one day's notice and flaunt it by walking through the emergency room. Besides, what they were about to do could get her fired. The fewer people who saw her the better.

Once inside the hospital, Graciela, her nurse's uniform and her familiar face, got them where they needed to go. She was like an ambassador for whom all barriers were lifted. No one stopped them. No one questioned them. They took a staff elevator to the fourth floor, arriving a few minutes past twelve.

Graciela had told McCaleb her plan on the way over. She figured they could count on having fifteen minutes to do what they had to do. That was the maximum – just the time it would take for the blood supplies coordinator to go down to the hospital cafeteria, get her lunch and then bring it back up to the pathology lab. The BSC actually had an hour lunch break but it was routine in that job to eat lunch at your desk because there was no replacement while you were gone. The BSC was a nursing position but because the job did not involve direct patient care, no one filled in the spot when the BSC went on break.

As Graciela expected, they got to the path lab at 12:05 and found the BSC desk empty. McCaleb felt his pulse quicken a little bit as he looked at the flying toasters floating across the screen of the computer sitting on the desk. However, the desk sat in a large open lab station. About ten feet from the computer desk was another desk where a woman in a nurse's uniform sat. Graciela showed nothing but ease with the situation.

'Hey, Patrice, what's the haps?' she said cheerfully.

The woman turned from the files she was dealing with in front of her and smiled. She glanced at McCaleb but then looked back at Graciela.

'Graciela,' she said, drawing each syllable out and overdoing the Latin inflection like a television news anchor. 'Nothing's happening, girl. How 'bout you?'

'Nada. Who's the BSC and where's the BSC?'

'It's Patty Kirk for a few days. She went down to get a sandwich a couple minutes ago.'

'Hmmmm,' Graciela said as if it had just dawned on her. 'Well, I'm going to make a quick connect.'

She came around the counter and headed toward the computer.

'We've got an SCW down in emergency with rare blood. I have a feeling this guy's going to run through everything we got and I want to see what's out there.'

'You could've just called up. I would've run it for you.'

'I know but I'm showing my friend, Terry, how we do things around here. Terry, this is Patrice. Patrice, Terry. He's pre-med, UCLA. I'm seeing if I can't talk him out of it.'

Patrice looked at McCaleb and smiled again, then her eyes studied him in an appraising way. He knew what she was thinking.

'I know, it's kind of late,' he said. 'It's a midlife crisis sort of thing.'

'I should say so. Good luck during residency. I've seen twenty-five-year-olds come out of that looking like they were fifty.'

'I know. I'll be ready.'

They smiled at each other and the conversation was finally over. Patrice went back to her files and McCaleb looked at Graciela, who was seated in front of the computer. The toasters were gone and the screen was awake. There was some sort of template with white boxes on it.

'You can come around,' she said. 'Patrice won't bite you.'

Patrice laughed but didn't say anything. McCaleb came around and stood behind her chair. She looked up at him and winked, knowing that he was blocking any view Patrice had of her. He winked back and smiled. Her coolness was impressive. He looked at his watch and then held his arm down so she could see it was now seven after twelve. She turned her attention to the computer.

'Now, we're looking for type AB blood, okay. So what we do is log on here and connect with BOPRA. That's short for Blood and Organ Procurement and Request Agency. That's the big regional blood bank we deal with. Most hospitals around here do.'

'Right.'

She reached up and ran her finger beneath a small piece of paper taped to the monitor above the screen. There was a six-digit number written on it. McCaleb knew this was the access code. On the drive over Graciela had explained how little security was attached to the BOPRA system. The code to access the computer was changed monthly. But the BSC position at Holy Cross was not a full-time position, meaning that nurses assigned to it were put through on rotation. This rotation was also routinely disrupted because nurses who had colds, viruses and any other maladies that did not require them to miss work but required that they be kept away from patients were often assigned to the BSC desk. Because of the high number of people working in the slot, the BOPRA code was simply taped to the monitor each month when it was changed. In eight years as a nurse, Graciela had worked at two other hospitals in Los Angeles. She had said that this practice was the same at each of those hospitals as well. BOPRA had a security system in place that was circumvented in probably every hospital it served.

Graciela typed in the code number followed by the modem command and McCaleb heard the computer dial and then connect to the BOPRA computer.

'Connecting to the mother station,' Graciela said.

McCaleb looked at his watch. They had eight minutes at the most left. The screen went through some welcome templates before settling on an identification and request checklist. Graciela quickly typed in the needed information and continued to describe what she was doing.

'Now we go to the blood request page. We type in what we are looking for and then ... hocus pocus, we wait.'

She held her hands in front of the screen and wiggled her fingers.

'Graciela, how's Raymond doing?' Patrice asked from behind them. McCaleb turned and looked back but Patrice was still working with her back to them.

'He's good,' Graciela answered. 'It still breaks my heart but he's doing good.'

'Ah, that's good. You gotta bring him in again.'

'I will but he has school. Maybe spring break.'

The screen started printing out an inventory of the availability of type AB blood and the hospital or blood bank location of each pint. While BOPRA was a blood bank itself, it also served as a coordinating agency for smaller banks and hospitals throughout the West.

'Okay,' Graciela said. 'So now we see that there is a pretty good supply of this around. The doctor wants to have at least six units on standby in case our patient with the sucking chest wound needs more surgery. So we click on the order window and put the hold on six. A hold only lasts twenty-four hours. If it's not updated by this time tomorrow, that blood is up for grabs.'

'Okay,' McCaleb said, acting like the student he was supposed to be.

'I'll have to remember to tell Patty to update this tomorrow.'

'What if you called this up and there was no blood?'

On the drive over she had told him to ask the question if there was anyone else in the nurses' station when they connected to BOPRA.

'Good question,' she said as she began moving the computer mouse. 'This is what we do. We go to this icon with the blood droplet on it. We click and that gets us to the donors file. We wait again.'

A few seconds went by and then the screen began filling with names, addresses, phone numbers and other information.

'These are all blood donors with type AB. It shows where they are, how they can be contacted and this other information shows when they gave blood last. You don't want to keep going to the same person all the time. You try to spread it out and you try to find someone either near to us, so they can just come in here, or near to a blood bank. You want it to be convenient for them.'

As she spoke she ran her finger down the list of names. There were about twenty-five of them, from all over the West. She stopped at her sister's name and tapped the screen with her fingernail. Then she kept going. Her finger reached the bottom without coming across the names James Cordell or Donald Kenyon.

McCaleb loudly let out his breath in disappointment but Graciela raised her finger in a *one-moment* gesture. She then hit the screen up key and a new screen of names appeared. There were maybe fifteen more. The name James Cordell sat on top of the new list. She ran her finger down the screen and found Donald Kenyon's name second from the last.

This time McCaleb's breath caught and he just nodded. Graciela looked up at him, the somber look of confirmation in her eyes. McCaleb leaned close to the screen and read the information that followed the names. Cordell hadn't given blood for nine months and it had been more than six years since Kenyon had spared a drop. McCaleb noticed that the final notation after each name was the letter *D* followed by an asterisk. Other names had one or the other but only a few had the combination of both. McCaleb reached down and tapped the screen below the letter.

'What's that? Deceased?'

'No,' Graciela said in a quiet voice. 'The *D* means donor. Organ donor. They signed papers, put it on their driver's licenses, all of that, so that if the time comes that they come into a hospital and die, they can take the organs.'

She looked at him the whole time she said this and McCaleb found it hard to look back at her. He knew what the confirmation meant.

'And the asterisk?'

'I'm not sure.'

She scrolled the screen until she got back to the legend at the top. She ran her finger along the symbols until she got to the asterisk.

'It means CMV negative,' she said. 'Most people carry a non-threatening blood virus called CMV. It's short for some big word. About a quarter of the population doesn't have it. It's something that has to be known to make a complete blood work match between donors and recipients.'

He nodded. It was information he already knew.

'So that's today's lesson,' Graciela said quietly.

She moved the mouse and McCaleb saw the arrow move to the disconnect icon at the top of the screen. He reached down and grabbed her hand before she could click the mouse button and sign off the BOPRA system.

Graciela looked back up at him, the question on her face. McCaleb looked back at Patrice. He couldn't talk. He looked around and saw a clipboard on the counter with some forms on it and a pencil connected to it with a string. He signaled with his hand to Graciela, pointing to Patrice and then back to her and making a talking sign with his fingers. He then grabbed the clipboard and started to write.

'Hey, uh, Patrice, how's Charlie doing?' Graciela asked.

'Oh, he's fine. Still an asshole.'

'Boy, you guys get along so *gooood*!'

'Yeah, we're real lovebirds.'

McCaleb held the clipboard in front of Graciela. He had written three questions.

1. *Can you print out that list?*
2. *Can you call up your sister's file?*
3. *Who got her organs?*

Graciela hiked her shoulders and mouthed the words *I don't know* to him. She then turned to the computer and went to work. First she printed out the list of type AB donors. Thankfully, the computer was attached to a laser printer which did the job almost silently and Patrice paid no notice. McCaleb quickly folded the list lengthwise and put it in his inside coat pocket. Next, Graciela went back to the original welcome screen and pulled down a window of commands. She clicked the mouse on an icon that showed a red heart. A screen that said ORGAN PROCUREMENT SERVICES appeared and there was another template seeking an access code. Graciela hiked her shoulders, looked up at the code taped above the screen and typed it in again.

Nothing.

The arrow switched to an hourglass and nothing happened. McCaleb looked at his watch. It was 12:15, the end of the window of opportunity they had agreed upon. Patty Kirk would be back any moment and they would be discovered. When she had planned all of this out, Graciela hadn't said anything about how they would explain what they were doing if they were caught.

'I think the computer's freezing,' Graciela said.

Out of frustration she whacked the side of the monitor with an open hand. McCaleb always considered it amazing how many people thought this might help a computer. He was about to tell her not to bother when he heard the wheels of Patrice's chair move. He turned to see her getting up. Maybe she was going to take a shot at the computer also.

'There it goes,' Graciela said.

McCaleb kept his body between Patrice's view and the computer.

'Damned thing,' Patrice said. 'It's always doing that. I'm going to go upstairs to the porch for a Coke and a smoke. See you later, Graciela.'

She smiled at McCaleb.

'And nice to meet you,' she added.

McCaleb smiled.

'Nice to meet you,' he said.

'See you later, Patrice,' Graciela added.

Patrice walked around the counter and out into the

hallway. She never looked at the computer screen as she passed. When she was gone, McCaleb looked down at the screen. There was a flashing message across it.

LEVEL 1 ACCESS ONLY
TRY AGAIN

'What's that mean?'

'It means I don't have the code to get into that file. What time is it?'

'Time to go. Sign off.'

She clicked on the disconnect button and McCaleb heard the *chick-chick* sound of the telephone connection being broken.

'What were you doing?' Graciela asked. 'What did you want?'

'I'll tell you later. Let's get out of here.'

She got up, moved the chair back the way she had found it and they hurried around the counter. Out in the hallway they took the first right and headed back toward the elevators. They walked quickly, as if they were thieves. There was a woman coming toward them, carrying a can of Coke and a Styrofoam sandwich box. She was about eighty feet away and she was smiling at Graciela.

'Oh, shit,' McCaleb whispered. 'Is that –'

'Yes. We're cool.'

'No, stall her.'

'Why? We're fine.'

He raised his hand to rub his nose and block his words from traveling to the approaching woman.

'The screen saver. They don't usually come on for at least a minute. She'll know.'

'It doesn't matter. We're not stealing government secrets.'

As it turned out, Graciela didn't have to stall. Patty Kirk stalled herself.

'Graciela, what are you doing here?' she said as they approached. 'I just saw Jane Tompkins in the cafeteria and she was bitchin' about you not coming in again.'

They stopped and Patty Kirk stopped.

'Don't tell her I was here!' Graciela urged.

'Well, what are you doing?'

She raised her hand to signal Graciela's uniform.

'This is my friend, Terry. He's pre-med. UCLA. I told him I would show him around today 'cause he might transfer his residency here. I thought with the pinks on, it would be a lot easier to get around. Terry, this is Patty Kirk.'

They shook hands and smiled. McCaleb asked how she was doing and she said fine. He had visions of those flying toasters finally returning to her computer screen.

Patty Kirk looked back at Graciela and shook her head.

'Janie's going to kill you if she finds out. She thought it was something with Raymond again. You owe me big time for this, girl.'

'I know, I know. Just don't tell her, okay? Everybody is mad at me down there. She's the only friend I've got left.'

They said their good-byes and McCaleb and Graciela moved on to the elevator. When Patty Kirk was out of earshot, Graciela asked if the stall was long enough.

'Depends on what the screensaver is set on. But it's probably okay. Let's get out of here.'

Back in the Rabbit, Graciela drove out of the hospital lot and headed to the 405 freeway to go south.

'Where to now?' she asked.

'I'm not sure. We have to get into BOPRA somehow. We need the list of recipients. But I doubt we could just drive up and they'd give them to us. Where is BOPRA anyway?'

'West LA, near the airport. But you are right, you're not going to just go in there and be given a list. The whole system is built on confidentiality. I only found you because somebody told me about that newspaper story.'

'Right,' he said.

He was already past that. His mind was racing and it finally snagged on an idea. They were coming up to the freeway entrance.

'Let's go over the hill. To Cedars. I think I know somebody who will help us.'

# 30

They first went to Bonnie Fox's office in the Cedars west tower. The waiting room was empty and Fox's receptionist, a woman named Gladys who never smiled, confirmed that the doctor was not in.

'She's up in north and I don't expect her back here today,' Gladys said, maintaining her frown. 'Are you here for your records?'

'No, not quite yet.'

McCaleb thanked her and they left. He knew the translation of what Gladys had told them was that Fox was making her rounds on the sixth floor of the north tower, the hospital. They took the third-floor bridge across to north and then the elevator up to the sixth-floor cardiology and transplant ward. McCaleb was growing tired of lugging the heavy leather bag with him.

McCaleb had been on six often enough not to seem out of place. Graciela, still in her nursing uniform, fit in even better. McCaleb led the way down the hall to the left of the elevators to where the transplant waiting and recovery rooms were located as well as the transplant nursing station. There was a good chance he would find Fox somewhere in the area.

As they made their way down the long hallway, McCaleb looked through the doors that were open. He didn't see Fox but he saw the frail forms of mostly older men on beds. These were the rooms for those who waited, hooked to machines, their time getting close and their chances dimming like the quieting of their hearts. As they passed one room, McCaleb saw the young boy he had seen before. The boy was sitting up on a bed, watching television. He appeared to be alone in the room. The wires and tubes snaked out of the sleeve of his hospital gown and ran to the machines and monitors. After he discerned that Fox was not in the room, McCaleb quickly looked away. The young ones were the hardest to take, to even acknowledge. Their organs so new yet inexplicably failing them, a terrible and sometimes fatal life lesson learned for nothing that they had done. For a moment, McCaleb's mind flashed on the Everglades, the gathering of investigators on airboats at Devil's Keep, the black hole into which disappeared his belief that there is a good and valid reason for everything.

They were in luck. As they made the turn to the nurses' station, McCaleb saw Bonnie Fox leaning over the counter and sliding a patient file out of a vertical rack. As she straightened up, she turned and saw them.

'Terry?'

'Hey, Doc.'

'What's wrong? Are you –'

'No, no, everything's fine.'

He held his hands up in a calming gesture.

'Then what are you doing up here? Your records are at my office.'

She seemed to notice Graciela then and clearly didn't recognize her. This added to the confusion already growing on her face.

'I'm not here about the records,' McCaleb said. 'Is there a room – an empty room – that we can use for a few minutes? We need to talk to you.'

'Terry, I'm in the middle of checking on my patients here. It's not right for you to come in here and expect me to –'

'It's important, Doctor. Very important. Give me five minutes and I'm sure you'll agree. If you don't, we're out of here. I'll go pick up my records and be gone.'

She shook her head in annoyance and turned to look at one of the nurses behind the counter.

'Anne, what do we have open?'

One of the nurses leaned to her left and ran her finger down a clipboard.

'Ten, eighteen, thirty-six, take your pick.'

'I'll be in eighteen, since it's close to Mr Koslow. If he rings, tell him I will be in there in five minutes.'

She looked sternly at McCaleb as she said the last two words.

Walking quickly, Fox led them back down the hallway and into room 618. McCaleb entered last and closed the door behind them. He put the heavy bag down on the floor. Fox leaned her hips against the empty bed, put the patient file down next to her and folded her arms. McCaleb could feel the anger coming from her and directed squarely at him.

'You have five minutes. Who is this?'

'This is Graciela Rivers,' McCaleb said. 'I told you about her.'

Fox studied Graciela with unsparing eyes.

'You're the one who started him on this,' she said. 'You know, he won't listen to me but you're a nurse, you should know better. Look at him. His color, the lines under his eyes. A week ago he was fine. He was perfect, goddammit! I'd already taken his file off my desk and put it away. That's how sure I was about him. Now –'

She gestured toward McCaleb's appearance as proof of her point.

'I only did what I felt I had to do,' Graciela said. 'I had to ask –'

'It's been my choice,' McCaleb interrupted. 'Everything. My choice.'

Fox dismissed their explanations with an annoyed shake of her head. She stepped away from the bed and signaled to McCaleb to sit down.

'Take off your shirt and sit down. Start talking. You're down to about four minutes now.'

'I'm not taking off my shirt, Doctor. I want you to listen to what I have to say, not how many times my heart is beating.'

'Fine. Talk. You want to take me away from patients I need to see, fine. Talk.'

She rapped her knuckles on the patient file on the bed.

'Mr Koslow here, he's in the same boat you were in a couple months ago. I'm trying to keep him alive until *maybe* a heart comes along. Then I've got a thirteen-year-old boy who –'

'Are you going to let me tell you why we're here or not?'

'I can't help it. I am so *angry* at you.'

'Well, listen to this and maybe it will change how you feel.'

'I think that's impossible.'

'Can I tell it or not?'

Fox held her hands up in surrender, pursed her lips and bowed to him. Finally, McCaleb began the story. He took ten minutes to summarize the story of his investigation but that was all right. By the five-minute mark, Fox was so transfixed that she wasn't noticing the time. She let him tell it without a single interruption.

'That's it,' he said when he was done. 'That's why we are here.'

Fox's eyes moved back and forth between them for a few moments while she tried to comprehend what McCaleb had just told her. She then began to move about the small space of the room as she recounted her understanding of the story. She wasn't pacing. It was more as though she needed to make room for the story in her mind and was manifesting that need in small movements back and forth that expanded the personal space around her.

'You are saying that you start off with a person who needs an organ – heart, lung, liver, kidney, whatever. But like you, they are of the rare blood group that is type AB with CMV negative. What that translates to is a long, long, possibly unsuccessful wait because only maybe one in two hundred people are in that group, meaning that likewise, only one in two hundred, let's say, livers, that come along would match this person. So have I got this right? You are saying this person decided to improve his odds by going out and shooting people who are in his group because then their organs would become available for transplant?'

She said it with too much sarcasm and that annoyed McCaleb but rather than object, he just nodded.

'And that he got the names of these people in his group from a list of blood donors in the BOPRA computer?'

'Right.'

'But you don't know how he got it.'

'We don't know for sure. But we do know that BOPRA's security system is highly vulnerable to compromise.'

From his pocket McCaleb took out the list that Graciela had printed at Holy Cross. He unfolded it and handed it to Fox.

'I was able to get that today and I don't know the first thing about hacking into computers.'

Fox took the page and waved it at Graciela.

'But you had her to help.'

'We don't know who this person is or who they had to help them. We have to assume that if this person has the connections and ability to hire a contract killer, then he or she could get into the BOPRA computer. The point is, it could be done.'

McCaleb pointed to the list.

'Right there is all that's needed. Everybody on that list is in the group. He would pick one of the donors. He would pick somebody young, do some research. Kenyon was young and fit. A tennis player, equestrian. Cordell was young and strong. Anybody who watched him over some time would know he was fit. A surfer, skier; mountain biker. They both were perfect.'

'Then why kill them – as some sort of practice?' Fox asked.

'No, not practice. It was the real thing but each time things went wrong. With Kenyon the shooter used a fragmenting bullet that pulped his brain and he was dead before they could even get him to the hospital. The killer refined his method. He switched to a full metal jacket load that was fired across the front of the brain. A fatal injury, yes, but not instantaneous. A man who drove up called it in on a cellular phone. Cordell was alive. But the address got screwed up and the paramedics went to the wrong place. Meantime, time goes by, the victim dies at the scene.'

'And again the organs were never harvested,' Fox said, understanding now.

'I hate that word,' Graciela said, her first words in a long time.

'What?' Fox asked.

'Harvested. I hate that. These organs aren't harvested. They're given. By people who cared about other people. They aren't crops on a farm.'

Fox nodded and looked silently at Graciela, seemingly taking her measure all over again.

'It didn't work with Cordell but it was not because of the method,' McCaleb continued. 'So the shooter just went back to his list of potential donors. He –'

'The list from the BOPRA computer.'

'Right. He goes back to the list and picks Gloria Torres. The process starts again. He watches, knows her routine, also knows she is healthy and will do.'

McCaleb looked at Graciela as he said this, afraid the harshness of it would bring another response. She remained quiet. Fox spoke.

'And so now you want to follow this trail of harvested organs and you think the killer – or the person who hired the killer – will have one of them. Do you realize what this sounds like?'

'I know how it sounds,' McCaleb said quickly before she could build on her doubts. 'But there is no other explanation. We need your help with BOPRA.'

'I don't know.'

'Think about it. What are the odds that it could be just a coincidence that the same man – a contract killer, most likely – just happens to gun down three different people from the exact same one-in-two-hundred blood group? You couldn't figure those odds with a computer. Because it can't be coincidence. It's the blood work. The blood work is the connection. The blood work is the motive.'

Fox walked away from them and to the window. McCaleb followed and stood next to her. The room looked down on Beverly Boulevard. He saw the string of businesses across the street, the mystery bookshop and the deli with the Get Well Soon! sign on the roof. He looked at Fox and it looked as though she was staring at her own reflection in the window.

'I have patients waiting,' she said.

'We need your help.'

'What exactly can I do?'

'I'm not sure. But I think you stand a better chance of getting information out of BOPRA than us.'

'Why don't you just go to the police? They have the best chance. Why are you involving me?'

'I can't go to them. Not yet. I go to them and I'm out of it, off the case. Think about what I just told you. I'm a suspect.'

'That's crazy.'

'I know that. But they won't. Besides, that doesn't matter. This is personal. I owe it to Glory Torres and I owe it to Graciela. I'm not going to sit on the sidelines on this one.'

A small bit of silence slipped by.

'Doctor?'

Graciela had come up behind them. They turned to her.

'You have to help. If you don't, then all of this – everything you do here – means nothing. If you can't protect the integrity of the system you work in, then you have no system.'

The two women stared at each other for a long moment and then Fox smiled sadly and nodded.

'Go to my office and wait for me,' she said. 'I have to see Mr Koslow and one other patient. It will take me a half hour at the most. After that I'll come to the office and make the call.'

# 31

'The coordinator's office.'

'Glenn Leopold, please, this is Bonnie Fox calling.'

They were in Fox's office with the door closed. Fox had the phone speaker on so McCaleb and Graciela could listen. They had waited for her a half hour before she had come in. Her demeanor was different. She was still going to help but McCaleb noticed that she was more agitated than she had appeared when they had gathered in the empty patient room in the north tower. They had gone over a plan McCaleb came up with while waiting, Fox had taken a couple of notes to refer to and then placed the call.

'Bonnie?'

'Hi, Glenn, how are you?'

'I'm fine. What can I do you for? I've got about ten minutes before a meeting.'

'This shouldn't take long. I've got a slight problem here, Glenn, and I think you might be able to help me.'

'Tell me.'

'I performed a transplant here February ninth – it was BOPRA file number ninety-eight thirty-six – and a complication has come up. What I'd like to do is speak with the surgeons who performed transplants with the donor's other organs.'

There was a brief silence before Leopold's voice came up on the speaker again.

'Uh, let's see ... I mean, this is kind of unusual. What sort of complication are we talking about, Bonnie?'

'Well, I know you have your meeting. To make it as brief as possible, the recipient's blood group was type AB with CMV negative. The organ we received through BOPRA matched that – according to the protocol. But now – what are we, nine weeks or so post-op – our recipient has developed CMV virus and we are showing rejection in the blood work from the latest biopsy. I am trying to isolate how this has happened.'

More silence.

'Well, I think it would have come up before now if it came in with the heart.'

'That's true but we weren't looking for it before. We assumed based on the protocol that there was no CMV. Don't get me wrong, Glenn, I am not saying it came in with the heart. But I have to find out where it came from and I want to cover everything. Best place to start is with the heart.'

'Are you trying to isolate this, as you say, at the request of attorneys? Because if that's what you are doing, then I think I need to get my –'

'No, no, Glenn, this is just me. I need to know if the virus came in with the organ or there was – is – a problem right here.'

'Well, what blood did you use?'

'That's just it, we only used the patient's own blood. I have the file right here. He stored eight units long before surgery. We only used six.'

'And you are sure you used *his* six?'

Leopold's voice was now showing some agitation. Fox was looking at McCaleb as she answered and he saw how uncomfortable it was for her to be deceitful with the BOPRA organ coordinator.

'All I can say is that we followed procedures and I

personally double-checked the bag labels before surgery. They were his labels. I have to assume it was his blood.'

'What do you want from us, Bonnie?'

'A list. What organ went to what patient, and the attending surgeon I can call.'

'I don't know. I think maybe I should –'

'Glenn, listen, it is nothing personal, but my patient is having this problem and I need to check this out for myself. I have to be satisfied myself. I will keep it contained, if that's what you are worried about. No one is talking about lawyers or malpractice. We just need to find out how this happened. For all we know, you are right, it's a blood mix-up. But I am sure you would agree that the place to start with something like this is with the new tissue that's been introduced to the patient.'

McCaleb held his breath. They were at the pivotal point. Fox needed to get the names herself. She couldn't let Leopold say he would check it out himself and get back to her.

'I suppose ...'

Leopold trailed off and Fox leaned forward, folded her arms on the desk and put her head down. In the silence McCaleb heard a sound from the phone that he identified as computer keys being tapped. He felt a slight charge as he realized that Leopold was probably calling up the file on his computer.

McCaleb stood up and leaned over the desk and gently tapped Fox on the elbow. She looked up at him and he made a circular motion with his hand, signaling her to keep going.

'Glenn?' she said. 'What do you think?'

'I'm looking at it right now ... Harvest occurred at Holy Cross ... There is nothing here on the donor profile indicating CMV. Nothing. This person was a long-time blood donor. I think it would have come up before if she –'

'That's probably true but I need to double-check. Even if just for my own peace of mind.'

'I understand.'

More sounds of the computer keyboard being played.

'Let's see, transportation was ... by MedicAir ... The liver was transplanted right there with the heart at Cedars. Do you know Dr Spivak? Daniel Spivak?'

'No.'

McCaleb grabbed a legal pad from his bag and started writing.

'Well, he did that one. Let's see, the lungs –'

'I'll call Spivak,' Fox interrupted. 'What's the patient's name?'

'Um ... really going to have to ask you to keep all of this in the strictest confidence, Bonnie.'

'Absolutely.'

'It was J. B. Dickey.'

McCaleb wrote it down.

'Okay,' Fox said. 'You were on to the lungs.'

'Uh, yes, lungs. No takers without the heart. Your patient got the heart.'

'Right. What about bone marrow transfer?'

'You want everything, I guess. The marrow ... uh, the marrow we did not do well with. We missed the window. The tissue was flown to San Francisco but by the time MedicAir got up there, they had a weather delay. They were redirected to San Jose but with the delay and the ground traffic and everything, it took too long getting up to St Joseph's. We missed the chance. From what I understand, the patient later expired. As you know, this blood group is tough. That was probably our one chance on that one.'

That brought another measure of silence. McCaleb looked at Graciela. Her eyes were downcast and he couldn't read her. For the first time he considered what she was going through. They were talking about her sister and the people she had helped save. But it was all said in such a clinical manner. Graciela was a nurse and was used to such discussions about patients. But not her sister.

McCaleb wrote 'bone marrow' on the page and then drew a line through the words. He then made the *keep-it-rolling* hand motion to Fox again.

'What about kidneys?' she asked.

'The kidneys ... The kidneys were split. Let's see what we've got on the kidneys ...'

Over the next four minutes Leopold went down the list of items mined from the body of Gloria Torres and redistributed to living patients. McCaleb wrote it all down, now keeping his eyes on the legal pad and not wanting to look at Graciela again to see how she was handling having to listen to such a grim inventory.

'That's it,' Leopold finally said.

McCaleb, energized by getting the names but exhausted by the cliff walk it took in getting them, blew his breath out loudly. Too loudly.

'Bonnie?' Leopold said quietly. 'Are you alone? You didn't tell me you were with –'

'No, it's just me, Glenn. I'm alone.'

Silence. Fox threw an angry look at McCaleb, then closed her eyes tightly and waited.

'Well, okay,' Leopold finally said. 'I thought I heard someone else there, that's all, and I have to reiterate that this information is highly confidential in –'

'I know that, Glenn.'

'– nature. I've broken my own rules by giving it to you.'

'I understand.' Fox opened her eyes. 'I will make my inquiries discreetly, Glenn, and ... I'll let you know what I find.'

'Perfect.'

After a few more exchanges of small talk, the call was

ended. Fox pushed the phone's disconnect button and brought her head back down on her folded arms.

'God ... I can't believe what I just did. I ... lied to this man. *Lied* to a colleague. When he finds out, he's ...'

She didn't finish. She just shook her head on the cradle of her arms.

'Doctor,' McCaleb tried. 'You did the right thing. There is no harm to him and he'll probably never know what was done with the information. Tomorrow you can call him and say you isolated the CMV problem and it wasn't from the donor. Tell him you destroyed the notes on the other recipients.'

Fox brought her head up and looked at him.

'It doesn't matter. I was deceitful. I hate having to be deceitful. If he finds out, he'll never trust me again.'

McCaleb just looked at her. He had no answer to that.

'You have to promise me one thing,' Fox said. 'That if your theory proves out, that if you are right, then you get whoever did this. That will be the only way I'll be able to accept this. It will be my only defense.'

McCaleb nodded. He came around the desk and leaned down and hugged Fox.

'Thank you,' Graciela said softly. 'You did good.'

Fox smiled weakly at her and nodded.

'One last thing,' McCaleb said. 'Do you have a copying machine?'

# 32

The elevator down was packed and silent except for the music piped in, which McCaleb identified as an old Louis Jourdan recording of 'Knock Me a Kiss'.

As they stepped out, McCaleb pointed Graciela in the direction of the doors leading to the tramway that would take her to the parking garage.

'You go that way.'

'Why? Where are you going?'

'I'm just going to take a cab back to the boat.'

'Well, what are you going to do? I want to go with you.'

He pulled her to the side of the busy elevator lobby.

'You've got to go back home to Raymond and your job. In fact, Raymond, he's your job. This is my job. This is what you asked me to do.'

'I know but I want to help.'

'You did help. You are helping. But you've got to go to Raymond. I'm going out through the emergency room. There are always cabs down there.'

She frowned. He could tell by her expression that she knew he was right but it didn't sit well. He reached into his pocket and pulled out the photocopy of the list he had made in Fox's office.

'Here, take this. If something happens to me, you have a copy. Give it to Jaye Winston at the sheriff's office.'

'What do you mean if something happens?'

Her voice was almost shrill and McCaleb immediately

regretted his choice of words. He moved her into a little alcove where there were pay phones. No one was using the phones and they had a small measure of privacy. He put the bag on the floor between his feet and leaned forward so his eyes were close to hers.

'Don't worry, nothing is going to happen,' he said. 'It's just that all this work I've done, ever since you came to the boat that day, it all has led to this. The names on this paper. I just think it's better if we both have a copy of it, that's all.'

'Do you really think the killer's name is on there?'

'I don't know. That's what I'm going to think about and work on when I get to the boat.'

'I can help you.'

'I know you can, Graciela. You already have. But right now you have to pull back a little bit and be with Raymond. You don't have to worry. I am going to be on the phone telling you everything that happens. Remember, I'm working for you.'

She tried a half smile.

'No, you're not. All I had to do was tell you about Glory and after that you were doing what your heart told you.'

'Maybe.'

'How about if I take you and just drop you off at the boat?'

'No way. That will take you into rush hour and you'll be driving for two hours. Go now, while you can. Go be with Raymond.'

She finally nodded. Still leaning down into her face, McCaleb brought his hands up to her shoulders and gently pulled her into a kiss.

'Graciela?'

'What?'

'There's something else, too.'

'What is it?'

'I want you to think about this, think about if I'm right. I have to think about this.'

'What do you mean?'

'If I'm right, if somebody killed Glory for something she had inside, then in a way they killed her for me as well. I got a part of her, too. If that's true, then can we ...'

He didn't finish the question and she didn't say anything for a long moment. Her eyes dropped their focus to his chest.

'I know that,' she finally said. 'But you didn't do anything. You didn't cause this.'

'Well, I want you to think about it and just be sure.'

She nodded.

'It's God's way of making something good out of something so bad.'

McCaleb leaned his forehead against hers. He didn't say anything.

'I know what you told me and I know that story about Aubrey-Lynn. It's all the more reason to believe. I wish you would try.'

He pulled her into an embrace and whispered into her ear.

'Okay, I'll try.'

A man with a thick briefcase stepped into the alcove and went to one of the phones. He glanced at them and did a double take when he saw Graciela's nursing uniform. He obviously believed it was a Cedars nurse engaging in some form of unprofessional conduct. It ended the moment for McCaleb. He broke the embrace and looked into Graciela's face.

'You be careful and say hello to Raymond for me. Tell him I want to go fishing again.'

She smiled and nodded.

'You be careful, too. And call me.'

'I will.'

She leaned forward and kissed him quickly and then

headed off in the direction of the parking garage. McCaleb glanced at the man on the phone and then walked away in the opposite direction.

# 33

There were no taxi cabs waiting at the curb outside the emergency room. McCaleb decided to change his plan. He hadn't eaten anything since breakfast and was growing weak with hunger. He felt a low-grade migraine beginning to throb at the base of his skull and knew if he didn't refuel, it would soon crawl over the top of him and encase his whole head. He decided to call Buddy Lockridge to come get him, then have a turkey and coleslaw sandwich from across the street at Jerry's Deli while he waited. The more he thought about the good sandwiches they made over there, the hungrier he got. Once Buddy arrived, they could drive over to Video GraFX Consultants in Hollywood to pick up the tape and the hard copy of the frame Tony Banks had enhanced for him.

He quickly stepped back into the ER lobby and over to the pay phone alcove. There was a young woman on one of the phones tearfully telling someone about somebody else who was apparently being treated in the ER. McCaleb noticed that one nostril and her lower lip were pierced with silver hoops connected by a chain of safety pins.

'He didn't know me, he didn't know Danny,' she wailed. 'He's totally fucked up and they're also calling the cops.'

Momentarily distracted by the safety pins and wondering what would happen if the woman yawned, McCaleb picked up the phone furthest from her and tried to tune her out. He was about to give up on Lockridge after six rings – on a boat like the *Double-Down*, you can't be more than four rings away – when Buddy finally picked up.

'Yo, Buddy, ready to go to work?'

'Terry?'

Before McCaleb could answer, Lockridge's voice dropped to a whisper.

'Man, where are you at?'

'Cedars. I need you to pick me up. What's the matter?'

'Well, I'll pick you up but I'm not sure you want to come back here.'

'Buddy, listen to me. Skip the bullshit and tell me exactly *what* is going on.'

'I'm not sure, man, but you've got people all over your boat.'

'What people?'

'Well, two of them are those two guys in the suits who were here yesterday.'

Nevins and Uhlig.

'They are *inside* my boat?'

'Yeah, inside. Also, they pulled the cover off your Cherokee and have a tow truck out there. I think they're going to take it. I went over there to see what was going on and they almost put me down on the boards. Showed me their badges and a search warrant and told me to get lost. They weren't nice about it. They're searching the boat.'

'Shit!'

McCaleb looked over and saw that his outburst had drawn the attention of the crying woman. He turned his back toward her.

'Buddy, where are you, up top or below?'

'Below.'

'Can you see my boat right now?'

'Sure. I'm looking out the galley window.'

'How many people you see?'

'Well, some are inside. But altogether I think there are four or five of them over there. And there's a couple more with the Cherokee.'

'Is there a woman?'

'Yeah.'

McCaleb described Jaye Winston as best as he could and Lockridge confirmed that a woman matching the description was on the boat.

'She's in the salon right now. It looked like before when I was looking at her that she was just sort of watching.'

McCaleb nodded. His mind was running over the possibilities of what was happening. Each way he looked at it, things added up the same way. The fact that Nevins and Uhlig knew he had FBI documents would not have engendered such a response – a warrant search with a full team. There was only one other possibility. He had become an official suspect. Accepting this, he thought about how Nevins and Uhlig would conduct an evidentiary search.

'Buddy,' he said, 'have you seen them taking anything off the boat? I'm talking about in plastic bags or brown paper bags, like from Lucky's.'

'Yeah, there's been some bags. They put them up on the dock. But you don't have to worry, Terror.'

'What do you mean?'

'I don't think they're going to find what they're really looking for.'

'What are you –'

'Not on the phone, man. You want me to come get you now?'

McCaleb stopped. What was he saying? What was going on?

'Hang tight,' he finally said. 'I'll call you right back.'

McCaleb hung up and immediately dropped in another

quarter. He called his own phone number. No one answered. The machine answered and he heard his own tape-recorded voice telling him to leave a message. After the beep he said, 'Jaye Winston, if you're there, pick up.'

He waited for a beat of silence and was about to say it again when the phone was picked up. He felt a slight sense of relief when he recognized Winston's voice.

'This is Winston.'

'This is McCaleb.'

That was all. He figured he would see how she wanted to play it. He would be better able to judge where he stood by the way she handled the call.

'Uh ... Terry,' she said. 'How did you – where are you?'

Whatever relief he was feeling now started to slip away. Its replacement was dread. He had given her the opportunity to talk to him obliquely, perhaps in code, acting as though she was talking to a fellow deputy or even Captain Hitchens. But she had used his name.

'Doesn't matter where I am,' he said. 'What are you doing on my boat?'

'Why don't you come here and we'll talk about it?'

'No, I want to talk about it now. I'm a suspect? That's what this is about?'

'Look, Terry, don't make this more complicated than it has to be. Why don't you –'

'Is there an arrest warrant? Just answer me that.'

'No, Terry, there isn't.'

'But I am a suspect.'

'Terry, why didn't you tell me you have a black Cherokee?'

McCaleb was stunned as he suddenly realized how things fit together with him in the middle.

'You never asked. Listen to what you are saying, what you are thinking. Would I get involved in all of this, the investigation, bring the bureau in, all of it, if I was the shooter? Are you serious?'

'You got to our only witness.'

'What?'

'You got to Noone. You got inside the investigation and got to the only witness. You hypnotized him, Terry. Now he's no good to us. The one person who might have been able to make the ID and we lost him. He –'

She stopped as there was a click as another phone was picked up.

'McCaleb? This is Nevins. What's your location?'

'Nevins, I'm not talking to you. You've got your head up your ass. I'm only –'

'Listen to me, I'm trying to be civil. We can do this easy and quiet or we can go big time. You decide, my friend. You have to come in and we'll talk about it and let the chips fall.'

McCaleb's mind quickly went over the facts. Nevins and the others had come to the same conclusion that he had come to. They had made the blood work connection. The fact that McCaleb was a direct beneficiary of the Torres killing made him a suspect. He imagined them running his name on the computer and coming up with the registration of the Cherokee. It was probably the piece that sent them over the top. They got a search warrant and went to the boat.

McCaleb felt the cold hand of fear clasp his neck. The intruder from the night before. It began to dawn on him that it wasn't a question of what he had wanted. It was *what had he planted*. He thought about what Buddy had said moments before about the agents not finding what they were looking for. And the picture was taking form.

'Nevins, I'll come in. But you tell me first, what have you got there? What have you found?'

'No, Terry, we don't play it like that. You come in and then we talk about all of this.'

'I'm hanging up, Nevins. Last chance.'

'Don't go in any post offices, McCaleb. Your picture's

going to be on the wall. As soon as we get the package together.'

McCaleb hung up, held his hand on the phone and leaned his forehead against it. He wasn't sure what was going on or what to do. What had they found? What had the intruder hidden in the boat?

'You okay?'

He jerked around and it was the girl with the pierced nose and lip.

'Fine. You?'

'I am now. I just had to talk to somebody.'

'I know the feeling.'

She left the phone alcove then and McCaleb picked up the receiver again and dropped another quarter. Buddy picked up on half a ring.

'All right, listen,' McCaleb said. 'I want you to come get me. But you're not going to be able to just walk out of there.'

'How come? It's a free –'

'Because I just talked to them and they know someone tipped me that they were there. So this is what I want you to do. Take off your shoes and put your keys and wallet inside them. Then get your laundry basket and stick your shoes in it and cover them up with clothes. Then carry the basket out of there and make –'

'I don't have any laundry in the basket, Terry. I did laundry this morning, before any of these people showed up.'

'Fine, Buddy. Take some clothes – clean clothes – and put them in the basket so it looks like you've got dirty clothes. Hide your shoes. Make it look like you are only going over to the laundry. Don't close the hatch on your boat and make sure you are carrying four quarters in your hand. They'll stop you but if you play it right, they'll believe you and let you go. Then get in your car and come get me.'

'They might follow me.'

'No. They probably won't even watch you once they let you go to the laundry. Maybe you should go to the laundry first, then to your car.'

'Okay. So where do I find you?'

McCaleb didn't hesitate. He had grown to trust Lockridge. Besides, he knew he could take precautions at his end.

After hanging up, McCaleb called Tony Banks and told him that he would be coming by. Banks said he would be there.

McCaleb walked into Jerry's Famous Deli and ordered a turkey sandwich with coleslaw and Russian dressing to go. He also ordered a sliced pickle and a can of Coke. After he paid for the sandwich, he took it out and crossed Beverly Boulevard back to Cedars. He had spent so many days and nights in the medical center he knew its layout by rote. He took the elevator to the third floor maternity ward, where he knew of a waiting room that looked out across the helipad to Beverly Boulevard and Jerry's. It was not unusual to see an expectant father wolfing down a deli sandwich in the waiting room. McCaleb knew he could sit up there and eat and wait and watch for Buddy Lockridge.

The sandwich lasted less than five minutes but the wait for Buddy Lockridge went on for an hour with no sighting of Lockridge. McCaleb watched two helicopters come in with deliveries of transplant organs packed in red coolers.

He was about to call the *Double-Down* to see if the agents had held Lockridge up when he finally saw Buddy's familiar Taurus pull up to the front of the deli. McCaleb walked to the window and looked long and far up and down Beverly Boulevard, then checked the sky for anything that looked like a law enforcement helicopter. He left the window and headed to the elevator.

A plastic laundry basket full of clothes was on the back seat of the Taurus. McCaleb got in, looked at it and then over at Lockridge, who was playing some unrecognizable tune on his harp.

'Thanks for coming, Buddy. Any problems?'

Lockridge dropped the harmonica into the door pocket.

'Nah. They stopped me like you said they would and asked their questions. But I played dumb; they let me go. I think it was 'cause I only had the four quarters on me that they let me go. That was a smart move, Terry.'

'We'll see. Who was it who stopped you? The two suits?'

'No, it was two other guys and they were cops, not agents. At least they said so, but they didn't give me their names.'

'Was one a big wide guy, Latino, with maybe a toothpick in his mouth.'

'You got it. That's him.'

Arrango. McCaleb found a little bit of satisfaction in putting one past the pompous jerk.

'So where to?' Buddy asked.

McCaleb had thought about this while he waited. And he knew he had to get to work on the list of transplant recipients. He had to get on it quickly. But before he did that, he wanted to make sure he had all his ducks in a row. He had come to look at investigations as being similar to the extension ladders on fire trucks. You kept extending the reach further, and the further out you went, the more wobbly it was out on the end. You could not neglect the base, the start of the investigation. Every loose detail that could be nailed down had to be put in its exact place. And so, he felt now, he had to finish the timeline. He had to answer the questions that he himself had raised before going on to the end of the ladder. It was his philosophy as well as instinct that told him to do this. He was playing out a hunch that within the contradictions he would find a truth.

'Hollywood,' he told Lockridge.

'That video place we went before?'

'You got it. We go to Hollywood first, then up to the Valley.'

Lockridge headed a few short blocks up to Melrose Boulevard before turning east toward Hollywood.

'All right, let's hear it,' McCaleb said. 'What were you talking about on the phone, about them not finding what they were looking for?'

'Check out the laundry basket, man.'

'Why?'

'Just take a look.'

He turned his head toward McCaleb and jerked it in the direction of the backseat. McCaleb unsnapped his seat belt and turned around to reach over the seat. As he did so, he checked the cars behind them. There was lots of traffic but no cars that raised any suspicion.

He dropped his eyes to the basket. It was full of underwear and socks. That had been a nice touch by Buddy. It made it less likely Nevins or anybody else would look through the basket when they stopped him.

'This stuff is clean, right?'

' 'Course. It's on the bottom.'

McCaleb brought his knees up onto the seat and leaned all the way over. He dumped the contents of the laundry basket on the backseat. He heard the dull thud of something heavier than clothes hitting the seat. He moved a pair of loud boxer shorts out of the way and saw a plastic Ziploc bag that contained a pistol.

Silently, McCaleb slid back into his seat, holding the bag containing the gun. He smoothed the plastic, which had been yellowed from within by a film of gun oil, so that he could get a better look at the weapon. He felt a sweat break across the back of his neck. The gun in the bag was an HK P7. And he didn't need any ballistics report to know it was *the* HK P7, the weapon that had killed Kenyon, then Cordell, then Torres. He bent down to look closely at the weapon and saw that the serial number had been burned away with acid. The gun was untraceable.

A tremor rolled through McCaleb's hands as he held the murder weapon. His body slumped against the door and his feelings jumped between the anguish of knowing the history of the object he now held in his hands and despair at the thought of his predicament. Someone was setting McCaleb up and the frame would probably have been all but unbreakable if Buddy Lockridge had not found the gun when he went into the dark waters beneath *The Following Sea*.

'Jesus,' McCaleb said in a whisper.

'Looks pretty mean, don't it?'

'Where exactly was it?'

'It was in a diving bag hanging about six feet below your stern. It was tied off on one of the underside eyelets. If you knew it was there, you could reach under with a gaff and hook the line and bring it up. But you had to know it was there. Otherwise, you wouldn't see it from up above.'

'Did the people doing the search go into the water today?'

'Yeah, one diver. He went down, but by then I'd already checked around like you asked. I beat him to it.'

McCaleb nodded and put the gun down on the floor between his feet. Staring down at it, he folded his arms across his chest as if protecting himself against a chill. It had been that close. And though he was sitting next to the man who had saved him for the time being, an overwhelming sense of isolation came over him. He felt completely alone. And he felt the flickering onset of something he had only read about before – the fight-or-flight syndrome. He felt an almost violent urge to forget about everything and run. Just cut and run and get as far away from all of this as he could.

'I'm in big trouble, Buddy,' he said.

'I kind of figured that,' his driver replied.

# 34

McCaleb had composed himself and was resolved by the time they reached Video GraFX Consultants. On the way he had examined the possibility of flight and then quickly discarded it. Fight was the only choice. He knew that he was tethered in place by his heart – to flee was to die, for he needed the carefully set post-op drug therapy to prevent his body from rejecting his new heart. To flee would also mean to leave Graciela and Raymond. And it felt already as if doing that would wither his heart just as quickly.

Lockridge dropped him off out front and waited in a red zone. The door was locked but Tony Banks had told him to ring the delivery buzzer if he arrived after closing. McCaleb pushed the button twice before Banks answered the door himself. He had a manila envelope with him and he handed it through the open door to McCaleb.

'This everything?'

'The tape and the hard copies. Everything is pretty clear.'

McCaleb took the package.

'What do I owe you, Tony?'

'Not a thing. Glad to help.'

McCaleb nodded and was about to head back to the car but stopped and looked back at Banks.

'I've got to tell you something. I'm not with the bureau anymore, Tony. I apologize if I misled you, but –'

'I know you're not with the bureau anymore.'

'You do?'

'I called your old office yesterday when you didn't return my call from Saturday. The number was on that letter you sent, the letter on the wall. I called and they said you hadn't worked there in something like two years.'

McCaleb studied Banks, really taking the young man's measure for the first time, and then held up the package.

'Then why are you giving me this?'

'Because you are after him, the man on that tape.'

McCaleb nodded.

'Then good luck. I hope you get him.'

Banks closed and locked the door then. McCaleb said thanks but by then the door was already closed.

The Sherman Market was empty save for a couple of young girls mulling choices at the candy rack and a young man behind the counter. McCaleb had been hoping to see the same older woman who had been there on his first visit, the widow of Chan Ho Kang. He spoke slowly and clearly to the young man, hoping he understood English better than the woman had.

'I am looking for the woman who works here during the daytime.'

The man – he was really no more than a teenager – looked sullenly at McCaleb.

'You don't have to talk like I'm some kind of retard,' he said. 'I speak English. I was born here.'

'Oh,' McCaleb said, taken aback by his clumsiness. 'Sorry about that. It's just that the woman that was here before, she had a hard time understanding me.'

'My mother. She lived her first thirty years in Korea speaking Korean. You try it sometime. Why don't you move over there and try to be understood in twenty years.'

'Look, I'm sorry.'

McCaleb held his hands up wide and palms out. This wasn't going well. He tried again.

'You are Chan Ho Kang's son?'

The boy nodded.

'Who are you?'

'My name is Terry McCaleb. I'm sorry about the loss of your father.'

'What do you want?'

'I am doing some work for the family of the woman that was killed in here that –'

'What work?'

'I am trying to find the killer.'

'My mother doesn't know anything. Leave her alone. She's had enough.'

'Actually, all I want to do is to look at her watch. I was in here the other day and I noticed she's wearing the watch your father was wearing that night.'

The young man stared blankly at him, then glanced away from him to check on the girls at the candy racks.

'Okay, girls, let's go. Make your choices.'

McCaleb looked back at the girls. They didn't look happy about being hurried about such an important decision.

'What about the watch?'

McCaleb looked back at him.

'Well, it's kind of complicated. There are things that don't add up on the police reports. I am trying to figure out why. To do that, I need to know the exact time the man with the gun came in here.'

He pointed at the video camera on the wall behind and above the counterman.

'The police gave me a copy of the tape. On the tape your father's watch is seen. I have had it enhanced. If your mother has not reset the watch since ... she started wearing it, then there is a way I can get the time I need.'

'You don't need the watch. The time is on the tape. You said you had the tape.'

'The police say the time on the tape is wrong. That's what I'm trying to find out. Will you call your mother for me?'

The girls came over to the counter then. The man didn't answer McCaleb as he silently took their money and gave them change. He watched them walk out before looking back at McCaleb.

'I don't understand this. It makes no sense to me what you want.'

McCaleb blew out his breath.

'I am trying to help you. Do you want the man who killed your father to be caught?'

'Of course. But this watch business ... what does it have to do with anything?'

'I could explain it all to you if you had about a half hour but –'

'I'm not going anywhere.'

McCaleb looked at him a moment and decided that it was going to be the only way to go. He nodded and told him to wait while he got a photo out of the car.

The young man's name was Steve Kang. Riding in the front passenger seat, he directed Buddy Lockridge into a neighborhood just a few blocks from where Graciela Rivers and Raymond Torres lived.

McCaleb had convinced him with his long version. The young man had then thought enough of McCaleb's theory to put a Be Back Soon sign on the door and lock up. He normally walked to and from the store, but Lockridge's car would save them time.

When they got to his home, Steve Kang led McCaleb inside while Lockridge waited in the car. The house was virtually identical in design to Graciela's and had probably been built in the early fifties by the same developer. Kang told McCaleb to sit in the living room and he then disappeared down a hallway leading to the bedrooms. McCaleb heard muffled talking from the hallway. After a few seconds he realized the conversation was in Korean.

While he waited, he thought about the similarities in the houses and envisioned the two different families grieving on the night of the shooting and the days after.

Steve Kang came back then. He handed McCaleb a remote phone and the watch his father had worn.

'She did not change anything,' he said. 'It's just the way it was that night.'

McCaleb nodded. From the corner of his eye he noticed movement. He looked to his left and saw Steve Kang's mother standing in the hallway, just watching him. He nodded to her but she didn't respond in any way.

McCaleb had brought the hard copy of the enhanced video frame in with him along with his notebook and phone book. He had told Steve Kang what he planned to do but was still uncomfortable carrying it out in front of him. He was about to impersonate a police officer, which was a crime, even if that officer was Eddie Arrango.

From his phone book he got the number for the Central Communications Center in downtown LA. He'd had the number since his days with the LA field office, when he would at times need to coordinate intra-agency activities. The CCC was the dark, cavernous dispatch center four floors below City Hall from which all police and fire department radio communications were transmitted. It was also where the clock was from which the official time of the murders of Gloria Torres and Chan Ho Kang had been set.

On the drive from Hollywood to the market McCaleb had pulled out the Torres file and gotten Arrango's badge number from the homicide report. He now placed the watch Steve Kang had given him on the arm of the couch and dialed the nonemergency number of the CCC. An operator answered in four rings.

'This is Arrango, West Valley homicide,' McCaleb said. 'That's serial one four one one. I'm not on the radio. I just need a ten-twenty for a surveillance commencement. And could you give me the seconds with that, too?'

'Seconds? Why, you're a precise man, Detective Arrango.'

'Precisely.'

'Hold one.'

McCaleb looked down at the watch. As the operator spoke, he noted the watch time was 5:14:42 P.M.

'That's seventeen fourteen thirty-eight.'

'Gotcha,' he said. 'Thanks.'

He hung up and looked at Steve Kang.

'Your father's watch is running four seconds ahead of the CCC clock.'

Kang narrowed his eyes and he came around the side of the couch to look over McCaleb as he wrote numbers down in his notebook, referred back to specific times listed on the timeline he had put together earlier, and then did the math.

They both arrived at the same conclusion at the same time.

'That means ...'

Steve Kang didn't finish. McCaleb noticed that he glanced over at his mother in the hallway and then back at the time McCaleb had underlined in the notebook.

'That bastard!' he said in a hateful whisper.

'He's more than that,' McCaleb said.

Outside, Buddy Lockridge started the Taurus as soon as he saw McCaleb leave the house. McCaleb jumped in.

'Let's go.'

'We giving the kid a ride back?'

'No, he's got to talk to his mother. Let's go.'

'Okay, okay. Where to?'

'Back to the boat.'

'The boat? You can't go there, Terry. Those people might still be there. Or they might be watching it.'

'It doesn't matter. I have no choice.'

# 35

........

Lockridge dropped McCaleb off at the curb on Cabrillo Way, about half a mile from the marina. He walked the rest of the way, keeping to the shadows cast by the small shops that lined the boulevard. The plan was for Buddy to leave his keys in the Taurus and then go to his boat as if everything about his life was routine and normal. If he saw anything unusual, anyone hanging around the marina who wasn't recognizable, he was to flick on the mast light on the *Double-Down*. McCaleb would be able to see the light from a good distance away and he would keep clear.

When the marina came into sight, McCaleb's eyes scanned the points of the dozens of masts. It was dark now and he saw no lights. Things looked good. He glanced around and spotted a pay phone outside a mini-market and went to it to call Lockridge anyway. It also gave him a chance to put the heavy leather bag down for a spell. Buddy picked up the phone right away.

'Is it safe?' McCaleb asked, remembering the line from a movie he had enjoyed some years before.

'Think so,' Buddy said. 'I don't see anyone and nobody grabbed me on the way in. I didn't see anything that looked like an unmarked cop car out in the lot, either.'

'What's my boat look like?'

There was a silence while Buddy took a look.

'It's still there. Looks like they got yellow tape strung

between the piers, like you're not supposed to go on it or something.'

'Okay, Bud, I'm coming in. I'm going to go into the laundry first and stick my bag in one of the dryers. If I go to the boat and get jumped by them, you come get the bag and sit on it until I get out. You okay with that?'

'Sure.'

'Okay, listen. If everything goes okay on the boat, I won't be staying long, so I'm going to say this now, thanks for everything, Buddy, you've been a big help.'

'No sweat, man. I don't care about what these bastards are trying to do to you. I know you're cool.'

McCaleb thanked him again and hung up, then picked up his bag and started carrying it under his arm as he headed toward the marina. He first ducked into the laundry and found an empty dryer in which to stow the bag. He then made it all the way to the boat without problem. Before unlocking the slider he took one last look around the marina and saw nothing amiss, nothing that raised an alarm. He noticed the dark form of Buddy Lockridge sitting in the cockpit of the *Double-Down*. He heard a *wah-wah* tremolo from a harmonica and he nodded toward the shadow figure. He then slid open the door.

The boat smelled stuffy and stale but there was still a lingering scent of perfume. He guessed Jaye Winston had left it behind. He didn't turn on a light but rather reached for the flashlight clamped on the underside of the chart table. He flicked it on and held the light down at his side and pointing at the floor. He headed below, knowing he had to move quickly. He just wanted to grab enough clothes, drugs and medical supplies to last him a few days. He figured, one way or the other, it would be all the time he would get.

He opened one of the hallway hatches and got out the large duffel bag. He then went into the master stateroom and gathered the clothes he would need. Doing it surreptitiously by flashlight slowed the process down but finally he had what he needed.

When he was done, he carried the bag across the hallway to the head to gather drugs, medical supplies and his clipboard. He put the open bag on the sink and was about to begin laying in the pharmaceutical boxes and vials when he realized something. When he had crossed the hallway, there had been a light on topside. The galley light. Or maybe one of the overheads in the salon. He momentarily froze and tried to listen for any sound from above while he reviewed his own movements. He was sure he had not put on a light when he had come in.

He listened nearly half a minute but there was nothing. He quietly stepped back into the hallway and looked up the stairway. He stood stock still and listened again while trying to weigh his options. The only way out besides going back up the stairs was the deck hatch in the roof of the forward stateroom. But it would be foolish to think that whoever was topside didn't have that escape route covered.

'Buddy,' he called. 'Is that you?'

The answer came after a long beat of silence.

'No, Terry, it's not Buddy.'

A female voice. McCaleb recognized it.

'Jaye?'

'Why don't you come on up?'

He looked back into the head. The flashlight was inside the duffel bag, illuminating little else but its contents. Otherwise he was in the dark.

'I'm coming up.'

She was sitting on the cushioned swivel chair near the teak coffee table. He had apparently gone right past her in the dark. He slid into the matching chair on the other side of the salon.

'Hello, Jaye. How's it going?'

'I've had better days.'

'Same here. I was going to call you in the morning.'

'Well, I'm here now.'

'And where are your friends?'

'They're not my friends. And they definitely aren't your friends, Terry.'

'Didn't sound like it. So what's going on? How come you're here and they're not?'

'Because every now and then one of us dopey locals turns out to be smarter than the bureau boys.'

McCaleb smiled without humor.

'You knew I'd have to come back for my medicine.'

She returned the smile and nodded.

'They figure you're already halfway to Mexico if you're not there already. But I saw that cabinet full of drugs and knew you had to come back. It was like a leash.'

'So now you get to take me in and get the bust and get the glory.'

'Not necessarily.'

He did not respond at first. He thought about her words, wondering how she was playing this.

'What are you saying, Jaye?'

'I'm saying my gut is telling me one thing, the evidence something else. I usually trust my gut.'

'Me too. What evidence are you talking about? What did you people find in here today?'

'Nothing much, just a baseball hat with the CI logo on it. We figured out it means Catalina Island and it matches the description James Noone gave of the cap the driver of the Cherokee was wearing. Then nothing else – until we opened up the top drawer of that chart table.'

McCaleb looked over at the chart table. He remembered opening the top drawer and checking it after the intruder had been scared off the night before. There was nothing in there amiss or that could hurt him.

'What was in it?'

'In it? Nothing. It was underneath. Taped underneath.'

McCaleb got up and went to the chart drawers. He pulled the top drawer out and turned it over. He ran his finger over the adhesive residue left by pieces of heavy tape. He smiled and shook his head. He thought about how quickly the intruder could have come in, taken a pretaped package and slapped it up under the open drawer.

'Let me guess,' he said. 'It was a plastic –'

'No. Don't say anything. You say anything and it could come back to hurt you. I don't want to hurt you, Terry.'

'I'm not worried about that. Not anymore. So let me guess. Under the drawer was a bag – a Ziploc type of bag. Inside it was the cross earring taken from Gloria Torres and a photograph of James Cordell's family. The one taken from his car.'

Winston nodded. McCaleb returned to his seat.

'You left out Donald Kenyon's cuff link,' she said. 'Sterling silver, in the shape of a dollar sign.'

'I didn't know about that. I bet Nevins and Uhlig and that asshole Arrango put on six inches apiece when they found that bag.'

'They were strutting all right,' she said, nodding. 'It made them very happy.'

'But not you.'

'No. It was too easy.'

They sat in silence for a few moments.

'You know, Terry, you don't seem very concerned that evidence linking you to three murders was found in your boat. Not to mention the obvious motive you have for those murders.' She nodded toward McCaleb's chest. 'No, you look like, at best, you are maybe moderately annoyed. You want to tell me why?'

McCaleb leaned forward, elbows on his knees. This brought his face more fully into the light.

'It was all planted, Jaye. The hat, earring, everything. Last night somebody broke in here. He didn't take anything. So he must've left things. I've got witnesses. I'm being set up. I don't know why, but it's a setup.'

'Well, if you're thinking Bolotov, forget it. He's been in Van Nuys jail since his parole officer picked him up Sunday afternoon.'

'No, I'm not thinking Bolotov. He's in the clear.'

'That sure sounds like a different tune.'

'Events have overtaken the possibility of him being a suspect. Remember, I figured him for that burglary near his work in which the HK P7 was taken. That would have given him the right gun to make him a suspect in Cordell and Torres. But that burglary occurred in December, near Christmas. Now add Kenyon. He was killed with a P7 in November. So it can't be the same gun, even if Bolotov did the burglary. So he's clear. I still don't know why he went ape shit on me and ran, though.'

'Well, like you said, he probably is good for that Christmas burglary. You went in there and spooked him, made it sound like you were going to put a couple of murders on him. He ran. That's all.'

McCaleb nodded.

'What's going to happen to him?'

'His boss is going to drop his complaint in lieu of restitution for the window that was broken. That's it. They'll release him after a hearing today.'

McCaleb nodded again and looked down at the carpet.

'So forget about him, Terry. What else have you got?'

He brought his eyes back up and looked intently back at her.

'I'm close. I'm just one or two steps away from putting this all together. I know who the shooter is now. And I'm just a few days away from knowing who hired him. I've got names, a list of suspects. I know the person we want is on that list. Trust your gut on this one, Jaye. You can hook me up now and bring me in and get the bust, but it's wrong and it won't fit. Eventually, I'll be able to prove it. But in the meantime, we'll miss the chance we've got right now.'

'Who is the shooter?'

McCaleb stood up.

'I have to get my bag. I'll show you.'

'Where's your bag?'

'In a dryer in the marina laundry. I stashed it there. I didn't know what to expect when I came in here.'

She thought a moment.

'Let me go get it,' he said. 'You've still got the pharmacy here. I'm not going anywhere. If you don't trust me, come with me.'

She waved him off.

'All right, go. Get your bag. I'll wait.'

On the way to the laundry McCaleb met Buddy Lockridge, who was holding the leather satchel taken from the laundry.

'Everything okay? You told me to go get this if I saw anybody put the moves on you.'

'Everything's fine, Buddy. I think.'

'I don't know what she's telling you, but she was one of them that was here today.'

'I know. But I think she's on my side.'

McCaleb took the bag from him and headed back to his boat. Inside, he turned on the television, put the Sherman Market tape in the VCR, and started playing it. He fast-forwarded the image and watched the jerking motions of the shooter coming in, shooting Gloria Torres and the market owner, then disappearing. Then the Good Samaritan came in and McCaleb put the tape on normal speed. At the moment the Good Samaritan looked up from his work on Gloria's stricken figure, McCaleb hit the pause button and the image froze.

He pointed at the man on the television screen and looked back at Jaye Winston.

'There. There's your shooter.'

She stared at the tube for a long moment, her face betraying none of her thoughts.

'Okay, tell me, how is that my shooter?'

'The timeline. Arrango and Walters never saw this as anything more than a common robbery and shooting. That's how it looked – who can blame them? But they were sloppy. They never bothered completing or verifying a timeline. They took what they saw at face value. But there was a problem between the time on the store video when the shooting went down and the time on the big clock downtown when the Good Samaritan called it in.'

'Right. You told me. What was the discrepancy, a half minute or so?'

'Thirty-four seconds. According to the store's video, the Good Samaritan called in the shooting thirty-four seconds before it happened.'

'But you said Walters or Arrango said they couldn't verify the accuracy of the video clock. They just assumed it was off because the old man – Mr Kang – probably set it himself.'

'Right, they assumed. I didn't.'

McCaleb backed the tape up to the point that Chan Ho Kang's watch was visible as his arm stretched across the counter. He played with it in slow motion, going back and forth until he had the time strip across the bottom at the right moment. He paused the image again. He then went to the bag and took out the hard copy of the video enhancement.

'Okay, what I did was triangulate the time to get an

accurate fix on when exactly this went down. You see the watch?'

She nodded. He handed her the hard copy.

'I had a friend who used to do work for the bureau enhance this image. That's the hard copy. As you can see, the time on the watch and the video match. To the second. Old man Kang must have set the camera clock right off his watch. You with me?'

'I'm with you. The video and the watch match. What does it mean?'

McCaleb held his hand up in a *hold-on* gesture and then got out his notebook and referred to his timeline notes.

'Now we know, according to the Central Communications Center clock downtown, that the Good Samaritan called in the shooting at 10:41:03, which was thirty-four seconds before the shooting took place according to the videotape. Okay?'

'Okay.'

He explained that evening's trip to the store and then to the Kang home, where he had been allowed access to the watch. He told her that the watch's setting had not been disturbed since the murders.

'I then called the CCC and got a time check and compared it to the watch. The watch is running only four seconds ahead of the CCC clock. Therefore, that means the video clock was running only four seconds ahead of CCC at the time of the murders.'

Winston narrowed her eyebrows and leaned forward, trying to follow his explanation.

'That would mean ...'

She didn't finish.

'It means that there is almost no difference – just four seconds – between the video clock and the CCC clock. So when the Good Samaritan called in the store shooting at ten forty-one oh three on the CCC clock, it was exactly ten forty-one oh seven on the store clock. There was only four seconds difference.'

'But that's impossible,' Winston said, shaking her head. 'There was no shooting at the time. That's thirty seconds too early. Gloria wasn't even in the store yet. She was probably just pulling in.'

McCaleb was silent. He decided to let her make the conclusions without having to be told or prompted. He knew it would have a stronger impact if she came to the same spot he was at on her own.

'So,' she said, 'this guy, this Good Samaritan, had to have called in the shooting before the shooting took place.'

McCaleb nodded. He noted the deepening intensity in her eyes.

'Why would he do that unless ... he knew. Unless he knew the shooting was going down? He's – damn! – he's got to be the shooter!'

McCaleb nodded once more, but this time he had a satisfied smile on his face. He knew he had her in his car now. And they were about to hit the gas pedal.

# 36

'Have you hashed this around, figured out how it all plays?'

'A little bit.'

'So then tell me.'

McCaleb was standing in the galley now, pouring himself a glass of orange juice. Winston had passed on a drink but was standing in the galley also. Her adrenaline would not allow her to sit. McCaleb knew that feeling.

'Wait a second,' he said.

He gulped down the orange juice in one tilt.

'Sorry, I messed with my blood sugar today, I think. Ate too late.'

'Are you all right?'

'Fine.'

He put the glass in the sink, turned and leaned against the counter.

'Okay, this is how I see it. You start with Mr X, somebody someplace that we'll assume to be a man for now. This person needs something. A new part. Kidney, liver, maybe bone marrow. Possibly corneas but that might be stretching it. It has to be something worth killing for. Something that he might die without. Or in the case of the cornea, possibly go blind and become non-functioning without.'

'What about a heart?'

'That would be on the list but, see, I got the heart. So scratch the heart unless you are Nevins and Uhlig and

Arrango and the rest of them who think I'm Mr X, okay?'

'Okay. Go on.'

'This guy, X, he's got money and access. Enough to be able to contact and hire a shooter.'

'With OC connections.'

'Maybe but not necessarily.'

'What about "Don't forget the cannoli"?'

'I don't know. I've been thinking about that. It's kind of showy for real organized crime, don't you think? Makes me think it's a deflection but for now that's just a guess.'

'All right, never mind for now. Go on with Mr X.'

'Well, besides being able to get to a shooter to do the job, he next has to have access to the computer at BOPRA. He's got to know who has the part that he needs. You know what BOPRA is?'

'I learned today. And I said the same thing about you to Nevins. "How could Terry McCaleb get access to BOPRA?" and he told me how bullshit their computer security is. Their theory is that you hacked in one day when you were at Cedars. You got a list of blood donors of type AB with CMV negative and went from there.'

'Okay. Now follow the same theory but instead of me, it's Mr X and he gets the list and then puts the Good Samaritan on the case.'

McCaleb pointed out into the salon, where the image of the Good Samaritan remained frozen on the television screen. They both looked at it for a few moments before he continued.

'The shooter goes down the list and lo and behold he sees a familiar name. Donald Kenyon. Kenyon is a famous man, mostly for all the enemies he has. He becomes the perfect choice because of that. All those enemies – investors and maybe even some mobster lurking behind the scenes, it makes for good camouflage.'

'So the Good Samaritan picks Kenyon.'

'Right. He picks him and then he watches him until he has his routine. And the routine is pretty simple because Kenyon's got a federal dog collar on and usually doesn't go anywhere outside of his house because of it. But the Good Sam is not discouraged. He gets the household routine down and he knows that for twenty minutes each morning Kenyon is in that house alone when the wife drives the kids to school.'

His throat dry from all the talking, McCaleb rescued the glass from the sink and poured himself another glass of orange juice.

'So he hits during that twenty-minute window,' he continued, after gulping down another half glass. 'And going in, he knows he has to do the job in such a way that Kenyon makes it to the hospital but no further. See, he's got to preserve the organs for transplant. But if he goes too far, Kenyon's dead on arrival and no good to him. So he comes into the house, grabs Kenyon and marches him to the front door. He then holds him there and waits for the wife to come back home from dropping the kids. He makes Kenyon look through the peephole and make sure it is her. Then he pops him and lays him out on the floor, fresh and ready when the wife opens the door.'

'But he doesn't make it to the hospital.'

'No. The plan was good but he fucked up. He used a Devastator in the P7. The wrong bullet for this kind of work. It's a frangible, it explodes and basically pulps Kenyon's brain, destroys all life support system controls. Death is almost instantaneous.'

He stopped there and watched Winston as she evaluated the story. Then he held up a finger, signaling her to wait before commenting. He went to his bag in the salon and pulled out a sheaf of documents, careful to keep his body between the bag and Winston. He didn't want her catching a glimpse of the P7, which was still in there.

At the galley counter he looked through the documents until he found what he needed.

'I'm not supposed to even have this but take a look. This is a transcript of the tape the bureau got from the illegal bugs in the Kenyon house. This is the part where he was hit. They didn't get everything that was said but what is there fits with what I just said.'

Winston stood next to him and read the section he had circled with a pen while riding with Buddy Lockridge on the way to the marina.

> UNKNOWN: Okay, look and see who ...
> KENYON: Don't ... She's got nothing to do with this. She ...

Winston nodded her head.

'He could have told him to look through the peephole,' she said. 'It obviously was the wife because Kenyon then tried to protect her.'

'Right, and notice that the transcript says that there were two minutes of silence before that last exchange and the gunshot. What else could he have been doing but waiting until she showed up so she would get to the body almost as soon as it happened?'

She nodded again.

'It fits,' she said. 'But what about the bureau people listening? You think the shooter didn't know about them?'

'I'm not sure. It doesn't seem like it. I think he just got lucky. But maybe he thought there was a slim chance the place was bugged. Maybe that's where the cannoli line came from. Just a little misdirection, just in case.'

McCaleb finished his orange juice and put the glass back into the sink.

'Okay, so he blew it,' Winston said. 'And it was back to the drawing board. Or, actually, back to the BOPRA list. And the next name he picked was my guy, James Cordell.'

McCaleb nodded and let her run with it. He knew that the more of the puzzle she fit together herself, the more apt she would be to believe in the whole thing.

'He changes the load, goes from frangible to hardball so that he would have a through-and-through wound with less immediate brain damage.

'He watches Cordell until he has the routine down and then he sets up the shoot in a way similar to Kenyon – the hit occurring almost instantaneous to the arrival of a second party who could get help. In Kenyon's case it was his wife. In Cordell's it was James Noone. The shooter probably stood behind Cordell until he saw Noone's car enter the turn lane to come into the bank. That was when he fired.'

'I think Noone was an accident,' McCaleb said. 'There is no way the shooter could have planned on a witness showing up. He was probably going to shoot Cordell and then call nine one one himself on the pay phone out at the curb – on the crime scene tape you can see the pay phone right there. But Noone came along and that forced him to just get the hell out of there. He probably thought the witness would make the call on the pay phone – a legitimate call for help. The bad break for him was that Noone made the call on a cell phone and the address was messed up, resulting in a terminal delay for Cordell.'

Winston nodded her agreement.

'Cordell was DOA,' she said. 'Another one goes to shit. He goes back to the list and it's Gloria Torres this time.

Only this time he's not taking a single chance. He calls the shooting in before it even happens.'

'Right, to get the paramedics rolling. He knew her routine. He was probably standing at that pay phone waiting. When he saw her car pulling in, he made the nine one one call.'

'He then goes in, does the job and splits. Outside he pulls off the mask and the jumpsuit and he becomes our Good Samaritan. He goes in, wraps her up and gets the hell out of there. This time it works. It is perfect.'

'It was a learning process. He learned from the mistakes of the first two, perfected it on the third.'

McCaleb folded his arms and waited for Winston to make the next jump.

'So we have to follow the harvest now,' she said. 'One of the people who received one of the organs will be Mr X. We have to go to BOPRA and get the – wait, you said you had a list of names?'

He nodded.

'From BOPRA?'

'From BOPRA.'

He went back to his bag and found the list Bonnie Fox had given him. He turned around and almost bumped into Winston, who had moved out of the galley. He handed her the sheet.

'There's the list.'

She studied it intently, as if she was expecting to see that one of the names on it would actually be Mr X or in some other way be readily identifiable as him.

'How did you get this?'

'Can't say.'

She looked up at him.

'For the time being I have to protect a source. But it's legit. Those people got organs from Gloria Torres.'

'Are you giving me this?'

'If you are going to do something with it.'

'I will. I'll start tomorrow.'

McCaleb was fully aware of what he was giving her. Of course, it might be the key to his exoneration and the capture of the worst kind of killer. But he was also handing her an E-ticket ride. If she was successful in breaking the case while the bureau and the LAPD were heading down the wrong road, her professional future would have no bounds.

'How are you going to run them down?' he asked.

'Anyway I can. I'll look for money, criminal records, anything that stands out. You know, the usual things, the full background. What are you going to be doing?'

McCaleb glanced over at his bag. It was bulging with documents, tapes and the guns.

'I don't know yet. Will you tell me something? How did this all turn on me? What pointed all you people at me?'

Winston folded the list into a neat square and slid it into the pocket of her blazer.

'The bureau. Nevins told me they got a tip. He wouldn't say from where. The tip was suspect-specific, though. He did tell me that. The source said you killed Glory Torres for her heart. They took it from there. They checked the autopsies of all three victims and found the blood matches. From there it was easy, everything fell into place. I have to admit they had me going. At the time, it all seemed to fit.'

'*How*?' McCaleb asked angrily, his voice rising. 'None of this would have even happened if I hadn't started looking into it. The ballistics match to Kenyon was made because of me. That brought the bureau in. You think that is what a guilty man would do? That's crazy.'

He was angrily pointing at his own chest.

'All of that was considered. We sat around and hashed it out this morning. The theory that emerged was that you had this woman – the sister – who had come to you and you figured she wasn't going to let this go. So you decided you better take the case before somebody else did. You took it and proceeded to sabotage it. You came up with this Bolotov goose chase. You hypnotized the only real witness and now he's lost to us as far as court goes. Yes, the ballistics match was made because of you but maybe that was a surprise, maybe you were expecting it to come up empty since a Devastator had been used the first time.'

McCaleb shook his head. He wouldn't allow himself to see their side of it. He still couldn't believe they had turned the focus on him.

'Look, we weren't sold on it one hundred percent,' Winston said. 'We felt there was enough to get and justify a warrant for the search – and there was. We felt the search was make or break. We would find evidence and go further with it, or we would drop it. But then we find out you drive a black Cherokee and then sitting under that drawer are three very damning pieces of evidence. The only thing that could have been worse for you would have been to find the gun.'

McCaleb thought of the gun sitting in his bag five feet away from them. Again he knew how lucky he had been.

'But like you said, it was too easy.'

'For me it was. The others didn't see it that way. Like I said before, they started strutting. They saw the headlines.'

McCaleb shook his head. The discussion had sapped his strength. He stepped over to the galley table and slid into the booth.

'I am being set up,' he said.

Winston came over.

'I believe you,' she said. 'And whoever he is, he's done a good job of it. Have you thought at all about why it is you that's been set up?'

McCaleb nodded as he drew a design in a spray of sugar that had been spilled on the table.

'When I look at it from the shooter's view, I see why.'

He brushed the sugar off the table with his palm.

'After Kenyon didn't work out and the shooter knew he had to go back to the list, he also knew he was doubling the risk. He knew there was an off chance that the cases might be connected through the blood. He knew he had to lay the groundwork for a deflection. He picked me. If he was in the BOPRA computer, then he knew I was next on the list for a heart. He probably backgrounded me like the others. He knew about the Cherokee I drove and used one himself. He took souvenirs from the victims so that he could plant them, if needed, here. Then it was probably him who made the tip call to Nevins when everything was set.'

McCaleb sat silently for a long moment, brooding about his situation. Then he slowly slid back out of the booth.

'I have to finish packing.'

'Where are you going to go?'

'I'm not sure.'

'I'll need to talk to you tomorrow.'

'I'll be in touch.'

He started down the stairs, his hands gripping the overhead rails.

'Terry.'

He stopped and turned to look back at her.

'I'm taking a big chance. My neck's a mile out there.'

'I know that, Jaye. Thanks.'

With that he disappeared into the darkness below.

# 37

McCaleb's Cherokee had been impounded during the search earlier in the day. He borrowed Lockridge's Taurus and drove it north on the 405. When he reached the 10 interchange, he went west to the Pacific and then continued north again on the coast highway. He was in no hurry and he was tired of freeways. He'd decided to drive along the ocean and then cut up to the Valley through Topanga Canyon. He knew Topanga was desolate enough for him to be able to tell if he was being followed by Winston. Or anybody else.

It was half past nine by the time he reached the shore and was skirting along the black water intermittently broken by the froth of crashing waves. The night fog was coming in heavy and pushing across the highway, butting into the sheer bluffs that guarded the Palisades. It carried with it the strong scent and feel of the sea and it reminded McCaleb of night fishing with his father when he was a boy. It always scared him when his father throttled down and killed the engines so they could drift in the dark. His breath held tight at the end of the night when the old man turned the key to restart. He had nightmares as a boy about drifting alone in the dark in a dead boat. He never told his father about those dreams. He never told him he didn't want to go night fishing. He always held his fears to himself.

McCaleb looked out to his left to try to find the line where ocean met sky but he couldn't see it. Two shades of darkness blending somewhere out there, the moon hidden in cloud cover. It seemed to fit his mood. He turned on the radio and fished around for some blues but gave up and turned it off. He remembered Buddy's collection of harmonicas and reached into the door pocket for one. He flipped on the overhead light and checked the etching on the top plate. It was a Tombo in the key of C. He wiped it off on his shirt and as he drove, he played with the instrument, mostly producing a cacophony that at times made him laugh out loud at how ugly it was. But every now and then he put together a couple of notes. Buddy had tried to teach him once and he'd gotten to the point where he could play the opening riffs of 'Midnight Rambler'. He tried for that now but couldn't find the chord and what he produced sounded more like a wheezing old man.

When he turned into Topanga Canyon, he put the harmonica down. The road through the canyon was a snake and he'd need both hands on the wheel. Fresh out of distractions, he finally began considering his situation. He first brooded about Winston and how much he could count on her. He knew she was capable and ambitious. What he didn't know was how well she would stand up to the pressure she would certainly encounter by going against the bureau and the LAPD. He concluded that he was lucky to have her on his side but that he couldn't sit back and wait for her to show up with the case wrapped up in a box. He could only count on himself.

He figured that if Winston did not convince the others, then at best he had two days before they had an indictment from a grand jury and would go to the media with their prize. After that, his chances of working the case would diminish rapidly. He'd be the lead on the six and eleven o'clock news. He'd have no choice but to give up the investigation, get a lawyer and surrender. The priority would then be clearing his name in the courtroom, never mind catching the real shooter and whoever it was who had hired him.

There was a gravel turnout on the road and McCaleb pulled over, put the car in park and looked out at the blackness of the drop-off to his right. Far off he saw the square lights of a house deep in the canyon and he wondered what it would be like to be there. He reached over to the seat next to him for the harmonica but it was gone, slipped over the side during one of the turns of the snaking road.

Three minutes went by and no car passed him. He dropped the car back into drive and continued on his way. Once he crested the mountain, the road straightened out some and dropped down into Woodland Hills. He stayed on Topanga Canyon Boulevard until he reached Sherman Way and then he cut east into Canoga Park. Five minutes later he stopped in front of Graciela's home and watched the windows for a few minutes. He thought about what he would say to her. He wasn't sure what he had started with her but it felt strong and right to him. Before he even opened the door to the car, he was mourning the possibility that it might already be over.

She opened the front door before he reached it and he wondered if she had been watching him sitting in the car.

'Terry? Is everything all right? Why are you driving?'

'I had to.'

'Come in, come in.'

She stepped back and allowed him in. They went to the living room and took the same seats on the sectional sofa that they had taken before. A small color television on a wooden stand played softly in the corner. The ten o'clock news on Channel 5 was just starting. Graciela used a remote to turn it off. McCaleb put his heavy bag down between his feet. He had left the duffel in the car, unwilling to presume that he would be asked to stay.

'Tell me,' she said. 'What is happening?'

'They think it was me. The FBI, LAPD, all of them but one sheriff's detective. They think I killed your sister for her heart.'

McCaleb looked at her face and then glanced away like a guilty man. He winced at the thought of what this must show to her but he knew down deep that he was guilty. He was the beneficiary, even if he had nothing to do with the actual crime. He was alive now because Glory was dead. A question echoed through his mind like the slamming of a dozen doors down a dark hallway. How can I live with this?

'That's ridiculous,' Graciela said angrily. 'How can they think that you –'

'Wait,' he said, cutting her off. 'I have to tell you some things, Graciela. Then you decide what and who to believe.'

'I don't have to hear –'

He held his hand up cutting her off again.

'Just listen to me, okay? Where's Raymond?'

'He's asleep. It's a school night.'

He nodded and leaned forward, elbows on his knees, hands clasped together.

'They searched my boat. While I was with you, they were searching my boat. They had made the same connection we made. The blood work. But they're looking at me for it. They found things on my boat. I wanted to tell you before you heard it from them or saw it on TV or the paper.'

'What things, Terry?'

'Hidden under a drawer. They found your sister's earring. The cross the shooter took.'

He watched her a moment before continuing. Her

eyes dropped from his to the glass-topped coffee table as she thought about his words.

'They also found the photo from Cordell's car. And they found a cuff link that was taken from Donald Kenyon. They found all the icons the killer took, Graciela. My source, the sheriff's detective, she tells me they are going to go to a grand jury and indict me. I can't go back to my boat now.'

She glanced at him and then away. She stood up and walked to the window, even though the curtain was closed. She shook her head.

'You want me to leave?' he said to her back.

'No, I don't want you to leave. This makes no sense. How can they – did you tell the detective about the intruder? He's the one who must have done this, who put those things in the drawer. He's the killer. Oh my God! We were that close to my sister's ...'

She didn't finish. McCaleb got up and went to her, relief coursing through him. She didn't believe it. None of it. He put his arms around her from behind and pushed his face into her hair.

'I'm so glad you believe me,' he whispered.

She turned around in his arms and they kissed for a long moment.

'What can I do to help?' she whispered.

'Just keep believing. And I'll do the rest. Can I stay here? Nobody knows that we're together. They might come here, but I don't think it will be to look for me. It might be just to tell you they think it's me.'

'I want you to stay. As long as you need or want to.'

'I just need a place where I can work. Where I can go through everything again. I get this feeling I missed something. Like the blood work. There's got to be some answers in all of that paper.'

'You can work here. I'll stay home tomorrow and help look through –'

'No. You can't. You can't do anything unusual. I just want you to get up in the morning and take Raymond to school and then go to work. I can do this. This part is my job.'

He held her face in his hands. The weight of his guilt was lessened by her just being there with him and he felt the subtle opening inside of some passage that had long been closed. He wasn't sure where it would lead but knew in his heart he wanted to go there, that he must go there.

'I was just about to go to bed,' she said.

He nodded.

'Are you coming with me?'

'What about Raymond? Shouldn't we –'

'Raymond's asleep. Don't worry about him. For right now let's worry about us.'

# 38

In the morning, after Graciela and Raymond were gone and the house was quiet, McCaleb opened his leather bag and spread all of the accumulated paperwork in six stacks across the coffee table. While contemplating it all, he drank a glass of orange juice and ate two untoasted blueberry Pop Tarts that he guessed were meant for Raymond. When he was done, he set to work, hoping his involvement in the paper would keep his mind off things beyond his control, mainly Jaye Winston's investigation of the names on the list.

Despite that distraction McCaleb could feel the flow of adrenaline start to kick in. He was looking for the tell. The piece of the puzzle that didn't fit before but would make sense now, that would tell him the story. He had survived in the bureau largely by following gut instincts. He was following one now. He knew that the larger the case file was – the larger the accumulation of facts – the easier it was for the tell to be hidden. He would go hunting for it now, in a sense looking for the perfect red apple in the stack at the grocery store – the one that when pulled brings the whole pile down and bouncing across the floor.

But as jazzed as McCaleb had been at eight-thirty in the morning, his spirits had immolated by late afternoon. In eight hours interrupted only by bologna sandwiches and unanswered calls to Winston, he had reviewed every page of every document he had accumulated in the ten days he had worked the case. And the tell – if it had ever been there – remained hidden. The feelings of paranoia and isolation were creeping back up on him. At one point he realized he was daydreaming about what would be the best place to flee to, the mountains of Canada or the beaches of Mexico.

At four o'clock he called the Star Center once more and was told for the fifth time that Winston was not in. This time, however, the secretary added that she was presumed gone for the day. In earlier calls the secretary had dutifully refused to reveal where Winston was or give him her pager number. For that he would have to speak to the captain and McCaleb declined, knowing the jeopardy he would place Winston in if it was revealed she was not only sympathetic to a suspect but was actually aiding him.

After hanging up, he called his phone on the boat and played back two messages that had come in during the last hour. The first was Buddy Lockridge checking in and the second was a wrong number, a woman saying she wasn't sure if she had the right number but was looking for someone named Luther Hatch. She left a callback number. McCaleb recognized the name Luther Hatch – the suspect in the case in which he had first met Jaye Winston. Once he made that connection, he recognized her voice on the message. She was telling him to call her.

As he punched in the numbers Winston had left, he recognized the exchange – it was the same for the bureau offices in Westwood, where he used to work. The phone was answered immediately.

'This is Winston.'

'This is McCaleb.'

Silence.

'Hey,' she finally said. 'I was wondering if you would get that message.'

'What's up? Can you talk?'

'Not really.'

'Okay, I'll talk, then. Do they know you are helping me?'

'No, obviously.'

'But you're there because they moved the investigation to the bureau, right?'

'Uh-huh.'

'Okay, have you had a chance to run those names down yet?'

'I've been out on it all day.'

'Do you have anything? Do any of them look good?'

'No, there's nothing there.'

McCaleb closed his eyes and cursed silently. Where had he gone wrong? How could this be a dead end? He was confused and his mind was running over the possibilities. He wondered if Winston had had enough time to thoroughly run out the list.

'Is there any place or time I can talk to you about this? I need to ask you some questions.'

'In a little while I probably can. Why don't you give me a number and I'll get back to you?'

McCaleb was silent while he thought about this. But he didn't take long. As Winston had said the night before, her neck was way out there for him. He believed he could trust her. He gave her Graciela's number.

'Call me back as soon as you can.'

'I will.'

'One last thing. Did they go to the grand jury yet?'

'No, not yet.'

'How long before they do?'

'I'll see you tomorrow morning, then. Bye.'

She hung up before she heard him curse out loud. The following morning they were going to seek an indictment against him for murder. And he was sure that obtaining it would be only a formality. Grand juries were always rigged in the prosecution's favor. In McCaleb's case, he knew that all they needed to do was show the Sherman Market tape and then introduce the earring found during the search of his boat. They would be staging press conferences by the afternoon – perfect timing for the six o'clock news.

While he was standing there contemplating his grim future, the phone rang in his hand.

'It's Jaye.'

'Where are you?'

'The federal cafeteria. A pay phone.'

McCaleb immediately envisioned her location, in an alcove with vending machines off to the side of the cafeteria dining room. It was private enough.

'What's going on, Jaye?'

'It's not good. They're putting the finishing touches on the package they're going to take to the DA's office tonight. They'll take it to the grand jury tomorrow morning. They're going to seek one murder charge for Gloria Torres. After that's in the pipeline, they'll take their time before adding on Cordell and Kenyon.'

'Okay,' McCaleb said, not sure how to respond. He decided there was no sense in continuing to curse out loud.

'My advice is that you come in, Terry. You tell them what you told me and convince them. I'll be on your side but right now I'm handcuffed. I have information about the Good Samaritan I shouldn't have. If I reveal it, I'll go into the shitter with you.'

'What about the list? Nothing at all?'

'Look, that much I did talk about with them. So I would have the time to work the list. I came in this morning and told them in order to be ready to counter your defense, we needed to investigate the other recipients of the organs from Gloria Torres. I said I had a source who would slip us the list of names without us having to get a search warrant, etcetera, etcetera, and they said great. They gave me the day. But nothing, Terry. I'm sorry but I checked out every name. I got nothing.'

'Tell me.'

'Well, I don't have the list with me but –'

'Hold on.'

McCaleb walked into Graciela's bedroom, where he had seen the copy of the list he had given her on the bureau. He grabbed it and read the first name to Winston.

'J. B. Dickey – he got the liver.'

'Right, okay, he didn't make it. He got the transplant but there were complications and he died three weeks after surgery.'

'But that doesn't mean it wasn't him.'

'I know that. But I talked to the surgeon at St Joseph's. It was a charity case. The guy was on MediCal and the hospital picked up the rest. This wasn't a guy with money or connections to a hit man, Terry. Come on.'

'Okay, next. Tammy Domike, one of the kidneys.'

'Right. She's a schoolteacher. She's twenty-eight, married to a carpenter and has two kids. She doesn't fit either. It just wasn't –'

'William Farley, the other kidney.'

'Retired Chippie from Bakersfield. He's been in a wheelchair for twelve years – since he took a bullet in the spine during a routine traffic pullover on the grapevine. They never caught the guy, either.'

'California Highway Patrol,' McCaleb mused out loud. 'He could have friends who could have pulled this off for him.'

Winston was silent for a long moment before responding.

'It seems unlikely, Terry. I mean, listen to what you're –'

'I know, I know, never mind. What about the eyes? Christine Foye got the corneas.'

'Right. She sells books for a living and just got out of college. It's not her, either. Look, Terry, we were hoping that one of these people would be some millionaire or a politician or anybody with the juice to do this. Somebody obvious. But it's just not there. I'm sorry.'

'So I'm still the best and only suspect.'

'Unfortunately.'

'Thanks, Jaye, you've been a big help. I've got to go.'

'Wait! And don't get mad at me. I've been the only one who has listened to you. Remember?'

'I know, I'm sorry.'

'Well, there was one other thing, I was thinking. I wasn't going to tell you until I had some time to check it out. I'm going to start on it tomorrow. I'm working on a warrant for information right now.'

'What? Tell me. I need something now.'

'Well, you were only thinking in terms of who got the organs that became available after the death of Gloria Torres, right?'

'Right. Cordell's and Kenyon's were not harvested.'

'I know. I'm not talking about that. But there is always a waiting list, right?'

'Yeah, always. I waited almost two years because of the blood type.'

'Well, maybe someone just wanted to move up the list.'

'Move up?'

'You know, they were like you, waiting, and they knew it would be a long wait. Maybe even a fatal wait. Weren't you told that with your blood type there was no telling when a heart would become available?'

'Yeah, they told me not to get my hopes up.'

'Okay, so maybe our guy is still waiting but by taking

out Gloria Torres, he has in effect moved up one notch on the list. Improved his chances.'

McCaleb thought about this. He saw the possibility. He suddenly remembered Bonnie Fox telling him that there was another patient on the ward who was in the same situation McCaleb had been in. He wondered now if she meant literally the same situation, waiting for a heart that was type AB with CMV negative. He thought of the boy he had seen in the hospital bed. Could he be the patient Fox meant?

McCaleb thought about what a parent would be willing to do to save a child. Could it be possible?

'It could work,' he said, his adrenaline returning and the monotonal quality of his voice gone now. 'What you're saying is that it could be somebody still waiting.'

'Right. And I am going to go to BOPRA with a warrant to get all their waiting lists and their blood donor records. It should be interesting to see how they respond.'

McCaleb nodded but his mind was skipping ahead.

'Wait a minute, wait a minute,' he said. 'It's too complicated.'

'What is?'

'The whole thing. If somebody wanted to move up on the list, why take out donors? Why not just knock people off the list?'

'Because that might be too obvious. If two or three people needing heart or liver transplants in a row get hit, it's bound to raise a question somewhere. But by hitting the donors, it's more obscure. No one noticed it until you came along.'

'I guess,' McCaleb said, still not sure he was convinced. 'Then if you're right, it could even mean the shooter's going to hit again. You've got to go down the list of AB donors. You've got to warn them, protect them.'

That possibility brought the excitement back. It was jangling in his veins.

'I know,' Winston said. 'When I get the warrant, I'm going to have to tell Nevins and Uhlig, all of them, what I am doing. That's why you have to come in, Terry. It's the only way. You have to come in with a lawyer and lay this all out, then take your chances. Nevins, Uhlig, these are smart people. They'll see where they went wrong.'

McCaleb didn't respond. He saw the logic in what she was saying but was hesitant to agree because it would be putting his fate in the hands of others. He would rather rely on himself.

'Do you have a lawyer, Terry?'

'No, I don't have a lawyer. Why would I have a lawyer? I haven't done anything wrong.'

He cringed. He had heard countless guilty individuals make the same statement before. Winston probably had, too.

'I meant do you know a lawyer who could help you?' she said. 'If you don't, then I can suggest a few. Michael Haller Jr would be a good choice.'

'I know lawyers in case I need one. I have to think about this.'

'Well, call me. I can bring you in, make sure everything is handled right.'

McCaleb's mind wandered and he was inside a holding cell at the county jail. He had been in the lockup on interviews as a bureau agent. He knew how loud jails were and how dangerous. He knew that innocent or not, he would never surrender himself to that.

'Terry, you there?'

'Yeah, sorry. I was just thinking about something. How can I reach you to arrange this?'

'I'll give you my pager and my home. I'll be here until

probably six but after that I'm heading home. Call me anywhere, any time.'

She gave him the numbers and McCaleb wrote them down in his notebook. He then put it away and shook his head.

'I can't believe this. I'm sitting here talking about turning myself in for something I didn't do.'

'I know that. But the truth is a powerful thing. It will work out. Just make sure you call me, Terry. When you decide.'

'I'll call you.'

He hung up.

# 39

Bonnie Fox's receptionist, the frowner, told McCaleb that the doctor had been in transplant surgery all afternoon and would probably not be available for another two to three hours. McCaleb almost cursed out loud but instead left Graciela's number and told the frowner to write down that he needed Fox to call back as soon as possible no matter what the hour. He was about to hang up when he thought of something.

'Hey, who is getting the heart?'

'What?'

'You said she was in surgery. Which patient? Was it the boy?'

'I'm sorry, I'm not at liberty to discuss other patients with you,' said the frowner.

'Fine,' he said. 'Then just make sure you tell her to call me.'

McCaleb spent the next fifteen minutes pacing between the living room and kitchen, hoping unrealistically that the phone would ring and Fox would be on the line.

He finally managed to shoehorn the anxiety into a side compartment of his brain and started thinking about the larger problems at hand. McCaleb knew he had to start making decisions, chief of which was to decide whether to get a lawyer. He knew Winston was right; it was the smart move to get legal protection. But McCaleb couldn't bring himself to make the call to Michael Haller Jr or anybody else, to give up on his own skills and rely on another's.

In the living room, there were no documents left on the coffee table. As he had gone through the pages, he had returned them to the leather bag until all that was on the table was the stack of videotapes.

Desperate for a diversion from his thoughts about what exactly Fox had said to him about the other patient, he picked up the videocassette on top of the stack and walked it over to the television. He popped it into the VCR without looking to see which tape it was. It didn't matter. He just wanted something else to think about for a while.

But as he dropped back onto the couch, he immediately ignored the tape that was playing. Michael Haller Jr, he thought. Yes, he would be a good attorney. Not as good as his old man, the legendary Mickey Haller. But the legend was long dead and Junior had taken his place as one of the most visible and successful defense attorneys in Los Angeles. Junior would get him out of this, McCaleb knew. But, of course, that would be after the reputation-destroying media blitz, the looting of his savings and the selling of *The Following Sea*. And even when it was over and he was clear, he would still carry the stigma of suspicion and guilt with him.

Forever.

McCaleb squinted his eyes and wondered what it was he was staring at on the TV. The camera was focused on the legs and feet of someone standing on a table. Then he recognized his own walking boots and placed what he was seeing. The hypnosis session. The camera had been running when McCaleb climbed onto the table to remove some of the overhead lighting tubes. James Noone appeared in the frame and reached up as one of the long fluorescent light tubes was handed down to him.

McCaleb grabbed the TV remote off the arm of the

couch and hit the fast forward button. Interested because he had forgotten to review the hypnosis session as he had promised Captain Hitchens he would, McCaleb decided to skip through the preliminaries. He moved the tape past the initial interview and relaxation exercises to the actual questioning of Noone under hypnosis. He wanted to hear James Noone's recounting of the details of the shooting and the killer's getaway.

McCaleb watched with total concentration and quickly found himself suffering the same physical effects of frustration he had felt during the actual session. Noone had been a perfect subject. It was rare that he had hypnotized a witness who could recall such detail. The cutting frustration was that he simply hadn't gotten a good look at the driver and the Cherokee's license plates had been covered.

'Damn,' McCaleb cursed out loud as the taped session drew to a close.

He reached for the remote, deciding to rewind and run the interview again, when he suddenly froze, his finger poised over the remote button.

McCaleb had just seen something that did not fit, something he had missed during the actual session because he was distracted by Winston, who had been sitting in. He rewound the tape but only briefly, then replayed the last few questions that were asked.

On the tape, McCaleb was wrapping it up, asking a scatter of leftover and wishful-thinking questions. They were long shots, thrown at Noone out of frustration. He had asked about any stickers on the Cherokee's windshield. Noone said no and then McCaleb was out of questions. He turned to Winston and asked her, 'Anything else?'

Even though McCaleb had broken his own rules by asking a question of a nonparticipant, Winston followed the rules and did not answer verbally. Instead, she shook her head in the negative.

'You sure?' McCaleb asked.

Again she shook her head no. McCaleb then began bringing Noone out of the trance.

But that was wrong and McCaleb had missed it at the time. Now he came around the coffee table, remote in hand, and leaned closer to the screen. He rewound the tape one more time to watch the sequence again.

'Son of a bitch,' he whispered after the play-through. 'You should've answered me, Noone. You should have answered!'

He punched the eject button and turned to grab another tape. He knocked the short stack across the coffee table and then quickly scrabbled through the plastic cassettes until he found the tape with the label marked Sherman Market. He put the tape into the machine, started playing it on fast forward and then paused the image when the Good Samaritan was on the screen.

The VCR could not hold the image still and McCaleb guessed the machine was an inexpensive model with only two tape heads. He ejected the tape and looked at his watch. It was four-forty. He slapped the remote down on top of the television and went to the kitchen for the phone.

Tony Banks agreed to stay once again after closing at Video GraFX Consultants until McCaleb could get there. Crossing the floor of the Valley on the 101, he initially made good time. Most of the rush-hour traffic was going the other way, the workforce of the city returning to the bedroom communities of the Valley. But when he dipped south on the freeway to go through the Cahuenga Pass into Hollywood, the brake lights were flared for as far as he could see and he got bogged down. He finally pulled

Buddy Lockridge's Taurus into the small employee lot at VGC at five after six. Once again, Tony Banks answered the door after McCaleb had pushed the night bell.

'Tony, thanks,' McCaleb said to the man's back as he was led down the hallway once again to one of the tech rooms. 'You are really helping me out here.'

'No problem.'

But McCaleb noted that there wasn't as much enthusiasm in the 'No problem' this time. They entered the same room they had sat in the week before. McCaleb handed Banks the two tapes he had brought with him.

'On each of these tapes there is a man,' he said. 'I want to see if they are the same man.'

'You mean, like, you can't tell.'

'Not for sure. They look different. But I think it's a disguise. I think they're the same man but I want to be sure.'

Banks put the first tape into the player on the left side of the console, turned it on and the Sherman Market robbery and shooting began playing on the corresponding overhead video display tube.

'This guy?' Banks said.

'Right. Freeze it when there's a good look.'

Banks froze the image at the moment the so-called Good Samaritan was looking off camera in right profile.

'How is that? I need the profile. It's hard to do a comparison front-on.'

'You're the boss.'

He handed Banks the second tape, which was placed in the righthand player, and soon the hypnosis session was playing on the right VDT screen.

'Back it up,' McCaleb said. 'I think there's a profile before he sits down.'

Banks reversed the tape.

'What are you doing to him on this?'

'Hypnosis.'

'Really?'

'I thought so at the time. But now I think he was playing me the whole – there.'

Banks paused the tape. James Noone was looking to his right, most likely at the door to the interview room. Banks played with the dials and the computer mouse and expanded the picture, then sharpened it. He did the same with the image on the left screen. He then leaned back and looked at the side-by-side profiles. After a few moments he spoke as he unclipped an infrared pointer from his pocket and turned it on.

'Well, the complexions don't match. One guy looks Mexican.'

'That would be easy. A couple hours in a tanning salon could give him that look.'

Banks played the pointer's red dot along the bridge of the Good Samaritan's nose.

'Look at the slope of the nose,' he said. 'See the double bump?'

'Right.'

The red dot jumped to the left screen and found the same double bump in the slope of James Noone's nose.

'It's an unscientific guess but it looks pretty close to me,' Banks said.

'Me too.'

'You've got different-color eyes but that can be done.'

'Contacts.'

'Right. And here, the expanded jawline on this guy on the right. A dental appliance – you know, like a rubber sleep guard – or even wads of tissue paper like Brando used in *The Godfather* could be used to make that appearance.'

McCaleb nodded, silently noting another possible connection to the gangster movie. Cannoli and now possibly wads of tissue paper as cheek implants.

'And hair is always changeable,' Banks was saying. 'In fact, this guy looks like he's got on a wig.'

Banks ran the red dot along the Good Samaritan's hairline. McCaleb silently chastised himself for seeing this only now. The hairline was a perfect line, the telltale indication of a hairpiece.

'Let's see what else we've got.'

Banks went back to the dials and pulled back on the image. He then used the mouse to delineate a new enhancement area. The Good Samaritan's hands.

'It's like chicks,' Banks said. 'They can put on makeup, wigs, even get their tits done. But they can't do nothing about their hands. Their hands – and sometimes their feet – always give 'em away.'

Once he had the Good Samaritan's hands blown up and in focus, he went to work on the other console until he had an enlargement of Noone's right hand on the opposite screen. Banks stood up so that he was at direct eye level with the screens and leaned to within a few inches of each tube as he studied and compared the hands.

'Okay, here, look.'

McCaleb stood up and looked closely at the screens.

'What?'

'The first one has got a bit of a scar here on the knuckle. You see it, the discoloration?'

McCaleb leaned in close to the image of the Good Samaritan's right hand.

'Wait a sec,' Banks said. He opened a drawer in the console and pulled out a photographer's eyepiece, the kind used to study and magnify negatives on a light table. 'Try this.'

McCaleb held the eyepiece over the knuckle in question and looked through it. He could see a swirl of white scar tissue on the knuckle. Though the whole image was distorted and blurry, he identified the scar as almost being in the shape of a question mark.

'Okay,' he said. 'Let's see the other.'

He took a step to his left and used the eyepiece to locate the same knuckle on James Noone's right hand. The hand was not held in the same posture or at the same angle but the thick white swirl of scar tissue was there. McCaleb held steady and studied the image until he was sure. He then closed his eyes for a moment. It was a lock. The man on each of the VDT screens was the same man.

'Is it there?' Banks asked.

McCaleb handed him the eyepiece.

'It's there. Any chance I can get hard copies of those two screens?'

Banks was looking through the eyepiece at the second screen.

'It's there all right,' he said. 'And yes, I can make hard copies. Let me put the images on a disk and take it back to the printer in the lab. It'll take a few minutes.'

'Thanks, man.'

'I hope it helps.'

'More than you know.'

'What's the guy doing anyway? Dressing up like a Mexican and doing good deeds?'

'Not really. Someday I'll tell you the whole thing.'

Banks let it go and went to work on the console, transferring the video images on the screens to a computer disk. He backed up the videos and transferred the headshots as well.

'Be back in a few minutes,' he said, getting up. 'Unless I have to warm up the machine.'

'Hey, is there a phone I can use while you're gone?'

'In the left drawer there. Hit nine first.'

McCaleb called Winston's home number and got her

machine. As he listened to her voice, he hesitated about leaving a message, aware of the consequences to Winston if it was ever proved that she had worked with the subject of a murder investigation. A tape of his voice could do that. But he decided that the discoveries he had made in the last hour made it worth the risk. He didn't want to page Winston because he didn't want to wait around for her to call. He had to move. He hatched a quick plan and left a message after the beep.

'Jaye, it's me. I'll explain all of this when I see you but for now just trust me. I know who the shooter is. It's Noone, Jaye, James Noone. I'm heading to his address now – the address on the witness report. Meet me there if you can. I'll run it all down for you then.'

He hung up and called her pager number. He then punched in her home phone number and hung up. With any luck, he thought, Winston would get the message and soon be heading toward Noone's address to back him up.

McCaleb pulled his leather bag onto his lap and opened the zippered center pouch. The two guns were there, his own Sig-Sauer P-228 and the HK P7 he now knew James Noone had planted under his boat. McCaleb reached into the bag and took his own weapon out. He checked the action and tucked the pistol into the waistband of his jeans at the small of his back. He pulled his jacket down over it.

# 40

When questioned on the night of James Cordell's murder, James Noone had provided deputies with a single address for both his home and workplace. Until McCaleb got there, the address on Atoll Avenue in North Hollywood defied identification as an apartment or an office. That area of the Valley was a hodgepodge mixture of residential, commercial and even industrial zoning.

He slowly crawled north on the 101, back through the Cahuenga Pass, and finally picked up some speed as he switched to the 134 north. He exited on Victory and drove west until he found Atoll Avenue. The neighborhood he turned into was decidedly industrial. He could smell a bakery and he passed a fenced yard where slabs of jagged granite were stacked and pointing at the sky. There were warehouses without names on them. There was a pool chemical supply wholesaler and an industrial waste recycling center. Just where Atoll dead-ended at an old railroad spur with tall weeds poking up between the rails, McCaleb turned the Taurus down a driveway bordered on both sides by a long row of small, single-garage-bay warehouses. Each unit was a separate small business or storage lockup. Some had the names of businesses painted over the aluminum roll-up doors, some had no identifying marks at all and were either unrented or used anonymously for storage. McCaleb stopped the car in front of the rusting door marked with the address James Noone had given deputies three months before. There were no other markings on the door but the address. He killed the car's engine and got out.

It was a black night. No moon, no stars. The row of warehouses was dark save for a single floodlight down at the entrance. McCaleb looked around. He heard the tinny sound of music – Jimi Hendrix singing *Let me stand next to your fire* – from somewhere seemingly far away. And further down the drive, six warehouses away, the door to one of the garages had been pulled down unevenly until it jammed, offering a three-foot slice of the warehouse's interior that looked like a crooked smile blacker than the sky.

He checked Noone's unit, dropping to a crouch to study the line where the garage door met the concrete pavement. He wasn't sure but there appeared to be a dim light emanating from within the warehouse. He stepped closer and could make out the padlock that attached a steel ring on the door to a matching ring embedded in the concrete.

He stood up and banged the door with an open palm. The noise was loud and he heard it reverberate inside. He stepped back and looked around again. Other than the sound of the music, there was only silence. The air was still. The night wind had not found its way down to the space between the rows of garages.

McCaleb got back in the car, started it and backed it up at an angle so that the headlights were at least partially focused on Noone's garage. He then killed the engine but left the lights on, got out and went to the trunk. After lifting up the trunk mat, he found the jack assembly intact. He removed the jack handle and came around the car to the garage door. He looked up and down the drive once more and then bent down to the padlock.

As a bureau agent, McCaleb had never once been

involved in an illegal break-in. He knew that they were a matter of routine but he had somehow avoided the ethical dilemma himself. But he felt no dilemma now as he worked the iron bar into the hasp of the lock. He wasn't carrying the badge anymore and, above that, this was personal. Noone was a killer and, worse yet, he had sought to pin his work on McCaleb. McCaleb didn't give a second thought to Noone's rights to protection from unlawful search and seizure.

Holding the jack handle on the far end for leverage, he slowly began pulling the steel bar in a clockwise motion. The padlock hasp remained strong but the steel ring attached to the door groaned under the pressure and then snapped off, its solder points giving way.

McCaleb straightened up and looked around and listened. Nothing. Just Hendrix covering Bob Dylan's 'All Along the Watchtower'. He quickly moved back to the Taurus and returned the jack handle to the spare-tire kit, pulled the trunk mat back over it and closed the trunk lid.

As he came around the car, he bent over next to the front tire and ran two fingers along the wheel rim, picking up a good amount of black carbon dust that had built up from the brake pads. He stepped over to the garage door and, squatting down by the lock, he smeared the carbon over the break points of the solder so that it would appear as though the ring had been broken off the door some time ago and the break points had been exposed to the elements. He then rubbed the rest of the dirt off his fingers onto one of his black socks.

When he was ready, he gripped the door's pull handle with his right hand. With his left he reached behind him and under his coat. He brought it back gripping his pistol, which he held at shoulder height, pointing skyward. With one move he stood and jerked the door up with him, using its momentum to keep it moving up until it was above his head.

His eyes quickly scanned the dim confines of the garage, his gun now pointed in the direction his eyes moved. The car's headlights illuminated about a third of the room. He could see an unmade cot and a stack of cardboard boxes against the left wall. Scanning right, he saw the outline of a desk and file cabinets. There was a computer on the desk, the monitor's screen apparently on and facing the rear wall, throwing a violet glow against it. McCaleb noticed the six-foot-long light hanging from the ceiling. In the shadowy light his eyes traced the aluminum conduit from the junction box along the ceiling and down the wall to a switch near the cot. He stepped sideways and reached for the switch without looking at it.

A fluorescent bulb blinked once, buzzed and then lit the garage with its severe light. McCaleb could now see that there was no one in the room and there were no closets to be checked. Just the approximately twenty-by-twelve-foot space cluttered with a mishmash of office furniture and equipment and the basic necessities of home – a bed, a chest of drawers, an electric space heater, a double-coil hot plate and a half-size refrigerator. No sink and no bathroom.

McCaleb stepped backward and then around the car. He reached in through the open window and shut off the lights. He then slipped the pistol back into his waistband, this time in the front for easier access. Finally, he stepped into the garage.

If the air had been still outside, then on the inside it seemed stagnant. McCaleb moved slowly around the old steel government desk and looked at the computer. The monitor was lit and a screen saver glowed on the screen. Random numbers of different sizes and colors floated on a sea of purple velvet. McCaleb stared at the screen for a few moments and he felt a tugging inside, almost a coiling of some deep muscle. In his mind the picture of a single red apple bouncing on a dirty linoleum floor appeared and then was gone. A tremble climbed the ladder of his spine.

'Shit,' he whispered.

He looked away from the computer screen, noticing that also on the desk was a collection of books clasped between brass bookends. Most were reference books on accessing and using the Internet. There were two volumes containing Internet addresses and two biographies of well-known computer hackers. There were also three books on crime scene investigation, a manual on homicide investigation, a book on an FBI investigation of a serial killer known as the Poet, and, finally, two books on hypnosis, the last about a man named Horace Gomble. McCaleb knew about Gomble. He had been the subject of more than one investigation by the bureau's serial crimes unit. Gomble was a former Las Vegas entertainer who had used his skills as a hypnotist, along with drug enhancers, to molest a series of young girls at county fairs throughout Florida. As far as McCaleb knew, he was still in prison.

McCaleb moved slowly all the way behind the desk now and sat down in the worn command chair facing the computer. Using a pen from his pocket, he pulled the desk's center drawer open. There was not much in it but a few pens and a plastic CD-ROM case. He used his pen to flip the case over and saw that it was called *Brain Scan*. He read the packaging and saw that the CD offered its user a guided tour of the human brain with detailed graphics and analysis of its workings.

He closed the drawer and used the pen again to open one of the two side drawers. The first one was empty except for an unopened box of Crackerjack. He closed it and below it was a file drawer. In this there were several manila files hanging in green folders hooked on two rails. Bending down to see better, McCaleb read the name on the tab of the first file:

GLORIA TORRES

He dropped the pen to the floor and in the same moment decided not to pick it up and that he didn't care anymore about leaving fingerprints or possibly infecting a crime scene. He pulled the file out and opened it on the desk. It contained photos of Gloria Torres in various clothing at various times of the day. In two of the photos Raymond was with her. In one she was with Graciela.

There were typewritten logs in the file. Surveillance logs. Detailed descriptions of Gloria's movements on a day-to-day basis. He quickly scanned these and saw repeated notations of her nightly stop at Sherman Market on her way home from work.

He closed the file, left it on the desk and reached for the next one in the drawer. He could have guessed the name written on the tab before he saw it:

JAMES CORDELL

He didn't bother opening it. He knew it would contain photos and surveillance notes just like the first one. Instead, he reached down and looked at the next file in line. It was as expected:

DONALD KENYON

He didn't pull that file, either. He used his finger to bend back the tabs on the remaining files so he could read them. As he did this, his heart lurched inside his chest, as if it had somehow come loose inside. He knew the names on the file tabs. Every single one of them.

'It's you,' he whispered.

And in his mind he saw the apples cascading onto the floor and going every which way.

He shoved the file drawer closed and the loud bang echoed off the concrete floor and steel walls, startling him like a shot. He looked out into the night through the open door and listened. He heard nothing, not even the music anymore. Only silence.

His eyes moved to the computer monitor and he studied the numbers moving lazily around on the screen. He knew the computer had been left on for a reason. Not because Noone was coming back; McCaleb knew he was long gone. No, it had been left on for him. McCaleb had been expected here. He knew this now, knew in his heart that Noone had choreographed every move.

McCaleb tapped the space bar and the screen saver disappeared. In its place was a prompt for a password. McCaleb didn't hesitate. He had the sense he was being played like a piano. He typed in numbers in an order he knew by heart.

903472568

He hit the enter key and the computer went to work. In a few moments the password was accepted and the screen flashed to the program manager template, a white screen with various icons spread across the field. McCaleb studied these quickly. Most were for accessing games. There also were icons for accessing America Online and Word for Windows. The last symbol he looked at was a tiny file cabinet and he guessed that was the computer's file manager icon. He found the electronic mouse on the side of the computer and used it to move the computer arrow to the file cabinet. He double-clicked and the screen flashed to the file manager. It was basic computer navigating. In the file manager the listing of files ran down the left side of the screen in a neat column. Choosing one of the files and clicking the arrow on it would bring up the titles of the documents contained in that file in a column on the right side of the screen.

Using the mouse, McCaleb ran the arrow down the files column, studying each one. Most were software files for the operation of various icon programs such as America Online, the Las Vegas Casino game and others. But eventually he came to a file titled CODE. He clicked the mouse and several document titles appeared on the right side of the screen. He read through these quickly and realized they corresponded with the names on the file tabs in the desk drawer.

All except for one document. McCaleb stared at it for a long moment, his finger raised and poised over the mouse button.

MCCALEB.DOC

He clicked the mouse and the document quickly filled the screen. McCaleb began to read it like a man reading his own obituary. The words filled him with dread, for he knew that they unalterably changed his life. They stripped his soul from him, took any meaning from his accomplishments and made a horrible mockery of them.

> Hello Agent McCaleb:
>
> It is you out there, I would hope.
>
> I will assume so. I will assume that you have lived up to that wonderful reputation you carried so nobly.
>
> I wonder? Are you alone? Are you running from them now as a wanted man? But, of course, now you have what you need to save yourself from them. But I am asking about before now, how did it feel to be the hunted one? I wanted you to know that feeling. My feelings ... A terrible thing to live with fear, no?

Fear never sleeps.

Most of all, what I wanted was a place in your heart, Agent McCaleb. I wanted always to be with you. Cain and Abel, Kennedy and Oswald, darkness and light. Two worthy opponents, chained together through time ...

I could have killed you. I had that power and opportunity. But it would have been too easy, don't you think? The man on the dock, asking directions. Your morning walk, the man on the rock jetty with the fishing pole. Do you remember me?

Now you do. I was there. But it would have been too easy, don't you agree? Too easy.

You see, I needed something more than vengeance or the vanquishing of a foe. Those are the goals of fools. I wanted – no. I needed and craved – something different. To test you first by turning you into me. The villain. The hunted one.

Then, when you emerged from that fire, your skin scorched but your body whole, to reveal myself as your most ardent benefactor. Yes, it was me. I followed her. I studied her. I chose her for you. She was my Valentine to you.

You are mine forever, Agent McCaleb. Every breath you take belongs to me. Every beat of that stolen heart is the echo of my voice in your head. Always. Every day.

Remember ...

Every breath ...

McCaleb folded his arms across his chest and held himself as though he had been flayed open with a blade. A deep shudder rolled through him and a moan escaped his throat. He pushed the chair back from the desk, away from the horrible message still on the screen, and bent his body forward into the crash position. His plane was going down.

# 41

His thoughts were blood red and black. He felt as though he were in some permanent void, surrounded by a velvet curtain of black space, his hands forever searching for the seam through which to escape but never finding it. He saw the faces of Graciela Rivers and Raymond as distant images receding into the darkness.

Suddenly, he felt a cold hand on his neck and he jumped, a shriek escaping from his throat like a prisoner going over the wall. He sat up. It was Winston. His reaction had scared her as much as she had scared him.

'Terry? Are you okay?'

'Yes. I mean, no. It's him. Noone is the Code Killer. He killed all of them. The last three for me. He did it until he got it right. He killed Gloria Torres for her heart. For me. So that I would live and be the testament to his glory.'

The coincidence of the name and Noone's purpose suddenly struck McCaleb.

'Wait a minute,' Winston said. 'Slow down. What are you talking about?'

'It's him. It's all here. Check the files, the computer. He killed those others. He then decided to save me. To kill for me.'

He pointed to the computer screen, where the message to McCaleb was still displayed. He waited while she read it but finally couldn't contain himself.

'All the pieces, they were right there. All the time.'

'What pieces?'

'The code. It was so simple. He used every digit but the number one. No one. Get it? I am no one. That's all he was saying.'

'Terry, let's talk about this later. Tell me how you got here? How did you know it was Noone?'

'The tape. The session we did with him.'

'The hypnosis? What about it?'

'Remember how I told you not to speak so the subject would not be confused?'

'Right. You said only you should ask questions of Noone. Anything between us should be signals or written down.'

'But at the end, when I knew it was all going to shit, I got frustrated. I said to you, "Anything else?" and you shook your head no. I asked, "Are you sure?" and you shook your head again. I broke my own rule by speaking to you. The thing is, I asked those questions to you out loud. So Noone should have answered me. If he was in a true hypnotic trance, he should have answered because he would not have known those questions were directed at you. But he didn't answer. It shows cognizance of the situation. He knew, either by the direction of my voice or its inflection, that I was talking to you instead of him. He shouldn't have known that. Not in a true trance. He should have answered every question spoken in that room unless it was specifically addressed to someone else. I never used your name.'

'He was faking.'

'Right. And if he was faking it, then his answers were bogus. It meant he was part of the setup. I had the videos compared before I came here. There are hard copies in my car. James Noone and the Good Samaritan are the same guy. The shooter.'

Winston shook her head as if to signal brain overload.

Her eyes scanned the room for a place to sit down. There was only the cot.

'You want to sit here,' McCaleb said, standing up.

'I want to sit down but not in here. We have to back out of here, Terry. I need to call Captain Hitchens and then the others, LAPD and the bureau. I better put out a pickup on Noone, too.'

McCaleb was amazed that she still didn't have all the pieces together.

'Aren't you listening? There is no Noone. He doesn't exist.'

'What do you mean?'

'The name. It goes with everything else. Noone. Break it down and you get *no one*. I am no one. The pieces were there all the time ...'

He shook his head and dropped back into the chair. He put his face in his hands.

'How am I ... I can't live with this.'

Again Winston put her hand on his neck but this time he didn't startle.

'Come on, Terry, let's not think about that. Let's go out to the car and wait. I have to get a crime scene crew in here, maybe get some prints so we can ID this guy.'

McCaleb stood up and walked around the desk and out toward the door. He spoke without looking back at her.

'He never left a print anywhere else before. I doubt he started now.'

Two hours later McCaleb was sitting in the Taurus, parked out on Atoll behind the yellow police lines that had been strung between the rows of garage warehouses. A hundred yards down the drive he could see the cluster of activity in and around Noone's brightly lit garage. There were several detectives – some McCaleb recognized from the Code Killer task force, technicians, videographers from at least two of the agencies involved, and a half dozen uniformed officers standing by.

Moths to the flame, he thought. He watched it all with a strange detachment. His thoughts were on other things. Graciela and Raymond. And Noone. He couldn't stop thinking about the man who called himself Noone. He had been in the same room with him. He had been that close.

He needed a drink, wanted the burning taste of whiskey in his throat, but he knew to take that taste would be the same as putting a gun to his head. He knew that despite the pain cutting through him, he would not give Noone, or whoever he was, that satisfaction. He decided in the darkness of the car that he would live. Despite it all he would live.

He didn't notice the men walking down the drive toward him until they were almost to the Taurus. He flicked on the lights and identified them as Nevins and Uhlig and Arrango. He turned the lights off and waited. They opened the doors of the car and got in, Nevins in the front, the other two in the back, with Arrango directly behind McCaleb.

'Got any heat in this thing?' Nevins asked. 'It's getting cold out here.'

McCaleb started the car but waited to turn the heater on until the engine got warm. He looked in the rearview mirror at Arrango. It was too dark to see if he had a toothpick in his mouth.

'Where's Walters?'

'Busy.'

'Okay,' Nevins said. 'Uh, we came down to tell you it looks like we were wrong about you, McCaleb. I'm sorry. We're sorry. Looks like Noone is the guy. You did good work.'

McCaleb only nodded. It was a half-assed apology but he didn't care about that. What he had found out in order to clear his name would be harder to live with than if he had been publicly accused of the murders. Apologies meant nothing to him.

'We know it's been a long night for you and we want to get you on your way. I was thinking we could just kind of get your rundown on how all of this shakes out and then maybe tomorrow you come in and give a formal statement. What do you think?'

'Fine. As far as the formal statement goes, I'll give it to Winston. Not you guys.'

'Fair enough. I can understand that. But for now, why don't you tell us how, in your view, how this whole thing works. Can you do that?'

McCaleb leaned forward and switched on the heater. He composed his thoughts for a few moments before beginning.

'I'll call him Noone because that's all we have and maybe all we'll ever have. It begins with the Code Killer. That was Noone. At that time I was the bureau's point man on the task force. By agreement with the LAPD, I became the media spokesman on the case. I led the briefings, requests for interviews went to me. For ten months my face became synonymous on TV with the Code Killer. And so Noone fixated on me. As we got closer to him, he fixated on me. He sent letters to me. In his mind, I was the nemesis. I was the embodiment of the task force that was hunting him.'

'Aren't you taking a lot of the credit for yourself?' Arrango asked. 'I mean, you weren't the only –'

'Shut up and listen, Arrango. You might learn something.'

McCaleb stared at him in the rearview and Arrango stared back. McCaleb saw Nevins hold a hand up in a calming motion directed at Arrango.

'*He* gave me the credit,' McCaleb said. 'I didn't take it. Eventually, when he knew the risks were too great, he dropped out. The killings stopped. The Code Killer disappeared. About that same time I went down with ... with my problems. I needed the transplant and it became news because I had been a face in the news. Noone saw this. He could have easily been aware of this. And he hatched what he would consider his grandest scheme.'

'He decided that rather than kill you, he would save you,' Uhlig said.

McCaleb nodded.

'It would give him the ultimate victory because it would last and last. To simply eliminate me, kill me, would bring only a fleeting sense of fulfillment. But by saving me ... now there was something unique, something that would get him into the hall of fame. And he'd always have me around as a reminder of how smart and powerful he is. Do you understand?'

'I understand,' Nevins said. 'But that's the psychological side. What I want to know is how he did it? How'd he get the names? How did he know about Kenyon and Cordell and then Torres?'

'His computer. Your techs are going to have to take that thing apart.'

'We've got Bob Clearmountain coming in,' Nevins said. 'You remember him?'

McCaleb nodded. Clearmountain was the LA field office's resident computer expert. A hacker extraordinary in his own right.

'Good. Then he'll be able to answer that question better than me. Eventually. My guess is that you'll find a hacking program in that computer. Noone got into BOPRA and from there got the names. He chose his targets based on age, physical fitness and proximity. And he went to work. With Kenyon and Cordell things went wrong. They went right with Torres. That is, according to Noone's view.'

'And he planned all along to lay it on you?'

'All I think is that he wanted me to follow the trail and find out for myself what he had done. He knew that would happen if I became a suspect. Because then I would have to look into it myself. But then that didn't happen at first because the case investigators missed the clues.'

He looked at Arrango in the mirror as he said this. He could see the detective's eyes turn dark with anger. He was about to explode.

'Arrango, the fact is, you treated it as an everyday stop-and-rob with the addition of shots fired, nothing more and nothing less. You missed it. So Noone jump-started the whole thing.'

'How?' Uhlig and Nevins asked in unison.

'My involvement came about because of an article in the *Times*. That article was prompted by a letter from a reader. Whatever name was on that letter, I bet it was Noone.'

He stopped there, waiting for disagreement. None came.

'The letter prompts the article. The article prompts Graciela Rivers. Graciela Rivers prompts me. Like dominoes.'

A thought suddenly occurred to him. He remembered the man in the old foreign car watching from across the street the first time he visited the Sherman Market. He realized the car matched the one he had seen speeding from the marina lot the night he chased the intruder.

'I think Noone was watching me all along,' he said. 'Watching his plan unfold. He knew when it was time to get into my boat and plant the evidence. He knew when to call you.'

He looked at Nevins, whose eyes shifted away and out the windshield.

'You got an anonymous call? What was said?'

'Actually it was an anonymous message. Taken down

by the overnight person. It just said, "Check the blood. McCaleb has their blood." That was it.'

'It fits. That was him. Just another move in the game.'

They were silent for a while. The windows were beginning to fog with the heat and their breath.

'Well, I don't know how much of this we'll ever confirm,' Nevins said. 'Certainly a lot of maybes.'

McCaleb nodded. He doubted any of it would ever be confirmed because he doubted Noone would ever be identified or found.

'Okay, then,' Nevins continued. 'I guess we'll be in touch.'

He opened his door and the others followed. Before he got out, Uhlig reached over the seat and tapped McCaleb's shoulder with a harmonica.

'It was on the floor back here,' he said.

As Arrango stepped out onto the asphalt, McCaleb lowered his window and looked up at him.

'You know, you could've busted it. It was all there in the book. It was waiting for you.'

'Fuck you, McCaleb.'

He walked away, following the two agents back toward Noone's garage. McCaleb smiled slightly. He had to admit that in spite of everything he still wasn't above the guilty pleasure of tweaking Arrango.

McCaleb sat in the car for a few more minutes before leaving. It was late, past ten o'clock, and he was wondering where to go. He had not talked to Graciela yet and he looked forward to the task with a mixture of dread and relief, the latter coming from knowing that one way or another their relationship would be clearly defined soon. The problem he had was that he wasn't sure that he wanted to deliver his tidings at night. His news seemed better delivered during the unflinching light of day.

He put his hand on the ignition and took one last look up the drive toward the lighted garage where his life had been so brutally changed. He saw that the light cast from the garage and across the driveway was moving. He guessed that the overhead light had been disturbed somehow and was swinging. Something occurred to him then and he took his hand off the ignition.

McCaleb stepped out of the Taurus and without hesitation ducked under the yellow tape. The uniform officer in charge of entry to the crime scene said nothing. He had probably inferred – wrongly – that McCaleb was a detective, having watched three of the lead investigators walk down and sit in the car with him.

He walked to the periphery of the light and waited until he could catch Jaye Winston's eye. She was standing with a clipboard and writing down descriptions of the warehouse's contents. Every item in the place was being tagged and taken.

When Winston stepped out of the way of one of the technicians, she glanced out into the darkness and McCaleb caught her attention with a wave. She walked out of the garage and over to him. She had a cautious smile on her face.

'I thought you were clear. Why aren't you gone?'

'I'm going. Just wanted to say thanks for everything. You gettin' anything in there?'

She frowned and shook her head.

'You were right. Place is clean. Latents guys haven't even found a smudge. There are prints on the computer but my guess is that they are yours. I don't know how we're going to track this guy. It's like he was never here.'

He signaled her closer when he noticed Arrango step out of the garage and put a cigarette in his mouth.

'I think he made a mistake,' he said quietly. 'Get your best latents man and go to the Star Center. Have him laser the light tubes in the ceiling of the interview room.

When I was setting up the hypnosis session, I took down some lights and handed them to Noone. He had to take them from me or he might give himself away. There might be prints.'

Her face brightened and she smiled.

'It's on the tape of the session,' he said. 'You can tell them it was your find.'

'Thanks, Terry.'

She clapped him gently on the shoulder. He nodded and started walking back to the car. She called after him and he looked back.

'Are you all right?'

He nodded.

'I don't know where you are going. But good luck.'

He waved and turned back toward his destination.

# 42

It seemed that every light was on in Graciela's home and this time McCaleb didn't linger in the car. He knew there was no longer any time to brood over choices. He had to face her and tell her the truth – tell her everything and accept the consequences.

Once again she opened the door before he got there. This woman who cares so much as to watch and wait for me, he thought as he stepped to the door. Now I must crush her heart.

'Terry, where have you been? I've been so worried.'

She rushed from the door and embraced him. He felt his will weaken but not break. He pulled her around to his side and led her back in with his arm around her shoulder, holding her close for what might be the last time.

'Let's go in,' he said. 'I have things to tell you.'

'Are you all right?'

'For now.'

They went to the living room and he sat next to her on the sectional. He held both her hands in his.

'Raymond in bed?'

'Yes. What is it, Terry? What's wrong?'

'It's over. They haven't caught him yet but they know who it is. Hopefully, they'll get him soon. I'm in the clear.'

'Tell me.'

He squeezed her hands. He realized that his were

sweating and let hers go. It felt as if he were letting loose a fallen bird that he had nursed back to health. He felt that he would never hold her hands again.

'Remember that night we talked about faith and how hard it is for me to have it?'

She nodded.

'Before I tell you everything, I want you to know that in the last few days – actually, in all the time that I've known you – I have felt something inside of me coming back. It's a faith of some sort. Maybe a belief in something. I don't know. But I do know it was a start, a beginning of something good ...'

'Was?'

He looked away from her for a moment to try to put the words together. It was hard. He knew he only had this one chance.

He looked back at her.

'But it's so new and so fragile, this change. And I don't know if it can last with what I have to tell you. But I want you to decide. I haven't prayed for anything in a long time. But I'll say a prayer that I see you – and Raymond – on my dock again. Or I'll pick up the phone and I'll hear your voice. I'm going to leave it up to you to decide.'

He leaned into her and kissed her gently on the cheek. She didn't resist.

'Tell me,' she said quietly.

'Graciela, your sister is dead because of me. Because of something I did a long time ago. Because I crossed a line somewhere and allowed my ego to challenge a madman's, Gloria is dead.'

His eyes dropped away from hers. The pain he had just put into them was too much for him to witness.

'Tell me,' she said again, even quieter this time.

And he did. He told her about the man known for the time being only as James Noone. He told her of the trail he had followed to the garage warehouse. He told her what he found there and what was waiting for him on the computer.

She began to cry as he told it, quiet tears that rolled down her cheeks and fell to the denim blouse she wore. He wanted to reach out to her, grab her and hold her close and kiss the tears on her cheeks. But he couldn't. He knew he was out of her world at that moment. He could not enter of his own choice. She would have to invite him back in.

When he was done, they sat quietly for a few moments. Graciela finally reached up and with open palms smeared the tears on her cheeks.

'I must look awful.'

'No, you don't.'

She looked down at the rug through the glass coffee table and a long period of silence passed by.

'What will you do now?' she finally asked.

'I'm not sure but I have a few ideas. I'm going to find him, Graciela.'

'Can't you leave it? Let the police find him?'

McCaleb shook his head.

'I don't think I can. Not now. If I don't find him and face him, I'll never know if I can get past this. I don't know if that makes sense or not.'

She nodded, still looking at the floor, and more silence went by. Finally she looked up at him.

'I want you to go now, Terry. I need to be alone.'

McCaleb nodded and slowly stood up.

'Okay.'

Again he fought an almost overwhelming urge to just touch her. Nothing more. He just wanted to feel her warmth once more. Like on the first day when she had touched him.

'Good-bye, Graciela.'

'Good-bye, Terry.'

He crossed the room and headed toward the door. On his way he glanced at the china cabinet in the living room and saw the framed photo of Gloria Torres. She was smiling at the camera on that happy day so long ago. It was a smile he knew would always haunt him.

# 43

After a night of fitful sleep with dreams of being dragged down through deep, dark water, McCaleb rose at dawn. He showered and then made himself a heavy breakfast – an onion and green pepper omelet, microwaved sausage and a half quart of orange juice. When he was done, he still felt hungry and didn't know why. Afterward he went down to the head and took another reading of his vital signs. Everything was fine. At five after seven he called Jaye Winston's office number. She was there and he could tell by her voice that she had worked straight through the night.

'Two things,' McCaleb said. 'When do you want to do this formal statement and when do I get my car back?'

'Well, the Cherokee you can have any time. I just have to call over to release it.'

'Where is it?'

'Right here. Our impound lot.'

'I suppose I have to come get it.'

'Well, you've got to come out here anyway to give me a statement. Why don't you do both at the same time?'

'Okay, when? I want to get this over with. I want to get out of here, take a vacation.'

'Where are you going?'

'I don't know. I just have to get away, try to work all of this poison out. Maybe Vegas.'

'Now that's a *great* place for mental rehabilitation.'

McCaleb ignored her sarcasm.

'I know. So when can we meet?'

'I've got to put the case together ASAP and I need your statement. So anytime this morning would be good for me. I'll just make room for you.'

'Then I'm on my way.'

Buddy Lockridge was sleeping on the cockpit bench. McCaleb rousted him and he woke with a start.

'What is – hey, Terror, you're back, man.'

'Yeah, I'm back.'

'How's my car, man?'

'It's still running. Listen, get up, I've got one more trip to make and I need you to drop me off.'

Lockridge slowly pulled himself up into a sitting position. He had been lying under a sleeping bag. He gathered it around him and rubbed his eyes.

'What time is it?'

'It's seven-thirty.'

'Fuck, man.'

'I know, but this will be the last time.'

'Everything okay?'

'Yeah, everything's fine. I just need you to drop me at the sheriff's office so I can get my car. I need to go by a bank on the way.'

'They're not open this early.'

'They'll be open by the time we get out to Whittier.'

'So if I'm driving you out to pick your car up, who is going to drive it back here?'

'Me. Let's go.'

'But you said you aren't supposed to be driving, man. Especially a car with an air bag.'

'Don't worry about it, Buddy.'

They were on the way a half hour later. McCaleb brought a duffel bag with a change of clothes and everything else he would need for his trip. He also brought a thermos of coffee and two cups. He poured coffee and filled Buddy in on the case and all that had happened while they drove. Buddy asked questions for most of the drive.

'I guess I'll have to buy a paper tomorrow,' he said.

'It will probably be on TV, too.'

'Hey, is it going to be a book? Will I be in it?'

'I don't know. The story will probably hit the news today. I guess it depends on how big a story it is before anybody decides on a book.'

'Do they pay you to use your name like that? In a book, I mean. Or like in a movie?'

'I don't know. I guess you could ask for something. You were an important part. You came up with that missing picture in Cordell's car.'

'That's right, I did.'

Lockridge seemed proud of his part and the prospect of possibly making some money from it.

'And the gun. I found the gun that prick hid under the boat.'

McCaleb frowned.

'You know what, Buddy? If there's ever a book or if any reporters or cops come around, I would like it a lot better if you never mentioned that gun. That would help me a lot.'

Lockridge glanced over at him and then back at the road.

'No problem, then. I won't say a word.'

'Good. Unless I tell you otherwise. And if anybody comes to me about a book, I'll be sure to tell 'em to talk to you.'

'Thanks, man.'

It was after nine by the time they fought through all the traffic to Whittier. McCaleb had Lockridge stop by a Bank of America branch while he went in and wrote a check for $1,000, taking the cash in twenties and tens.

A few minutes later the Taurus pulled into the Star

Center parking lot. McCaleb counted out $250 and handed it to Lockridge.

'What's this for?'

'That's for letting me use the car and for the ride today. Also, I'm going to be away for a few days. Will you keep an eye on the boat for me?'

'Will do, man. Where you going?'

'Not sure yet. And I don't know when I'll be back.'

'That's okay. Two-fifty goes a long way.'

'Remember that woman who visited me? The pretty one?'

'Sure.'

'I'm hoping she'll come by the boat looking for me. Watch for her.'

'Okay. What do I do if she shows up?'

McCaleb thought a moment.

'Just tell her I'm still gone but that I was hoping she'd come by.'

McCaleb opened the car door. Before getting out, he shook Lockridge's hand and told him again that he had been a lot of help.

'Okay, I'm out of here.'

'Sure thing, man, have a good one.'

'Oh, hey, know what? I'll probably be doing a lot of driving. You mind if I borrow one of those harps you got?'

'Take your pick.'

He fished around in the door storage pocket and came out with three harmonicas. McCaleb picked the one he had been playing during the drive the other night along the coast highway.

'That's a good one. You start with the key of C.'

'Thanks, Buddy.'

'You sure took your sweet-ass time,' Winston said as

McCaleb walked up to her desk. 'I've been wondering where the hell you've been.'

'I've been dicking around at the impound yard for an hour,' McCaleb responded. 'I can't believe you people. You take my car on a bullshit warrant and *I* have to pay towing and impound fees. A hundred and eighty bucks. There is no justice in this world, Jaye.'

'Look, just be lucky they didn't lose it and you got it back in one piece. Have a seat. I'm not quite ready.'

'Then what're you complaining about me being late for?'

She didn't answer. McCaleb took the chair at the side of her desk and watched as she went through a typed report, apparently proofreading and then initialing the bottom of each page.

'Okay,' she said. 'I was going to use one of the interview rooms. The tape's already set up. Shall we?'

'Wait a sec. What's happened since last night?'

'Oh, that's right. You haven't been around.'

'You get any prints off the light tubes?'

She broke into a smile and nodded.

'Why didn't you tell me?' McCaleb protested. 'What did you get?'

'Everything. Two palms, both thumbs, four fingers. We put it on the box and got a hit. Our boy is local. Name is Daniel Crimmins, thirty-two years old. And you remember that profile you did for the Code Killer task force? Well, you were dead-on, McCaleb. A slam dunk.'

McCaleb was beside himself with energy, though he outwardly tried to remain calm. The last pieces of the puzzle were dropping into place. He tried to recall the suspect's name from the case files but drew a blank.

'Tell me.'

'He was an LAPD academy washout. That was five years ago. As near as we can tell, since then he's had a number of private security jobs. I don't mean tin badge stuff. Computer stuff. He advertised on the Internet, had a web page, sent mailers to businesses. He basically sold computer security. We're hearing that he sometimes got work by hacking into a company's computer and then sending the CEO E-mail telling him how easy it was and why they should hire him to make their system hackproof.'

'BOPRA?'

'You got it. We've got a team over there now but they called in a little while ago. There's an executive who remembers getting E-mail from Crimmins last year. But he blew it off as a prank. He killed the message and never got another one. But it shows that Crimmins was inside BOPRA.'

McCaleb nodded.

'Anybody get his LAPD file yet?'

'Yeah, Arrango. He's being a prick with it, dealing it out on a need-to-know basis. But basically the guy lasted five months. Reason for his termination was – quote – failure to thrive in the collegial atmosphere of the academy. Translation: the guy was an introvert who would never last in a squad car. No partner would take him. So they washed him out. The problem for him was he was second generation. His old man retired up to Blue Heaven ten years ago. Uhlig had someone in the Idaho field office look dad up. He said as far as he knew, his son was currently on the LAPD. He didn't know Danny boy had been a washout because Danny boy didn't tell him. He says he hasn't seen his son in something like five or six years but when they talk on the phone, the boy always has good war stories.'

'Yeah, they're just made up.'

McCaleb saw that it all fit. The authority complex. Crimmins had transferred it from the father to the LAPD after he was washed out. The expulsion from the academy could have provided the psychic break that turned a harmless fantasy life into a deadly pastime. The murders were all on LAPD turf. He was showing the institution that deemed him unworthy just how smart, clever and worthy he was.

It occurred to McCaleb that when he had profiled the Code Killer three years before, he had suggested that dismissed officers and academy washouts be questioned as a priority. As far as he knew, that had been done.

'Wait. This guy should have been questioned back then. Failed law enforcement career was in the profile.'

'He *was* questioned. That's why Arrango is dicking around with the file. Somehow, Crimmins passed the test. He was interviewed by a team from the task force but he didn't raise an eyebrow or warrant a second look. Still, it must've scared him. He was interviewed four weeks after the last Code killing. Maybe it's the reason he stopped.'

'Probably. Still, it's not going to look very good when it comes out this guy was interviewed and skated.'

'Too fucking bad. I say, let the chips fall. We've got the press conference scheduled for three o'clock.'

McCaleb considered what she had said about the killings stopping after Crimmins had been interviewed. He felt a thrill of satisfaction that it might have been his directive to interview academy washouts that had halted the killings. While he was savoring the thought, Winston opened a file and took a color photo off a stack of them. She handed it to him. It showed Crimmins in his academy uniform. Clean cut, clean shaven, a thin face and hopeful eyes that seemed to betray his confidence. It was as if he knew when the photo was taken that he would not make it, that there would be no graduation photo.

'So it looks like when he was Noone, there was not much of a disguise used,' he said. 'The glasses and something inside his cheeks to make his face look fuller.'

'Right. Probably because he knew he would have direct contact with cops and a full-on disguise would show.'

'Can I keep this?'

'Sure, we'll be giving them out today.'

'What's next? You got addresses?'

'Nothing good. The warehouse you already found was the only thing current. But there's got to be another place. His web page was still operational even after we unplugged the warehouse. It means he's got another computer somewhere. Running as we speak.'

'Can't they just trace the phone line in?'

'He's got an anonymous provider.'

'What's that?'

'Anything going to or from the web page goes through this anonymous provider of Internet access. We can't trace and we can't crack open the provider because of First Amendment bullshit. Besides, the expert over at the bureau, Bob Clearmountain, told me guys like him now use microwaves instead of hardwire phone lines. Makes it harder to trace and locate.'

The technology was beyond McCaleb. He changed the subject.

'You going to ID him at the press conference?'

'Think so. We'll get the photo out, show the hypnotism video, see what it brings. By the way, Keisha Russell at the *Times*. Did you tip her off?'

'I owed her the call. She helped me at the beginning of this thing. I left her a voice mail this morning. Thought I'd give her a head start on it. Sorry.'

'No, that's okay. I like her. I needed to talk to her anyway. Nevins told me what you said last night, about it probably being our guy who sent the letter that prompted the story about you in the *Times*.'

'Right. Did she keep the letter?'

'No. She only remembered it was signed Bob something or other. It was probably him. He had this thing so wired.'

McCaleb suddenly thought of something. Graciela had told him that she had not become aware of the *Times* story on him until a man who claimed he had worked with Glory called and told her of the story. She then went to the library to read it. McCaleb realized that the caller could have been Crimmins setting his plan into motion.

'What is it?' Winston asked.

'Nothing. I was just thinking.'

He decided not to tell Winston his hunch yet. He would check it out himself. It would give him a reason to break his promise not to call Graciela. He could make it an official call.

'So,' Winston said. 'Where do you think he is?'

'Crimmins?' He hesitated. 'In the wind, I guess.'

Winston studied his face a moment.

'I thought you might have an idea.'

He looked away from her and down at the desk.

'Well, the wind doesn't blow forever,' she said, letting it go. 'He's got to come down somewhere.'

'Hope so.'

They were silent then, finished with each other except for the formality of the statement he would have to tape.

'It may be none of my business,' Winston said, 'but how are you going to deal with this?'

'I'm working on it.'

'Well, if you ever need somebody to talk to ...'

He nodded his thanks.

'Okay, then should we go get this over with?'

An hour later McCaleb was alone in the interview room. He had told his story to Winston and she had left with the tape to get it transcribed. She had given him permission to use the phone that was on the table and told him he had the room for as long as he needed it.

He composed his thoughts for a few moments and then punched in the number for the nursing station in the emergency room at Holy Cross. He asked for Graciela but the woman who answered said Graciela was not there.

'Is she on break?'

'No, she's not here today.'

'Okay, thank you.'

He hung up. He guessed that she had called in sick. He couldn't blame her. Not with the news he had delivered the night before. He punched in her home number. But after five rings the call was picked up by an answering machine. After the beep he fumbled through the message he wanted to leave.

'Uh, Graciela, it's me, Terry, you there?'

He waited a long moment and then continued.

'Um, I just wanted ... they told me you weren't at work and I, uh, I wanted to say hello and there's a couple of questions I need to ask you about things. Loose ends mostly ... but it would help to – anyway, I'm gonna go and I'll probably try to call you later on. Um, I'll probably be on the road so you don't have to worry about calling me back.'

He wished he could erase the message and start over. He cursed to himself and hung up, then wondered if the curse had been recorded. He shook his head, got up and left the room.

# 44

It took him two days to find the picture that Daniel Crimmins as James Noone had drawn during the hypnosis session. McCaleb started at Rosarita Beach and then worked his way south. He found it between La Fonda and Ensenada on a remote stretch of the coast. Playa Grande was a small village on a two-tiered rock flow overlooking the sea. The village mostly consisted of a motel with six small detached bungalows, a pottery store, a small restaurant and market and a Pemex station. There was also a small stable for renting horses to ride down on the beach. The commercial core, if it was big enough to be called that, was at the edge of a cliff overlooking the beach. On the stepped bluff above it was a wide scattering of small houses and trailer homes.

What made McCaleb stop was the stable. He remembered Crimmins describing horses on the beach. He got out of the Cherokee and walked down a steep trail cut through the rock outcroppings to the beach. The wide, white beach was a private enclave about a mile long and enclosed on each end by huge, jagged rock flows into the sea. Near the south end, McCaleb saw the rock overhang that Crimmins had described during the hypnosis session. McCaleb knew that the best and most convincing way to lie is to tell as much truth as possible. So he had taken his subject's description of the place at which he felt most relaxed in the world to be a true description of a place he knew. Now, McCaleb had found it.

He had arrived at Playa Grande through simple deduction and legwork. The description Crimmins had given during the session had obviously been the Pacific Coast. He had said he liked to drive *down* to this place and since McCaleb knew there was no California beach south of LA as remote as he had described or with horses on it, that obviously made the destination Mexico. And since Crimmins had said he drove there, that pretty much eliminated Cabo and the other points far south along the Baja peninsula. It took two days to cover the coastline that was left. McCaleb stopped at every village and every time he saw a cutoff from the highway to the beach.

Crimmins had been right. It was a truly beautiful and restful spot. The sand was like sugar and a million years of crashing waves had carved a deep bite into the cliff face, creating the overhang that resembled nothing so much as a rock wave, curled and about to break over the beach.

McCaleb was the only person on the beach to be seen in either direction. It was a weekday and he guessed that this stretch of sand lay largely unpopulated until the weekends. That was why Crimmins had liked it.

Three horses were on the beach. They milled around an empty feed trough while waiting for customers. There was no need to tie them. The beach was completely enclosed by water and rock. The only way off it was the steep trail back up to the stable.

McCaleb wore a baseball cap and sunglasses as protection against the power of the midday sun. He wore long pants and a windbreaker as well. But, entranced by the beauty of the spot, he remained on the beach long after he determined Daniel Crimmins was nowhere to be seen. After a while a teenager wearing shorts and a sweatshirt with no sleeves came down the trail and approached.

'You would like horse ride?'

'No, *gracias*.'

From the pocket of his coat McCaleb pulled the folded

photos Tony Banks had made from the videotapes. He showed them to the boy.

'You seen? This man ... I want to find.'

The boy stared at the photos and made no indication he understood. Finally he just shook his head.

'No, no find.'

He turned and headed back to the trail. McCaleb returned the photos to his jacket and after a few minutes headed back up the steep incline himself. He stopped twice on the way up but the climb still left him exhausted.

McCaleb ate lobster enchiladas at the restaurant for lunch. It cost him the equivalent of $5 American. He showed the photos a few more times but got no takers. He walked to the Pemex station after lunch and used the pay phone there to check the machine on his boat for messages. There were none. He then called Graciela's number for the fourth time while he had been on the road and once again got her machine. He didn't leave a message this time. If she was ignoring his calls, it was probably because she simply no longer wanted to talk to him.

McCaleb checked into the Playa Grande Motel, paying cash and using a phony name. As an afterthought he showed the photos to the man behind the counter in the small office and got another negative response.

His bungalow had a partial view of the beach below and a wide view of the Pacific. He checked what he could see of the beach and it was still empty except for the horses. He took off his windbreaker and decided to take a nap. It had been a wearying two days of driving bad roads, walking on sand and climbing steep trails.

Before lying down, he opened his duffel bag on the bed, put his toothbrush and toothpaste in the bathroom and then arranged the plastic vials containing his medicines and the box of disposable thermometer strips on the bed table. He took the Sig-Sauer out of the bag and put it on the table as well. It was always a marginal risk taking weapons across the border. But at the crossing, as expected, McCaleb had been simply waved through by the bored Mexican *federales*.

As he dropped off to sleep with his head between two musty pillows, he decided he would try the beach again at sunset. Crimmins had described the sunset during the hypnosis session. Maybe he would be on the beach then. If not, McCaleb decided he would begin looking for Crimmins in the scattered neighborhood above the village. McCaleb was confident he would find him. He felt no doubt that he had found the place Crimmins had described.

He dreamed in colors for the first time in months, his eyes darting under tight eyelids. He was on a runaway horse, a huge Appaloosa the same color as the wet sand, galloping down the beach. He was being chased but his unsteady mount prevented him from turning to see who it was behind him. He only knew that he must run, that if he stopped he would perish. The animal's hooves were throwing great clods of wet sand in the air as it galloped.

The rhythmic cadence of the horse's gallop was replaced by the pounding sound of his own heart. McCaleb came awake and tried to calm his body. After a few moments he decided he should check his temperature.

As he sat up and put his feet down on the carpet, his eyes checked the bed table by habit. He was looking for the clock that was on the table next to his own bed on the boat. But there was no clock here. He looked away and then his eyes darted back to the table as he realized the gun was gone.

McCaleb quickly stood up and looked around the room, an eerie feeling of dislocation coming over him. He knew he had placed the gun on the table before sleeping.

Someone had been in the room while he slept. Crimmins. He had no doubt. Crimmins had been in the room.

He hastily checked the windbreaker and duffel bag and found nothing else missing. He scanned the room again and his eyes came across a fishing pole standing in the corner of the room next to the door. He went to the corner and grabbed it. It was the same model rod and reel combination he had bought for Raymond. As he turned it in his hands and studied it, he found the initials RT had been cut into the cork hand grip. Raymond had marked the pole as his. Or someone had marked it for him. Regardless, the message was clear: Crimmins had Raymond.

McCaleb was fully alert now, his chest filling with the constricting ache of dread. He punched his fists into the arms of the windbreaker as he put it on and then left the bungalow after studying the door and finding no sign that the lock had been tampered with. He moved quickly to the motel office, the bell ringing loudly overhead as he shoved the door open. The man who had taken his money stood up from the chair behind the counter, an uneasy smile on his face. He was about to say something when McCaleb, in one unhesitating motion, stepped to the counter, reached over it and grabbed the man by the front of his shirt. He jerked him forward until his body was prone over the top of the counter, the edge of the Formica digging into his substantial gut. McCaleb bent down until he was in the man's face.

'Where is he?'

'*Qué?*'

'The man, the one you gave the key to my room. Where is he?'

'*No habla* –'

McCaleb pulled down on the man's shirt harder and put his forearm on the back of his neck. McCaleb could feel his own strength flagging but pushed down harder.

'*Bullshit, you don't. Where is he?*'

The man sputtered and moaned.

'I don't know,' he finally said. 'Please. I don't know where he is.'

'Was he alone when he came here?'

'Alone, yes.'

'Where does he live?'

'I do not know this. Please. He say he your brother and have surprise for you. I give him the key so he surprise you.'

McCaleb let go and pushed the man back over the counter so hard that he fell backward right into his chair. He held his hands up in a beseeching manner and McCaleb realized he must be truly scaring the man.

'Please.'

'Please, what?'

'Please, I don't want to have trouble.'

'It's too late. How did he know I was here?'

'I call him. He pay me. He come here yesterday and say you might come. He give me phone number. He pay me.'

'And how did you know it was me?'

'He give me picture.'

'All right, give it to me. The number and the picture.'

Without hesitation the man reached to a drawer in front of him. McCaleb quickly reached over and grabbed his wrist and roughly jerked it away from the drawer. He opened the drawer himself and his eyes held on a photograph sitting on top of a clutter of paperwork. It was a photo of McCaleb walking along the rock jetty near the marina with Graciela and Raymond. McCaleb could feel his face turning red as the anger pushed hot blood into the tightened muscles of his jaw. He held the photo up and studied the back. There was a phone number written on the back.

'Please,' the motel man said. 'You take the money.

One hundred American dollars. I don't want trouble for you.'

He was reaching into his shirt pocket.

'No,' McCaleb said. 'You keep it. You earned it.'

He yanked the door open then, hitting the overhead bell so hard that the twine it hung from snapped and the bell bounced into the corner of the office.

He went through the gravel parking lot and over to the phone at the Pemex station. He dialed the number on the back of the photograph and listened to a series of clicks on the line as the call went through at least two call-forwarding circuits. McCaleb cursed to himself. He would not be able to trace the number to an address, even if he could get someone in local authority to do it for him.

Finally the call reached the last circuit and started ringing. McCaleb held his breath and waited but the call was not picked up by human or machine. After twelve rings he crashed the receiver down onto its hook but it bounced off and dropped, swinging erratically back and forth beneath the phone. McCaleb stood frozen by anger and the impotence of his position, the light sound of the still-ringing phone buzzing from below.

After a long moment he realized he was staring through the glass pane of the phone booth at the motel parking lot. His Cherokee was there and one other car. A dusty white Caprice with a California plate on the back.

Quickly, he left the booth, crossed the parking lot to the trail and headed down to the beach. The trail cut between rock outcroppings and obscured any view below. McCaleb didn't see the beach until he got to the bottom and made the final turn to the left.

The beach was empty. He walked straight out to the water's edge looking both ways but the sand in both directions was deserted. Even the horses had been taken in for the day. His eyes were eventually drawn to the pocket of deep shadows beneath the rock overhang. He headed that way.

Beneath the overhang the sound of the surf was amplified to a magnitude that sounded like the cheering in a stadium. Moving from the bright light of the open beach into the deep shadows temporarily blinded McCaleb. He stopped, closed his eyes tightly and reopened them. As his focus returned, he saw the outlines of the jagged rock surrounding him. Then from the deepest pocket of the enclave stepped Crimmins. He held the Sig-Sauer in his right hand, the muzzle of the weapon pointing at McCaleb.

'I don't want to hurt you,' he said. 'But you know I will if I have to.'

He spoke loudly so that his voice would carry above the din and echo of waves.

'Where is he, Crimmins? Where is Raymond?'

'Don't you mean, "Where are they?"'

McCaleb had assumed as much but the confirmed knowledge of the terror Graciela and Raymond were feeling at that moment – if they were still alive – cut into him. He took a step toward Crimmins but then stopped when Crimmins raised the aim of the weapon to his chest.

'Easy now. Let's be calm. They are safe and sound, Agent McCaleb. Not to worry about that. Their safety, in fact, is in your hands. Not mine.'

McCaleb made a quick study of Crimmins. He had jet black hair and a mustache now. He was growing a beard or needed a shave. He wore pointed-toe boots, black jeans and a denim cowboy shirt with double pockets and a design seam across the chest. His current look put him somewhere between the Good Samaritan and James Noone.

'What do you want?' McCaleb demanded.

Crimmins ignored the question. He spoke in a calm voice. He was confident he had the upper hand.

'I knew if anyone would come, it would be you. I had to take precautions.'

'I said, what do you want? You want me, is that it?'

Crimmins stared wistfully out past McCaleb and shook his head. McCaleb studied the weapon. He could see the safety was off. But the hammer was not cocked back. It was impossible to tell whether Crimmins had chambered a round.

'My last sunset here,' Crimmins said. 'I have to leave this place now.'

He looked back at McCaleb, smiling as though inviting McCaleb to acknowledge the loss.

'You performed much better than I had anticipated.'

'It wasn't me. It was you, Crimmins. You fucked up. You left your fingerprints for them. You told me about this place.'

Crimmins frowned and nodded, acknowledging the mistakes. A long beat of silence went by.

'I know why you came here,' he finally said.

McCaleb did not reply.

'You want to take from me the gift that I gave you.'

McCaleb felt the bile of hate rising and burning in his throat. He remained silent.

'A vengeful man,' Crimmins said. 'I thought I told you how fleeting the fulfillment of vengeance is.'

'Is that what you learned, killing all of those people? I bet when you closed your eyes at night, the old man was still there, no matter how many you killed. He wouldn't go away, would he? What did he do to you, Crimmins, to fuck you up so bad?'

Crimmins tightened his grip on the gun and McCaleb could see his jaw take on a more pronounced line.

'This is not about that,' he responded angrily. 'It's about you. I want you to live. I want to live. None of it will have been worth it unless you live. Don't you see that? Don't you feel the bond between us? We are tied together now. We are brothers.'

'You're crazy, Crimmins.'

'Whatever I am, it is not of my doing.'

'I don't have time for your excuses. What do you want?'

'I want you to thank me for your life. I want to be left alone. I want time. I need time to move my things and find a new place. You will have to give it to me now.'

'How do I know you even have them? You have a fishing pole. It's nothing.'

'Because you know me. You know I have them.'

He waited and McCaleb said nothing.

'I was there when you called and groveled to her machine, when you pleaded for her to pick up like a pathetic schoolboy.'

McCaleb felt his anger become shaded with embarrassment.

'Where are they?' he yelled.

'They are close.'

'Bullshit. How'd you get them across the border?'

Crimmins smiled and gestured with the gun.

'The same way you took this across. No questions asked going south. I gave your Graciela a choice. She and the boy could ride up in the front and be on their best behavior or they could ride in the trunk. She acted accordingly.'

'You better not have hurt them.'

McCaleb realized how desperate he sounded and wished he hadn't said it.

'Whether that happens depends on you.'

'How?'

'I leave now. And you do not follow. You do not attempt to track me. You get in your car and go back up to your boat. You stay by the phone and I will call you from time to time to make sure you are there and not following me. When I know I am safe from you, I will let the woman and the boy go.'

McCaleb shook his head. He knew it was a lie. Killing Graciela and Raymond would be the final misery Crimmins would joyfully and without guilt bestow on him. The ultimate victory. He knew that no matter what happened after, he couldn't let Crimmins off the beach alive. He had come to Mexico for one reason. He now had to act on it.

Crimmins seemed to know his thoughts and smiled.

'No choice, Agent McCaleb. I walk away from here or they die alone in a black hole. You kill me and no one will find them. Not in time. Starvation, darkness ... it is an awful thing. Besides, you forget something.'

He held the gun up again and waited a beat for McCaleb to reply but there was nothing.

'I hope you think of me often,' Crimmins said. 'As I shall think of you.'

He started walking toward the light.

'Crimmins,' McCaleb said. 'You have nothing.'

Crimmins turned and his eyes dropped to the gun now in McCaleb's hand. McCaleb took two steps toward him and raised the muzzle of the P7 to his chest.

'You should have checked the duffel bag.'

Crimmins countered by raising the Sig-Sauer to McCaleb's chest.

'Your gun's empty, Crimmins.'

McCaleb saw doubt flick through the other man's eyes. It went by fast but he caught it. He knew then that Crimmins had not checked the gun. He didn't know that it contained a full clip but no round had been chambered.

'But this one isn't.'

They stood there, each man holding the muzzle of his gun a foot from the other's heart. Crimmins looked down at the P7, then up to McCaleb's eyes. He stared intently, as if trying to read something. In that moment McCaleb thought about the photo in the newspaper article. The piercing eyes that showed no mercy. He knew then that he had those eyes again.

Crimmins pulled the trigger of the Sig-Sauer. The hammer snapped on an empty chamber. McCaleb fired the P7 and watched as Crimmins jerked backward and fell flat on his back on the sand, his arms outstretched at ninety-degree angles, his mouth open in surprise.

McCaleb moved over him and quickly grabbed away the Sig-Sauer. He then used his shirt to wipe off the P7 and dropped it on the sand, just out of the dying man's reach.

McCaleb got down on his knees and leaned over Crimmins, careful not to get blood on himself.

'Crimmins, I don't know if I believe in a God, but I'll hear your confession. Tell me where they are. Help me save them. Finish it with something good.'

'Fuck you,' Crimmins said forcefully, his mouth wet with blood. 'They die and that's on you.'

He raised a hand and pointed a finger at McCaleb. He then dropped it to the sand and seemed drained by the outburst. He moved his lips once more but McCaleb couldn't hear him. He bent over closer.

'What did you say?'

'I saved you. I *gave* you life.'

McCaleb stood up then, brushed the sand off his pants and looked down at Crimmins. His eyes were tearing and his mouth was moving as he labored for his final breaths. Their eyes connected and held.

'You're wrong,' McCaleb said. 'I traded you for me. I saved myself.'

# 45

McCaleb drove along the gravel roads on the bluff over the village of Playa Grande and studied each house and trailer he passed, looking for the telltale sign of a telephone line hookup or a mounted microwave dish. He had all the windows of the car open and each time he came upon a property that fit the search profile, he pulled the car in close, turned it off and listened.

Not many of the properties were connected to the outside world by telephone or airwaves. McCaleb assumed most of the people who lived in so remote a location chose to do so because they didn't want that connection. They were expatriates and recluses, people who wanted to be cut off from the rest of the world. It was another reason Crimmins had chosen the place.

Twice people came out of their homes to ask McCaleb what he wanted. He showed them the photos but got negative responses. He apologized for the intrusion and moved on.

By the time the sun was close to the horizon, he was growing desperate. Without daylight he knew his search would be untenable. He would have to stop at every house or wait until the following morning. That would leave Graciela and Raymond alone somewhere for the night, without food and light, probably no heat, scared, bound or held captive in some way.

He increased his speed and quickly moved through an entire trailer park, stopping only once to show the photos to an old woman sitting on the front porch of a decrepit trailer. She shook her head no at the photos and he moved on.

Finally, after the sun was gone and the sky held the last of the day's light, he passed a crushed-shell drive leading over a small rise and then out of sight. A gate was pulled across it and posted with a No Trespassing sign printed in Spanish and English. McCaleb studied the gate for a few moments and saw that it was tied closed with just a short length of wire through the hasp. He got out, pulled the wire free and pushed the gate open.

Once over the first rise, McCaleb could see that the drive led to a trailer home set on the next rise. The ticking of anticipation began in his chest when he saw the small dish mounted on the flat roof. As he got closer, he could see there was no car parked under the aluminum carport. He also noticed a small Quonset-style storage shed at the back of the property near an old fence. Sitting on top of several of the fence posts were bottles and jars, as if set out for shooting practice.

The sound of the Cherokee's tires turning on the crushed shells obliterated any possibility of a quiet approach. It also robbed McCaleb of the chance to listen until he stopped the car.

He pulled into the carport and stopped. He turned the key off and sat frozen still and listened. There was only silence for two seconds and then he heard it. The sound was muffled by the trailer's aluminum siding, but he heard it. The ringing of a telephone inside the trailer. McCaleb held his breath and listened to it ring over and over until he was sure. He blew out his breath and felt a jolt go through his heart. He knew he had found them.

He got out and approached the trailer's door. The phone kept ringing, at least ten times now since he had stopped the car. He knew it would keep ringing until he got inside and answered it or somebody ventured into the phone booth at the Pemex station and hung up the receiver.

He tried the door and found it locked. Using the ring of keys he had taken from Crimmins's pants, he tried several in the knob until he had the door open. He stepped into the quiet and warm trailer and looked around what seemed to be a small living room. The shades had been drawn and it was dark except for the glow of a computer screen that sat on a table against the wall to the right. McCaleb reached to the wall to the left of the door and found a light switch. He flicked it and the room was illuminated.

It was much like the warehouse he had discovered in LA, crowded with computers and other equipment. There was a small sitting area apparently reserved for relaxation. None of it meant anything to McCaleb. He didn't care anymore. He had come for only two reasons.

He stepped into the trailer and called out.

'Graciela? Raymond?'

He heard nothing in reply. He thought about what Crimmins had said, about them being in a black hole. He turned and looked out the door, his eyes scanning the desolate landscape. He saw the Quonset shed and started that way.

With the heel of his palm he banged on the padlocked door and the noise echoed loudly inside but there was no answer. He fumbled as he got the keys out again and quickly jammed the small key with the Master Lock logo on it into the lock. Finally, he swung the door open and stepped into the darkness. The shed was empty and McCaleb felt a great tearing inside.

He turned and braced himself in the doorway, his eyes downcast as his mind filled with a vision of Graciela and Raymond, their arms around each other, in complete darkness somewhere.

That was when he saw it. On the crushed-shell drive

in front of him there was a clear depression pattern crossing the two patterns made by a vehicle's tires. There was a trail across the drive, heading in the direction of the sloping hill's crest. It looked to McCaleb as if there was nothing out that way, yet someone had walked there enough times to leave the trail across the drive.

His strides increased to a full run as he headed in the direction the trail led. He came over the crest and in the drop-off below he saw the flat concrete foundation of a structure that had never been built. He slowed to a walk as he approached, wondering what he had found. Rusted iron rebars and plumbing pipes protruded from the concrete. An old pick and a shovel had been left lying on it. There was a step up onto the slab at the spot where a door obviously was to be placed but never was. McCaleb stepped up and looked around. There were no doors to a basement, nothing he saw that matched what Crimmins had said.

He kicked at one of the brass water pipes and looked down into the four-inch main pipe upon which a toilet was supposed to have been placed. In that moment he knew where they were.

He spun around and his eyes covered the ground around the slab. Noting that the step would be the front of the structure, he concentrated on the ground to the rear, looking for the spot where the plumbing would lead: a septic tank. His eyes immediately picked up an area of dirt and rock that he could tell had recently been turned. He grabbed the shovel and ran.

It took him five minutes to clear the dirt and rock off the top of the tank. He knew they had air; the pipes up to the slab would provide it. But he worked as if they were suffocating below him. As he finally opened the manhole-sized cover of the tank, the sky's dying light swept in and he saw their faces. They were scared but alive. McCaleb felt a great lifting of weight off him as he reached down to them.

He helped them out of the darkness, their eyes crinkled against even the weak early-evening light. Then he held them so tight he thought that he might hurt them. Graciela was crying, her body shaking against his.

'It's all right,' he said. 'It's over now.'

She pulled her head back and looked in his eyes.

'It's over now,' he repeated. 'He won't hurt anybody ever again.'

# 46

The bilge was a claustrophobic crawl space full of the dizzying fumes of gasoline. McCaleb had an old T-shirt wrapped around his face like a bandit but still the fumes filled his lungs. There were nine bolts that held the fuel filter he was changing in place. He had three in and tightened down. He was struggling with the fourth, angling his face forward in a vain effort to keep the sweat from running into his eyes, when he heard her voice above him.

'Hello? Anybody home?'

McCaleb dropped what he was doing and jerked the shirt from around his face. He crawled to the open hatch and came up. Jaye Winston was standing on the dock waiting for him.

'Jaye. Hey, what's up? Come on aboard.'

'No, I'm on the run. I just wanted to stop by and let you know they found him. I'm on my way down to Mexico.'

McCaleb raised his eyebrows.

'He's not alive. He killed himself.'

'Really?'

'We're dealing with the Baja Judicial Police so nothing is for sure until I get down there, but they found him washed up on the beach in a place called Playa Grande. Down on the coast. Shot himself in the heart. A boy who takes care of horses on the beach found him. That was two days ago. We just got the news.'

McCaleb looked around. He saw a man in a white shirt and tie loitering near the gate to the gangway. Her partner, he assumed.

'Are they sure it was him?'

'They say so. The description is close. Plus they tracked him back to a trailer off the beach. They found computers, photos, all kinds of stuff. Looks like our guy. Plus he left a good-bye note on the computer screen.'

'What did he say?'

'Well, this is all secondhand, but essentially he took responsibility for his actions and said he deserved to die for them. It was short and sweet.'

'They find a weapon?'

'Not yet but they're sweeping the beach with metal detectors today. If they find it, it will probably be our HK P7. The bullet taken during the autopsy was a Federal FMJ. We'll see if we can borrow it for comparison to our cases up here.'

McCaleb nodded.

'So how are they playing it out?'

'Pretty simple. The guy knows we're on to him, gets an attack of remorse, writes his note and goes down to the beach, where he puts one in his heart. The tide took him into the rocks there and the body got hung up. That's why it wasn't carried out to sea. We're going down to have a look at things. And to get prints. Probably won't get gunshot residue because the body was in the water. But one thing's for sure, we're not going to close it unless we're absolutely sure it was Crimmins.'

'Yeah, that's a good idea.'

'I just want to make sure because it just didn't seem like it was heading toward a suicide, know what I mean?'

She was looking at him intently.

'Well ... you never know.'

She nodded and for the first time she looked away from him. She checked on her partner, who was watching them from a distance that put him well out of earshot.

'How was Vegas, Terry?'

He sat down on the gunwale and put the wrench he had been working with down next to him.

'Uh ... well, I didn't really go anywhere. I decided that if I didn't get this thing running, it might never happen. I turned off the phone and just worked on the boat. I think it's finally ready to go.'

'Good. I hope you catch a lot of fish.'

'I will. You come over some day, I'll take you out to catch a marlin.'

'I might take you up on that.'

She nodded and took another look around the marina.

'Well, I guess I better go. It's a long drive down there and we're getting a late start.'

'Happy hunting.'

'Thanks.'

She made a move to go but then hesitated and looked back at him.

'I saw your Cherokee up there in the lot. You ought to get it washed, Terry. There's an awful lot of sand on it.'

Their eyes held each other's for a long moment then, the silent transmission clear.

'I'll do that,' McCaleb finally said. 'Thanks.'

# 47

*The Following Sea* was cutting south at trolling speed across the low swells toward Catalina. Up on the bridge, McCaleb stood braced against the wheel. He had the forward wind curtain down and the chill air coming up off the surface hit him fully, hardening his skin beneath his clothes. Ahead in the mist the island rose like a huge rock cathedral on the horizon. The outbuildings and some of the taller boats of Avalon were coming into view. He saw the circular terra-cotta roof of the casino, the town's signature structure, clearly now.

He turned to look astern. The mainland was out of sight, discernible only by the haze of smog that hung over it like a sign warning *Do Not Come Here!* He was happy to be free of it.

He thought about Crimmins for a moment. He had no regrets about the way he had left things in Mexico. There would be no questions about his motives and choices now. But he was protecting more than himself. Graciela and Raymond had spent thirty-six hours with Crimmins. Though he had not physically harmed them, they still needed private time to heal, to put the ordeal behind them. McCaleb couldn't see how bringing more cops and questions into their lives could help with that. Graciela had agreed.

From the bridge he looked down into the cockpit and secretly watched the two of them. Raymond was in the fighting chair, his small hands grasping the trolling set.

Graciela stood next to him, holding the chair for support. If McCaleb could, he would have willed a big black marlin onto the line for the boy. But he wasn't worried. There would be plenty of time to catch fish.

Graciela seemed to sense his gaze and she looked up at him. They shared a smile of intimacy. McCaleb could feel his heart seize when she smiled at him that way. It made him so happy that it hurt.

The boat trip was a test. Not only for the boat but for the two of them. That was what she had called it. A test to see if they could overcome the thing between them, the painful knowledge of what had happened and what he had done, of why he was here and others were not. Especially Gloria. They would see if they could put that behind them, too, or at least to the side, to be taken out and looked at only when needed.

It was all McCaleb could hope for. It was all he wanted, just the chance. The fact that it was now in his grasp made his faith in her feel requited, fulfilled. For the first time in a long time he was feeling as though there was purpose.

He looked forward again and checked the boat's course. He could see the bell house up on the hill and next to it the roof of the home where the writer and sportsman Zane Grey had lived. It was a beautiful town and he couldn't wait to be back and to show it to them.

He stole another glance down into the stern. Graciela's hair was tied back against the wind and he studied the lovely lines of the nape of her neck. He had been feeling something almost like faith lately and was confused by where it would lead him now. Confused but not concerned. He knew it was of no real matter. His faith was in Graciela Rivers. He had no doubt as he gazed down at her that he was looking at the rock upon which he would make his stand.

# Acknowledgments

*Blood Work* is a work of fiction but it was inspired by conversations with my friend Terry Hansen, who received a heart transplant on Valentine's Day 1993. I thank him for his openness in discussing the emotional and physical changes such an event brought to his life.

I would also like to thank all those who offered their advice and expertise to me during the writing of this novel. Any mistakes in these pages are my own. Particularly, I would like to thank Linda and Callie for putting up with me; William Gaida, LAPD-retired, for teaching me the art of hypnotic interrogation; and Jim Carter for showing me around boats and Cabrillo Marina. Also, thanks go to Gene Riehl, FBI-retired, Scott Anderson, computer czar, Larry Sulkis, first gunner, and Scott Eyman, the writing guru who helped talk me off the ledge after I spiked 240 pages – on purpose! – and had to start again.

The book and the author were benefited immensely by the thoughts of those who read it along the way. They include Mary Connelly Lavelle, Susan Connelly and Jane Connelly Davis, Joel Gotler, Brian Lipson, Philip Spitzer, Ed Thomas, Bill Gerber, Melissa Rooker and Clint Eastwood. (Special thanks to Joel for the harmonica riffs.) My editor, Michael Pietsch, did his usual superb job in taking a massive manuscript and making smooth sense of it.

Lastly, once again thanks to the booksellers who help me tell my stories.

Michael Connelly
Los Angeles

If you have enjoyed *Blood Work*
here is a taste of Michael Connelly's new book

ANGELS FLIGHT

Published by Orion Books
December 1998
ISBN: 0 75282 137 7
Price: £16.99

# ONE

The word sounded alien in his mouth, as if spoken by someone else. There was an urgency in his own voice that Bosch didn't recognize. The simple hello he had whispered into the telephone was full of hope, almost desperation. But the voice that came back to him was not the one he needed to hear.

'Detective Bosch?'

For a moment Bosch felt foolish. He wondered if the caller had recognized the faltering of his voice.

'This is Lieutenant Michael Tulin. Is this Bosch?'

The name meant nothing to Bosch and his momentary concern about how he sounded was ripped away as an awful dread entered his mind.

'This is Bosch. What is it? What's wrong?'

'Hold please for Deputy Chief Irving.'

'What is –'

The caller clicked off and there was only silence. Bosch remembered who Tulin was now – Irving's adjutant. Bosch stood still and waited. He looked around the kitchen, only the dim oven light on. With one hand he held the phone hard against his ear, the other he instinctively brought up to his stomach, where fear and dread were twisting together. He looked at the glowing numbers on the stove clock. It was almost two, five minutes past the last time he had looked at it. This isn't right, he thought as he waited. They don't do this by phone. They come to your door. They tell you this face to face.

Finally, Irving picked up on the other end of the line.

'Detective Bosch?'

'Where is she? What happened?'

Another moment of excruciating silence went by as Bosch waited. His eyes were closed now.

'Excuse me?'

'Just tell me, what happened to her? I mean . . . is she alive?'

'Detective, I'm not sure what it is you are talking about. I'm calling because I need to muster your team as soon as possible. I need you for a special assignment.'

Bosch opened his eyes. He looked through the kitchen window into the dark canyon below his house. His eyes followed the slope of the hill down toward the freeway and then up again to the slash of Hollywood lights he could see through the cut of the Cahuenga Pass. He wondered if each light was someone awake and waiting for something or someone that wasn't going to come. Bosch saw his own reflection in the window. He looked weary. He could make out the deep circles etched beneath his eyes, even in the dark glass.

'I have an assignment, Detective,' Irving repeated impatiently. 'Are you able to work or are you –'

'I can work. I just was mixed up there for a moment.'

'Well, I'm sorry if I woke you. But you should be used to it.'

'Yes. It's no problem.'

Bosch didn't tell him that he hadn't been awakened by the call. That he had been roaming around in his dark house waiting.

'Then get it going, Detective. We'll have coffee down here at the scene.'

'What scene?'

'We'll talk about it when you get here. I don't want to delay this any further. Call your team. Have them come to Grand Street between Third and Fourth. The top of Angels Flight. Do you know where I'm talking about?'

'Bunker Hill? I don't –'

'It will be explained when you get here. Seek me out when you are here. If I am at the bottom, come down to me before you speak with anyone.'

'What about Lieutenant Billets? She should –'

'She will be informed about what is happening. We're wasting time. This is not a request. It is a command. Get your people together and get down here. Am I making myself clear to you?'

'You're clear.'

'Then I will be expecting you.'

Irving hung up without waiting for a reply. Bosch stood with the phone still at his ear for a few moments, wondering what was going on. Angels Flight was the short inclined railroad that carried people up Bunker Hill in downtown – far outside the boundaries of the Hollywood Division homicide table. If Irving had a body down there at Angels Flight the investigation would fall under the jurisdiction of Central Division. If Central detectives couldn't handle it because of caseload or personnel problems, or if the case was deemed too important or media sensitive for them, then it would be bumped to the bulls, the Robbery-Homicide Division. The fact that a deputy chief of police was involved in the case before dawn on a Saturday suggested the latter possibility. The fact that he was calling Bosch and his team in instead of the RHD bulls was the puzzle. Whatever it was that Irving had working at Angels Flight didn't make sense.

Bosch glanced once more down into the dark canyon, pulled the phone away from his ear and clicked it off. He wished he had a cigarette but he had made it this far through the night without one. He wouldn't break now.

He turned his back and leaned on the counter. He

looked down at the phone in his hand, turned it back on and hit the speed dial button that would connect him with Kizmin Rider's apartment. He would call Jerry Edgar after he talked to her. Bosch felt a sense of relief come over him that he was reluctant to acknowledge. He might not yet know what awaited him at Angels Flight, but it would certainly take his thoughts away from Eleanor Wish.

Rider's alert voice answered after two rings.

'Kiz, it's Harry,' he said. 'We've got work.'

# TWO

Bosch agreed to meet his two partners at the Hollywood Division station to pick up cars before they headed downtown to Angels Flight. On the way down the hill to the station he had punched in KFWB on his Jeep's radio and picked up a breaking news report on a homicide investigation under way at the site of the historical funicular railroad. The newsman on the scene reported that two bodies had been found inside one of the train cars and that several members of the Robbery-Homicide squad were on the scene. But that was the extent of the reporter's information as he also noted that the police had placed an unusually wide cordon of yellow tape around the crime scene, prohibiting him from getting a closer look. At the station Bosch communicated this bit of thin information to Edgar and Rider while they signed three slickbacks out of the motor pool.

'So it looks like we're gonna be playing sloppy seconds to RHD,' Edgar concluded, showing his annoyance at being rousted from sleep to spend probably the whole weekend doing gopher work for the RHD bulls. 'Our guts, their glory. And we aren't even on call this weekend. Why didn't Irving call out Rice's got-damned team if he needed a Hollywood team?'

Edgar had a point. Team One – Bosch, Edgar and Rider – wasn't even up on call rotation this weekend. If Irving followed proper call out procedure he would have called Terry Rice, who headed up Team Three, which was currently on top of the rotation. But Bosch already figured that Irving wasn't following any procedures, not if the deputy chief had called him directly before checking with his supervisor, Lt. Grace Billets.

'Well, Jerry,' Bosch said, more than used to his partner's whining, 'you'll get the chance to ask the deputy chief personally in a little while.'

'Yeah, right, I do that and I'll find my ass down in Harbor the next ten years. Fuck that.'

'Hey, Harbor Division's an easy gig,' Rider said, just to rag Edgar a bit. She knew Edgar lived in the Valley and that a transfer to Harbor Division would mean a miserable ninety-minute commute each way – the pure definition of Freeway Therapy, the brass's method of unofficially punishing malcontents and problem cops. 'They only pull six, seven homicides a year down there.'

'That's nice but count me the fuck out.'

'Okay, okay,' Bosch said. 'Let's just get going and we'll worry about all of that stuff later. Don't get lost.'

Bosch took Hollywood Boulevard to the 101 and coasted down the freeway in minimal traffic to downtown. Halfway there he checked the mirror and saw his partners cruising in the lanes behind him. Even in the dark and with other traffic he could pick them out. He hated the new detective cars. They were painted black and white and looked exactly like patrol cruisers with the exception that they did not carry the emergency lights across the roof. It had been the former chief's idea to replace unmarked detective cars with the so-called slickbacks. The whole thing had been a scam perpetrated to fulfill his promises to put more cops on the street. By changing unmarked cars into clearly marked cars, he was giving the public the erroneous impression that there were more cops patrolling the streets. He also counted the detectives using slickbacks when he addressed community groups and proudly reported that he had increased the number of cops on the street by hundreds.

Meantime, detectives trying to do their jobs drove around like targets. More than once Bosch and his team had sought to serve an arrest warrant or had attempted to quietly come into a neighborhood in the course of an investigation only to have their presence signaled by their own cars. It was stupid and dangerous but it was the chief's edict and it was carried out throughout the department's divisional detective bureaus, even after the chief was not asked back for a second five-year term. Bosch, like many of the department's detectives, hoped the new chief would soon order the detective cars back to normal. Meanwhile, he no longer drove the car assigned to him home from work. It had been a nice detective supervisor's perq having a take-home car but he didn't want the marked car sitting in front of his house. Not in L.A. You never knew what menace that could bring to your door.

They got to Grand Street by two-forty-five. As Bosch pulled to a stop he saw an unusually large number of police and related vehicles parked along the curb at California Plaza. He noted the crime scene and coroner's vans, several patrol cars and several more detective sedans – not the slickbacks, but the unmarked cars still used by RHD bulls. While he waited for Rider and Edgar to pull up he opened his briefcase, took out the cellular phone and called his home. After five rings the machine picked up the call and he heard his own voice telling him to leave a message. He was about to click off but decided to leave a message.

'Eleanor, it's me. I've got a call out . . . but page me or call me on the cell phone when you get in so I know you're okay . . . Um, okay, that's it. Bye – oh, it's about two-forty-five right now. Saturday morning. Bye.'

Edgar and Rider had walked up to his door. He put the phone away and got out with his briefcase. Edgar, the tallest, held up the yellow crime scene tape and they crossed under, gave their names and badge numbers to a uniform officer with the crime scene attendance list, and then walked across California Plaza.

The plaza was the centerpiece of Bunker Hill, a stone courtyard formed by the conjoining of two marble office towers, a high-rise apartment building and the Modern Museum of Art. There was a huge fountain and reflecting pool at its center, though the pumps and lights were off at this hour, leaving the water still and black.

Past the fountain was the Beaux Arts revival-style station and wheelhouse at the top of Angels Flight. It was next to this small structure that most of the investigators and patrol officers milled about as if waiting for something. Bosch looked for the gleaming shaven skull that belonged to Deputy Chief Irving but didn't see it. He and his partners stepped into the crowd and moved toward the lone rail car sitting at the top of the tracks. Along the way he recognized many of the faces of Robbery-Homicide detectives. They were men he had worked with years earlier when he had been part of the élite squad. A few of them nodded to him or called him by name. Bosch saw Francis Sheehan, his former partner, standing off by himself, smoking a cigarette. Bosch broke from his partners and stepped over.

'Frankie,' he said. 'What's going on?'

'Harry, what are you doing here?'

'Got called out. Irving called us out.'

'Shit. Sorry, partner, I wouldn't wish this one on my enemy.'

'Why, what's going –'

'You better talk to the man first. He's putting the big blanket on this one.'

Bosch hesitated. Sheehan looked worn down but Bosch hadn't seen him in months. He had no idea what had put the dark circles under his hound dog eyes or when they had been cut into his face. For a moment Bosch remembered the reflection of his own face that he had seen earlier.

'You okay, Francis?'

'Never better.'

'Okay, I'll talk to you.'

Bosch rejoined Edgar and Rider who were standing near the rail car. Edgar nodded slightly to Bosch's left.

'Hey, Harry, you see that?' he said in a low voice. 'That's Sustain Chastain and that bunch over there. What are those pricks doin' here?'

Bosch turned and saw the grouping of men from Internal Affairs.

'Got no idea,' he said.

Chastain and Bosch locked eyes for a moment but Bosch didn't hold it. It wasn't worth the waste of energy to get worked up over just seeing the IAD man. Instead, he focused on trying to put the whole scene together. His curiosity level was at maximum. The number of RHD bulls hanging around, the IAD shines, a deputy chief on the scene – he had to find out what was going on.

With Edgar and Rider behind him in single file, Bosch worked his way to the rail car. Portable lights had been set up inside and the car was lit up like somebody's living room. Inside, two crime scene techs were at work. This told Bosch that he was quite late arriving at the scene. The crime scene techs didn't move in until after the coroner's techs had completed their initial procedures – declaring victims dead, photographing the bodies in situ, searching them for wounds, weapons and identification.

Bosch stepped to the rear of the car and looked through the open door. The technicians were at work around two bodies. A woman was sprawled on one of the stepped seats about midway through the car. She was wearing gray leggings and a white thigh-length T-shirt. A large flower of blood had blossomed on her chest where she had been hit dead center with a single bullet. Her head was snapped back against the sill of the window behind her seat. She had dark hair and features, her lineage obviously stretching somewhere south of the border. On the seat next to her body was a plastic bag filled with many items Bosch couldn't see. A folded newspaper protruded from the top of it.

On the steps near the rear door to the car was the facedown body of a black man wearing a dark grey suit. From his viewpoint Bosch could not see the man's face and only one wound was visible – a through and through gunshot wound at the center of the victim's right hand. Bosch knew it was what would later be called a defensive wound in the autopsy report. The man had held his hand up in a futile attempt to ward off gunfire. Bosch had seen it often enough over the years and it always made him think about the desperate actions people take at the end. Putting a hand up to stop a bullet was one of the most desperate.

Though the techs were stepping in and out of his line of sight, Bosch could look straight down through the inclined train car and down the track to Hill Street about three hundred feet below. A duplicate train car was down there at the bottom of the hill and Bosch could see more detectives milling about by the turnstiles and the closed doors of the Grand Central Market across the street.

Bosch had ridden the incline railroad as a kid and had studied how it worked. He still remembered. The two matching cars were counter-balanced. When one went up the side by side tracks the other went down, and vice versa. They passed each other at the midpoint. He remembered riding on Angels Flight long before Bunker Hill had been reborn as a slick business center of glass and marble towers, classy condominiums and apartments, museums and fountains referred to as water gardens. Back then the hill had been a place of once grand Victorian homes turned into tired looking rooming houses. Harry and his mother had taken Angels Flight up the hill to look for a place to live.

'Finally, Detective Bosch.'

Bosch turned around. Deputy Chief Irving stood in the open door of the little station house.

'All of you,' he said, signaling Bosch and his team inside.

They entered a cramped room dominated by the large old cable wheels that once moved the train cars up and down the incline. Bosch remembered reading that when Angels Flight was rehabilitated a few years earlier after a quarter century of disuse, the cables and wheels had been replaced with an electric system monitored by computer.

On one side of the wheel display was just enough room for a small lunch table with two folding chairs. On the other side was the computer for operating the trains, a stool for the operator and a stack of cardboard boxes, the top one open and showing stacks of pamphlets on the history of Angels Flight.

Standing against the far wall, in the shadow behind the old iron wheels, his arms folded and his craggy, sun-reddened face looking down at the floor, was a man Bosch recognized. Bosch had once worked for Captain John Garwood, commander of the Robbery-Homicide Division. He knew by the look on his face that he was very put out about something. Garwood didn't look up at them and the three detectives said nothing.

Irving went to a telephone on the lunch table and picked up the loose handset. As he began talking he motioned to Bosch to close the door.

'Excuse me, Sir,' Irving said. 'It was the team from Hollywood. They are all here and we are ready to proceed.'

He listened for a few moments, said good-bye and hung up the phone. The reverence in his voice and his use of the word *sir* told Bosch that Irving had been talking to the chief of police. It was one more curiosity about the case.

'All right, then,' Irving said, turning around and facing the three detectives. 'I am sorry to roust you people, especially out of rotation. However, I have spoken with Lieutenant Billets and as of now you have been cut free of the Hollywood rotation until we get this handled.'

'What exactly is *this* that we are handling?' Bosch asked.

'A delicate situation. The homicides of two citizens.'

Bosch wished he would get to the point.

'Chief, I see enough RHD people around here to investigate the Bobby Kennedy case all over again,' he said, glancing at Garwood. 'And that's not to mention the IAD shines hovering around the edges. What exactly are we doing here? What do you want?'

'Simple,' Irving said. 'I am turning the investigation over to you. It is your case now, Detective Bosch. The Robbery-Homicide detectives will be withdrawing as soon as you people are brought up to speed. As you can see, you are coming in late. That's unfortunate but I think you will be able to overcome it. I know what you can do.'

Bosch stared at him blankly for a long moment, then glanced at Garwood again. The captain had not moved and continued to stare at the floor. Bosch asked the only question that could bring understanding to this strange situation.

'That man and woman on the train car, who are they?'

Irving nodded.

'*Were* is probably the more correct word. *Were*. The

woman's name was Catalina Perez. Who exactly she was and what she was doing on Angels Flight we do not know yet. It probably does not matter. It appears that she was just in the wrong place at the wrong time. But that will be for you to officially determine. Anyway, the man in there, he is different. That was Howard Elias.'

'The lawyer?'

Irving nodded. Bosch heard Edgar draw in a breath and hold it.

'This is for real?'

'Unfortunately.'

Bosch looked past Irving and through the ticket window. He could see into the train car. The techs were still at work, getting ready to shut off the lights so they could laser the inside of the car. His eyes fell to the hand with the bullet wound through it. Howard Elias. Bosch thought about all of the suspects there would be. Many of them standing around outside at that very moment, watching.

'Shit,' Edgar said. 'Don't suppose we could take a pass on this one, could we, Chief?'

'Watch your language, Detective,' Irving snapped, the muscles of the jaw bulging as he grew angry. 'That is not acceptable here.'

'Look, Chief, all I'm sayin' is if you're looking for somebody to play department Uncle Tom, it ain't going to be –'

'That has nothing to do with this,' Irving said, cutting him off. 'Whether you like it or not, you have been assigned to this case. I expect each of you to do it professionally and thoroughly. Most of all, I expect results, as does the chief of police. Other matters mean nothing. Absolutely nothing.'

After a brief silence, during which Irving's eyes went from Edgar to Rider and then to Bosch, the deputy chief continued.

'In this department there is only one race,' he said. 'Not black or white. Just the blue race.'